CRISTINA GARCÍA

¡Cubanísimo!

Cristina García was born in Havana and grew up in New York City. She is the author of *Dreaming in Cuban, The Agüero Sisters,* and *Monkey Hunting.* Ms. García has been a Guggenheim Fellow, a Hodder Fellow at Princeton University, and the recipient of a Whiting Writers' Award. She lives in Los Angeles with her daughter.

ALSO BY CRISTINA GARCÍA

Dreaming in Cuban

The Agüero Sisters

Monkey Hunting

¡CUBANÍSIMO!

¡Cubanísimo!

THE VINTAGE BOOK OF CONTEMPORARY CUBAN LITERATURE

EDITED AND WITH AN INTRODUCTION BY

CRISTINA GARCÍA

VINTAGE BOOKS
A Division of Random House, Inc.
New York

SPECIAL THANKS TO THOMAS COLCHIE FOR HIS INVALUABLE ASSISTANCE IN THE EARLY STAGES OF THIS PROJECT AND TO GUSTAVO PELLÓN FOR HIS SUGGESTIONS AND LEADS. ALSO, MY GRATITUDE TO ALICE VAN STRAALEN, WHOSE DEDICATION TO THIS BOOK HAS MADE HER AN HONORARY *CUBANA*.

FIRST VINTAGE BOOKS EDITION, MAY 2003

 Published in the United States by Vintage Books, a division of Random House, Inc., New York, and simultaneously in Canada by Random House of Canada Limited, Toronto.

Permissions acknowledgments can be found at the end of the book.

Library of Congress Cataloging-in-Publication Data
¡Cubanísimo! : the Vintage Book of contemporary Cuban literature / edited and with an introduction by Cristina García.—1st Vintage Books ed.
p. cm.
Contents: José Martí—Fernando Ortiz—Antonio Benítez-Rojo—Lydia Cabrera—Dulce María Loynaz—Alejo Carpentier—Miguel Barnet—Guillermo Cabrera Infante—Nancy Morejón—Calvert Casey—José Lezama Lima—Heberto Padilla—Lourdes Casal—Lino Novás Calvo—Nicolás Guillén—Virgilio Piñera—Gustavo Pérez-Firmat—Severo Sarduy—Reinaldo Arenas—Zoé Valdés—Ernesto Mestre—María Elena Cruz Varela—José Manuel Prieto—Ana Menéndez—Rafael Campo.
ISBN 0-385-72137-4
1. Cuban literature—20th century—Translations into English. I. García, Cristina, 1958–
PQ7383.5.E5 C83 2003
860.8'097291—dc21
2002038076

Author photograph © Norma Quintana
Book design by Debbie Glasserman

www.vintagebooks.com

Printed in the United States of America
10 9 8 7 6 5 4 3 2 1

TO PILAR, CARI, AND GRACE

CONTENTS

CLAVE 5: *Salsa* 307

INTRODUCTION

Writers distinguish themselves by the quality and music of their sentences. And, of course, by their history. On both counts, Cuban writers are richly blessed. In the last forty-plus years, three distinct Cuban cultures have evolved: that of the Revolution, uneasily in place since 1959; that of nostalgia in Miami, where the exiles' dream of reclaiming the homeland is kept alive daily at the dinner table and on radio shows that proclaim "Next year in Havana!"; and that of the cultural hybridism found in the thriving Cuban diasporas in New York, Mexico City, Madrid, and other hospitable cities. Today's Cuban writers often are identified or identify themselves by where they stand in relation to the Revolution.

Yet, there is a palpable longing, too, for a common identity, a sense of "us" within all these variances that dates back to Cuba's wars of independence. *Criollos,* former slaves, and even Chinese immigrants fought side by side to finally overthrow Spanish rule in 1898. One element ties the longing for identity together, and that is music. Most images we think of as Cuban are accompanied by bongos or congas, the *tres* guitar, the *maracas* (*el ritmo de semillas secas*—"the rhythm of dry seeds" as García Lorca described them), the *güiro,* the trumpets, and the swaying bass. For Cubans, there is nothing more fundamental than music. In Cuba, children clap out dance rhythms before they can walk.

A day in the life of Cubans anywhere includes rhythm. A lilting *cha-cha-chá* danced across the kitchen. Back-to-back *boleros* sung in the shower. The infectious afternoon swing of a *son.* No matter their politics, few Cubans can sit still listening to *"El cuarto de Tula,"* a song about the fiery goings-on in one room of a provincial brothel. Or resist the rhythms of the island's premier dance band, Los Van Van, who've been going as strong as the Rolling Stones for over thirty years. (One side effect of the Revolution, at least musically, was the preservation, training, and support of musicians by the Cuban government even as this "support" served at times to stifle freedom and experimentation.)

Underlying all of this music is the *clave,* a simple five-beat cadence, three slow beats followed by two fast: 1-2-3, 1-2 (or the other way around). The *clave,* the mother of all Cuban rhythms, is embedded in every song and dance step. Its beat is clapped out by a set of paired hardwood sticks, also called the *clave,* and decrees the tempo for the song. It's the one instrument in a Cuban band that never improvises, so basic is its syncopation. No matter the complexity of the composition or the size of the orchestra, the *clave* anchors the music.

Yet the *clave* has other meanings in Spanish, that of "key," as in the key to a code or mystery and that of an architectural keystone, the wedge-shaped piece at the crown of an arch that locks the other pieces in place. The multiple spirits of the *clave* are what inform this anthology of contemporary Cuban writing—its rhythm, its spirit, its mystery, its function, and the multicultural essence of Cuban identity.

There is a song by bass player Israel "Cachao" López called *"Como mi ritmo no hay dos"* (*Nobody's Got a Rhythm Like Mine*). López's song is a *descarga,* a jam session, and that is what this anthology aims to be, with the *clave* as its organizing principle—uniquely Cuban, emerging from its soil and the synergies of its extraordinary mix of inhabitants. The selections in the anthology are loosely grouped according to different musical and dance modes. The five sections have *clave*-like "beats" that embrace the style and reflect something of the flavor of each. It is my wish that they capture something indispensably Cuban.

The initial grouping, *danzón,* is very much turn-of-the century, with the traditional structure and charm of a classical concerto. From the late 1800s until about 1920, the *danzón* was Cuba's national dance and an extraordinary variety of *danzones* were written: to celebrate the establishment of the Cuban Republic, to salute Italian operas, even to lament the fate of Warsaw during World War I.

The first excerpts in the *danzón* section are from the writings of José Martí, the fallen hero of Cuba's independence movement and the father of its modernist literature (and himself subject of a *danzón* called *"Martí no debió morir," Martí Shouldn't Have Died.*) In the last entry of his war diaries, Martí writes from a makeshift riverside camp: "They roast plantains and pound jerked beef with a stone for newcomers. The rising waters of the Contramaestre are very murky, and Valentín brings me a jug, boiled and sweetened, with fig leaves in it." As Guillermo Cabrera Infante has said: "That pure prose is actually the man himself. José Martí is a man made of prose—and of poetry, too."

In the early *danzones,* couples first began to dance arm-in-arm, a departure from previous dance forms. Fernando Ortiz beautifully articulates this *danzón* duality (with its implied notions of gender) in his multidimensional exploration of the island's two major crops in his classic study, *Cuban Counterpoint: Tobacco and Sugar:*

> There is no rebellion of challenge in sugar, nor resentment, nor brooding suspicion, but humble pleasure, quiet, calm, and soothing. Tobacco is boldly imaginative and individualistic to the point of anarchy. Sugar is on the side of sensible pragmatism and social

integration. Tobacco is as daring as blasphemy; sugar as humble as prayer.

In the same section, sociologist and folklorist Lydia Cabrera explores the myths and origins of Afro-Cuban culture in her short story "The Hill of Mambiala." The early *danzones* relied heavily on the *cinquillo,* music that came from the Haitian blacks of Santiago de Cuba and which finally gained legitimacy when it was expressed through the more socially acceptable *danzón.* Cabrera's allegorical story subtly addresses this racial accommodation (along with its many prejudices) and is typical of her work as one of the foremost interpreters of the island's African legacies and traditions.

In a different vein, Antonio Benítez-Rojo's "A View from the Mangrove" offers a powerful, hallucinatory account of one man's struggle during the last War of Independence (1895–1898). One can almost imagine a slow *danzón* as its accompaniment. And with her delicately wrought poetry and considerations of place and belonging, Dulce María Loynaz also embodies the formality and refinement of the *danzón.*

The *rumba,* as Alejo Carpentier points out, is "above all a fiery dance, whose rhythms served to accompany a kind of choreography that conjured up ancient sexual rites." It is, he insists, more than a genre; it is an *atmosphere,* and recognizable to any Cuban. Derived from the religious practices of Cuba's African slaves, the *rumba* emerged around the great sugar mills and docks of Matanzas. It was first played on *cajones,* or wooden crates used to pack candles and salt cod, and is a seductive mixture of the spiritual and the secular, the divine and the profane, the magical and the quotidian.

The *rumba* section begins with Carpentier's influential essay that was the prologue to his 1949 novel, *The Kingdom of This World.* In it, he asks: "But what is the history of the Americas but a chronicle of the real marvelous?" And in those words (*lo real maravilloso*), the concept of an innate magical realism in Latin America—in contrast to Europe's more constructed idea of surrealism—was born.

Many Cuban writers exuberantly occupy this *rumba* category. Miguel Barnet's race-sensitive *Biography of a Runaway Slave* is a pioneering (and now classic) work of oral history, chronicling the life of a 103-year-old slave named Esteban Montejo. Guillermo Cabrera Infante's novel *Three Trapped Tigers* vibrates with sensual energy and verbal pyrotechnics, subverting its own narrative with a hilarious assemblage of vignettes, parodies, dreams, and even psychiatric sessions that capture, pitch-perfectly, the decadent multiracial nightlife of 1950s Havana. Cabrera Infante is also well known as an essayist—his "Lorca the Rainmaker Visits Havana" is included here—and is a sharp critic of the Castro regime.

Nancy Morejón's poem, "Love, Attributed City," is a verbal *rumba* to her beloved Havana, with every line suffused with the city's rhythms.

> *". . . who am I*
> *the guerilla, the roving madwoman, the Medusa, a*
> *Chinese flute,*
> *a warm chair, the coast guard's cannon, anguish,*
> *the blood of martyrs, the ovum of* Ochún *on this earth . . ."*

Conversely, Calvert Casey's short story, "The Walk," is a gentler tale of the quiet, deliberate initiation of a Cuban boy. In it, one senses a *rumba* in the making.

The rhythm of the *son* is what most people associate with Cuban music. Originating in Oriente, the easternmost province of the island, *son* is the most widely influential element in Latin music and the foundation of contemporary *salsa.* Invented by black and mulatto musicians during the 1880s, including the descendants of refugees from Haiti's revolution nearly a century earlier, the *son* was disseminated by soldiers during the War of Independence who carried its basic instruments—*clave, maracas, güiro*—in their pockets and on their backs, and then by the popularity of radio in the 1920s.

Like the *rumba,* the *son* is wholly dependent on the *clave* as the percussion weaves and improvises counterpoints around its basic rhythm. "Thanks to the *son,*" wrote Carpentier, "Afro-Cuban percussion, confined to the slave barracks and the dilapidated rooming houses of the slums, revealed its marvelous expressive sources, achieving universal status."

In his labyrinthine novel, *Paradiso,* José Lezama Lima (who until its publication was known primarily for his poetry) masterfully employs such "counterpoint" while exploring the many strata of Havana society. The notorious "Chapter VIII" of the novel—an erotic tour de force—created a scandal when it first appeared in 1966. With its baroque and deftly layered sophistications, *Paradiso* is considered by many critics as one of the great, underappreciated Latin American novels of the last century.

A few years later Heberto Padilla created another furor with his novel, *Heroes Are Grazing in My Garden,* a critical portrait of the Revolution. Padilla imbues all his work with a historical sensibility, suggesting in his poem "A prayer for the end of the century" that we are an extension of all who have come before us and that our choices can be as burdensome as history. "Doors are things there are too many of!" he writes in "Self-portrait of the other." Padilla's imprisonment in 1971 inspired worldwide literary support. Similarly shunned by the Revolution was Lino Novás Calvo, a fine short-story writer who has been nearly forgotten even by Cubans. He is represented here by the somber, thoughtful piece "As I Am . . . As I Was."

Another version of the *son* sensibility can be found in Lourdes

Casal's story, "The Founders: Alfonso." In it, she highlights a key ingredient in the *ajiaco* stew that is the Cuban identity: the Chinese, who, beginning in the late 1840s, were imported in great numbers as contract laborers to work the island's sugarcane fields, though in reality, they were little more than slaves. Over time their culture (and even a shrill instrument called *la corneta china*) found its way into the larger Cuban mix, accenting its language, cuisine, literature, and music.

The section ends with Nicolás Guillén's essay, "Josephine Baker in Cuba," which reflects his preoccupation with the importance of race, and the lasting impact of slavery and racism in Cuba. Probably best known for his poetry (many of his earlier poems were set to music, specifically to the *son*), Guillén dedicated himself to integrating Afro-Cuban identity and its consciousness into the island's cultural and intellectual life.

The *mambo* is Cuba's fastest and most impassioned music. Only the most assured venture onto the dance floor when a *mambo* is in full swing. Despite conflicting histories about its origins, most musicologists agree that the *mambo* developed in Havana during the late 1930s. Did Arsenio Rodríguez, who enjoyed using the word interchangeably with *diablo,* or devil, start the craze? Were the López brothers, Cachao and Orestes, responsible for the term? (They claimed to have borrowed the word from Lucumí, an Afro-Cuban language.) Or was it Pérez Prado? He was said to have heard "mambo" used in political circles for a kind of dirty dealing and decided to use it musically.

Literarily, the *mambo* section also comprises a brash audacity. For example, little known in the English-speaking world, Virgilio Piñera is an innovative master of the macabre and the absurd. His short story "The Face" illustrates his fixation with the nature of love and obsession. Who could resist a story that begins like this?

One morning I got a phone call. The person on the other end said he was in grave danger. To my obvious question: "With whom do I have the pleasure of speaking?" he replied that we had never seen each other and never would.

Severo Sarduy is another Cuban original who freely mixes genres for his outrageous yet profoundly tragicomic works. An excerpt from his novel, *From Cuba with a Song,* about a courtesan and poet named Dolores Rondón ("Courtesan all her life. Poet for a day.") gives readers a feverish spin of his talents in the form of fast-paced comic theater. Sarduy's works are as much transgressive performance pieces as they are literature.

Although probably best known for his memoir *Before Night Falls,* which was made into a movie, Reinaldo Arenas is the author of numerous radically inventive works. Persecuted both for his writings and his homosexuality, Arenas's improvisations have inspired subsequent generations of Cuban writers. He is the consummate *mambo* writer—confident, insistent, erotic. Similarly, Gustavo Pérez-Firmat, with his brief, pungent essays, speaks to the hilarity and challenges of "living on the hyphen" while Zoé Valdés, in her novels and short stories, addresses with a mambo-like fury the equally extravagant adaptations often required to survive the Cuban Revolution.

The last selections are those grouped as *salsa,* a music whose roots are in *son,* but which has been a product of multiple exiles, of combining the here and there into a fusion of *sabores,* or flavors. *Salsa* was first used in the mid-1970s to describe a style of music that blended Cuban and Puerto Rican sounds with jazz and which often reflected the culture of the New York *barrios.*

In his epic novel, *The Lazarus Rumba,* Ernesto Mestre captures the many contradictions of present-day Cuban reality, not the least of which is by writing a Cuban book in English that is itself filled with plenty of Spanish asides and aphorisms. How do you convincingly reflect in American English a world that takes place in Cuban Spanish and not call it a translation?

Such elasticity of identity is also the concern of José Manuel Prieto, who spent his formative years in the former Soviet Union and Eastern Europe and who now teaches Russian literature in Mexico City. His novel, *Nocturnal Butterflies of the Russian Empire,* is indebted as much to Vladimir Nabokov and the Russian masters as to José Lezama Lima and José Martí. It's a story of a Cuban smuggler-cum-lepidopterist negotiating the collapse of Communism and his own fractured identity. What, then, does it mean to be a Cuban today? Where do we call home? What are the trade-offs and betrayals we make with our choices?

Although the poet María Elena Cruz Varela knows where she belongs, she can no longer live there. Forced to leave Cuba in the early 1990s after her arrest and imprisonment for human rights activities and her outspokenness against the Castro regime, Cruz Varela is a reluctant exile whose ecstatic sadness at her fate informs each line of her poetry.

Perhaps there will be no more light. Maybe no more fire.
Perhaps I will return to the country of eternal snow.
To my orphaned costume of winter. An angel in the medley.
Careful accord from a poor blinded bard.
Ready to recite my filth . . .

In contrast, the old Cuban men in Ana Menéndez's short story, "In Cuba I Was a German Shepherd," humorously dream and scheme of returning to their native island as they play their interminable domino games. But as their lives wind down, it is their very exile that most defines them. Rafael Campo, a poet and a physician raised in the United States, writes of the body's own estrangement from itself, the participant-observers we've become in our own corporeal dramas. One wonders how much of this alienation is culturally based.

Because my body speaks the stranger's language,
I've never understood those nods and stares . . .

Still, it is ultimately in the body that Cuba's rhythms lodge themselves—in the twist of a hip, the bent knees, a just-so jut of an elbow. It is a legacy of flesh, encoded by the *clave,* and passed on to the island's daughters and sons. Cuban literature is a product of these very same rhythms, of a passion for its roots and loyalties. If in reading this anthology, you find yourself eager for more, there is plenty to explore. Celia Cruz, the queen of Cuban music, always ends her concerts with the same exhortation: *¡Azúcar!* It means everything Cuban and sweet. It means keep dancing, and reading, to the *clave.*

—Cristina García
July 30, 2002
Los Angeles

CLAVE 1

Danzón

JOSÉ MARTÍ

Love in the City

Times of gorge and rush are these:
Voices fly like light: lightning,
like a ship hurled upon dread quicksand,
plunges down the high rod, and in delicate craft
man, as if winged, cleaves the air.
And love, without splendor or mystery,
dies when newly born, of glut.
The city is a cage of dead doves
and avid hunters! If men's bosoms
were to open and their torn flesh
fall to the earth, inside would be
nothing but a scatter of small, crushed fruit!

Love happens in the street, standing in the dust
of saloons and public squares: the flower
dies the day it's born. The trembling
virgin who would rather death
have her than some unknown youth;
the joy of trepidation; that feeling of heart
set free from chest; the ineffable
pleasure of deserving; the sweet alarm
of walking quick and straight
from your love's home and breaking
into tears like a happy child;—
and that gazing of our love at the fire,

as roses slowly blush a deeper color,—
Bah, it's all a sham! Who has the time
to be noble? Though like a golden
bowl or sumptuous painting
a genteel lady sits in the magnate's home!

But if you're thirsty, reach out your arm,
and drain some passing cup!
The dirtied cup rolls to the dust, then,
and the expert taster—breast blotted
with invisible blood—goes happily,
crowned with myrtle, on his way!
Bodies are nothing now but trash,
pits, and tatters! And souls
are not the tree's lush fruit
down whose tender skin runs
sweet juice in time of ripeness,—
but fruit of the marketplace, ripened
by the hardened laborer's brutal blows!

It is an age of dry lips!
Of undreaming nights! Of life
crushed unripe! What is it that we lack,
without which there is no gladness? Like a startled
hare in the wild thicket of our breast,
fleeing, tremulous, from a gleeful hunter,
the spirit takes cover;
and Desire, on Fever's arm,
beats the thicket, like the rich hunter.

The city appals me! Full
of cups to be emptied, and empty cups!
I fear—ah me!—that this wine

may be poison, and sink its teeth,
vengeful imp, in my veins!
I thirst—but for a wine that none on earth
knows how to drink! I have not yet
endured enough to break through the wall
that keeps me, ah grief!, from my vineyard!
Take, oh squalid tasters
of humble human wines, these cups
from which, with no fear or pity,
you swill the lily's juice!
Take them! I am honorable, and I am afraid!

TRANSLATED BY ESTHER ALLEN

from WAR DIARIES

April 17, 1895

Morning in the camp. Yesterday a cow was slaughtered and as the sun comes up, groups are already standing around the cauldrons. Domitila, agile and good, in her Egyptian kerchief, springs up the mountain and brings back the kerchief full of tomatoes, cilantro, and oregano. Someone gives me a piece of malanga. Someone else, a cup of hot cane juice and leaves. A bundle of cane is milled. At the back of the house is the slope facing the river, with its houses and banana trees, cotton and wild tobacco; below, along the river, a cluster of palms; in the clearings, orange trees; and all around are mountains, rounded and peaceable; and the blue sky above, with its white clouds, and a palm tree, half in cloud—half in the blue.—Impatience makes me sad. We'll leave tomorrow. I tuck the *Life of Cicero* into the same pocket where I'm carrying 50 bullets. I write letters. The General makes a sweet of coconut shavings with honey. Tomorrow's departure is arranged. We buy honey from a rancher with a short beard and alarm in his eyes. At first it's four reales a gallon, but then, after the sermon, he gives away two gallons. "Jaragüita" comes, Juan Telesforo Rodríguez, who doesn't want to go by Rodríguez anymore because he used that name as a guide for the Spaniards, and now he's leaving with us. He has a wife now. When he goes, he slips away. The villainous El Pájaro plays with the machete; his foot is tremendous; his eye shines like marble where the sun hits the ebony black spot. Tomorrow we leave the home of José Pineda: Goya, his wife. (Toward Jojó Arriba.)

April 24

Across the wide gulch, over the Monte de Acosta, across crumbling stone, with pools of clear water where the mockingbird drinks, and a bed of dry leaves, we haul ourselves along the exhausting path from sunup to sundown. The danger is palpable. Since El Palenque they've been following our tracks closely. Garrido's Indians could fall on us here. We take shelter on the porch of Valentín, overseer of the Santa Cecilia sugar plantation. Strong Juan, with good teeth, comes out to give us his warm hand, and his uncle Luís calls him over: "And you, why aren't you coming?" "But don't you see how the bugs are eating me up?" The bugs, the family. Ah, rented men, corrupting salary! The man who is his own man, who belongs to himself, is different. And these people? What does he have to leave behind? The house of yagua palms, which the land gives them and they make with their own hands? The pigs, which they can raise on the mountainside? Food the earth gives; shoes, the yagua and the majagua; medicine, herbs, and bark; sweets, honey. Farther along, digging holes for fence posts, is an old man, bearded and big-bellied, in a dirty shirt and pants that reach his ankles, his skin earth-colored, his eyes viperish and shrunken: "And what are you men doing?" "Well, we're here to build these fences." Luís swears and raises his long arm into the air. He strides away, his chin quivering.

April 26

We form ranks at sunrise. To horse, still sleepy. The men are shaky, haven't yet recovered. They barely ate last night. About 10, we rest along both sides of the path. From a small house they send a hen, as a gift to "General Matías," and honey. In the afternoon and at night I write, to New York, to Antonio Maceo who is nearby and unaware of our arrival, and the letter for Manuel Fuentes, to the *World,* which I finished, pencil in hand, at dawn. Yesterday I cast an occasional glance over the calm, happy camp: the sound of a bugle; loads of plantains carried on shoulders; the bellow of the seized cattle when their throats are slit. From his hammock, Victoriano Garzón, a sensible black man with a mustache and goatee and fiery eyes, tells me, humble and fervent, about his triumphant attack on Ramón de las Yaguas: his words are restless and intense, his soul is generous, and he has a natural authority: he pampers his white aides, Mariano Sánchez and Rafael Portuondo, and if they err on a point of discipline, he lets them off. Stringy, sweetly smiling, in a blue shirt and black pants, he watches over each and every one of his soldiers. The formidable José Maceo parades his tall body past: his hands are still raw from the brambles in the pine forest and on the mountainside, when the expedition from Costa Rica was pursued and took flight, and Flor was killed, and Antonio took two men with him, and José was left all alone, sinking beneath his load, dying from cold amid the damp pines, his feet swollen and cracked: and he arrived, and now he triumphs.

May 1

We leave the camp of Vuelta Corta. That was where Policarpo Pineda, alias the *Rustan,* or the Moth, had Francisco Pérez, the one from the Escuadras, hacked to pieces. One day the Moth executed Jesus Christ himself: he was wearing a big crucifix on his chest and a bullet sent an arm of the cross into his flesh, so later he fired four shots into the cross. We were talking about this during the morning, when the path, now in the blooming region of the coffee plantations, among plantains and cacao, emerged into a magical hollow called the Tontina; from the depths of the vast greenness its roof of palm trees can hardly be seen and on all sides are mahogany trees with their purple flowers. Not much farther was the Kentucky, Pezuela's coffee farm, the large brick driers in front of the house, which is cheerful, spacious, and white, with balconies, and a low area nearby where the machines are. At the door is Nazario Soncourt, a slender mulatto, with rum and a pitcher of water on a small table, and glasses. The Thoreau brothers come out to see us from their vivid coffee farm, with its little houses of brick and tile: the youngest one, red with effort, his eyes anxious and misty, stammers: "But we can work here, right? We can go on working." And he says nothing but that, like a madam.—We reach the forest. Estanislao Cruzat, a good mountaineer, Gómez's groom, cuts a slash near the base of two trees, pounds two forked sticks in front of each one, and others to support the trunk, and some crosspieces, and sticks laid lengthwise: and there's a bench. After a short rest, we continue along an overgrown footpath in the fertile region of Ti Arriba. Sunlight glitters on the cool rain: oranges dangle from airy trees: high grass covers the wet ground. Slender white tree trunks weave through the green forest, from their roots to the blue sky; liana twists around delicate bushes in spirals of even rings that look man-made, and copey trees grow down into the earth from above, swaying in the air. I drank clear water from a bromeliad clinging to a hog plum tree: crickets were chirping in broad daylight.—To sleep, in the house of the "bad Spaniard": he fled to Santiago de Cuba: the house has a zinc roof and a filthy floor: the men devour the bunches of plantains hanging from poles along the roof, two pigs, doves and ducks, a heap of cassava in a corner. This is La Demajagua.

May 4

Bryson leaves. Soon after that: the court-martial of Masabó. He raped and robbed. Rafael presides and Mariano reads the charges. Somber, Masabó denies them, his face brutal. His defender invokes our arrival and asks for mercy. Death. As the sentence was read out, a man was peeling a piece of sugarcane at the back of the crowd. Gómez holds forth: "This man is not our comrade: he is a *vil gusano,* a vile worm." Masabó, who hasn't sat down, lifts his eyes toward him with hatred. The troops, in great silence, hear and applaud: *"¡Que viva!"* And as the march gets in order, Masabó remains standing; his eyes do not fall nor can any fear be seen in his body: his pants, wide and light, flap constantly, as if in a fast wind. At last they go, the horses, the prisoner, the entire force, to a nearby hollow, in the sun. A weighty moment: the troops silent, standing on tiptoe. The shots ring out, and then one more, and another to finish him off. Masabó died a valiant man. "How do I stand, Colonel? Front or back?" "Front." He was brave in battle.

May 16

Gómez goes out to visit the surrounding area. First, a search of the bags of Lieutenant Chacón, Officer Díaz, and Sergeant P. Rico—who grumble—to find a stolen half-bottle of lard. Conversation with Pacheco, the captain: the Cuban people want affection and not despotism; because of despotism many Cubans went over to the government and they'll do it again; what exists in the countryside is a people that has gone out in search of someone to treat it better than the Spaniard, and that thinks it only fair for its sacrifice to be acknowledged. I soothe—and deflect his demonstrations of affection toward me, as well as everyone else's. Marcos, the Dominican: "Even your footprints!" Gómez returns from Rosalío's house. The mayor of La Venta is going free: the soldiers in La Venta, Andalusians, want to come over to our side. Rain, writing, reading.

May 17

Gómez goes with 40 horsemen to give the Bayamo convoy some trouble. I stay behind, writing, with Garriga and Feria, who are copying the *General Instructions* to the commanders and officers, twelve men with me under Lieutenant Chacón, with three guards at the three roads, and next to me, Graciano Pérez. Rosalío, riding his lead pack mule, mud up to his knees, brings me, in his own basket, a fond lunch: "for you, I give my life." The two Chacón brothers arrive, just come from Santiago, one of them the owner of the herd that was seized the day before yesterday, and his blond brother, an educated, comical man, and José Cabrera, a shoemaker from Jiguaní, sturdy and frank, and Duane, a young Negro like a carving, in shirt, pants, and a wide belt, and . . . Ávalos, shy, and Rafael Vásquez, and Desiderio Soler, 16 years old, whom Chacón brings along like a son. There's another son here, Ezequiel Morales, 18 years old, his father dead in the wars. And those who arrive tell me about Rosa Moreno, the widowed campesina who sent her only son, Melesio, 16 years old, to Rabí: "Your father died in that: I can't go now: you go." They roast plantains and pound jerked beef with a stone for the newcomers. The rising waters of the Contramaestre are very murky, and Valentín brings me a jug, boiled and sweetened, with fig leaves in it.

TRANSLATED BY ESTHER ALLEN

FERNANDO ORTIZ

Tobacco and Sugar

from CUBAN COUNTERPOINT

Tobacco is born, sugar is made. Tobacco is born pure, is processed pure and smoked pure. To secure saccharose, which is pure sugar, a long series of complicated physiochemical operations are required merely to eliminate impurities—bagasse, scum, sediment, and obstacles in the way of crystallization.

Tobacco is dark, ranging from black to mulatto; sugar is light, ranging from mulatto to white. Tobacco does not change its color; it is born dark and dies the color of its race. Sugar changes its coloring; it is born brown and whitens itself; at first it is a syrupy mulatto and in this state pleases the common taste; then it is bleached and refined until it can pass for white, travel all over the world, reach all mouths, and bring a better price, climbing to the top of the social ladder.

"In the same box there are no two cigars alike; each one has a different taste," is a phrase frequent among discerning smokers, whereas all refined sugar tastes the same.

Sugar has no odor; the merit of tobacco lies in its smell and it offers a gamut of perfumes, from the exquisite aroma of the pure Havana cigar, which is intoxicating to the smell, to the reeking stogies of European manufacture, which prove to what levels human taste can sink.

One might even say that tobacco affords satisfaction to the touch and the sight. What smoker has not passed his hand caressingly over the rich *brevas* or *regalías* of a freshly opened box of

Havanas? Do not cigar and cigarette act as a catharsis for nervous tension to the smoker who handles them and holds them delicately between lips and fingers? And what about chewing tobacco or snuff? Do they not titillate their users' tactile sense? And, for the sight, is not a cigar in the hands of a youth a symbol, a foretaste of manhood? And is not tobacco at times a mark of class in the ostentation of brand and shape? At times nothing less than a *corona coronada,* a crowned crown. Poets who have been smokers have sung of the rapt ecstasy that comes over them as they follow with eyes and imagination the bluish smoke rising upward, as though from the ashes of the cigar, dying in the fire like a victim of the Inquisition, its spirit, purified and free, were ascending to heaven, leaving in the air hieroglyphic signs like ineffable promises of redemption.

Whereas sugar appeals to only one of the senses, that of taste, tobacco appeals not only to the palate, but to the smell, touch, and sight. Except for hearing, there is not one of the five senses that tobacco does not stimulate and please.

Sugar is assimilated in its entirety; much of tobacco is lost in smoke. Sugar goes gluttonously down the gullet into the intestines, where it is converted into muscle-strengthening vigor. Tobacco, like the rascal it is, goes from the mouth up the turnings and twistings of the cranium, following the trail of thought. *Ex fumo dare lucem.* Not for nothing was tobacco condemned as a snare of the devil, sinful and dangerous.

Tobacco is unnecessary for man and sugar is a requisite of his organism. And yet this superfluous tobacco gives rise to a vice that becomes a torment if it is denied; it is far easier to become resigned to doing without the necessary sugar.

Tobacco contains a poison: nicotine; sugar affords nourishment: carbohydrates. Tobacco poisons, sugar nourishes. Nicotine stimulates the mind, giving it diabolical inspiration; the excess of glucose in the blood benumbs the brain and even causes stupidity.

For this reason alone tobacco would be of the liberal reform group and sugar of the reactionary conservatives; fittingly enough, a century ago in England the Whigs were regarded as little less than devils and the Tories as little less than fools.

Tobacco is a medicinal plant; it was so considered by both Indians and Europeans. Tobacco is a narcotic, an emetic, and an antiparasitic. Its active ingredient, nicotine, is used as an antitetanic, in cases of paralysis of the bladder, and as an insecticide. In olden times it was used for the most far-fetched cures; according to Father Cobo, "to cure innumerable ailments, in green or dried leaf form, in powder, in smoke, in infusion, and in other ways." Cuban folklore has preserved some of these practices in home remedies. Snuff was used as a dentifrice. At the beginning of the nineteenth century a very bitter-tasting variety, known as Peñalver, was manufactured in Havana and exported to England for this purpose; it contained a mixture of powdered tobacco and a kind of red clay. Tobacco has always been highly prized for its sedative qualities, and was regarded as a medicine for the spirit. For this reason, if long ago the savages censed their idols in caves with tobacco to placate their fury with adulation, today one burns the incense of tobacco in the hollows of one's own skull to calm one's worries and breathe new life into one's illusions.

Sugar, too, has its medicinal side and is even a basic element of our physiological makeup, producing psychological disturbances by its deficiency as by its excess. For this reason, and because of their scarcity, sugar and tobacco were sold centuries ago at the apothecary's shop. But in spite of their old association on the druggist's shelves, tobacco and sugar have always been far removed. In the opinion of moralists tobacco was vicious in origin, and was abominated by them and condemned by kings as much as it was exalted by the doctors.

Tobacco is, beyond doubt, malignant; it belongs to that dangerous and widespread family of the Solanaceæ. In the old Eurasian world the Solanaceæ were known to inspire terror, torment, visions, and delirium. Mandragora produced madness and dreams and acted as an aphrodisiac. Atropa gave its name to one of the Fates. Belladonna gave the sinful blackness of hell to the pupils of beautiful women's eyes. Henbane was the narcotic poison of classic literature. The various Daturas were the source of alkaloids that the Indians of Asia as well as those of America employed in their rites, spells, and crimes. In our New World this family of cursed plants was regenerated. Even though the Datura, of which the lowly Jimsonweed is a species, still works its diabolical will here, inspiring the mystic frenzy of Aztecs, Quechuas, Zuñis, Algonquins, and other native tribes, America has paid its debt of sin with interest, bestowing on mankind other plants of the solanaceous family, but upright, edible members, such as the potato, which today is cultivated more extensively throughout the world than wheat; the tomato, the "love apple" of the French, whose juice is considered a stimulating wine today; and the pepper, that king of spices, which carries to all the globe the burning and vitamin-rich stimulus of the tropical sun of America.

But in addition to these exemplary plants with their nutritious, homely, respectable fruits, the Solanaceæ of America set afoot in the world that scamp of the family, tobacco, neither fruit nor food, sly and conceited, lazy and having no other object than to tempt the spirit. The moralists of Europe were fully aware of the mischief-making properties of that irresistible Indian tempter. Quevedo said in Spain that "more harm had been done by bringing in that powder and smoke than the Catholic King had committed through Columbus and Cortés." But those were rogues' days and nothing could be devised to halt this Indian tobacco which, like the Limping Devil, went roving all over the world because everywhere it found a longing for dreams and indulgence for rascalities.

In Europe tobacco became utterly degraded, the instrument of crime, the accomplice of criminals. In the eighteenth century there was a general fear of being poisoned by deadly poison mixed with snuff. "Perfumed snuff was at times the vehicle of poison," says the historian of tobacco, Fairholt. "In 1712 the Duke of Noailles presented the Dauphine of France with a box of Spanish snuff, a gift which pleased her mightily. The snuff was saturated with poison, and after inhaling it for five days the Dauphine died, complaining of a severe pain in her temples. This caused great excitement, and there was great fear of accepting a pinch of snuff, and likewise of offering it. It was generally believed that this poisoned snuff was used in Spain and by Spanish emissaries to get rid of political opponents, and also that it was employed by the Jesuits to poison their enemies. For this reason it was given the name of 'Jesuit snuff.' This fear persisted for a long time." In 1851 tobacco was guilty of murder. The Count of Bocarme was put to death in Mons for poisoning his brother-in-law with nicotine that was extracted from tobacco for this purpose.

As though to heighten the malignity of tobacco, there is that special virus, or ultra-virus, which attacks it, and produces the dread disease known as mosaic. Sugarcane, too, suffers from a mosaic; but that which preys upon tobacco is produced by the first of the filtrable viruses, which was not only the first to be discovered, in 1857, but is the most infectious of all. It is stubbornly immune to ether, chloroform, acetone, and other similar countermeasures. There is something diabolical about this virus of tobacco mosaic. Its behavior is almost supernatural. It has not yet been ascertained whether it is a living molecule at the bottom of the life scale, or merely a macromolecule of crystallized protein. As though it had a double personality, the virus is as inert as distilled water, as inoffensive as a cherub, until it comes into contact with tobacco. But as soon as it penetrates the plant it becomes as active and malignant as the worst poison, like a mischievous devil in a vestry room. It almost seems as though it were in the essence of the tobacco that the virus finds the evil power by which it mottles the plant, dressing it up like a devil or a harlequin. The instant the tiniest particle of the infernal virus establishes contact with the protoplasm of tobacco, all its evil powers come to life, it infects every healthy plant, reproduces by the million, and in a few days a whole crop is stricken and destroyed by the virosis. As though the virulence of tobacco were the most deadly, when the Indians had to sleep in places infested by poisonous animals they were in the habit of spreading tobacco around themselves as a defense, for, as Father Cobo says, "it has a great malevolence against poisonous animals and insects" and drives them away as by magic.

Now to the traditional malignity of tobacco another and more cruel is being attributed: the power to cause cancer by means of the tars extracted from it. An Argentine doctor (Dr. Ángel H. Roffo) smeared these tars on the skin of rabbits, and cancer resulted "in every case." This did not occur with the tars distilled from Havana tobacco, but even with these half of the cases experimented with developed cancer.

At the same time scientists are still studying the possibility that cancer may be produced by an ultra-virus, that is to say, one of those protein viruses which, although chemical compounds, behave with lifelike activity, multiplying when in contact with certain living organisms, growing and dying like living cells. A scientist (Dr. W. W. Stanley) who achieved fame by isolating certain viruses in the form of crystals, holds the belief that whether those viruses that are invisible even with the microscope are the cause of cancer or not, they hold the secret of those irritations of the tissues, and in them are to be found the governing factors of the vital process in all cells, whether normal or cancerous. The puzzling feature of this horrible disease, which seems to consist in a wild reproduction of living cells out of harmony with hereditary structural rhythms, and the no less puzzling phenomenon of this ultra-virus of tobacco mosaic, which also manifests itself as the unforeseen coming to life of certain molecules that suddenly lose their inertia on coming into contact with tobacco, and reproduce and proliferate madly, carrying the germs of life, add a new mystery to the nature of tobacco. Can it be that there is something in tobacco that is a powerful stimulant of life, that can make cells proliferate in this wild manner and give to inert molecules the vital power of reproductivity, just as its smoke stimulates the weary, guttering spirit so it may flame up anew and live with renewed vigor?

There is always a mysterious, sacral quality about tobacco. Tobacco is for mature people who are responsible to society and to the gods. The first smoke, even when it is behind one's parents' backs, is in the nature of a *rite de passage,* the tribal rite of initiation into the civic responsibilities of manhood, the test of fortitude and control against the bitterness of life, its burning temptations, and the vapors of its dreams. The Jívaro Indians of South America, as a matter of fact, use tobacco in the celebration of *kusupaní,* the ceremony that marks the coming of age of the youths of the tribe. Among certain Indians of America, like the Jívaros, and some of the Negro peoples of Africa, such as the Bantus, the spirit of tobacco is masculine, and only men may cultivate the plant and prepare it for the rites. Sugar, on the other hand, is not a thing for men, but for children in their tender infancy, something mothers give their little ones as soon as they can taste, like a symbolic omen of the sweetness of life. "With sugar or honey, everything tastes good," goes the old saying.

Tobacco was always a thing of consequence. It was the glory of the conquerors of the Indies, then the mariner's companion on his ocean voyages, and the comrade of old soldiers in distant lands, or settlers returning from America, of self-satisfied magnates, rich businessmen; and it became the seal and emblem of every man who was able to buy himself a pleasure and display it in defiant opposition to the conventionalisms that would put a check-rein upon pleasure.

In the fabrication, the fire and spiraling smoke of a cigar, there was always something revolutionary, a kind of protest against oppression, the consuming flame and a liberating flight into the blue of dreams. For this reason the reciprocal offering of tobacco is a fraternal rite of peace, like the swearing of blood brotherhood among savages or the firing of salvos between battleships. When Europe met America for the first time, the latter offered tobacco in sign of friendship. When Christopher Columbus stepped on American soil for the first time in Guanahaní on October 12, 1492, the Indians of the island greeted him with an offertory rite, a gift of tobacco: "Some dried leaves, which must be a thing highly esteemed among them, for in San Salvador they made me a present of them." To give leaves of tobacco or a cigarette was a gesture of peace and friendship among the Indians of Guanahaní, among the Taínos, and among others of the continent. Just as it is today among the whites of civilized nations. Smoking the same pipe, taking snuff from the same snuffbox, or exchanging cigarettes is a rite of friendship and communion like sharing a bottle of wine or a loaf of bread. It is the same among the Indians of America, the whites of Europe, and the Negroes of Africa.

Tobacco is a masculine thing. Its leaves are hairy, and as though weathered and tanned by the sun; its color is that of the earth. Twisted and enveloped in its wrapper as a cigar, or shredded and smoked in a pipe, it is always a boastful and swaggering thing, like an oath of defiance springing erect from the lips. In days gone by, the country women of Cuba, who shared with their men the joys and tasks of their rustic existence, smoked their homemade cigars, and not a few in the cities preserved these rural customs in their own homes. All through Europe certain highborn and emancipated ladies of the aristocracy smoked in the seductive intimacy of their boudoirs. Even the daughters of the Grand Monarch smoked, although Louis XIV himself abhorred tobacco. The custom spread, but then gradually disappeared until finally only the peasant women of certain countries continued to smoke a pipe. Among the upper classes some ladies went on smoking Havana cigars, but this was an eccentricity that occasioned much comment. In the present age, which has attenuated the social dimorphism between the sexes, women smoke perhaps more than their hardy mates. But even today they limit themselves to cigarettes, the babies of cigars, of embryonic masculinity, all wrapped in rice paper, and with gold tips, and even perfumed, sweetened, and perverted like effeminate youths. The women who smoke cigarettes today remind one of those exquisite abbés of the eighteenth century who mixed their snuff with musk, ambergris, rose vinegar, and other exotic perfumes. They do not smoke real cigars, *puros,* pure in content and in name, as they were invented by the Indians of Cuba, in their pristine simplicity, naked, unadorned, without the adulterations, mixtures, wrappings, perfume, and refinements of a decadent civilization. A cigar is smoked with "the five senses" and with meditation, which comes as sensation is transformed into thought and ideals; but one smokes a cigarette without thinking or reflecting, as a habit one has fallen into, which among women is a mark of smartness and frivolous coquetry.

If tobacco is male, sugar is female. The leaves of its stalk are always smooth, and even when burned by the sun are still fair. The whole process of sugar-refining is one continual preparation and embellishment to clean the sugar and give it whiteness. Sugar has always been more of a woman's sweetmeat than a man's need. The latter usually looks down upon sweets as a thing below his masculine dignity. But if where tobacco is concerned women invade man's field smoking cigarettes, which are the children of cigars, men return the compliment in their consumption of sugar, not in the form of sweets, syrups, or candy, but as alcohol, which is the offspring of the sugar residues.

There is no rebellion or challenge in sugar, nor resentment, nor brooding suspicion, but humble pleasure, quiet, calm, and soothing. Tobacco is boldly imaginative and individualistic to the point of anarchy. Sugar is on the side of sensible pragmatism and social integration. Tobacco is as daring as blasphemy; sugar as humble as a prayer. Don Juan, the scoffer and seducer, probably smoked tobacco, while the little novitiate Doña Inés must have munched caramels. Faust, that discontented philosopher, probably puffed at a pipe, while the gentle, devout Marguerite nibbled at sugar wafers.

Character analysts would classify sugar as a *pycnik,* tobacco as a leptosomae type. If sugar was the treat that Sancho, the gluttonous peasant, relished, tobacco might well have answered the purpose for Don Quixote, the visionary hidalgo. Sancho was too poor to get his fill of sugar; tobacco was too dear to reach La Mancha in time to delight the impoverished squire. But it is reasonable to believe that the one would have stuffed himself on cakes and the other would have seen visions and fabulous monsters in the puffs of smoke. And if Don Quixote had ever come upon a smoker puffing out smoke, he would have considered this one of his most fantastic adventures, which is what they tell happened in 1493 to one of the early users of tobacco, who as he was smoking in his home at Ayamonte in Cuba was believed to be possessed of a devil and was denounced by the officials of the Holy Inquisition, who refused to tolerate any smoke that was not that of incense or the faggots heaped about the stake.

Psychologists would say that sugar is an extrovert, with an objective, matter-of-fact soul, and that tobacco is an introvert, subjective and imaginative. Nietzsche might have called sugar Dionysian and tobacco Apollonian. The former is the mother of the alcohol that produces the sacred joy and well-being. In tobacco's spirals of smoke there are fallacious beauties and poetic inspirations. Perhaps old Freud wondered whether sugar was narcissistic and tobacco erotic. If life is an ellipsis with its two foci in stomach and loins, sugar is food and nourishment while tobacco is love and reproduction.

In their origins sugar and tobacco were equally pagan, and still are by reason of their sensual appeal. In both their pagan beginnings go far back, even though they were unknown to the old gods and peoples of the Mediterranean world, who used bread and wine in their orgies, mysteries, and communions. Jehovah promised his people a land flowing with milk and honey, not with tobacco and sugar. The Hebrew knew neither sugar nor tobacco, nor did Jesus and his apostles, or the Christian faithful. These latter learned the taste of sugar from the Arabs during the crusades to Jerusalem, on the Moslem-held islands of Cyprus and Sicily, from the Moors in the gardens of Valencia or on the plains of Granada. The white peoples of the Middle Ages did not know tobacco, but sugar was familiar to them. The Archpriest of Hita could gorge himself on sugared delicacies. In the fourteenth century he was writing (*Libro de Buen Amor,* stanza 1,337):

All kinds of sugar with these nuns are plentiful as dirt,
The powdered, lump, and crystallized, and syrups for dessert;
They've perfumed sweetmeats, heaps of candy—some with spice of wort,
With other kinds which I forget and cannot here insert. *

But the roguish clergyman knew nothing of tobacco and its delights.

The Christians discovered tobacco when they discovered the Indians of the New World, first in Cuba, then in the other islands of the West Indies, and then in the countries of the Spanish Main. This was toward the end of the fifteenth century, at the very

*Translation by E. K. Kane.

beginning of the modern era. And was not this moment marked by the discovery of a New World by the white men of Europe?

It would seem as though tobacco had lived in hiding, exercising its powers in the jungles of an unknown world, until civilization was ready to receive its stimuli with the arrival of the Renaissance and rationalism.

Tobacco is "the gracious plant that gives smoke, man's companion," wrote the Cuban José Martí. And with this steady company for every hour, even those of solitude and vigil, those hours of man's mysterious fecundations, he found in it consolation for his spirit, a spur for thought, and a ladder of inspiration. To Martí tobacco's role in history has been "to comfort the thoughtful and delight the musing architects of the air." America surprised Europe with tobacco, that genie who built castles in the air, and the sixteenth century was the century of Utopias, of the cities of dreams.

Tobacco smoke wafted the breath of a new spirit through the Old World, analytic, critical, and rebellious. In the end the smoke of the Indian tobacco proved itself more powerful by arousing the minds of men than that of the Inquisition's pyres hounding them mercilessly.

Tobacco and sugar were children of the Indies; but the latter was born in the East, the former in the West. One's name is of Sanskrit origin; the other still keeps its native savage nomenclature. In the far-off Indies they believe that sugar came to them as a gift of the gods with the dew from heaven, to nourish and sustain the joys of the flesh, and then goes into the earth and is absorbed by it after the body that consumed it has rotted away. In these Indies of ours it was believed that tobacco sprang from the earth through the action of the spirit of the caverns, and that after being burned in the human mouth and dissipated in trances of delight, its volatile essence rises carrying a message to the heavenly powers.

Despite the fact that both plants originated among heathen peoples, sugar was never frowned upon by the Church and was considered veritable ambrosia. But tobacco was regarded as an invention of the devil and was savagely persecuted to the lengths of excommunication and the gallows for its users. The devils are very astute, and to deceive the unsuspecting they often added to tobacco something to give it a sweet taste and an exotic perfume. Vanilla, mustard, anisette, caraway seed, and even molasses were all used to cover up the rascality of tobacco with the blessed cape of sweetness. Especially tobaccos of inferior quality, whose power of temptation was slight, and which were generally rejected as being unquestionably "infernal" if they were not disguised by some sweet, sugary flavor and given an odor that might be confused with that of sanctity. This was what the devil used to do with inexperienced and reluctant smokers, in the case of twist for pipes, and snuff; today he does it with ladies' cigarettes. Virtuous perfumes, sanctimonious flavors—perversions fomented by greed or inspired by Satan.

In the smoking of a cigar there is a survival of religion and magic as they were practiced by the *behiques,* the medicine men, of Cuba. The slow fire with which it burns is like an expiatory rite. The smoke that rises heavenward has a spiritual evocation. The smoke, which is more pleasing than incense, is like a fumigatory purification. The fine, dirty ash to which it turns is a funereal suggestion of belated repentance. Smoking tobacco is raising puffs of smoke to the unknown, in search of a passing consolation or a hope which though fleeting beguiles for a moment. For this reason tobacco has been called "the anodyne of poverty" and the enemy of heartache.

Take a little tobacco
And your anger will pass.

These are the words Lope de Vega puts into the mouth of a Spaniard in the third act of *La mayor desgracia de Carlos V.* "When things go bad, try tobacco," says the old proverb, to express the hope-filled calm that settles over a man as the smoke of his cigar curls upward. Tobacco, according to the Cuban poet Federico Milanés, is:

The fragrant leaf that, turned to gentle smoke,
Drives from man's brow the leaden cares away.

For, as George Sand said, "It assuages grief and peoples solitude with a thousand pleasant images."

Even in the manner of lighting a cigar there is a sort of liturgical foretaste of mystery; whether it is by means of a spark struck from flint by steel, or by a phosphorous match whose scratched head bursts into flame. The devil has caused more wax to be employed in the tiny vestas burned in the rites of tobacco than the gods in the votive candles before their shrines. In this machine age the century-old liturgical traditions are dying out, and automatic lighters are being introduced for the smoker and electric bulbs for the churches. But in both cases the flickering flame of fire that ignites, illuminates, and burns like the spirit still persists. There is no trace of ritual observed in the consumption of sugar.

Sugar is the product of human toil, but it may be consumed by a beast; tobacco is rough and natural, but it has been set apart by Satan for the exclusive use of the being that calls himself the lord of creation, perhaps because he considers himself the last animal fashioned by the Maker and the only one having the right to sin.

There are those who might think that because of these concomitances between the devil and tobacco, the clergy might have been averse to its delights and cultivation, although, naturally, they did not refuse the tithes on the tobacco fields, which were carefully collected by the diligent tithers. There were probably churchmen who owned tobacco plantations; but, to the best of our knowledge, priests in Cuba did not count tobacconists' shops or cigar factories among their worldly goods, though it would be risky to deny the possibility of their having a share in such businesses, especially in these days of anonymous stockholders in great commercial enterprises which make possible easy and inconspicuous investments in the large tobacco companies. If the churchmen did not have plantations it was not because of fear of the devil, nor yet because of a distaste for the worldly attractions of trade or repugnance to owning slaves and treating them after the custom of the country. It is a well-known fact that from the beginning of the sixteenth century the clergy of these islands had numerous slaves for their service and their business undertakings, at times "more Negroes and plantations than the laity," according to a complaint made to the King in 1530 by the lawyers Espinosa and Zuazo. And there is no question that there were clergymen who raised cane, and were even plantation owners, openly and aboveboard, for the Jesuits had several sugar refineries here, each with its complement of Negro slaves, obedient to the work bell and the crack of the overseer's whip. In any case, the churchmen quickly came to terms with tobacco, and the factories of Havana even made the finest-quality cigars especially for the clergy, as well as for the royal family.

While it was possible for sugar, no matter where it was grown, always to be equally sweet, it was never possible to produce anywhere else in the world tobacco comparable to that of Cuba or a cigar to rival a pure Havana. This explains that folk song of Andalusia referring to tobacco, in the form of a riddle:

In Havana I was born
And in all the world known.

The manufacture of sugar quickly achieved a uniformity of product as a result of the complete similarity of industrial processes. Almost all plants contain sugar, some in abundance, like sugarcane, beets, and many others; they are cultivated in many lands, and different methods are used to extract their juice and, from this, the more or less refined crystals; but in the end there is only one kind of sugar. All saccharoses are the same. Even in the canefield each variety of cane reproduces itself without variation every year, not only because the same root sends up new shoots each year, but through the canes themselves, which come up from their own cuttings if these are rooted down for new plantings. In this reproduction of sugarcane there can be no breeding, genetic crossings, or variations. But no matter what the initial juice-yielding capacity of the cane, the unity of the final product is always the same.

Uniformity has never been possible, and never will be, where tobacco is concerned. The botanical varieties that contain nicotine are few; but even within each variety, and even in tobacco itself, each field, each crop, each plant, and perhaps each leaf has its own unique quality. And since the reproduction of tobacco is by means of seed, which each plant produces in great abundance, it is not to be wondered at that each crop contains many variations, the result of infinite crossbreedings and mixtures, of the carefully studied selections of the planter and the strange mutations and chromosomic caprices of nature. One of the greatest and most difficult problems of tobacco-planters and manufacturers is to maintain an unchanging standard in the quality of their product, which has an established reputation. The infinite and constant variety, natural or induced, is the secret of the success or failure of the tobacco industry, depending on the taste of the smoker. The planter and miller of sugarcane has no such problem, for he knows that, in the last analysis, all saccharose is the same, an amorphous mass, of similar granulation, without class or distinction.

The taste, the color, and the aroma of a cigar depend not only on its being of real tobacco, but on its being a Havana (which is the best in the world); on the region where it was grown (Vueltabajo, Semivuelta, Vueltarriba, Partidos, etc., if it is Cuban; or from Virginia, Java, Sumatra, Turkey, Egypt . . . or the devil's little acre); on its year, on the fertilizer that was used on the fields, on the weather conditions, on its fermentation, stripping, selection, stacking, leaf, wrapper, filler, blend, rolling, moisture, shape, packing, ocean shipping, the way it is lighted, the way it is smoked; in a word, each and every one of the steps in its life, from the plant that produces the leaf to the smoker who transforms it into smoke and ashes. For this reason the tobacco industry employs *escogedores* and *rezagadores,* who by touch, sight, smell, and taste can distinguish and select the leaves and tobacco, just as wine tasters do with the fermented juice of the vine. For each product of the tobacco industry a constant selection of the tobacco used is necessary. From the time tobacco is set out in the field until it goes up in smoke an innumerable series of selections and eliminations are required. In the color-field alone the nomenclature of smoking tobacco in Cuba is as finely shaded as that employed by anthropologists to describe the human race. The color of the different types of cigar, like that of women, cannot be simply reduced to blondes and brunettes. Just as a Cuban distinguishes among women every shade from jet-black to golden white, with a long intervening series of intermediary and mixed pigmentations, and classifies them according to color, attractiveness, and social position, so he knows the different types of tobacco: *claros, colorado-claros, colorados, colorado-maduros, maduros, ligeros, secos, medios-tiempos, finos, amarillos, manchados, quebrados, sentidos, broncos, puntillas,* and many others down to *botes y colas,* these last "from the wrong side of the railroad track," used only in the proletarian mass of cut tobacco. There are selectors who can distinguish seventy or eighty different shades of tobacco, with the technical exactitude of the most painstaking anthropologist. It is not to be wondered at that there are "tobaccologists" as bold and self-seeking as certain proponents of racial theories today who, for the sake of defending the tobacco interests of their own countries, have created varieties, blends, names, and brands as absurd and artificial as the imaginary races invented by the race theorists of the present. And the races of tobacco, as well as its mixtures and adulterations, are so on the increase at present that outside of Cuba there are hybrid cigars, of unconfessable ancestry, some not even of tobacco; and the Havana cigar of good family has always to be on the alert for innumerable and hateful bastards who would usurp the legitimacy of his good name.

As the taste of all refined sugars is the same, they always have to be taken with something that will give them flavor. No one, except a child with a sweet tooth, would think of eating sugar by itself. When people are starving, they will take it dissolved in water: the Cuban revolutionists, the *mambises,* drank *canchánchara* sometimes in the everglades, and the slaves drank cane juice as it ran from the press, just as today poor Cubans buy a glass of cane juice for a penny to fill their bellies and quiet their hunger. When one chews pieces of peeled cane and sucks out the juice, there is a mixture of flavors in it, and the same is true of cane syrup and raw sugar. From the time the Arabs with their alchemy brought "*alçucar,*" as it was still called in the royal decrees having to do with America, into our Western civilization, it has been used in syrups, frosting, icings, cakes, candy, always with other flavors added to it.

Tobacco is proud; it is taken straight, for its own sake, without company or disguise. Its ambition is to be pure, or to be so considered. Sugar by itself surfeits and cloys, and for this reason it needs company and uses a disguise or a chaperon. It must have some other substance to lend it a seductive flavor. And it, in turn, repays the favor by covering up the flatness, insipidness, or bitterness of other ingredients with its own sweetness. A miscegenation of flavors.

This basic contrast between sugar and tobacco is emphasized even more throughout the whole process of their agricultural, industrial, and commercial development by the amorphism of the one and the polymorphism of the other.

Sugar is common, unpretentious, undifferentiated. Tobacco is always distinguished, all class, form, and dignity. Sugar is always a formless mass whether as cane, juice, or syrup, and then as sugar, whether in loaf, lump, grain, or powder, the same in the sack as in the sugar-bowl, or when it is absorbed in syrup, compote, preserves, candy, ice cream, cake, or other forms of pastry. Tobacco may be good or bad, but it always strives for individuality.

Sometimes, even when an attempt is made to bring about a similarity and even a confusion between different types, the indomitable individualism of tobacco thwarts the effort and turns the tables on the designing manufacturers. When during the past century cigars were manufactured in Seville with Virginia filler and Havana wrapper for the Spanish market, to the detriment of the Cuban product, the critical smokers could detect at a glance the difference between the two by the fact that the wrapper of the Havana cigars was rolled from right to left, and that of the Peninsular article from left to right. It almost amounted to saying that the Cubans were leftists, and the inhabitants of Seville rightists. Perhaps the distinction still holds good.

The best smoker looks for the best cigar, the best cigar for the best wrapper, the best wrapper for the best leaf, the best leaf for the best cultivation, the best cultivation for the best seed, the best seed for the best field. This is why tobacco-raising is such a meticulous affair, in contrast to cane, which demands little attention. The tobacco-grower has to tend his tobacco not by fields, not even by plants, but leaf by leaf. The good cultivation of good tobacco does not consist in having the plant give more leaves, but the best possible. In tobacco quality is the goal; in sugar, quantity. The ideal of the tobacco man, grower or manufacturer, is distinction, for his product to be in a class by itself, *the best.* For both sugar-grower and refiner the aim is *the most;* the most cane, the most juice, the most bagasse, the most evaporating-pans, the most centrifugals, the highest crystallization, the most sacks, and the most indifference as to quality for the sake of coming as close as possible in the refineries to a symbolic hundred percent chemical purity where all difference of class and origin is obliterated, and where the mother beet and the mother cane are forgotten in the equal whiteness of their offspring because of the equal chemical and economic standing of all the sugars of the world, which, if they are pure, sweeten, nourish, and are worth the same.

The consumer of sugar neither knows nor asks where the product he uses comes from; he neither selects it nor tries it out. The smoker seeks one specific tobacco, this one or the other. The person with a sweet tooth just asks for sugar, without article, pronoun, or adjective to give it a local habitation and a name. When, in the process of refining, sugar has achieved a high degree of saccharose and of chemical purity it is impossible to distinguish one from the other even in the best-equipped laboratory. All sugars are alike; all tobaccos are different.

Sugar is, strictly speaking, a single product. To be sure, cane always yielded, in addition to crystallized saccharose, alcohol, brandy, or rum. But this was a by-product and not sugar, just as the nicotine extracted from tobacco is not tobacco. All through the Antilles alcohol was distilled from molasses, and liquors were made from it: rum in Cuba, eau-de-vie in the French West Indies, rum in Jamaica, bitters in Trinidad, curaçao, and so on. Alcohol was always the cargo for the slaver's return trip, for with it slaves were bought, local chieftains bribed, and the African tribes corrupted and weakened. Out of this strongly flavored, caramel-colored alcohol manufactured in the West Indies for the slave-runners, mixed with the sugar with which they were provisioned along with jerked beef, codfish, and other foods designed to withstand the long crossings, and the lemons that the sailing ships always carried to ward off epidemics of scurvy, a mixed drink indigenous to the slave-trading boats came into being. It is known today as a Daiquirí, its name coming from the place where the United States soldiers first made its acquaintance. But rum was never a prime factor in the social economy of Cuba any more than were the heartwoods, hides, shellfish, and other secondary products. It is also true that the sugar-refiners in olden times manufactured different kinds of sugar, such as muscovado, loaf sugar, brown sugar, white sugar, and so forth. But these sugars were all the same product of the cane, refined to varying degrees, within the same mill, varying only in crystallization or purity.

Tobacco, on the other hand, from its first appearance in history as an article of trade, came in different forms, which were prepared in different ways. In the industrial field, tobacco has yielded six typical products. The first was that which we Cubans call tobacco by antonomasia and by adhering strictly to history, for this was the name given it by the Cuban Indians. Tobacco, strictly speaking, consists, as in the days of the Indians, of a variable number of dried tobacco leaves, called *tripa,* rolled up and enveloped in another leaf called *capa,* all forming a cylindrical roll about half an inch thick and four to eight inches long, pointed at both ends. It was in this form that the Spaniards first made the acquaintance of tobacco, and they gave it the popular name *cigarro.*

In addition to tobacco, or cigar, there were and are other products of the same plant: namely, *andullo,* or plug tobacco; twist, for chewing or pipe smoking; *picadura,* or fine-cut tobacco to be smoked in a pipe or rolled in husk or paper; *cigarrillos,* which are not little cigars or *tabaquitos,* but leaf or cut tobacco rolled in paper; and snuff, or powdered tobacco. These products of the tobacco industry do not represent successive phases in the same process of manufacture. They are all different products, and in their fabrication the tobacco from the start is handled differently, depending on the article desired. Tobacco is also exported in bulk to be made up abroad, to the detriment of Cuba's commercial standing. In this case tobacco occupies the status of a semi-raw material, like the raw sugar that is bought up by foreign refiners for the benefit of the country where it is processed rather than Cuba. These last years have seen the development of a new industrial tobacco product, the stripped leaf, in the preparation of which cheap Cuban labor is employed, and which is then exported and sold to foreign factories, which save the difference in the salaries they would have to pay and then, as though they were tobacco refineries, utilize this high-grade Cuban product, depriving our country of the profits of its final elaboration.

In any case the cultivation, processing, and manufacture of tobacco is all care, selection, attention to detail, emphasis on variety; this extends from the different botanical varieties to the innumerable commercial forms to satisfy the individual taste of the consumer. In the production of sugar the emphasis is on indifference to selection, lumping all the cane together, milling, grinding, mixing with an eye to uniformity. It passes from the botanical mass to the chemical product with the sole aim of satisfying the largest and most general tastes of the human palate.

The consumption of tobacco—that is to say, smoking—is a personal, individualized act. The consumption of sugar has no specific name; it is the humdrum satisfaction of an appetite. For this reason there is a word for smoker; there is no such word as "sugarer."

TRANSLATED BY HARRIET DE ONÍS

ANTONIO BENÍTEZ-ROJO

A View from the Mangrove

TO PACHÍN MARÍN AND NICOLÁS ROJO

The heron, a white arrow, shoots down from the yagruma limb. As it hits the water's surface, it extends its wings, clamps its beak around one of the crabs on the mangrove's roots, and flies back up to the same branch. Then it tosses its head back, gives a quick shake from side to side, and swallows the crab.

From his hammock he has seen the heron repeat this feat about a dozen times, always with the indifferent regularity of a cuckoo clock. But nevertheless, and in spite of their methodical extermination, the crabs stay motionless, as if they were just empty shells or something growing from the exposed mangrove roots. He tries to explain these little crabs' stupidity to himself. Perhaps they're very young. At the moment he can't think of any better reason. After a while he concludes that they're not stupid. The crabs are following an instinct: the least movement of a leg or claw would draw the heron's immediate attention. There are thousands of crabs on the mangrove roots, and only one bird to prey on them. Statistics favor the individual who doesn't move.

The heron leaves its branch and starts to fly above the swamp. It disappears in the direction of the coast. The crabs begin to stir themselves, devouring the roots' tiny parasites. He feels a surge of nausea. Finally he falls asleep.

. . .

The hammock has been strung between two yagrumas, the only two trees growing on his tiny islet. His rifle, a Mauser, hangs from one of the branches overhead. The old man slung it from the stock and barrel, and now it dangles by his right cheek. The captain wanted to leave him with just a machete, with firearms scarce, and anyway, what use would a man have for a Mauser if he is dying of yellow fever? But someone said that to kill an alligator you have to have a rifle, and the general, already mounted on his horse, said: Leave the Mauser with that man and let's get the hell out of here! Leave him a bottle of my gin, too!

There are many little alligators all around the islet, but of the big ones he has only caught a look at two. They had arrived together. They came out of the black water and began to lumber toward the hammock. He grabbed the Mauser and aimed it at the first in line. He didn't have to shoot. On seeing him stir, both halted their advance. Then the trailing one bit into the other's tail and began to eat it, chewing with a desolate torpor, like a cow. The alligator that had been attacked stayed motionless for a long while. When it had lost a good part of its tail, it moved back slowly toward the water. The other followed nonchalantly.

There is a time of day at which the swamp's scenario shows some coloration. At noontime, when the sky is not cloudy, the sunlight washes away the carbonous coating that covers everything around. Then the twisted mangrove branches take on a rusty shade, and in their leaves one sees dark green, maroon, and yellow. Beyond, at a distance of two hundred feet from the islet, there is a clump of mahogany trees. Hidden among its highest branches there must be a parrots' nest; he has seen them fly by several times with worms in their beaks. At midday the gaudy pair always come out to enjoy the sun; they delouse each other and then approach the other's head as if about to kiss. Below, the water is still black, but in the fat, oily bubbles rising from the turbid depths there are all the colors of the rainbow. It is a beautiful moment. That is when he uncorks the bottle, takes a little sip of gin, and starts to read the English botanist's book in the vibrant clarity of the breeze that wafts in from the sea. Luckily the crazy old man who looks after him never comes by at this enchanted hour.

Look here, old man, my fiancée, what do you think?

I like those green eyes.

How'd you know they're green? They look gray in the photo.

Are you going to marry her?

Of course I am. As soon as the war ends. Her name is Julia. She works at the Cuban Revolutionary Junta in New York. How long do you think the war will last?

Wars last forever.

The general thinks this one will end in 1900. This war is not what I expected. It's shit. The things you do won't go away. But there's no choice, you have to keep on fighting. After the last shot is fired, I'm sailing to New York. We'll get married there and come back to live in Havana. I miss her. I can't show her letters to you because I left them with the general. You never know.

I'll see you tomorrow. The tide is going out and the rowboat will get stuck. It happened the other day.

The old man lives inland, at the edge of the swamp. He makes charcoal there out of mangrove wood. It isn't easy to make charcoal, the old man says. If a person doesn't know how to make an oven in the earth, the mangrove turns into ashes and all that work is lost.

Shortly before dawn, when the creatures in the swamp are resting and the inland air blows strong, he can smell the smoke from the old man's ovens. He feels less lonely then, and starts thinking of the good things left for him to do.

What do you do with all that charcoal?

I stuff it into gunnysacks. Then I sew them up and sell them to a man who comes by in an oxcart. That man sells them to another man who has a big wagon with four mules. My charcoal gets to Havana, and from there they take it by boat to New York and London.

You're crazy.

I've been looking at the mangroves for too long.

To get to the islet, the old man has to set out two hours earlier in his little boat and open a path through the narrow channels of the mangrove swamp. A few days earlier, he had made this trip along with the old man, but he had the yellow fever then and he hardly remembers anything: just an atrocious headache and the certainty that he was going to die.

The general gave me money to take care of you. You'll be fine here. The enemy won't find you. I'll hitch the hammock to those two yagrumas. I'll work a herbal cure on you. You'll see, the old man says.

Here's *Ricinus communis* for your headache.

Hibiscus abelmoschus to sweat out the fever.

Pimpinela anisum to expel the gas.

Ammona squamosa to quiet the nerves.

Are you sure you're going to cure me?

Nothing is for sure. You have to survive a relapse. One morning you'll wake up feeling better and you'll think you're cured. But you won't be. The next day the relapse will strike. It always happens like that with yellow fever, the old man says.

I feel better this morning. I've only thrown up once.

That's a good sign. When you're stronger I'm going to arrange things so that you can go back home, the old man says.

I can't go back there. My town is occupied by a Spanish regiment. And besides, I don't have any family there.

Where do you want to go?

I'd like to go to New York. I'd like to see my fiancée. Even for just a few weeks. Sometimes I touch my face and I think my hands are hers. Afterwards, I'd come back to Cuba with any group that wants to fight.

I think I can arrange your trip, the old man says with assurance. Inexplicably, neither his face nor his hands have coal stains on them.

He lifts up his hand from the edge of the hammock and examines it, turning it over from one side to the other. His skin is still yellow.

It was the fever. It attacks the liver. But now you're over the fever. Only the memory of it is left. You're weak now, the old man says, as he feeds him cold rice and sardines. You'll have the relapse tomorrow. When it's over, you'll be out of danger and I'll take you in my boat.

How do you feel?

I didn't sleep too well, he says. He reaches out toward the tree with his yellow hand. A white owl had been perched there for a long time. The crabs, as well.

At night the mosquitoes don't bother him much. But the big crabs still climb up the tree trunks and get into his hammock. They don't bite. They like to wander over his body. That always wakes him. Then he takes his hat off his face and brushes them off.

Come on. It's time to go. I'll help you get to the boat. You can lean on your rifle.

The old man starts rowing at an incredible rate. The mangroves pass by his eyes as though he saw them from a galloping horse. Who would have his horse now? Too fast. *Muntingia calabura* for dizziness.

On his arrival, he vomits a thick substance, black and congealed.

The house has a modest porch with two mahogany armchairs. The old man walks indecisively toward the door, stares at the iron ring that functions as a knocker, and turns around very slowly to face him: We'd better stay on the porch. The house is crammed with charcoal bags. If I leave them outside, they soak up rain and no one buys them. We'll wait here for the man with the cart.

He slumps into one of the armchairs. The wound on his back starts burning and he squirms to the edge of the seat. I'm dead tired. Do you live alone?

I live with myself, the old man answers. The other me is inside.

If you hadn't taken care of me, I would have died. Where do you think the general is? He's a bad-tempered man, but he values me. He left me the Mauser and a bottle of his own gin. I'm on his general staff, he says, looking at the old man's worried eyes.

Nobody knows where he is. He had to retreat. The Spanish column brought artillery along. You asked them yourself to hide you in the swamp. You couldn't stay on your horse anymore.

I heard him say that he'd come back for me.

Don't worry. We've got to keep on going now. The swamp is full of Spanish soldiers and my house isn't safe.

He had thought he wouldn't be able to breathe inside the gunnysack. But he could. The old man put him in there, curled up like a fetus. He lay some charcoal over his hat and sewed it up.

What if the Spaniards stick their bayonets into the bags?

They never do, says the old man's friend. And he feels them loading him up into the cart. Everything is set.

I'm coming with you on this trip. Don't think I'm doing it for the money.

Thanks, old man, he says from inside the sack. What about your work?

It doesn't matter. I've been crazy for a long time.

It isn't bad inside the sack. He feels a lot more protected there than in the hammock. He's not trembling any more. It's not as if the swamp was cold; the coldness was inside him. *Costos picatus* to warm up the stomach. The charcoal is protecting him as well. Why is that? It must retain the oven's heat. He sticks out his tongue and licks the charcoal. It is warm and tastes like toasted bread, with a crackling crust.

The oxen pulling on the cart move quickly. It feels as though he's going by train. It is all right, much better than the swamp.

The old man places his mouth on the sack and tells him in a quiet voice that they've arrived.

Where are we?

Nowhere.

The old man's crazy, he thinks.

Now the wagon will take you. When you get to Havana, tell the cook at the Hotel Inglaterra that I sent you. He'll let you know how you can travel to New York.

What's your name, old man?

I think my name is Eudelio.

What are you doing in there? Get out of that sack! We're going to hang you by the balls, says the Spanish sergeant, an energetic man with a thick, red face. The sergeant has ripped open the sack with a knife, and he emerges dusting off the charcoal soot with his hat. It's too bright there in the street. He looks around, squinting: a big avenue with trees, buildings, carriages, and Havana's walls as backdrop. The people who pass by stop to have a look at him. They inspect him from head to toe without saying anything, as if he were a circus attraction, the alligator man. One of the mules is peeing a thick stream of beer, good quality, with a head on it. Two soldiers help him get off the cart. They are blond and very young. They must be conscripts from Galicia or Catalonia. We're dying like flies, yellow fever, malaria, dysentery, typhoid, says one of them as he ties his hands behind his back, exactly where the wound is. You're going to die too. They're going to take you to Cabaña Castle and they'll shoot you there this very night. They always shoot spies.

I'm not a spy. I'm a soldier.

If you're a soldier, where's your rifle? asks the other conscript.

They put him under guard in the pantry at the Hotel Inglaterra because the colonel is taking his siesta and can't be disturbed. The room is crowded with chickens and sacks of charcoal. The chickens are jammed inside some wire cages; they flap and cackle without end. They are gray and black, the colors of the swamp before the magic hour and just after. He doesn't like chickens, particularly their yellow, horny feet, there's something horribly human about them, the last thing he would eat, he thinks, is a chicken foot. The smell of chicken shit is nauseating him. He goes to a corner to vomit; he gags but nothing comes up. He sits down on a charcoal sack. Being below street level, he can pass the time watching the vertiginous feet of passersby through the basement window bars. After a while he feels queasy and stops looking at the anonymous feet. Below the window, by the wall, there is a crate with three guinea hens inside. They're not making any noise. They are not moving either. They look stuffed. The young roosters will be eaten first, he concludes.

The water of the swamp, at sunrise, is always covered with a whitish vapor, but it's not a big thing, it is as if down below the peat were burning quietly. At nine o'clock the black water stops smoking, and then it's possible to see the little alligators, as long as one's arm, eating crabs and conches among the mangrove roots. That day, nevertheless, the swamp was hidden under a persistent fog bank. When midday came, his hammock seemed to float in the resplendent vapors like a fantastic ship; for a moment he felt like a navigator of the mists, an astral being who crossed spaces not belonging to this world; for a moment the root of the universe seemed his and he felt close to God. Then, beyond the islet, the enchanted mist began to break apart in sections, and suddenly the sunlit heads of the mahoganies appeared. The parrots were right there, as always, picking lice from one another with their curving beaks and showing off their colors. There was something indecent in their disdain for the grandeur of the spectacle. Without thinking it over, he grabbed the Mauser, drew it up before his face, and fired. One of the parrots fell into the cloud bank. In the echoing of the rifle shot, he heard the alligators splashing. The other parrot did not move. It stayed there, rigid, perched on the branch like an unbearable, big, stuffed bird. When the old man arrived, there was hardly any fog left.

What's the matter? What are you brooding about?

I did something I shouldn't have. I don't know why I did it. You're old, you ought to know.

I've brought you some *Picramnia pentandra.* It helps you when your soul is sick.

Come on, old man. Don't play deaf. You ought to know.

Ask me some other time. Today I came here just to tell you not to look at the mangrove trees too much. You can lose your sanity. Just look at me.

Late in the afternoon the pantry door opens, and he thinks they're going to shoot him now. It is the cook, an old man, short and thin. His moustache looks like the general's. The man pretends not to see him. He opens a cage, puts his arm in, and takes out one of the noisiest chickens. He has it by the neck. After examining it in the basement window light, he starts to whip it around like a windmill with his arm. The chicken drops a cloud of black feathers and stops its cackling. The man takes it by its feet with his other hand and walks toward the door. Are you the cook? he asks him. The man turns facing him and feigns surprise.

Who are you? What are you doing in my pantry?

I was sent here by Eudelio, the charcoal maker.

Come on with me. I owe a lot to him. How is he doing?

He's crazy.

The man smiles. He likes to play at being mad. But you seem

in bad shape. I'm going to make you a good soup with this chicken's feet and head. I'll hide you in an empty room. There are a lot of them now because it's summer and there's a yellow fever epidemic.

I can't eat chicken feet.

That doesn't matter, you won't see them in the dish. Follow me confidently and don't close the door. The colonel will think you've run away into the street.

But the guards . . . ?

What guards?

There were two of them.

Oh, those! They ran away. You look contagious.

The cook shows him an iron spiral staircase. It is very dark and he doesn't see the steps. He goes up falteringly, clinging to the handrail. It's for serving the guests who don't want to come down to the dining room, says the cook, raising his voice as if he were far away. You're really dirty and you smell terrible, he shouts. I'll tell one of the bellboys to bring you up some hot water. What country are you heading to?

There's something I have to do in New York.

That's no problem. I'll get the papers so they'll let you out of here and into there. I've got good connections.

Are we almost to the room? I'm out of breath. My heart is pounding.

Rivea corymbosa for heart palpitations.

Go slow. One more floor and we're there. The higher you get, the safer you'll be. I'm putting you with another one who's going to New York. So you'll have company. He's a Spanish soldier. A deserter like you.

I'm not a deserter. I had yellow fever and I'll come back to fight with another expedition. They organize the expeditions in New York. Haven't you heard of the New York Revolutionary Junta?

I don't care. They all say the same thing.

I'm ready to die for the cause.

You're a fool. Didn't the old man tell you that?

Of course I know you, the soldier says. He has just come out from underneath the bed. He is almost an adolescent. He has a tender blond moustache and a pimply nose.

You're mistaken. I've never seen you.

You seemed very sick this morning. Also, you didn't get a good look at my face. I was the one who tied your hands behind your back. My name is Pere. What's yours?

You're my enemy.

Forget that. I'm an anarchist like my father. My whole village is for Cuba's independence. This war is shit. We're dying like flies, malaria, typhoid, dysentery . . .

I'm really tired, he says, interrupting the soldier. He sits down on the bed.

What you are is really dirty. You shouldn't lie down in that bed.

I don't care if I get the sheets dirty.

That's not what I mean. The mattress is full of crab lice and bedbugs. I've already got the crabs. It itches like hell. I've got soldier's ointment in my pack. It's very good for the crabs, but I left it at the barracks. I don't even have a comb here.

Ask the cook for one.

I don't have a cent left. I gave everything to that man to get to New York. I've got an uncle there who has a bakery. He makes good money.

Let me get a little sleep. Wake me up when the hot water comes.

He lies down on his side to keep from aggravating his wound.

In the swamp it rains every day between two and three in the afternoon. When the first drops start falling on the leaves, he gets set to leave the hammock's sticky embrace and lie down on the grass with his eyes shut. The water is warm and very sweet. It does many things for him. Above all, it helps him to remember. But now he can't remember anything. It is as though his memories were no longer his. They are there, he knows, but they are outside of him. He imagines them as a deck of cards that someone shuffles in the rain. *Lepidium virginicum* to keep memory intact.

It is raining on his face, on his hammock and the white leaves of the yagruma, on the mangrove trees, on the swamp's black oily water, on mahoganies in the distance, a memory at last, New York, Chinatown, smell of sesame oil and ginger, and the man who's walking toward him. He saw him from a distance. His pallid face emerged from among the open umbrellas of the passersby. He was talking to himself. People were avoiding him. But he hounded them. He stuck his palm under their umbrellas and asked for money. He carried a deep anger. He pushed some of them up into the shop doors, and others he shoved off the sidewalk. He had never seen a person ask for charity like that, so desperately. Suddenly the man was staring him in the face. He understood right away that it was a special, private look, just for him. He felt lifted above the people and the rain, and he realized that the two of them were alone in the street. He put his hand in his pocket and felt the coins' hard edges. He stopped and waited. He saw him come nearer dragging his clogs, his feet yellow and horny. He couldn't walk straight any more. He weaved from side to side as though carrying a great weight on his shoulders. His arms stopped beating on the umbrellas. Only his hand remained extended, his face a tightened knot of supplication. At first he couldn't explain to himself what he was feeling. He lowered his eyes. The man's open hand grazed a button on his coat. When he turned his head, the man had already disappeared behind the undulating black tide of the umbrellas. He thought of making his way among the crowd and catching up with him. But something kept him there, under his umbrella, outside the doors of the little Chinese restaurant. The rain stopped and the street looked different. He folded his umbrella and went in. He went up to the counter. He asked for a gin and a bowl of soup. The old woman at the counter shouted something that he didn't understand. He put his hand into his pocket and pulled out a fistful of coins. They were damp with sweat. He drank the gin down with one gulp and left all the coins on the counter.

What's wrong with you tonight? Julia asked him as they left the theater. It was raining again and he looked for the man among the umbrellas and the carriages.

I don't know. It must be the rain. I was thinking about Cuba.

Let's not talk about the war tonight. How about having dinner at Delmonico?

After the rain, in midafternoon, the low tide comes. The water retreats toward the coast, leaving behind an unbearable stink. The black mud that surrounds his islet then stretches out as far as he can see, giving up the secret of its genesis. Jutting from its puddle-ridden surface there are bones and carcasses of alligators, rats, amphibians, fish backbones. In this cemetery, everything is black, tarry, just this side of turning into peat. He can always get to sleep at this time of day. He wakes up when the bats begin to squeal.

Your hot water's here, he hears the soldier say. He takes off his hat, turns to face him, and sees him seated on the floor, scratching himself between his legs. He has taken off his boots and his stockings. His feet are horny and yellow. By the door there is a pewter bucket steaming faintly. Leave me a little water if you can, my feet are really rotten. My unit came from Sancti Spíritus on foot.

You can have it all. Spare me your feet and all your crabs for now, he says, pulling the hat down over his face. He'll sleep until the bats come out, he thinks.

Amelia patens for eczema and inflammations of the feet.

Are you sure you're crazy, old man?

Nothing is for sure.

Why do you think I couldn't give a quarter to the beggar in Chinatown?

I'm not here to answer that.

Don't play crazy now, he says, sitting up with difficulty in the hammock. You know the answer. Why did I keep my hand in my pocket? Why didn't I run after him? My money would never have saved him, but I would have given him something. Don't laugh. You don't get it. My quarter could have been a little match light, a shooting star, a firefly, something to grab onto in the darkness. What came over me, old man? Don't think I'm a bad person. I know you know the answer. I know you know.

I don't know anything about anything. Turn over on your front so the wound can keep improving. It's going well, there are worms in there already.

I told you. Don't bug me any more about your feet and your crabs.

They've brought the dinner. Aren't you hungry? I'm turning up the light, the soldier ventures timidly, as if he had to ask permission for his every move. He watches him approach the wall and move the switch on the gas lamp. The room fills up with pallid light.

What a shitty light!

The switch won't turn any farther, the soldier says. I wouldn't have thought that in this hotel they'd be so cheap. But after all it's named the Hotel Inglaterra.

What is there to eat?

I don't know. I haven't opened the door. Someone knocked for supper. I'm going to go look for it.

Chicken soup, the soldier announces from the door. There aren't any chairs or tables in here. I'll put the tray down on the floor.

What's in that bottle, water?

Smells like gin to me.

You can have all the soup. Pass me the bottle. He sits down on the bed and takes a big swallow. They haven't brought any spoons and the soldier drinks the soup directly from the bowl. He holds it with both hands and draws it slowly to his mouth in a respectful gesture. Before swallowing, he keeps it for a moment in his mouth, as if it were a sacred food. What did you say? the soldier asks.

Nothing.

I thought you were praying.

I asked you if the soup was any good.

A little cold, but nourishing, the soldier says, putting the bowl on the floor and scratching at his crotch lice.

No chicken feet in it?

How'd you know, the soldier asks, his eyes wide with surprise. I left them for the end. Now I'm going to chew on them.

Go to hell, he says. He takes another long drink from the bottle and stretches out again on the bed.

Salva officinalis for insomnia.

You know what, Eudelio? It's a pity juniper doesn't grow in tropical swamps. Instead of making charcoal, you could make a living by distilling gin. Imagine if all these mangrove trees were junipers weighed down with berries. You'd be a rich man.

I'm fine the way I am, the old man says as he covers the wound with a herb plaster.

Would you like a little gin? There's not much left in the bottle.

Keep it for yourself. I only drink *aloe vera* water. It's good for asthma and for liver ailments. Also for the kidneys.

How do you know so much about tropical plants?

I wrote the book you're reading.

You're crazy, Eudelio. The book was published in London.

You want to go to London?

No. I told you already. I have to go to New York. I want to see my fiancée. Afterwards, I'll come back with another expedition.

I'm happy for you. New York is very close. It's right there, below the mahoganies, where the parrot you shot landed.

The noise of the door makes him turn his head. The soldier is no longer in the room. He must have gone to wash his feet. The bucket of water has disappeared. There is nothing left on the floor but the soup bowl and the yellowish, half-chewed chicken feet. He thinks about the soldier with his tender blond moustache, a poor boy forced to fight in Cuba. They're dying like flies, the general had told him. Our strongest allies are the climate and the diseases, yellow fever, malaria, typhoid, dysentery . . .

Chrysobalanus icaco for dysentery.

One of the worst moments in the swamp comes at around midnight, the hour of the owls and the rats, of the nocturnal hunt. The owls sit perched above his hammock. They try to hide their plumage in the white leaves of the yagrumas. From there, with their specialized eyes, they scrutinize the mangroves. They hunt silently, solemnly, like exterminating angels; they hunt quite differently from the way the herons go about it, plunging head first without the least elegance; they hunt patiently, choosing their captives, lifting them upward in an open-winged glide, describing an arc in the night, to sit blandly back upon the branch. Over his hammock, they eat like pigs. They splatter him all over with the blood and bits of rat flesh.

Why don't the rats sit still, Eudelio? Maybe they wouldn't draw the owls' attention then.

They can't help it. Rats have lots of energy. They eat too much. They're just like chickens.

What would happen if they ate less?

In that case they would not be rats.

Which one am I, Eudelio, a white owl or a rat? Tell me. I know you have the answer.

You're an alligator. And stop calling me Eudelio, my name's

Ezequiel. I've something for you here. *Rondoleta stellata,* very good for dog bites.

I haven't been bitten by a dog.

Of course you have. Don't you remember? They bit you at my house.

Shortly before dawn, when the creatures in the swamp are resting and the inland air blows strong, he can smell smoke from the old man's ovens. He feels less lonely then and starts to think of the good things left for him to do.

How do you feel?

I didn't sleep too well, he says. He reaches out toward the tree with his yellow hand. A white owl had been perched there for a long time. The crabs, as well. I've got to scare them with my hat. Do you think I've gotten past the relapse?

Of course you've gotten through it. Now you have to get through being dead.

You're crazy, old man. Leave me alone.

They say that you start seeing ghosts, and you've been seeing them already.

I haven't seen a thing.

A minute ago you said you had.

I don't recall talking to you about any ghosts. I don't recall anything. I just remember when it rains. Go to hell, old man.

It's raining now. Can't you hear the noise the rain makes on the mangrove?

That can't be true. There aren't any mangroves here. I'm in Havana, in a room in the Hotel Inglaterra. Tomorrow I'm going on a trip. I want to go to New York. Lift my head out of this hammock and breathe city air, just for a few days even, a hot bath, a garden, piano music, something to get hold of. Afterwards, I'd come back.

You must have been dreaming.

No. You're my dream. When I wake up, you won't be here.

You're wrong. It's at this moment that I'm not here. The only things here now are the mangroves and the rain.

In the swamp it rains every day between two and three in the afternoon. The water is warm and very sweet. It does many things for him. Above all, it helps him to remember, to remember the houses in the town, in a line beside the road of red earth. That day his horse goes by. It's with the other horses in the general's retinue. The people recognize the general and they always have something for the troops, cheese, jerked meat, beans, rice, clothing, sometimes a little money. The people are for the revolution, for a free Cuba, and the general is popular. The girl is running alongside the horses, she is running barefoot and she catches up to the general's black horse, reaches out with her arm and grabs the stirrup: A Spaniard! There's a Spanish soldier in my house! The general turns his head around, looks at the girl and then looks back at him. He could have looked at someone else, but he looks at him and he guides his horse off the road and follows the girl. The house has a modest porch with two mahogany armchairs. It is surrounded by trees, avocadoes, mangoes, lemon trees, and behind there is a banana grove. He dismounts, takes his Mauser from the saddle and follows the girl to the door. He picks up and drops the iron ring three times and the man with close-cropped hair opens up for him. The whole family starts to shout at once, and he scarcely understands what they are saying, a Spanish soldier, the banana grove, the dogs. They push him down the corridor and exit with him through the far door. The black dogs begin barking, showing their fangs. If it weren't for their chains they would tear him to pieces. He knows their breed, there aren't many left, bloodhounds, years ago they hunted runaway slaves. Beyond the latrine, his back against a banana plant, is the Spanish soldier. He thinks that he must be seriously wounded. He's sitting in a pool of blood. He is almost an adolescent, a deserter. He has seen many others like him, barefoot, ragged, hiding in the canebrakes and in caves below the hills. At night they go marauding through the fields in search of something to eat, bananas, mangoes, melons. Almost all of them are conscripts from Catalonia, the last ones to arrive, village boys who scarcely know how to use a rifle. In the barracks they are dying like flies, dysentery, typhoid, yellow fever. They flee to the countryside to escape the epidemics. The general doesn't take them prisoner. Sometimes he takes pity on them and gives them a little food. Now the boy is raising his head toward the heavy bunch of bananas that hangs above his head. He knows he's being watched and he doesn't dare to look around him. His face is yellow with fever and with fright. He is clutching his genitals with both hands. Thick blood is seeping through his fingers. The dogs broke loose and they attacked him, the close-cropped man says, lying in self-justification. He's been there since daybreak. We knew the general was going to come, says an old woman, wringing her hands. Now he is your prisoner. Take charge of him, she adds imperatively. The boy's trousers are ripped and soaked in blood; his feet are horribly destroyed. He will never walk again. All of a sudden he feels the Mauser lifting up his arm. He watches how the barrel nears the boy's head. Don't kill me, *Cubanito!* A tender blond moustache, a pimpled nose. Looking to enkindle his compassion, the boy pulls apart his bloody hands, a thick and black coagulate. He fired without knowing why.

Ocinum sanctum for the soul in torment.

I think I'm dying, old man.

We're always dying. Once we're born.

The high tide hasn't come in yet. How did you get here? Look at the swamp. Nothing but tarry bones. Look at the mangrove roots, how long they are.

Mangroves are always mangroves. I already told you not to

look at them too much. Get ready to travel. I'm taking you to New York to kiss the green-eyed girl.

Wait a bit, old man. I can't get out of the hammock. And I've been lying to you. The green-eyed girl no longer exists for me. I lost her.

I know. You told me. You've told me everything.

She's the only woman who's ever mattered to me. I'm not a bad person. Do you think I'll ever see her again? Sometimes I've thought your hands were hers.

I've got some chicken soup here for you. It will give you some energy.

Thank you.

Why are you pouring it out? It was a good soup, with the feet and head in it. I was thinking of making a fire to heat it up. It would have given you some strength for the trip.

Do me a favor, old man. Grab the Mauser and put it on top of me. I need to hold on to something hard.

I understand.

Now answer me. Why did I do the things I told you? I swear I won't ask you anything more. But answer me. Answer me if only this one time.

The general's adjutant entered the tent and came to attention, making his spurs resound.

The general lifted his head from the cot, wiped his eyes, and told his adjutant to be at ease.

We've found him, general.

Don't tell me he's still alive!

No, general, sir, the birds in the mangrove swamp had eaten him already. In the hammock there were only his bare bones with this Mauser on them.

The general sat down on the cot and took the rifle that his

adjutant held out to him. He examined it carefully. He ascertained that it was loaded and he handed it back very slowly, holding it in the palms of his hands as though it were a sword of honor. That's how my men die, God damn it, with their rifle in their hands and ready to shoot! Give this Mauser to a brave man!

TRANSLATED BY JAMES MARANISS

LYDIA CABRERA

The Hill of Mambiala

It was no secret in the village that El Negro Serapio Trebejos would do anything except work for a living.

He never ran out of excuses, reasons for following this calling. And since he had charm, a gift of the gab, and the guitar, it was hard in the end not just giving him what he asked for: especially since it seemed he asked for nothing. Small change for cheap tobacco and liquor, any leftover food and, once in a while, some old, worn-out clothes—as it was no longer possible to go simply naked.

The shack he lived in with his family had neither owner nor bill collector and, hesitating about collapsing once and for all when a strong wind blew or a storm picked up speed, was held in suspense. (There among palm trees, in front of the little hill of Mambiala, where the road twists in leaving the village and lowers like a reptile to the coast.)

Not complicating his life with anything beyond begging, there was food on the table regularly enough, praise the Lord, for him, his wife, and their children: two potbellied black girls, with their kinky hair tangled and full of lice—dirty, shiftless, forever sprawled out on a wobbly cot, already at an age to be earning their keep: and two long-legged black boys, ragged, troublemakers—without work, worth, or good intentions. In other words, the kind of people you could not count on to be up to any good. But there came a time, a bad time, very bad—as never before imagined—and food was scarce for everyone . . .

No one came to the rescue of El Negro Serapio . . .

No one ever remembered seeing him cut sugarcane, hoe a piece of earth—or even plant a yam. In vain he now went about playing the guitar, improvising verses, holding out his hat that had been drilled by cockroaches . . .

"Why don't you go to work? There's no soup left and no more guarachas to dance. Lazybones!"

And the good housewives, lovers of justice:

"Tell El Negro—at the gate—don't let him in!—that today's leftovers are for the hens."

"Sorry, brother, come back another day."

Which is how he and his offspring began to feel the pain of hunger.

The little hill of Mambiala, which rose up not far in the distance—a light green, plush and round like an orange—was covered with pumpkin vines at the top. It was a pumpkin patch without pumpkins, and everyone knew that it bore no fruit.

For several days El Negro and his family had gone to sleep without a bite to eat, and one morning, a Palm Sunday, Serapio awoke dreaming that he had been placed inside of a pumpkin, as lucky as an unborn baby in its mother's womb; and with all his teeth intact, he bit down on the pulp, and the pumpkin started to jump and run, bouncing and screaming: "Help! Police!"—something was tickling her and it was driving her crazy . . .

"Could this be a sign from heaven?" El Negro asked, crossing himself. "What if I find Señora Pumpkin on Mambiala today!"

And after telling the dream to his family—feeling greatly comforted—he climbed to the top of the hill and spent a long, hard time searching eagerly. Leaves and stalks and more leaves! In all of that bushy, tangled, overgrown pumpkin patch there was not one miserable pumpkin; and there was no place left to search. He looked and looked until about twelve o'clock in the afternoon—the hour when other men were sitting down for lunch.

Serapio cried, begging to God and Mambiala. He went back patiently to explore the pumpkin patch from one end to the other, leaf by leaf, plant by plant.

> *"Give it to me Mambiala, Mambiala,*
> *Oh, God, Mambiala!*
> *Poor man that I am, Mambiala*
> *Oh, God, Mambiala!"*

"I'm dying of hunger, Mambiala, Mambiala!"

He was completely worn out, but before giving up he knelt down and, in one last effort, raised his arms to the sky. Remembering a picture that recounted a miracle, he started to cry it out to the heavens.

Heaven paid him not the least bit of attention. Not one pumpkin rained down on his head. At the height of his suffering, he dropped flat down on his face. When, after crying to the ground all the tears from his eyes, he picked himself up to leave, Serapio saw, there next to him, a little clay pot, on whose edges the sun reflected like damp gold. The most youthful and gracious ever to leave a potter's hands. So attractive that he felt happy and wanted to caress it . . . He spoke to the pot as if it were the most natural thing in the world that it understood him, and even more natural that it should be able to comfort him.

"Oh, how pretty, and round, and new you are! Who brought you up here? Some poor soul like me looking for a pumpkin?" Then he asked it, sighing, "What's your name, my little fat Negrita?"

The pot, moving its hips flirtatiously, answered:

"Me name is Dishy Good Cooking."

"Is hunger making me hear things?" thought Serapio. "Are you the one talking or am I two people, one sane and the other crazy, and both of us hungry? What did you say your name was?"

"Dishy Good Cooking."

"Well, then, cook for me."

The pot shot up in the air. It spread out the whitest of tablecloths on the grass, and with fine plates and silverware served a delicious lunch to the poor man who did not know how to use utensils other than his fingers; but he ate until he could no more and drank until he felt the hill of Mambiala sway . . .

And the hill became detached from the earth; it was a globe that was bounding up in gentle tumbles, through the deep azure, higher each time, when El Negro, clinging to some foliage so as not to fall, fell asleep . . .

When the sun began to lose its strength, Serapio put the pot under his arm and went home.

His starving family was waiting. As soon as they spotted him, they started to scream: "The pumpkin! The pumpkin!" But he made a strange gesture to them, a gesture that none of them recognized—and what's more was difficult to interpret—which by the time El Negro joined them, turned out to be negative. Dismay was painted on the faces of the luckless who had spent one more day on sugar and water, trusting in the miracle of Mambiala; and they turned against Serapio, accusing him of eating it by himself. Up there alone, taking advantage of the fact that no one could see him!

Only the mother, a shriveled-up old woman who was indifferent to everything, did not move or get excited. She remained nailed to her stool. Either hunger had turned her into a stick, or she was made of wood. She was a long, hard stick, La Mamá Tecla. She never spoke. In a kind of confused way, she perhaps grumbled to herself, or gave curt, unintelligible answers to someone whom only she could see, and who seemed to be bothering her with useless questions. Even so, they basically must have agreed with each other, as probably what Mamá Tecla spluttered out, looking impatiently out of the corner of her eye and moving slightly her lower lip where an extinguished butt of tobacco hung, was:

"You don't have to tell me anything: I know, I know."

Most of the time the old woman, so stiff and silent in her corner of misery, was only there like an object, expressing in its abstraction, intensely . . . nothing.

And no one paid attention to her; already it was asking a lot to give her what was left—if anything remained—from a hodgepodge of leftovers. The long, dry fingers of Má Tecla rolled around the scraps, gave them the shape of a ball, and she swallowed mechanically, not bothering to taste or chew, with an indifference that reached the perfection of scorn.

"Go invite the neighbors—sí, señor—to eat their fill with us tonight," ordered El Negro, showing them the pot with pride; but one of his daughters, the one who looked like she had the mumps, replied:

"Eat their fill of what? Rats? This was the last thing we needed. Have you heard? My father has gone crazy!"

And not one of his children obeyed him. Serapio had to go himself to invite the black folks of the village and get, where and how he could, some planks of wood and two sawhorses.

Some came to laugh, others out of curiosity; the guests did not keep their host waiting. In fact, many of them—people of good faith—who saw the table set up across the road with a clean, tiny, empty pot in the middle without a speck of food declared it an insult and wanted to leave without accepting an explanation.

It took a lot of effort for Serapio to gather everyone together . . .

"Chameleon's Banquet," said the limping Cesáreo Bonachea, who used to carry vats of food and was always in a good mood. "Open your mouth and flies enter!"

But then Serapio signaled the little clay pot with a "mofori-vale,* and in a tender voice asked:

"What's your name?"

"Dishy Good Cooking."

"Well, then, cook for these people like you know how, you pretty thing, you."

And before anyone could recover from astonishment, the clay pot had covered the table with the most succulent and appetizing of dishes. Such chickens, stuffed turkeys and pâté! And what roasted hams, sausages, suckling piglets, vegetables, fruit, and all kinds of sweets. A never-ending supply of everything, and it was all excellent. The entire village ate, and there was no one who did not get drunk on the delicious wine that flowed incessantly from a tiny source at the bottom of each glass.

Dancing all night was inevitable; and the entire next day with its night.

One feast followed another, with the same lavish splendor at all hours. And so Serapio, from a beggar, was transformed into the beloved benefactor of the region. Even those closest to him now called him "Don" Serapio without realizing it. Together with the "Don"—and also along with his belly that was growing (worthy of a gold watch chain with a diamond stud)—the black man felt something new entering his soul and speaking to him in a language that was as obscure to him as the brief mutterings of Mamá Tecla, who, by the way, remained nailed to her stool in the same silence, looking at them all with the same eyes—fixed, impassive, and hard.

Finally the affair caused such a stir that it became known throughout the five corners of the world. The newspapers spoke about it, and before the evidence of the miracle, the Pope made

*Sign of respect that the blacks of the Lucumí sect address to their *aylochas* and *babalaos*—their priests and sorcerers.

haste to send an encyclical to the pumpkins, prohibiting that they perform another one without his consent.

While at Mambiala, the little hill was left bald from all the pilgrims.

But the luck that suddenly comes to the humble man rarely does not go hand in hand with his downfall.

The very wealthy went to dine with Serapio, and at dessert one of them said—one whose beard was blackened with varnish like shoes:

"I'll give you one hundred and forty good hectares already sown with sugarcane for your clay pot."

"No, señor," answered Serapio. "With her I have more than enough sugarcane, and brown sugar, and cane syrup and everything sweet . . ."

"I," said another gentleman, belching with elegance, "would give you one of my coffee plantations."

"I," said the owner of the Company of Navigation, a very honorable slave trader, "would give you my schooner *Seagull.* There's not a more beautiful ship sailing the seas with an ebony cargo . . ."

And among the rich and ostentatious there was a millionaire—very much a usurer—a certain Don Cayetano, Marquis of Zarralarraga, who, so as not to lose an opportunity to make money, sold the hair, teeth, flesh, and bones of his dead relatives. In his head of rock, he was making calculations, adding and subtracting while he was eating . . .

"I," said Zarralarraga, dreaming to himself about having a monopoly on world food, "offer you . . . one million pesos for the Good Cooking pot, and not another centavo!"

When El Negro heard "one million pesos," he left running to find a notary public whom, in a short while, he had dragged back by his shirttails. There and then the sales contract was drawn up. At the bottom of a sheet of paper, with a sun that looked like a fried egg, stamped and then crossed by a ribbon, Zarralarraga wrote his illustrious signature—thick letters ending in a point and a triple flourish locked in a belt of ink.

"Sign here, Don Serapio."

"The only problem is, I don't know how to write," said the black man, noticing this for the first time in his life. "And now that I think about it, I can't read either."

"It's not necessary. We're among gentlemen!"

And there you have it: the document was null and void. The Marquis of Zarralarraga, that same night, getting out of his coach, slipped on a mango peel and broke the pot; El Negro Serapio—who already envisioned himself surrounded by pomp and riches, in a three-piece suit, diamonds on every finger and all his teeth in gold, dashing off in a car by day, and at night sleeping on a feather mattress—was left as miserable as the day he was born.

In the course of the days that followed, bitter ones, as the memory of the good so badly lost was still fresh, Serapio looked back one morning at the little hill of Mambiala. His stomach had shrunk to the eye of a needle.

"Who knows," said Serapio to his daughters (the daughters who could have been dressed in silk and instead were barefoot in rags that unavoidably displayed their rear ends), "maybe Mambiala feels sorry for us and will do another little miracle! If I don't find a clay pot, maybe I'll find a pumpkin."

He climbed up the hill. By now there was no pumpkin patch. Just some poor blades of grass between the rocks.

"Oh, God, Mambiala!
Mambiala, leave it for me, Mambiala.
Poor man that I am, Mambiala
Oh, God, Mambiala!"

"I'm dying of hunger, Mambiala, Mambiala!" And he repeated his request, wailing, without expecting anything, when his big toe on his right foot tripped over a staff. A staff made from manatee, the skin of a sea cow.

"What's your name?" he immediately asked, pouncing on it, radiant with joy.

"Mistah Manatí, Good Distribution!" answered the staff in the gruff voice of a man with few friends . . .

"Well, then, come and distribute with me, Mr. Manatí."

Manatí instantly slipped out of his hands, and executing his duty with jealous zeal—Zúava! Zúava! Zúava!—gave him a beating . . . and would have finished him off if the poor black, after going down half of Mambiala under a hail of unerring blows, had not said to him between whacks, spitting out a piece of tongue, two molars and an eyetooth:

"All right, Mr. Manatí, that's e-nough!"

El Manatí stopped suddenly in midair and, calming down, stationed himself next to Serapio, motionless, awaiting orders.

"What will I do?" El Negro asked himself, perplexed, counting the lumps he had on his forehead. "I don't know if it's a good idea to introduce this Mr. Manatí to the family . . . (Yet, it would serve them right!) When I took Good Cooking home, everyone ate their fill and fattened up: neither I nor she skimped on anything for anyone. Isn't it fair that they also share in the beating?"

Down on the main road, the family was waiting impatiently.

They had warned the friends and neighbors. They were very sure, they felt it in their bones, that their father would not come back empty-handed!

"The pot, the pot!" they screamed, seeing that he moved toward them in a strange way that they did not recognize.

"Are we having guests over to eat?"

"Some."

"Go and tell the Mayor, the Judge, the Priest, the Notary Public: all of the authorities! That Mr. Zarralarraga who broke the pot. Don't leave anyone out, there will be enough for everyone;

oh, and one more thing . . . tell the doctor and the owner of the funeral parlor!"

It was immediately known that Serapio had come back with another marvel from Mambiala, which gloriously demonstrated how God will protect a bum two times and that there is no reason to get discouraged, but follow the example and wait.

They got everything ready, just as he ordered, a long table in the road, while a crowd flocked in, anxious to witness Serapio's latest discovery.

The rich and ostentatious and all the leading citizens were the first to appear. Green with envy, they took their places, Zarralarraga in the seat of honor.

The rest of the riffraff circled the table, overjoyed, promising each other a banquet and then dancing. Serapio went back to hearing himself called Don Serapio, a garden wall of flattery and smiles.

("But it's not a pot . . . hmmm. They say that it's a staff," insisted an old woman; and wrapped in a cloak, she went back to her fleabag shack, remembering that she had left some beans on the stove that might burn.)

"Attention," Serapio cried out at last, placing El Manatí in the middle of the table. "Don't anyone move."

"Papa, I want ham!"

"Papa, some chicken!" asked the girls.

A wide-eyed hush, as everyone held their breath.

Serapio got as far away as he could.

He climbed up a tree. But no one could move away from the eyes of the staff. Hid among the branches, Serapio said, not without a slight tremor in his voice:

"You there, on the table . . . What is your name?"

"Mistah Manatí, Good Distribution."

"Well, then, distribute fairly, Mr. Manatí."

Pákata! Pákata! Pákata! Pákata!

The thrashing began. Zumba! Tumba! El Manatí beat and struck . . . Pákata! Pákata! was the only thing heard, quick and dry, everywhere and at the same time; stars of fire instantly broke out over the surprised heads. In less than a second, a whirlwind of blows had swept the crowd that escaped tooth and nail, carrying off their share of the feast by the barrelful.

The harshest blows rained on the ribs of the leading citizens; no sooner had the staff turned against whoever was closest than it had attacked someone far away trying to escape with their life on all fours . . . They fell in bunches, one on top of the other, bones broken and flesh opened like ripe pomegranates. And Serapio, up in the tree, shaking the branches with glee like his monkey forefather, was goading the staff on . . .

"Let the Mayor have it, Mr. Manatí, for all the fines he imposes! Hard, even harder; knock the block off the usurer! And the Civil Guard . . . right in the kisser!"

With the Authorities splayed out, their feet in the air and letting out their last groans, El Manatí went into Serapio's shack, where his children were hiding, crouched up in a ball around the imperturbable Mama Tecla. With each strike that Mistah Manatí landed, Mamá Tecla said to the other—to her invisible friend—widening a little more her terrible white eyes:

"I know that already! I know it!"

The shack understood that that was the precise moment to collapse.

When Serapio saw everyone lifeless—the Marquis of Zarralarraga, with his mouth monstrously diagonal, his nose like an eggplant, one eye hanging like a tear, his head of rock a scramble of brains and chips . . . his four children in pieces, his old lady dead, sitting on her stool, erect among the debris—and still the glug glug of the blood that the earth kept sucking—he picked up his staff and walked away from the village . . .

"Don't you think we got a little carried away, Mr. Manatí!"

He wandered aimlessly all night long, leaning on his staff, led by his staff.

"Ay, Mambiala, some wonderful gift you gave me! I didn't ask for much, Mambiala, Mambiala! A poor man like me who never wanted to hurt anybody . . . making his way, just going down the road of hard knocks. What's left for me now? Send me . . . But not one of those parasites left to support . . ."

At dawn, the birds broke into song in the morning light of the trees. Serapio found himself seated on the edge of a well that exhaled its protected freshness, its smell of deeply hidden water, of damp stone untouched by the sun. He looked inside and the water signaled him.

"Yes," said Serapio, "it's better to rest!"

He let the staff drop inside the well, and threw himself after it.

This is the Well of Yaguajay.

The black women knew the story. They told it to their children who, enchanted by fear, went to throw stones into the silence at the bottom. With faces hanging inside, they spit in the water. Looking inside, looking, they would never tire of looking into the Soul of the well; at the Drowned One, whom they could not see, but who saw them, sinking ever deeper.

At night, the well would wake them; it was the Drowned One, who made the frogs sing in the hollow sockets of their eyes: and they would return to their dream body, attracted to the intense mystery—to the delight of fear—to look at him, to break, with another throw of a stone, the black sunken mirror, the pupil of his eye round like a plate. To spit, leaning dangerously over its darkness, into the calm, irresistible presence. The Well of Yaguajay at night! Then the Drowned One rose up in the still water; from the deep, the silent, he scaled the silence.

A deaf splashing that dissolved the fallen stars, and the Drowned One came back whole, two open and desperate hands, climbing up on the smell of mint leaves. The black women, who after dark did not go near the well, had seen it. Too late to save themselves, too late for their cries to be heard, alone in their dream at the well, the hands that appeared over the edge seized them, cold and hard like stone, and plunged them to the terrifying bottom of unspeakable secrets.

TRANSLATED BY LISA WYANT

DULCE MARÍA LOYNAZ

Eternity

I want my favors not to disappear, but to live
and last, if possible, all my friend's life.
—SENECA

There are roses in my garden:
I do not want to give
you roses, for tomorrow—
tomorrow you'll have none.

The birds are in my garden
chanting crystal songs:
I won't give them, for they
have wings to fly away.

In my garden bees are
building well-wrought combs:
the sweetness of a moment—
I won't give that to you!

For you, infinity
or nothing; what lasts all time
or this unspoken sadness
that you can't understand.

The unnamed sadness of
having nothing to give
to one whose own looks carry
hints of eternity.

Leave, then, leave this garden.
Do not touch this rose:
The things that death will carry
off, never should be touched.

TRANSLATED BY DAVID FRYE

Certainty

All the rivers will reach the sea:
reach it with their cargo of landscapes—
green ones, pink ones,
fleeting ones . . .
Landscapes
gathered up
all along
the riversides, the riversides:
the land will travel to the sea
along the rivers' trembling paths!
And for us, the sea will be made sweet
and warm . . .
All the rivers will reach the sea!
And I will not kiss you.

The great sea will come to the land;
will dangle pearls in bunches
from the trees . . .
It will scour roofs clean of daily
sorrows;
will soften the husks
of dead ages that oppress
the fresh bud and the blind seed
that instinctively seeks the sky . . .
The sea will come to cleanse the earth
for us! . . .
The sea will come upon the land . . .
And I will not kiss you.

Our world will turn yellow
with gold and wheat:
A dark dust cloud
kicked up by herds of sheep
as they run downhill
will for a moment blot out
the sun's light . . .
A song will be on every tongue
and over every roof a spiral of smoke
and over every face, new loveliness . . .
The peacefulness of
a sleeping child will lie upon the land!
And I will not kiss you . . .

Towards twilight hatred will swell,
ballooning like
a shade upon the earth:
Towards twilight dull hatred
will explode upon the earth;

at twilight a cloud of dust,
pale as death,
will blot out the sun. Tumultuous
warhorses will run downhill
—torrents of steaming flesh—
horses, black and red!
Startled in his cave,
the wolf will watch them pass:
and man will devour
man. And a flower of the field
will be crushed by a horse's hoof . . .
At twilight hatred
will walk upon the earth!
And I will not kiss you . . .

Men will come, new men,
old men,
always men:
Better times will come.
And another truth, and other lies . . .
North will be south, south will be north.
We will eat apples harvested
at the Poles, still tasting
of blue ice . . .
The Equator's waist will be
girt in cold sequins of hoarfrost . . .
We will switch the stars around
like chessmen
on the celestial board;
we'll switch our ideas,
our dreams, our joys . . .
(our sorrows will always remain the same,
but we know quite well that

they combine mathematically,
in different ways each time,
until the end of time . . .)
new men will come
with new Life,
new dawn.
With their newborn Truth
cradled in their strong arms!
And I will not kiss you . . .

The earth will roll and roll along,
through riverbeds of dead stars.
The earth will wear itself away
along the edge of night,
along the muddy tracks of stars.
The earth will grow smaller
and smaller, rolling and rolling along.
Smaller and slower;
wearing itself out along a riverbed
that never meets an end nor a beginning.
The earth will wear itself out,
rose by rose, stone by stone . . .
(God above! God below!)

And I will not kiss you!

TRANSLATED BY DAVID FRYE

CLAVE 2

Rumba

ALEJO CARPENTIER

Prologue

from THE KINGDOM OF THIS WORLD

What we are to understand in this matter of metamorphosis into wolves is that there is an illness doctors call lupine mania.
—THE TOILS OF PERSILES AND SEGISMUNDA

Toward the end of 1943, I had the good fortune to be able to visit the kingdom of Henri Christophe—the poetic ruins of Sans-Souci, the massive citadel of La Ferrière, impressively intact despite lightning bolts and earthquakes—and to acquaint myself with the still Norman-style Cap-Haïtien (the Cap Français of the former colony) where a street lined with long balconies leads to the cut-stone palace inhabited once upon a time by Pauline Bonaparte.

After feeling the in no way false enchantment of this Haitian earth, after discovering magic presences on the red roads of the Central Plateau, after hearing the drums of Petro and Rada, I was moved to compare this marvelous reality I'd just been living with the exhaustingly vain attempts to arouse the marvelous that characterize certain European literatures of these last thirty years. The marvelous, sought for by means of the old clichés of the Forest of Broceliande, the Knights of the Round Table, Merlin the Magician, and Arthurian cycle. The marvelous, poorly suggested by the acts and deformities of sideshow characters—will the young poets of France ever get tired of the freaks and clowns of the fête foraine, to which Rimbaud bade farewell in his *Alchemy of the Word*?

The marvelous, obtained through sleight-of-hand, through bringing together objects ordinarily never found in the same place: the old, lying tale of the fortuitous encounter of the umbrella and the sewing machine on an operating table, which engendered ermine spoons, the snails in the rainy taxi, the head of a lion on the pelvis of a widow in surrealist exhibitions. Or, even more to the point, the literary marvelous: the king in Sade's *Juliette,* Jarry's supermacho, Lewis's monk, the hair-raising theatrical props of the English gothic novel: ghosts, walled-up priests, lycanthropy, hands nailed to the castle door.

But, by attempting to arouse the marvelous at all costs, the thaumaturges become bureaucrats. Invoked by means of all-too-well-known formulas that make certain paintings into a monotonous mess of molasses-covered clocks, of seamstresses' dummies, of vague phallic monuments, the marvelous is left behind in the umbrella, the lobster, the sewing machine, wherever, on an operating table, within a sad room, a stony desert. Miguel de Unamuno said that having to memorize rule books meant a poverty of imagination. And today there exist rule books of the fantastic based on the principle of the burro devoured by the fig, posited in the *Chants de Maldoror* as the supreme inversion of reality, to which we owe many of André Masson's *Children Menaced by Nightingales* or *Horses Devouring Birds.*

But we should note that when André Masson tried to draw the forest on the island of Martinique, with the incredible entangling of its plants and the obscene promiscuity of certain fruits, the marvelous truth of the subject devoured the painter, leaving him virtually impotent before the empty page. And it had to be a painter from America, the Cuban Wifredo Lam, who showed us the magic of tropical vegetation, the uncontrolled Creation of Forms in our nature—with all its metamorphosis and symbiosis—in monumental paintings whose expression is unique in contemporary art. In the face of the disconcerting poverty of imagination of a Tanguy, for example, who for twenty-five years now has been painting the same petrified larvae under the same gray sky, I feel the urge to recite a phrase that was the pride of the surrealists of the first generation: *Vous qui ne voyez pas, pensez à ceux qui voient.*

There are still too many "adolescents who take pleasure in raping the cadavers of beautiful, freshly murdered women" (Lautréamont), without realizing how marvelous it would be to rape them alive. It's that so many people forget, because it costs them so little to dress up as magicians, that the marvelous begins to be marvelous in an unequivocal way when it arises from an unexpected alteration of reality (a miracle), from a privileged revelation of reality, from an illumination that is either unusual or singularly favorable to the unnoticed riches of reality, from an amplification of the scale and categories of reality perceived with particular intensity by means of an exaltation of the spirit that leads it to a kind of "limit-state."

In the first place, the sensation of the marvelous presupposes a faith. Those who do not believe in saints cannot be cured by the miracles of saints, in the same way that those who are not Quixotes cannot enter, body and soul, the world of Amadis of Gaul or Tirant lo Blanc. Certain remarks about men being transformed into wolves made by the character Rutilio in Cervantes's *Toils of Persiles and Segismunda* are prodigiously believable because in Cervantes's day it was believed there were people afflicted with lupine mania. The same applies to the character's journey from Tuscany to Norway on a witch's cape. Marco Polo allowed that certain birds flew carrying elephants in their talons; Martin Luther saw the Devil right before his eyes and threw an inkwell at his head. Victor Hugo, so exploited by the bookkeepers of the marvelous, believed in ghosts, because he was sure of having spoken, while in Guernsey, with the ghost of Leopoldina.

All Van Gogh needed was to have faith in the Sunflower to capture its revelation on a canvas. Thus the idea of the marvelous invoked in the context of disbelief—which is what the surrealists did for so many years—was never anything but a literary trick, and a boring one at that after being prolonged, as was a certain "arranged" oneiric literature, as were certain praises of folly, which we left behind long, long ago. But by the same token, we are not, for all that, going to yield to those who advocate a *return to the real*—an expression that takes on, in this context, the value of a political slogan—because they are merely replacing the magician's tricks with the commonplaces of "committed" literary hacks or the scatological delights of some existentialists.

But it is unquestionably true that it is hard to make a case for poets and artists who praise sadism without practicing it, who admire the supermacho because of their own impotence, who invoke spirits without believing they answer their chants, and who found secret societies, literary sects, vaguely philosophic groups, with passwords and arcane goals—never achieved—without being able to conceive a valid mysticism or to abandon their pettiest habits and risk their souls on the play of a frightening card of faith.

All of that became particularly evident to me during my stay in Haiti, where I found myself in daily contact with something we could call the *real marvelous*. I was treading earth where thousands of men eager for liberty believed in Mackandal's lycanthropic powers, to the point that their collective faith produced a miracle the day of his execution. I already knew the prodigious story of Bouckman, the Jamaican initiate. I entered the La Ferrière citadel, a structure without architectonic antecedents, portended only in Piranesi's *Imaginary Prisons*. I breathed the atmosphere created by Henri Christophe, monarch of incredible undertakings, much more surprising than all the cruel kings invented by the surrealists, who are very fond of imaginary, though never suffered, tyrannies.

With each step I found the real marvelous. But I also realized that the presence and authority of the real marvelous was not a privilege unique to Haiti but the patrimony of all the Americas, where, for example, a census of cosmogonies is still to be established. The real marvelous is found at each step in the lives of the men who inscribed dates on the history of the Continent and who left behind names still borne by the living: from the seekers after the Fountain of Youth or the golden city of Manua to certain rebels of the early times or certain modern heroes of our wars of independence, those of such mythological stature as Colonel Juana Azurduy.

It's always seemed significant to me that in 1780 some perfectly sane Spaniards from Angostura, set out even then in search of El Dorado, and that, during the French Revolution—long live Reason and the Supreme Being!—Francisco Menéndez, from Compostela, traversed Patagonia hunting for the Enchanted City of the Caesars. Looking at the matter in another way, we see that while in western Europe dance-related folklore has lost all its magic, spirit-invoking character, it is rare that a collective dance in the Americas does not contain a profound ritual meaning that creates around it an entire initiatory process: the *santería* dances in Cuba or the prodigious Black version of the Feast of Corpus Christi, which may still be seen in the town of San Francisco de Yare in Venezuela.

There is a moment in the sixth song of Maldoror when the hero, chased by all the police in the world, escapes from "an army of agents and spies" by taking on the shape of diverse animals and making use of his ability to transport himself instantly to Peking, Madrid, or Saint Petersburg. This is "marvelous literature" at its peak. But in the Americas, where nothing like that has been written, there existed a Mackandal who possessed the same powers because of the faith of his contemporaries and who used that magic to inspire one of the most dramatic and strange uprisings in History.

Maldoror—Isidore Ducasse himself confesses it—was nothing more than a "poetic Rocambole." All he left behind was a short-lived literary school. The American Mackandal, on the other hand, has left behind an entire mythology, accompanied by magical hymns, preserved by an entire people, who still sing them at Vaudou ceremonies. (There is, on the other hand, a strange coincidence in the fact that Isidore Ducasse, a man who had an exceptional instinct for the fantastic-poetic, was born in the Americas and bragged so emphatically at the end of one of his chapters of being "Le montevidéen.") Because of the virginity of its landscape, because of its formation, because of its ontology, because of the Faustian presence of the Indian and of the Black, because of the Revelation its recent discovery constituted, because of the fertile racial mixtures it favored, the Americas are far from having used up their wealth of mythologies.

The text that follows, even though I didn't propose it to myself in a systematic fashion, responds to this order of concerns. It tells a sequence of extraordinary events that occurred on the island of Saint–Domingue over the course of a period which does not exceed an entire human life. It allows the *marvelous* to flow freely from a reality followed strictly in all its details. The reader must be warned that the story he is going to read is based on an extremely rigorous documentation which not only respects the historical truth of the events, the names of the characters (even the minor ones), of the places, and even the streets but which hides under its apparently nonchronological façade, a minute collation of dates and chronologies.

And yet, because of the dramatic singularity of the events, because of the fantastic bearing of the characters who met, at a given moment, in the magical crossroads of Cap-Haïtien, everything seems marvelous in a story it would have been impossible to set in Europe and which is as real, in any case, as any exemplary event yet set down for the edification of students in school manuals. But what is the history of all the Americas but a chronicle of the real marvelous?

TRANSLATED BY ALFRED MACADAM

Journey Back to the Source

I

"What d'you want, pop?"

Again and again came the question, from high up on the scaffolding. But the old man made no reply. He moved from one place to another, prying into corners and uttering a lengthy monologue of incomprehensible remarks. The tiles had already been taken down, and now covered the dead flower beds with their mosaic of baked clay. Overhead, blocks of masonry were being loosened with picks and sent rolling down wooden gutters in an avalanche of lime and plaster. And through the crenellations that were one by one indenting the walls, were appearing—denuded of their privacy—oval or square ceilings, cornices, garlands, dentils, astragals, and paper hanging from the walls like old skins being sloughed by a snake.

Witnessing the demolition, a Ceres with a broken nose and discolored peplum, her headdress of corn veined with black, stood in the backyard above her fountain of crumbling grotesques. Visited by shafts of sunlight piercing the shadows, the gray fish in the basin yawned in the warm weed-covered water, watching with round eyes the black silhouettes of the workmen against the brilliance of the sky as they diminished the centuries-old height of the house. The old man had sat down at the foot of the statue, resting his chin on his stick. He watched buckets filled with precious fragments ascending and descending. Muted sounds from the street could be heard, while overhead, against a basic rhythm of steel on stone, the pulleys screeched unpleasantly in chorus, like harsh-voiced birds.

The clock struck five. The cornices and entablatures were depopulated. Nothing was left behind but stepladders, ready for tomorrow's onslaught. The air grew cooler, now that it was disburdened of sweat, oaths, creaking ropes, axles crying out for the oil can, and the slapping of hands on greasy torsos. Dusk had settled earlier on the dismantled house. The shadows had enfolded it just at that moment when the now-fallen upper balustrade used to enrich the façade by capturing the sun's last beams. Ceres tightened her lips. For the first time the rooms would sleep unshuttered, gazing onto a landscape of rubble.

Contradicting their natural propensities, several capitals lay in the grass, their acanthus leaves asserting their vegetable status. A creeper stretched adventurous tendrils toward an Ionic scroll, attracted by its air of kinship. When night fell, the house was closer to the ground. Upstairs, the frame of a door still stood erect, slabs of darkness suspended from its dislocated hinges.

II

Then the old Negro, who had not stirred, began making strange movements with his stick, whirling it around above a graveyard of paving stones.

The white and black marble squares flew to the floors and covered them. Stones leaped up and unerringly filled the gaps in the walls. The nail-studded walnut doors fitted themselves into their frames, while the screws rapidly twisted back into the holes in the hinges. In the dead flower beds, the fragments of tile were lifted by the thrust of growing flowers and joined together, raising a sonorous whirlwind of clay, to fall like rain on the framework of the roof. The house grew, once more assuming its normal proportions, modestly clothed. Ceres became less gray. There were more fish in the fountain. And the gurgling water summoned forgotten begonias back to life.

The old man inserted a key into the lock of the front door and began to open the windows. His heels made a hollow sound. When he lighted the lamps, a yellow tremor ran over the oil paint of the family portraits, and people dressed in black talked softly in all the corridors, to the rhythm of spoons stirring cups of chocolate.

Don Marcial, Marqués de Capellanías, lay on his deathbed, his breast blazing with decorations, while four tapers with long beards of melted wax kept guard over him.

III

The candles lengthened slowly, gradually guttering less and less. When they had reached full size, the nun extinguished them and took away the light. The wicks whitened, throwing off red sparks. The house emptied itself of visitors and their carriages drove away in the darkness. Don Marcial fingered an invisible keyboard and opened his eyes.

The confused heaps of rafters gradually went back into place. Medicine bottles, tassels from brocades, the scapulary beside the bed, daguerreotypes, and iron palm leaves from the grill emerged from the mists. When the doctor shook his head with an expression of professional gloom, the invalid felt better. He slept for several hours and awoke under the black beetle-browed gaze of Father Anastasio. What had begun as a candid, detailed confession of his many sins grew gradually more reticent, painful, and full of evasions. After all, what right had the Carmelite to interfere in his life?

Suddenly Don Marcial found himself thrown into the middle of the room. Relieved of the pressure on his temples, he stood up with surprising agility. The naked woman who had been stretching herself on the brocade coverlet began to look for her petticoats and bodices, and soon afterward disappeared in a rustle of silk and a waft of perfume. In the closed carriage downstairs an envelope full of gold coins was lying on the brass-studded seat.

Don Marcial was not feeling well. When he straightened his cravat before the pier glass he saw that his face was congested. He went downstairs to his study where lawyers—attorneys and their clerks—were waiting for him to arrange for the sale of the house by auction. All his efforts had been in vain. His property would go to the highest bidder, to the rhythm of a hammer striking the table. He bowed, and they left him alone. He thought how mysterious were written words: those black threads weaving and unweaving, and covering large sheets of paper with a filigree of estimates; weaving and unweaving contracts, oaths, agreements, evidence, declarations, names, titles, dates, lands, trees, and stones; a tangled skein of threads, drawn from the inkpot to ensnare the legs of any man who took a path disapproved of by the Law; a noose around his neck to stifle free speech at its first dreaded sound. He had been betrayed by his signature; it had handed him over to the nets and labyrinths of documents. Thus constricted, the man of flesh and blood had become a man of paper.

It was dawn. The dining-room clock had just struck six in the evening.

IV

The months of mourning passed under the shadow of ever-increasing remorse. At first the idea of bringing a woman to his room had seemed quite reasonable. But little by little the desire excited by a new body gave way to increasing scruples, which ended as self-torment. One night, Don Marcial beat himself with a strap till the blood came, only to experience even intenser desire, though it was of short duration.

It was at this time that the Marquesa returned one afternoon from a drive along the banks of the Almendares. The manes of the horses harnessed to her carriage were damp with solely their own sweat. Yet they spent the rest of the day kicking the wooden walls of their stable as if maddened by the stillness of the low-hanging clouds.

At dusk, a jar full of water broke in the Marquesa's bathroom. Then the May rains came and overflowed the lake. And the old Negress who unhappily was a maroon and kept pigeons under her bed wandered through the patio, muttering to herself: "Never trust rivers, my girl; never trust anything green and flowing!" Not a day passed without water making its presence felt. But in the end that presence amounted to no more than a cup spilled over a Paris dress after the anniversary ball given by the Governor of the Colony.

Many relatives reappeared. Many friends came back again. The chandeliers in the great drawing room glittered with brilliant lights. The cracks in the façade were closing up, one by one. The piano became a clavichord. The palm trees lost some of their rings. The creepers let go of the upper cornice. The dark circles around Ceres' eyes disappeared, and the capitals of the columns looked as if they had been freshly carved. Marcial was more ardent now, and often passed whole afternoons embracing the Marquesa.

Crow's-feet, frowns, and double chins vanished, and flesh grew firm again. One day the smell of fresh paint filled the house.

V

Their embarrassment was real. Each night the leaves of the screens opened a little farther, and skirts fell to the floor in obscurer corners of the room, revealing yet more barriers of lace. At last the Marquesa blew out the lamps. Only Marcial's voice was heard in the darkness.

They left for the sugar plantation in a long procession of carriages—sorrel hindquarters, silver bits, and varnished leather gleamed in the sunshine. But among the pasqueflowers empurpling the arcades leading up to the house, they realized that they scarcely knew each other. Marcial gave permission for a performance of native dancers and drummers, by way of entertainment during those days impregnated with the smells of eau de cologne, of baths spiced with benzoin, of unloosened hair and sheets taken from closets and unfolded to let a bunch of vetiver drop onto the tiled floor. The steam of cane juice and the sound of the angelus mingled on the breeze. The vultures flew low, heralding a sparse shower, whose first large echoing drops were absorbed by tiles so dry that they gave off a diapason like copper.

After a dawn prolonged by an inexpert embrace, they returned together to the city with their misunderstandings settled and the wound healed. The Marquesa changed her traveling dress for a wedding gown and the married pair went to church according to custom, to regain their freedom. Relations and friends received their presents back again, and they all set off for home with jingling brass and a display of splendid trappings. Marcial went on visiting María de las Mercedes for a while, until the day when the rings were taken to the goldsmiths to have their inscriptions removed. For Marcial, a new life was beginning. In the house with the high grilles, an Italian Venus was set up in place of Ceres, and the grotesques in the fountain were thrown into almost imperceptibly sharper relief because the lamps were still glowing when dawn colored the sky.

VI

One night, after drinking heavily and being sickened by the stale tobacco smoke left behind by his friends, Marcial had the strange sensation that all the clocks in the house where striking five, then half past four, then four, then half past three . . . It was as if he had become dimly aware of other possibilities. Just as, when exhausted by sleeplessness, one may believe that one could walk on the ceiling, with the floor for a ceiling and the furniture firmly fixed between the beams. It was only a fleeting impression, and did not leave the smallest trace on his mind, for he was not much given to meditation at the time.

And a splendid evening party was given in the music room on the day he achieved minority. He was delighted to know that his signature was no longer legally valid, and that worm-eaten registers and documents would now vanish from his world. He had reached the point at which courts of justice were no longer to be feared, because his bodily existence was ignored by the law. After getting tipsy on noble wines, the young people took down from the wall a guitar inlaid with mother-of-pearl, a psaltery, and a serpent. Someone wound up the clock that played the *ranz-des-vaches* and the "Ballad of the Scottish Lakes." Someone else blew on a hunting horn that had been lying curled in copper sleep on the crimson felt lining of the showcase, beside a transverse flute brought from Aranjuez. Marcial, who was boldly making love to Señora de Campoflorido, joined in the cacophony, and tried to pick out the tune of "Trípili-Trápala" on the piano, to a discordant accompaniment in the bass.

They all trooped upstairs to the attic, remembering that the liveries and clothes of the Capellanías family had been stored away under its peeling beams. On shelves frosted with camphor lay court dresses, an ambassador's sword, several padded military jackets, the vestment of a dignitary of the Church, and some long cassocks with damask buttons and damp stains among their folds. The dark shadows of the attic were variegated with the colors of amaranthine ribbons, yellow crinolines, faded tunics, and velvet flowers. A picaresque *chispero*'s costume and hair net trimmed with tassels, once made for a carnival masquerade, was greeted with applause. Señora de Campoflorido swathed her powdered shoulders in a shawl the color of a Creole's skin, once worn by a certain ancestress on an evening of important family decisions in hopes of reviving the sleeping ardor of some rich trustee of a convent of Clares.

As soon as they were dressed up, the young people went back to the music room. Marcial, who was wearing an alderman's hat, struck the floor three times with a stick and announced that they would begin with a waltz, a dance mothers thought terribly improper for young ladies because they had to allow themselves to be taken round the waist, with a man's hand resting on the busks of the stays they had all had made according to the latest model in the *Jardin des Modes.* The doorways were blocked by maidservants, stableboys, and waiters, who had come from remote outbuildings and stifling basements to enjoy the boisterous fun. Afterward they played blindman's buff and hide-and-seek. Hidden behind a Chinese screen with Señora de Campoflorido, Marcial planted a kiss on her neck, and received in return a scented handkerchief whose Brussels lace still retained the sweet warmth of her low-necked bodice.

And when the girls left in the fading light of dusk, to return to castles and towers silhouetted in dark gray against the sea, the young men went to the dance hall, where alluring *mulatas* in heavy bracelets were strutting about without ever losing their high-heeled shoes, even in the frenzy of the guaracha. And as it was carnival time, the members of the Arará Chapter Three Eyes Band were raising thunder on their drums behind the wall in a patio planted with pomegranate trees. Climbing onto tables and stools, Marcial and his friends applauded the gracefulness of a Negress with graying hair, who had recovered her beauty and almost become desirable as she danced, looking over her shoulder with an expression of proud disdain.

VII

The visits of Don Abundio, the family notary and executor, were more frequent now. He used to sit gravely down beside Marcial's bed, and let his acana-wood cane drop to the floor so as to wake him up in good time. Opening his eyes, Marcial saw an alpaca frock coat covered with dandruff, its sleeves shiny from collecting securities and rents. All that was left in the end was an adequate pension, calculated to put a stop to all wild extravagance. It was at this time that Marcial wanted to enter the Royal Seminary of San Carlos.

After doing only moderately well in his examinations, he attended courses of lectures, but understood less and less of his master's explanations. The world of his ideas was gradually growing emptier. What had once been a general assembly of peplums, doublets, ruffs, and periwigs, of controversialists and debaters, now looked as lifeless as a museum of wax figures. Marcial contented himself with a scholastic analysis of the systems, and accepted everything he found in a book as the truth. The words "Lion," "Ostrich," "Whale," "Jaguar" were printed under the copper-plate engravings in his natural history book. Just as "Aristotle," "St. Thomas," "Bacon," and "Descartes" headed pages black with boring, close-printed accounts of different interpretations of the universe. Bit by bit, Marcial stopped trying to learn these things, and felt relieved of a heavy burden. His mind grew gay and lively, understanding things in a purely instinctive way. Why think about the prism, when the clear winter light brought out all the details in the fortresses guarding the port? An apple falling from a tree tempted one to bite it—that was all. A foot in a bathtub was merely a foot in a bathtub. The day he left the seminary he forgot all about his books. A gnomon was back in the category of goblins; a spectrum a synonym for a phantom; and an octandrian an animal armed with spines.

More than once he had hurried off with a troubled heart to visit the women who whispered behind blue doors under the town walls. The memory of one of them, who wore embroidered slippers and a sprig of sweet basil behind her ear, pursued him on hot evenings like the toothache. But one day his confessor's anger and threats reduced him to terrified tears. He threw himself for the last time between those infernal sheets, and then forever renounced his detours through unfrequented streets and that last-minute faintheartedness which sent him home in a rage, turning his back on a certain crack in the pavement—the signal, when he was walking with head bent, that he must turn and enter the perfumed threshold.

Now he was undergoing a spiritual crisis, peopled by religious images, paschal lambs, china doves, Virgins in heavenly blue cloaks, gold paper stars, the Magi, angels with wings like swans, the Ass, the Ox, and a terrible St. Denis, who appeared to him in his dreams with a great space between his shoulders, walking hesitantly as if looking for something he had lost. When he blundered into the bed, Marcial would start awake and reach for his rosary of silver beads. The lampwicks, in their bowls of oil, cast a sad light on the holy images as their colors returned to them.

VIII

The furniture was growing taller. It was becoming more difficult for him to rest his arms on the dining table. The fronts of the cupboards with their carved cornices were getting broader. The Moors on the staircase stretched their torsos upward, bringing their torches closer to the banisters on the landing. Armchairs were deeper, and rocking chairs tended to fall over backward. It was no longer necessary to bend ones knees when lying at the bottom of the bath with its marble rings.

One morning when he was reading a licentious book, Marcial suddenly felt a desire to play with the lead soldiers lying asleep in their wooden boxes. He put the book back in its hiding place under the washbasin, and opened a drawer sealed with cobwebs. His schoolroom table was too small to hold such a large army. So Marcial sat on the floor and set out his grenadiers in rows of eight. Next came the officers on horseback, surrounding the color sergeant; and behind, the artillery with their cannon, gun sponges, and linstocks. Bringing up the rear were fifes and tabors escorted by drummers. The mortars were fitted with a spring, so that one could shoot glass marbles to a distance of more than a yard.

Bang! . . . Bang! . . . Bang!

Down fell horses, down fell standard-bearers, down fell drummers. Eligio the Negro had to call him three times before he could be persuaded to go to wash his hands and descend to the dining room.

After that day, Marcial made a habit of sitting on the tiled floor. When he realized the advantages of this position, he was surprised that he had not thought of it before. Grown-up people had a passion for velvet cushions, which made them sweat too much. Some of them smelled like a notary—like Don Abundio—because they had not discovered how cool it was to lie at full length on a marble floor at all seasons of the year. Only from the floor could all the angles and perspectives of a room be grasped properly. There were beautiful grains in the wood, mysterious insect paths and shadowy corners that could not be seen from a man's height. When it rained, Marcial hid himself under the clavichord. Every clap of thunder made the sound box vibrate, and set all the notes to singing. Shafts of lightning fell from the sky, creating a vault of cascading arpeggios—the organ, the wind in the pines, and the crickets' mandolin.

IX

That morning they locked him in his room. He heard whispering all over the house, and the luncheon they brought him was too delicious for a weekday. There were six pastries from the confectioner's in the Alameda—whereas even on Sundays after Mass he was only allowed two. He amused himself by looking at the engravings in a travel book, until an increasing buzz of sound coming under the door made him look out between the blinds. Some men dressed all in black were arriving, bearing a brass-handled coffin. He was on the verge of tears, but at this moment Melchor the groom appeared in his room, his boots echoing on the floor and his teeth flashing in a smile. They began to play chess. Melchor was a knight. He was the king. Using the tiles on the floor as a chessboard, he moved from one square to the next, while Melchor had to jump one forward and two sideways, or vice versa. The game went on until after dusk, when the fire brigade went by.

When he got up, he went to kiss his father's hand as he lay ill in bed. The Marqués was feeling better, and talked to his son in his usual serious and edifying manner. His "Yes, Father's" and "No, Father's" were fitted between the beads of a rosary of questions, like the responses of an acolyte during Mass. Marcial respected the Marqués, but for reasons that no one could possibly have guessed. He respected him because he was tall, because when he went out to a ball his breast glittered with decorations; because he envied him the saber and gold braid he wore as an officer in the militia; because at Christmas time, on a bet, he had eaten a whole turkey stuffed with almonds and raisins; because he had once seized one of the *mulatas* who were sweeping out the rotunda and had carried her in his arms to his room—no doubt intending to whip her. Hidden behind a curtain, Marcial watched her come out soon afterward, in tears and with her dress unfastened, and he was pleased that she had been punished, as she was the one who always emptied the jam pots before putting them back in the cupboard.

His father was a terrible and magnanimous being, and it was his duty to love him more than anyone except God. To Marcial he was more godlike even than God because his gifts were tangible, everyday ones. But be preferred the God in heaven because he was less of a nuisance.

X

When the furniture had grown a little taller still, and Marcial knew better than anyone what was under the beds, cupboards, and cabinets, he had a great secret, which he kept to himself: life had no charms except when Melchor the groom was with him. Not God, nor his father, nor the golden bishop in the Corpus Christi procession was as important as Melchor.

Melchor had come from a very long distance away. He was

descended from conquered princes. In his kingdom there were elephants, hippopotamuses, tigers, and giraffes, and men did not sit working, like Don Abundio in dark rooms full of papers. They lived by outdoing the animals in cunning. One of them had pulled the great crocodile out of the blue lake after first skewering him on a pike concealed inside the closely packed bodies of twelve roast geese. Melchor knew songs that were easy to learn because the words had no meaning and were constantly repeated. He stole sweetmeats from the kitchens; at night he used to escape through the stable door, and once he threw stones at the police before disappearing into the darkness of the Calle de la Amargura.

On wet days he used to put his boots to dry beside the kitchen stove. Marcial wished he had feet big enough to fill boots like those. His right-hand boot was called Calambín; the left one Calambán. This man who could tame unbroken horses by simply seizing their lips between two fingers, this fine gentleman in velvet and spurs who wore such tall hats, also understood about the coolness of marble floors in summer, and used to hide fruits or a cake, snatched from trays destined for the drawing room, behind the furniture. Marcial and Melchor shared a secret store of sweets and almonds, which they saluted with *"Urí, urí, urá"* and shouts of conspiratorial laughter. They had both explored the house from top to bottom, and were the only ones who knew that beneath the stables there was a small cellar full of Dutch bottles, or that in an unused loft over the maids' rooms was a broken glass case containing twelve dusty butterflies that were losing their wings.

XI

When Marcial got into the habit of breaking things, he forgot Melchor and made friends with the dogs. There were several in the house. The large one with stripes like a tiger; the basset trailing its teats on the ground; the greyhound that had grown too old to play; the poodle that was chased by the others at certain times and had to be shut up by the maids.

Marcial liked Canelo best because he carried off shoes from the bedrooms and dug up the rose trees in the patio. Always black with coal dust or covered with red earth, he devoured the dinners of all the other dogs, whined without cause, and hid stolen bones under the fountain. And now and again he would suck dry a new-laid egg and send the hen flying with a sharp blow from his muzzle. Everyone kicked Canelo. But when they took him away, Marcial made himself ill with grief. And the dog returned in triumph, wagging his tail, from somewhere beyond the poorhouse where he had been abandoned, and regained his place in the house, which the other dogs, for all their skill in hunting, or vigilance when keeping guard, could never fill.

Canelo and Marcial used to urinate side by side. Sometimes they chose the Persian carpet in the drawing room, spreading dark, cloudlike shapes over its pile. This usually cost them a thrashing. But thrashings were less painful than grown-up people realized. On the other hand, they gave a splendid excuse for setting up a concerted howling and arousing the pity of the neighbors. When the cross-eyed woman from the top flat called his father a "brute," Marcial looked at Canelo with smiling eyes. They shed a few more tears so as to be given a biscuit, and afterward all was forgotten. They both used to eat earth, roll on the ground, drink out of the goldfish basin, and take refuge in the scented shade under the sweet-basil bushes. During the hottest hours of the day quite a crowd filled the moist flower beds. There would be the gray goose with her pouch hanging between her bandy legs; the old rooster with his naked rump; the little lizard who kept saying *"Urí, urá"* and shooting a pink ribbon out of his throat; the melancholy snake, born in a town where there were no females; and the mouse that blocked its hole with a turtle's egg. One day someone pointed out the dog to Marcial.

"Bow-wow," Marcial said.

He was talking his own language. He had attained the ultimate liberty. He was beginning to want to reach with his hands things that were out of reach.

XII

Hunger, thirst, heat, pain, cold. Hardly had Marcial reduced his field of perception to these essential realities when he renounced the light that accompanied them. He did not know his own name. The unpleasantness of the christening over, he had no desire for smells, sounds, or even sights. His hands caressed delectable forms. He was a purely sensory and tactile being. The universe penetrated him through his pores. Then he shut his eyes—they saw nothing but nebulous giants—and entered a warm, damp body full of shadows: a dying body. Clothed in this body's substance, he slipped toward life.

But now time passed more quickly, rarefying the final hours. The minutes sounded like cards slipping from beneath a dealer's thumb.

Birds returned to their eggs in a whirlwind of feathers. Fish congealed into roe, leaving a snowfall of scales at the bottom of their pond. The palm trees folded their fronds and disappeared into the earth like shut fans. Stems were reabsorbing their leaves, and the earth reclaimed everything that was its own. Thunder rumbled through the arcades. Hairs began growing from antelope-skin gloves. Woolen blankets were unraveling and turning into the fleece of sheep in distant pastures. Cupboards, cabinets, beds, crucifixes, tables and blinds disappeared into the darkness in search of their ancient roots beneath the forest trees. Everything that had been fastened with nails was disintegrating. A brigantine, anchored no one knew where, sped back to Italy carrying the marble from the floors and fountain. Suits of armor, ironwork, keys, copper cooking pots, the horses' bits from the stables, were melting and forming a swelling river of metal running into the earth through roofless channels. Everything was undergoing metamorphosis and being restored to its original state. Clay returned to clay, leaving a desert where the house had once stood.

XIII

When the workmen came back at dawn to go on with the demolition of the house, they found their task completed. Someone had carried off the statue of Ceres and sold it to an antique dealer the previous evening. After complaining to their trade union, the men went and sat on the seats in the municipal park. Then one of them remembered some vague story about a Marquesa de Capellanías who had been drowned one evening in May among the arum lilies in the Almendares. But no one paid any attention to his story because the sun was traveling from east to west, and the hours growing on the right-hand side of the clock must be spun out by idleness—for they are the ones that inevitably lead to death.

TRANSLATED BY FRANCES PARTRIDGE

MIGUEL BARNET

Life in the Woods

from BIOGRAPHY OF A RUNAWAY SLAVE

I have never forgotten the first time I tried to run away. That time I failed and spent a number of years enslaved by the fear they would put the shackles on me again. But I had the spirit of a cimarrón in me, and it didn't go away. I kept quiet about things so nobody could betray me because I was always thinking about escaping. It went round and round in my head and wouldn't leave me in peace. It was an idea that never left me and sometimes even sapped my energy. The old blacks were not kindly towards running away. The women even less so. Runaways, there weren't many. People were afraid of the woods. They said that if some slaves escaped, they would be caught anyway. But for me that idea went around in my head more than any other. I always had the fantasy that I would enjoy being in the forest. And I knew that working in the fields was like living in hell. You couldn't do anything on your own. Everything depended on the master's orders.

One day I began to watch the overseer. I had already been studying him. That dog got stuck in my eyes, and I couldn't get him out. I think he was a Spaniard. I remember that he was tall and never took his hat off. All the blacks had respect for him because one of the whippings he gave could strip the skin off of just about anybody. The thing is, one day I was riled up, and I don't know what got into me, but I was mad, and just seeing him set me off.

I whistled at him from a distance, and he looked around and then turned his back. That's when I picked up a rock and threw it at his head. I know it hit him because he shouted for someone to grab me. But he never saw me again because that day I made it into the woods.

I traveled many days without any clear direction. I was sort of lost. I had never left the plantation. I walked uphill and downhill, all around. I know I got to a farm near Siguanea, where I had no choice but to camp. My feet were full of blisters and my hands were swollen. I camped under a tree. I stayed there no more than four or five days. All I had to do was hear the first human voice close by, and I would take off fast. It would have been real shitty if you got caught right after escaping.

I came to hide in a cave for a time. I lived there for a year and a half. I went in there thinking that I would have to walk less and because the pigs from around the farms, the plots, and the small landholdings used to come to a kind of swamp just outside the mouth of the cave. They went to take a bath and wallow around. I caught them easy enough because big bunches of them came. Every week I had a pig. That cave was very big and dark like the mouth of the wolf. It was called Guajabán. It was near the town of Remedios. It was dangerous because it had no way out. You had to go in through the entrance and leave by the entrance. My curiosity really poked me to find a way out. But I preferred to remain in the mouth of the cave on account of the snakes. The majases are very dangerous beasts. They are found in caves and in the woods. Their breath can't be felt, but they knock people down with it, and then they put people to sleep to suck out their blood. That's why I always stayed alert and lit a fire to scare them away. If you fall asleep in a cave, be ready for the wake. I didn't want to see a majá, not even from a distance. The Congos, and this is true, told me that those snakes lived more than a thousand years. And as they approached two thousand, they became serpents again, and they would return to the ocean to live like any other fish.

Inside, the cave was like a house. A little darker, naturally. Oh, and dung, yes, the smell of bat dung. I walked on it because it was as soft as a mattress. The bats led a life of freedom in the caves. They were and are the masters of them. All over the world it's like that. Since no one kills them, they live a long time. Not as long as the snakes, for sure. The dung they drop works afterward as fertilizer. It becomes dust, and it's thrown on the ground to make pasture for animals and to fertilize crops.

One time that place nearly burned up. I lit a fire, and it spread all through the cave. The bat shit was to blame. After slavery I told the story to a Congo. The story that I had lived with the bats, and that joker, they could sometimes be more jokers than you might imagine, he said: "Listen here, boy, you know nothin'. In my country that thing what you call a bat is big like a pigeon." I knew that was a tall tale. They fooled nearly everyone with those stories. But I heard it, and smiled inside.

The cave was quiet. The only sound always there was the bats going: "Chwee, chwee, chwee." They didn't know how to sing. But they talked to each other and understood each other. I saw that one would say "Chewy, chewy, chewy," and the bunch would go wherever he went. They were very united about things. Bats have no wings. They're nothing but a cloth with a little black head, very dirty, and if you get up real close, you'll see they look like rats. In the cave I was summering, you might say. What I really liked was the woods, and after a year and a half I left that darkness behind. I took to the footpaths. I went into the woods in Siguanea again. I spent a long time there. I took care of myself like a spoiled child. I didn't want to be chained to slavery again. For me that was disgusting. I've always thought so. Slavery was a nuisance. I still think so today.

I was careful about all the sounds I made. And of the fires. If I left a track, they could follow my path and catch me. I climbed up and down so many hills that my legs and arms got as hard as sticks. Little by little I got to know the woods. And I was getting to like them. Sometimes I would forget I was a cimarrón, and I would start to whistle. Early on I used to whistle to get over the fear. They say that when you whistle, you chase away the evil spirits. But being a cimarrón in the woods you had to be on the lookout. I didn't start whistling again because the guajiros or the slave catchers could come. Since the cimarrón was a slave who had escaped, the masters sent a posse of rancheadores after them. Mean guajiros with hunting dogs so they could drag you out of the woods in their jaws. I never ran into any of them. I never seen one of those dogs up close. They were trained to catch blacks. If a dog saw a black man, he ran after him. If by chance I heard one barking nearby, I took my clothes right off because the dog can't smell anybody naked like that. When I see a dog now, nothing happens, but if I seen one then, all of me you would see would be my heels. I've never been attracted to dogs. To my mind they have wicked instincts.

When a slave catcher caught a black, the master or the overseer gave him an ounce of gold or more. In those years, an ounce was like saying seventeen pesos. Who knows how many guajiros were in that business!

Truth is that I lived well as a cimarrón, very hidden, very comfortable. I didn't even allow other cimarrones to spot me: "cimarrón with cimarrón sells a cimarrón."

I didn't do many other things. For a long time I didn't speak a word to anyone. I liked that tranquility. Other cimarrones always went around in groups of two or three. But that was dangerous because when it rained, their footprints stayed in the mud. That's how they caught many foolish groups.

. . . .

There was a kind of black who was a freeman. I used to see them in the woods searching for herbs and guinea pigs, but I never called to them or approached them. Just the opposite, when I saw one of those blacks what I did was hide more carefully. Some worked in the crop lands, and when they left the field, I took the opportunity to go in and carry off the 'taters and pigs. They almost always had pigs on their conucos. But I would rather rob things from the small landholdings because they had more of everything. And it was easier. The small landholdings were bigger than the conucos. Much bigger! They were more like farms. The blacks didn't have those luxuries. The guajiros sure did live easy, in houses of thatch, cane thatch or real palm. From the distance I could see them playing music. Sometimes I could even hear them. They played little accordions, guitars, bandor guitars, kettle-drums, calabash, maracas, and hollow gourds. Those were their main instruments. When I left the woods was when I came to learn their names because as a cimarrón I was ignorant of everything.

They liked to dance. But they didn't dance to the music of the blacks. They tended toward the zapateo and the caringa. All the guajiros got together in the afternoon, around five to dance the zapateo. The men put a kerchief around their necks, and the women put them on their heads. If a guajiro really danced well, his woman would come to put a hat on top of the one he had on. It was the prize. I came up to them carefully, and I was able to take it all in. I even seen the pianolas. They played all the instruments there. They made a lot of noise, but it was real pretty. From time to time a guajiro grabbed for a gourd to accompany the pianola. It was on those instruments that you could hear the popular music of the times, the danzón.

On Sundays the guajiros dressed all in white. The women wore their hair down and put flowers in it. Then they went to the partidos, and they got together there in the taverns made out of wood to have parties. The men like to wear canvas and heavy drill cloth. They made long shirts that resembled guayaberas with open pockets. Guajiros in those years lived better than people imagine. Almost every day they got a bonus from the masters. They were friendly with each other and did their dirty work together. I think that the cimarrón lived better than the guajiro. The cimarrón was more free.

To look for food you had to be carrying things back and forth, but there was always enough food. "The cautious tortoise carries its house on its back." What I liked most were 'taters and pig meat. I think it was because of pig meat that I've lasted so long. I ate it every day, and it never did me any harm. To catch little pigs I went up to the small farms at night, making sure no one heard me. The first one I saw I grabbed by the neck, and swung him up on my shoulder with a rope tight around him and took off running, with a hand over his snout. When I found a place to camp, I lay him down on one side, and I began to look him over. If he was fed well and weighed about twenty pounds, then I had food for sure for fifteen days.

You live half wild when you're a cimarrón. I myself hunted animals like the guinea pigs. The guinea pig is fast as the devil, and to catch it you have to have lightning in your feet. I liked smoked guinea pig a great deal. Nowadays, I don't know what people think of that animal, but no one eats it. I used to catch a guinea pig and smoke it without salt and it would last me for months. The guinea pig is the healthiest food there is, although 'taters are the best thing for your bones. If you eat them every day, especially taro, you won't have bone trouble. In the woods there are lots of those wild 'taters. The taro has a big leaf that shines at night. You recognize it right away.

All the leaves in the woods have uses. Tobacco or mulberry leaves work for bites. Whenever I saw that the bite of some bug was going to get swollen up on me, I took hold of the tobacco leaf, and I chewed it well. Then I put it on the bite, and the swelling went down. Often when it was cold, an ache seeped into my bones. It was a dry pain that didn't go away. To rid myself of it I made a brew of rosemary leaves, and it went away right then. The cold also gave me a bad cough. The sniffles and a cough was what I got. That was when I picked a big leaf and put it on my chest. I never found out the name of that leaf, but it gave off a whitish liquid that was very warm. That soothed my cough. When I got very cold my eyes would water up, and they itched in a very bothersome way. The same thing happened to me with the sun. In that case I would put out a few leaves of the ítamo plant to catch the dew, and the next day clean my eyes with them. Ítamo is the best thing there is for that. Nowadays what they sell in the pharmacy is ítamo. What happens is that they put it in little jars, and it seems like something else. As one gets old, the thing with your eyes goes away. I haven't suffered from itching for many years.

I smoked the leaf of the macaw tree. I made well-rolled, tightly packed cigars with it. After I left the woods, I didn't smoke tobacco anymore, but while I was a cimarrón, I smoked it all the time.

And I drank coffee. I made coffee with guanina leaf. I had to grind the leaf with a bottle. After it was well broken up, I boiled it, and then it was coffee. You could always put a little wild honey in it to give it flavor. With the honey the coffee gave strength to the body. You're always fortified when you live in the woods.

Being weak comes from town life because people go crazy over lard when they see it. I never liked it because it makes you weak. If you eat a lot of lard, you get fat and sort of dumb. Lard does bad things to the circulation and strangles people. One of the best remedies to keep your health is bee honey. You can get it easy in the woods. Anywhere you wanted there was bee honey. I found loads of it in the hollows of trees. Honey was used to make canchánchara which was a delicious water drink. It was made with river water and honey. The best thing was to drink it cold. That water was better for you than any of today's medicine. It was natural. When there was no river nearby, I used to go deep into the woods to look for a spring. In the woods there are enough springs to make sweet water. They ran downhill and brought the coldest, clearest water I ever seen in my life.

The simple truth is that I never needed anything in the woods. The only thing I couldn't have was sex. Since there were no women, I had to get by with my desire bottled up. You couldn't even step up to a mare because they neighed like the dickens. And when the guajiros heard that clamor they would come right away, and nobody was going to put cuffs on me just for a mare.

I never went without fire. The first days I spent in the woods I carried matches. Then they ran out, and I had to use tinder. It was a black ash that I kept in a tinderbox the Spaniards sold in the taverns. It was very easy to make a fire. All you had to do was strike the tinderbox with a stone till it made a spark. I learned that from the Canary Islanders when I was a slave. I never liked the Islanders. They were very bossy and very stingy. The Galicians were better people and got along better with the blacks.

Since I've always liked to be my own boss, I kept myself away from them. From everyone. I even stayed away from the animals. So the snakes wouldn't come up close, I lit a thick log and left it to burn all night long. The snakes didn't approach because they thought the fire was the devil or one of their enemies. That's why I say I felt good being a cimarrón. Because I was my own boss, and I defended myself on my own. I used knives and short Collin machetes which were the ones the rural police used. Those weapons were used to cut down the forest or to hunt animals. And I had them ready in case some slave catchers wanted to catch me by surprise. Though that would have been hard because I kept on the move. I walked so much in the sun that my head would begin to get hot and sort of red, for me. Then I would get some hot spells that were so fierce that to get over them I had to wrap up some, almost always with a plantain leaf, or put fresh herbs on my forehead. The trouble was that I had no hat, which is why my head would get all heated up that way. I used to figure that the heat got into my insides and softened up my brains.

Once the hot spell passed (sometimes it lasted for many days), I would slip into the first river I saw without making a sound and come out like new. River water did me no harm. I think river water is the best thing for your health because it's cold. That cold is good because it makes you hard. Your bones feel in place. Rainwater gave me some sniffles, which I got rid of with a brew of cuajaní berries and bee honey. To stay dry I covered myself with yagua palm fronds. I folded them over a stand I made with four forked stakes, and I fashioned a shelter. Those shelters were seen all around after slavery and during the war. They looked like lean-tos.

What I did most was walk and sleep. When it got to be midday or five in the afternoon, I used to hear the conch shell that the women would use to call their husbands. It sounded like: "foooo, foo, foo, foo, foo." At night I slept like a log. That's why I was so fat. I didn't think about a thing. It was only eat and sleep and watch. I used to like to go to the hillsides at night. The hills were quieter and safer. Slave catchers or wild animals were unlikely to go there. I almost reached Trinidad. From up on those hills you could see the town. And the ocean.

The closer I got to the coast, the bigger the ocean became. I always figured it was a giant river. At times I stared at it, and it became the strangest white and got lost in my eyes. The ocean is another big mystery of nature. And it's very important because it can carry men off, swallow them, and never give them back. Those are what are called shipwrecked people.

What I do remember well are the birds in the woods. I haven't forgotten that. I remember them all. There were pretty ones and some right ugly ones. At first, they put a lot of fear into me, but later I became accustomed to hearing them. I really believed they were watching out for me. The cotunto was the most bothersome one. It was a black bird, pitch black, that sang: "You, you, you, you, you ate the cheese I had over there." And it repeated that until I answered, "Get out of here!" and it flew away. I used to hear him crystal clear. There was another one that answered him like a ghost, going "coo, coo, coo, coo, coo, coo."

The gnome owl was one of the ones that scared you the most. It always came at night. The ugliest thing in the woods was that critter! It had white feet and yellow eyes. It screamed something like this: "cous, cous, couououous."

The barn owl sang a sad song, but it was a witch. It searched for dead mice. It sang "chew-ah, chew-ah, chew-ah, kuwee, kuwee," and it flew off like lightning. When I saw an owl in my path, especially when she went back and forth, I wouldn't go on because by doing that she was giving warning that there was an enemy or death itself nearby. The owl is wise and strange. I remember that the male witches had a lot of respect for her and did magic with the barn owl or sunsundamba, which is what she is called in Africa. The owl has probably left Cuba. I haven't seen her again. Those birds change their territory.

The house sparrow came from Spain and has produced quite a number of offspring here.

And the tocoloro which is more or less green. The tocoloro has a scarlet band across his chest that's the same as the sash the King of Spain wears. The overseers said he was the King's messenger. What I know is that you couldn't even look at the tocoloro. The black man who killed one of those birds was killing the King. I seen many blacks get the lash for killing tocoloros and sparrows. I liked that bird because it sang as though it was hopping around, going, "coh, co, coh, co, coh, co."

The one that sure was a mother's whore was the ciguapa owl. It whistled just like a man. Anybody would get a chill hearing it. I don't want to think about how many times those creatures bothered me.

In the forest I got used to living with the trees. They also have their sounds because the leaves whistle in the wind. There is a tree with a big white leaf. At night it seems like a bird. In my opinion, that tree spoke. It made "ooch, ooch, we, we, ooch, ooch." Trees have shadows too. The shadows don't do harm, though at night you shouldn't walk on them. I think the shadows of trees are like a man's spirit. The spirit is the reflection of the soul. You can see that.

What men are surely not able to see is the soul. We can't say that the soul has such and such a color. The soul is one of the greatest things in the world. Dreams are made for making contact with it. The old Congos said that the soul was like witchcraft one had on the inside. They also said that there were good spirits and evil spirits, that is, good souls and bad souls. And that everybody had them. In my opinion, there are some who have a soul for witchcraft and nothing more. Other people have natural ones. I prefer the natural one because the other means a pact with the devil. And the soul can leave the body. That happens when a person dies or when he sleeps. That is, when the soul leaves on its own and begins to move around. It does that to rest because so much struggle all the time would be unbearable.

There are people who don't like to be called when they're sleeping because they frighten easily, and they can die all of a sudden. That happens because during sleep the soul leaves the body. It leaves a person empty. I sometimes have the shakes at night. It was the same in the woods. So I cover myself good because that's the warning God sends you so you'll take care of yourself. If you suffer from the shakes, you have to pray a lot.

The heart is very different. It never leaves its place. Just by putting your hand on the left side you can prove that it's beating. But the day it stops, you have to be ready to go. That's why you shouldn't trust it.

Now, the most important thing about this subject is the angel. The Guardian Angel. He's the one who makes you go forward or go backward. For me the angel ranks higher than the soul and the heart, always at the foundation of a person, caring for him, watching everything. It will not leave for anything in the world. I've thought a lot about these things, and I still see them a little in the dark. All these thoughts come while one is alone. A man thinks at all hours. Even when he's dreaming it's as though he was thinking. It's not good to speak about those thoughts. There is the danger that decay will set in. You can't trust people very much. How many people ask you questions to find out about you, and then split your hide down the middle! Besides, the question about spirits is infinite, like numbers that never come to an end. No one knows where they end.

Truth is that I don't even trust the Holy Ghost. That's why as a cimarrón I remained alone. I did nothing but listen to the birds and the trees, and eat, but I never met anyone. I remember I was so hairy that my kinka got all tangled up together. That was scary. When I went into town, an old man called Tá Migué cut my hair with a big scissors. He gave me a trim that made me like a fancy horse. I felt strange with all that wool off. I was awful cold. Within a few days my hair began to grow again. Blacks have that tendency. I never seen a bald black man. Not one. The Spaniards brought baldness to Cuba.

All my life I've liked the woods. But when slavery ended I stopped being a cimarrón. I found out about the end of slavery from all the people shouting, and I left the woods. They shouted, "We're free now." But I wasn't affected. To my mind, it was a lie. I don't know . . . fact was that I went up to a mill, and without touching the boilers or the cans or anything, I stuck my head out little by little until I came out altogether in the open. That was when

Martínez Campos was governor because the slaves said he was the one who let them go free. Even so, many years passed in Cuba, and there were still slaves. It lasted longer than people believe.

When I came out of the woods I started in walking, and I met an old woman with two children in her arms. I called to her from a distance, and when she came up to me I asked her: "Tell me, is it true that we're no longer slaves?" She answered me: "No, son, now we're really free." I kept walking the way I was headed, and I started to look for work. Many blacks wanted to be friends of mine. And they asked me what I did as a cimarrón. And I told them: "Nothing." I've always liked independence. Sassy talk and idle gossip do no good. I went for years and years without talking to anyone.

TRANSLATED BY W. NICK HILL

GUILLERMO CABRERA INFANTE

Lorca the Rainmaker Visits Havana

Address to the Ibero-American Institute in Madrid on the fiftieth anniversary of the poet's murder, 20 *May* 1986

In the spring of 1930 (which was summer in Cuba as usual: a "violent season," as the poet Paz warns), Federico García Lorca, the Spanish poet, travelled to Havana by sea, the only way to get to the island then. At the same time Hart Crane, the American poet, homosexual and alcoholic, travelled from Havana to New York—and never arrived. He jumped overboard to disappear forever, leaving behind as cargo a long poem and various virulent verses as testimony to his mincing steps on earth. Lorca, on the other hand, was in his prime. He had just finished *Poet in New York* with its splendid "Ode to Walt Whitman." I am not going to comment on this book, that long lucid lament, except to touch on its musical, merry coda, that "*Son** of Blacks in Cuba" which transformed Cuban popular poetry and the American vision of Lorca.

Around that time, apart from the more lamentable than lamented Crane, writers and artists who would later have as much of a name as Lorca visited Cuba. Some lived in Havana "for free." Never, by grace or disgrace, did they meet Lorca. Not in Old Havana nor in El Vedado nor in La Víbora nor in Jesús del Monte, not in Cayo Hueso nor in San Isidro nor in Nacanor del Campo, which was not called Nicanor del Campo then.

*The Cuban dance rhythm.

Hemingway for instance was living in Old Havana, in a hotel whose name would have pleased Lorca, *Ambos Mundos.* There, in the best of both worlds, Hemingway wrote a novel of love and death (of little love and dour death) whose first chapter offers a view of a city of dreams and nightmares.

The novel, *To Have and Have Not,* deals in a violence that Lorca never knew. In any case not before his end in Granada. But it is possible that in 1930 he would have known by sight one of those three men who now

> started for the door, and I watched them go. They were good-looking young fellows, wore good clothes; none of them wore hats, and they looked like they had plenty of money. They talked plenty of money, anyway, and they spoke the kind of English Cubans with money speak.

At that time, in that country, Lorca must have dressed like them and worn pomaded, plastered down hair. Dark as he was, for Hemingway he could have been a rich Cuban boy, and he would know what happened to a rich Cuban boy when he played games of death.

> As they turned out of the door to the right, I saw a closed car come across the square toward them. The first thing a pane of glass went and the bullet smashed into the row of bottles on the show-case wall to the right. I heard the gun going and, bop, bop, bop, there were bottles smashing all along the wall.
>
> I jumped behind the bar on the left side and could see looking over the edge. The car was stopped and there were two fellows crouched down by it. One had a Thompson gun and the other had a sawed-off automatic shotgun. The one with the Thompson gun was a nigger. The other had a chauffeur's white duster on . . .

> Old Pancho . . . hit a tire on the car . . . and at ten feet the nigger shot him in the belly . . . He was trying to come up, still holding onto the Luger, only he couldn't get his head up, when the nigger took the shotgun that was lying against the wheel of the car by the chauffeur and blew the side of his head off. Some nigger.

Lorca never knew that terrible Cuban violence nor those Havana blacks, *sbirri eccellenti.* His blacks were sons of the *son, reyes* of the rumba. Lorca had this habit of doing the rounds of the popular districts of Havana, like Jesús Maria, Paula and San Isidro and sometimes reached the Plaza de Luz, the Caballería dock there beside it and even La Machina dock, where the opening action of *To Have and Have Not* takes place. But he never knew the obscene night that ended with sleeping beggars and dead rich kids. Although at the end, like Hemingway, he found out what a violent death at dawn was.

Another American who came to Havana in those first years of the thirties to leave in the bay a wake of art was the photographer Walker Evans. Evans recalls: "I did land in Havana in the midst of the revolution." I don't know how these Americans always manage to fall right into the middle of a revolution in Cuba! As Evans was in Havana in 1932 and the dictator Machado did not fall until 1933 to be replaced by Batista months later, Evans could not have fallen into the middle of any revolution, except the revolting solutions that a feisty rum gives you. But Evans insists: "Batista was taking over" and Evans was drinking Bacardi. "I had a few letters to newspapermen, which turned out to be lucky because it brought me to Hemingway. So I met him. I had a wonderful time with Hemingway. Drinking every night." What did I tell you? It's the revolution called Cuba-libre. One part rum to one part Coke. Stir. Serves two. According to Evans, Hemingway "was at loose ends." Easily explained. Those are the uncertain years of *To Have and Have Not,* his first Cuban novel. But Evans did know where he was going and his photos of Havana are like "Son de negros en Cuba," a graphic romance in which the blacks of Havana are revealed as dapper dandies in white.

I can't even attempt to describe these masterful photos that now belong in the museums. But there is a black dressed in pure white linen, with a straw hat and shoes just shined by the shoeshine boy seen in the background. Well dressed with a brown tie and matching handkerchief, a dandy detained forever on a corner of Old Havana, next to a magazine stand, his sharp stare directed towards an object hidden by the frame of the photo that we now know is time: this makes the photograph a portrait, a work of art, a thing that *To Have and Have Not* never was, never will be and that Lorca's sinuous *son* is.

But Havana was not so violent or so violet a city.

The writer Joseph Hergesheimer, as American as Hemingway and Evans, says of Havana in his *San Cristóbal de La Habana,* one of the most beautiful travel books that I have read:

> watching the silver greenness of Cuba rising from the blue sea, I had a premonition that what I saw was of peculiar importance to me . . . Undoubtedly their effect belonged to the sea, the sky, and the hour in which they were set . . . The Cuban shore was now so close, Havana so imminent, that I lost my story in a new interest. I could see low against the water a line of white buildings, at that distance purely classic implication.

These are poetic not historical visions of the city. But, one moment, there is a second—or maybe a third—opinion about this *ancien régime* Havana. I found this description in the *Encyclopedia Britannica,* at times our contemporary:

> Capital and commercial metropolis and the largest port of Cuba. The city, which is the largest in the Antilles and one of the first

tropical cities of the New World, lies on the north coast of the island, towards its western extreme. Its location on one of the best bays of the hemisphere made it commercially and militarily important from colonial times and is the greatest factor responsible for its constant growth from the 235,000 inhabitants that it had in 1899 to the 978,000 of 1959. Other factors that contributed to its growth are its healthful climate and its picturesque setting and those cheerful entertainments that once made it a Mecca of tourism. The average annual temperature varies by only ten degrees Celsius with a mean of 24 degrees. Although many mansions of the residential districts have been expropriated, from a physical point of view the view is no less impressive. *The appearance of Havana from the sea is splendid.*

That was the Havana that Lorca saw. There he composed one of his freest, most spontaneous pieces. It is a letter to his parents in Granada published in Madrid not long ago. Lorca speaks of his successes as a lecturer, quite real, and of his imaginary risk when witnessing a crocodile hunt and taking part in it in cold (and sometimes burning) blood. Fortunately Lorca was not a hunter and exempts us from the corpse count of wild animals that Hemingway would have made. Maybe it would sadden Lorca to know that in that region of Cuba, the Zapata swamp, where he saw uncountable crocodiles, there was *circa* 1960, scarcely thirty years after his tale, a pen that was only a low wood fence, where a single immobile crocodile dozed in the sun, as if he were already stuffed. A sign at the side begged the visitor: "Please do not throw rocks at the gator."

Lorca sees in Havana (how could he not see them?) what he calls "the most beautiful women in the world." Then he makes the local Cuban woman into a whole world and says: "This island has more feminine beauties of an original type" and immediately the celebration becomes an explanation: "owing to the drops of black blood that all Cubans carry." Lorca reaches a conclusion: "The blacker, the better." (Which is also the opinion of Walker Evans, photographer, for whom an elegant black is the acme of the dandy.) Finally Lorca praises the land ("this island is a paradise") to warn his parents in Granada: "If I get lost look for me . . . in Cuba." The letter ends with an extraordinary hyperbole: "Don't forget that in America being a poet is something more than being a prince." Unfortunately it is not true now—nor was it true then. Not in Cuba at least. I have known poor poets, sick poets, persecuted poets, imprisoned poets, moribund and finally dead poets. They were all treated not like princes but like pariahs, like the plague: suffering the leprosy of letters. But for Lorca Havana was a party and so it should have been. There is no need to contaminate his poetry with my reality.

On Lorca's visit to Buenos Aires Borges accused him of a crime of *lèse legerté.* Lorca told the young Borges that he had discovered a crucial character. In him was hidden the destiny of all humanity, a saviour. His name? Mickey Mouse! It's strange that Borges, with his sense of humour, did not find that behind the statement by Lorca there was nothing but a joke: silly sallies by a poet with a comic sense of life. To Borges the joke was a yoke. Lorca wanted to amaze: *pour épater le Borges.* In Havana, on the contrary, he delighted his Havanan friends, fans of the silent cinema, with his piece "El paseo de Buster Keaton," composed only two years before. Buster Keaton is not here a redeemer who tries to return to Bethlehem on his second coming. But neither is he the sobbing Mickey Messiah, with his always open eyes, his four-fingered gloves and his shoes of a mouse with hundred league boots. Mickey is insufferable, Keaton is insuperable. The motto of this last little piece is "In America there are nightingales," which is another way of saying that poets can be princes. Lorca in Havana, by not wanting to amaze anyone, amazed everyone.

An anonymous author at the time describes Lorca's stay in

Havana as "the agitated rhythm of his Havana existence, full of gifts, of chats and of homages and burdened with the sweet and social tyranny of friendship." But Lorca did not go only to Havana. So much did Lorca declare in Havana that he would go to Santiago that he almost didn't make it. Many people still doubt whether Lorca really went to Santiago de Cuba. They are the people who think of poetry as a metaphor in action. Indeed, after several failed attempts, Lorca finally went to Santiago. Not in a "coach made of black water" and with the blond head of Fonseca, but in Santiago de Cuba he really stayed in the Venus Hotel. Lorca truly was the poet of love. Those who doubt it, should read his "Romance de la casada infiel," or the unfaithful Andalusian bride. Few poems written in Spanish are as erotic.

As a poet Lorca was a definitive influence for Cuban poetry. This, after the Modernist lay-back, was beginning a phase of a populism called in the Caribbean *negrismo.* It was a vision of the poetic possibilities of the black and his dialects that was then more alien than alienating. The word might be exotic but exotic in Cuba is a Scandinavian seaman not a black stevedore. The best poets of that generation, who would have been Lorca's age, cultivated *negrismo* as an amenable fashion. Others were like Al Jolsons of poetry: whites in black faces. The poem was thus becoming some kind of greasepaint.

Lorca's brief visit was a hurricane that came not from the Caribbean but from Granada. His influence extended throughout Cuban literature. That kind of poetry was made to be recited; the mouth chanting couplets. That is the sorcery of poetry (and that other form of poetry, song lyrics): it demands at the same time silent reading and reading aloud and will even stand reciting. Poetry, then, is another form of music, as Verlaine wanted: *"De la musique avant toute chose."* Lorca, in his "Son de negros en Cuba," murmurs an exotic song that becomes instantly familiar. "I will go to Santiago" is in effect the refrain of a *son.* As in the *Cuban Overture* by Gershwin, the melody is familiar and the harmony lingers on.

Lorca arrived in Havana at the Machina dock. The trip he made was the reverse of Crane's. Although *La zapatera prodigiosa,* a piece full of Andalusian sun, dates from the time he lived in New York, he also wrote there his dark in mood *Poeta en Nueva York,* that opens like a premonition, "Asesinado por el cielo" ("Murdered by the Sky"), and ends with his "Huída de Nueva York" ("Flight from New York"). Almost immediately, in the book and in life, the poet composes his "Son de negros en Cuba," where he invokes a sortilege to the moon:

When the full moon rises
I will go to Santiago de Cuba.

His poem, which has the poetic form of a *son,* a Cuban love song to dance to, blooms here like a tropical flower: spontaneous, exceptionally beautiful. The poet flees from civilization to native life, exotic nature. Almost like Gauguin did. Although I seem to be hearing the Shakespeare of *The Tempest:*

the isle is full of noises,
Sounds and sweet airs, that give delight, and hurt not.

After the discovery Lorca now wants to sail around the isle where

The roofs of palm will sing.
I will go to Santiago . . .
I will go to Santiago . . .
With the blond head of Fonseca
I will go to Santiago
And with the rosebush of Romeo y Julieta . . .
Oh Cuba! Oh rhythm of dry seeds!

Oh warm waist and drop of wood!
Harp of live trunks, crocodile, tobacco flower!

There is a traditional *son* that sings:

Mamma I want to know
where the singers come from . . .

Lorca knew: those singers, like the *son,* came from Santiago de Cuba. Deciphering poems is the work of academicians, but I want to show how Lorca made a poem from the obvious, for Cubans, that turned into poetry for all. The "palm roofs" are the roofs of the *bohíos,* traditional peasant dwellings, built with leaves, trunks and fibres from the royal palm tree. No one in Cuba would call the *palma, palmera* as Lorca does. Not even in a poem. "The blond head of Fonseca," which intrigued so many, doesn't belong to any of his Cuban friends but to the cigar maker of that name, whose red head appears as a chromo on the boxes of his brand. "The rosebush of Romeo y Julieta" is not that thicket where Romeo gives Juliet what she gave him the other day, but another brand of Havana cigars. The rosebush is a lithograph. "The dry seeds" are of course inside the maracas and the "drop of wood" is the musical instrument called *claves,* a couple of percussion sticks. I hope not to have to explain what a "warm waist" is.

This poem written in Cuba wears a luminous aura such as one only sees in Havana. This is attested to by the fragment of Hergesheimer, that is a frieze from a tropical edifice and, especially, the photographs by Walker Evans with the fruit stands in the sun, the women who adorn a patio and the motley façades of the numerous, numinous movie-houses with their open invitation to the grand tour.

In that laughing and confident era, gone with the wind of history, Lorca was blinded by Havana, but managed to open the eyes of Havanans who were indifferent to the brilliance of their city, as capital as a sin. There are still some who remember Lorca as if they were seeing him alive and kicking the flamenco floor. One of those Havana dwellers is Lydia Cabrera. Lydia recalls Lorca from the beginning. She met him in the house of another Cuban in Madrid, José María Chacón y Calvo, who was later instrumental in Lorca's trip to Havana. "What charm he had!" says Lydia. "What a vital child he was!" Until she went back to Havana she used to see Lorca every day in that Madrid, the reverse of Havana, that has not been lost but won. Celebrating the occasion, Lorca dedicated to Lydia the poem she would like most. The poem (and maybe the dedication) scandalized one of Lydia's brothers, alarmed perhaps by all the erotic imagery that Lorca displays from the first line until the revelation of this virgin with a husband. She, Lydia, was not in the least put off and it is still her favourite poem by Lorca. She recalls that after five minutes of conversation with Lorca she was bewitched. (The word is hers, she who knows so much about bewitching.) She always called him Federico.

Lydia Cabrera says about Lorca's end: "When I learned about the tragic details of his death, I thought with consternation of the horror that Federico must have felt. He was so delicate! So horrible a death must have caused him unimaginable horror. It was an unforgivable death. I thought a lot, a great deal about him." Everyone who knew Lorca in Havana, and even those who didn't know him, lamented his death. About his assassination Lezama Lima had a curious opinion. It is not a political but a poetic version of the death of the poet: "What killed Lorca was vulgarity." Cryptic rather than a critic, Lezama adds: "Not politics."

That was the end. At the beginning Lorca arrived in Havana and surprised everyone when he introduced himself: "I'm Federico García." Choosing to use his common middle name excited speculation. Someone asked: "Are you gentlemen really sure that this García man is Lorca?" As there were so many Garcías in

Cuba, from the general of the wars of independence, Calixto García, to the most vulgar politicians, many Cubans felt related to Lorca.

At that time the Colombian poet Porfirio Barba Jacob, a man of successive and sonorous pseudonyms, lived in Havana. Formerly he had been called by his proper name, an obscure Osorio, then he had been Ricardo Arenales and Maín Ximénez, until finally he hit upon that twice queer pseudonym with porphyria. All these names and that man make up a considerable Modernist poet, an endangered species. Barba Jacob was famous in Havana for a verse and its obverse. The writer declared in a poem: "In nothing I believe, in nothing." The man was a pederast poet. Very ugly, he was called "the man who looked like a horse."

Barba Jacob added to those hurdles of love a new one. He was missing a front tooth which he always insisted on replacing with a false one made not of chalk, as some historians have it, but of cotton or paper. His conversation began in the evening on the Acera del Louvre, in the vespers Hergesheimer talked about. As the night progressed that tooth whiter than the other teeth would disappear only to reappear towed by his tongue not to its goal but to another part of his mouth. Barba Jacob's tooth shone white now in the forest of his mouth, now on his livid lip, or it just flew to alight on the beard of Barba. The poet believed that his conversation was truly fascinating, to judge by the faces of his listeners. But the fascination actually came from that ambulatory mock tooth. Or better, shipwrecked tooth: a sailor in white who sailed on the raft of his tongue, between dental Charybdis and the Scylla of his gums.

The mention of a mariner, even a metaphorical one, leads us to the great amorous transport of Barba. It is said that the poet of Modernist decadence found his sinning sailor when he, literally, "covered the waterfront." Littorally they found each other on the docks. The sailor became the lover of the pederast and pessimist rhymester (remember, please, his motto: "In nothing I believe, in nothing") and, beneath it all, a poor poet. It was 1930 when the bard Barba was showing off his freshly caught mariner. It was Barba's bad luck (or poetic injustice) that the sodomite sailor and he crossed Federico García's path. He who was the opposite of the Colombian: graciously gypsy-like and, to top it all, a famous poet. Lorca proceeded, with all his charm and all his teeth shining bright in his dark face, to rescue the Scandinavian sailor stranded in the tropics. Barba lost his soft tooth forever.

Around 1948, almost twenty years after the amorous *double entente,* it was still possible to see that pseudo-Swedish sailor walking the night (up Prado, down Prado) like a shipwreck from another age. His clothes were, yes, navy blue: he wore a windbreaker to make hallucinatory the tropical night. A dirty blond, an anchorite with the anchor still around his neck, perhaps Norwegian, perhaps Galician, he wandered like the shade of a wandering sailor, without seeing anyone. For, you see, no one saw him. But invariably pedestrians and poets that gathered on the corner of Prado and Virtudes, where the least virtuous neighbourhood of Havana by night began, looked towards the odd parapet of the central promenade hoping to catch sight of this mariner shipwrecked in Havana, to whom Barba the bard sang: "There are days when we are so lubricious, so lubricious" (a sigh), "And there are days when we are so lugubrious, so lugubrious." Now an irreverent index appeared to finger him and a vile voice came to reveal: "That one too!" The laugh was like the draught that moved the cotton tooth of Porfirio Barba Jacob, who believed in no one, in no one.

The culmination of Lorca's visit to Havana occurred when he was offered a farewell meal, a banquet, a lunch was launched in the dining room of the Hotel Inglaterra at the end of the Acera del Louvre, at times called del *Livre.* Lorca and his future disciples were there. Literary Havana was also there, the one that did not write poems but was disposed to write prose as Lorca wrote verse. Through the open doors of the hotel (the air was not conditioned yet) could be seen the numerous columns, all white in the sun, the pavement of the Louvre and the park in the background, with the sunny solid statue of another poet, José Martí, who was killed, like Lorca, by that bullet with a name that always comes to kill poets when they are most needed.

Suddenly, as happens in the tropics, it started to rain. To rain for real, without warning, without anyone expecting it and without a break. The water was falling everywhere from everywhere. It was raining behind the undaunted columns, it was raining on the pavement, it was raining on the asphalt and on the paving of the park and its trees that could no longer be seen from the hotel. It was raining on the statue of Martí and its livid marble arm and the accusing hand and the pointing finger were all liquid now. It was raining on the Centro Gallego, on the Centro Asturiano and on the Manzana de Gómez and even further, on the little Plaza de Alvear, on the fountain of the beggars and on the façade of the Floridita where Hemingway used to come to drink. It was raining on the Cytherea of Hergesheimer and on the black-and-white landscape of Walker Evans. It was raining all over Havana.

In the dining room where the diners were devouring the hot meal indifferent to the rain that was melted crystal, humid mirror, liquid curtain, Lorca, only Lorca, saw the rain. He stopped eating to watch it and on an impulse he leapt to his feet and went to the open door of the hotel to see how it rained. Never had he seen it rain so for real. The rain of Granada sprinkled the villas, the rain of Madrid converted the never distant dust into mud, the rain of New York was an alien enemy—frozen like death. Other rains were not rain: they were drizzle, they were dew compared with this rain. "And the windows of heaven were opened," says Genesis—and the Hotel Inglaterra became an ark and Lorca was Noah. There were giants in poetry back then! Lorca continued his vigil, on his watch (there would be no siesta that afternoon), looking at the rain alone, seeing the deluge organize itself before his very eyes.

But soon they noted his absence from the banquet and they came, sole and solicitous, then two by two to make a rude circle around him, as happened to Noah with his zoo. Lorca had already written that the Cubans talk loud and louder talk the Havanans, the *hablaneros.* Lorca lifted a finger to his lips as a sign of respectful silence before the rain.

The racket of the banquet had ended in the roaring of the torrent. For the first time for the journalists, writers and musicians who met in that simple symposium, Federico García Lorca, poet (poet as we know means *maker* in Greek), had made rain in Havana as no one had seen it rain before, as no one saw it again afterwards.

TRANSLATED BY KENNETH HALL WITH THE AUTHOR

I Heard Her Sing

from THREE TRAPPED TIGERS

I knew La Estrella when she was only Estrella Rodríguez, a poor drunk incredibly fat Negro maid, long before she became famous and even longer before she died, when none of those who knew her well had the vaguest idea she was capable of killing herself but then of course nobody would have been sorry if she did.

I am a press photographer and my work at that time involved taking shots of singers and people of the *farándula,* which means not only show business but limelights and night life as well. So I spent all my time in cabarets, nightclubs, strip joints, bars, *barras, boîtes,* dives, saloons, *cantinas, cuevas, caves* or caves. And I spent my time off there too. My job took me right through the night and into dawn and often the whole morning. But sometimes, when I had nothing to do after work at three or four in the morning I would make my way to El Sierra or Las Vegas or El Nacional, the nightclub I mean not the hotel, to talk to a friend who's the emcee there or look at the chorus flesh or listen to the singers but also to poison my lungs with smoke and stale air and alcohol fumes and be blinded forever by the darkness. That's how I used to live and love that life and there was nobody or nothing that could change me because time passed so fast by my time that the days were only the waiting room of evening and evenings became as short as appointments and the years turned into a thin picture spread, and I went on my way, which means preferring nights to evenings, choosing night instead of day, living by night and squeezing my night, I mean my life, into a glass with ice or into a negative or into memory.

One of those nights I arrived at Las Vegas and I met up with all those people who like me had nobody who could change them and suddenly a voice came up to me from the darkness and said, *Fotógrafo,* pull up a seat please. Let me buy you a drink, and it was no longer just a voice but none other than Vítor Perla. Vítor has a magazine entirely devoted to half-naked girls or naked half-girls and captions like: A model with a future in sight—or rather two! Or: The persuasive arguments of Sonia Somethin, or: The Cuban BB says it's Brigitte who is her look-alike, and so on and so forth, so much so that I don't know where the hell they get their ideas from, they must have a shit factory in their heads to be able to talk like that about a girl or girls who only yesterday were or was probably just a *manejadora,* that is half maid and half baby-sitter, and now is half mermaid and half baby doll, or a part-time waitress who is now a full-time temptress, or who only yesterday worked in the garment center in Calle Muralla and who today is hustling her way to the top with all she's got. (Fuck, here I am, already talking like those people.) But for some mysterious reason (and if I were a gossip columnist I would spell it my$terious) Vítor had fallen into the deep, which was why it surprised me to find him in shallow waters and such spirits. I'm lying, of course. The first thing that surprised me was that he wasn't in the clink. So I told myself, He's loaded with shit but still manages to keep afloat: that's grace under morass, and I said it to him too but what I really said was, You keep afloat like good Spanish cork, and he burst out laughing. You're right, he said, but it's loaded cork! Confidentially, I must have a bit of lead somewhere inside—I'm keeling over. And so we began talking and he told me many things confidentially, he told me all his troubles, confidentially, and many other things, always confidentially, but I'm not going to repeat them because I'm a photographer not a press gossip, as I've said. Besides, Perla's problems are his own and if he solves them so much the better and if not it's curtains for Vítor. Anyway, I was fed up listening to his troubles and the way he twisted his face right and twitched his mouth left and as I had no wish to look at such ugly curly lips I changed the subject and we started talking about nicer things, namely women, and suddenly he said, Let me introduce you to Irena, and out of nowhere he produced the cutest little blonde, a doll who'd have looked like Marilyn Monroe if the Jívaros had abducted her and cut her down to size, not just shrinking her head but all the rest—and I mean *all* the rest, tits and all. So he hauled her by the arm like fishing her up from the sea of darkness and he said to me or rather to her, Irena, I want you to meet the best photographer in the world, only he didn't say the world but *el mundo,* meaning that I work for *El Mundo,* and the cutest little blonde, this incredible shrinking version of Marilyn Monroe smiled eagerly, turning up her lips and flashing her teeth like she was raising her skirt to show her thighs and her teeth gleaming in the darkness were the prettiest thing I've ever seen: perfectly even, well-formed and sensual like a row of thighs, and we started talking and every so often she would show off her teeth without blushing and I liked them so much that after a while I was meaning to ask her to let me touch her teeth or at least fondle her gums, and we were sitting at the table talking when Vítor called the waiter with this Cuban sucking sound we use to call waiters that is exactly like an inverted kiss and the drinks came as if by themselves but actually via an invisible waiter, his swarthy face and dirty hands lost in the darkness, and we started drinking and talking some more and in next to no time I'd very delicately as if I hadn't meant to place my foot on top of hers and I swear I almost didn't notice it myself, her foot was so tiny, but she smiled when I said sorry and I knew instantly that she noticed it and in the next next to no time I was holding her hand, which by now she couldn't help noticing that I meant it but I lost one fucking hour looking for it because her hand disappeared into my hand, playing hide-and-seek in between my yellow fingers that are permanently smeared with these hypo spots I pretend are nicotine stains, after Charles Boyer, naturally, and now already after I had finally found her hand I started caressing it without saying excuse me or anything because I was calling her Irenita, the name was just her size, and in next to next to no time we were kissing and all that, and when I happened to look around, Vítor had already got up to leave, tactful as ever, very discreetly, and so there we were on our own for a long time alone touching each other, feeling each other up, oblivious to everybody and everything, even to the show, which was over now anyway, to the orchestra playing a dance rhythm, to the people who were dancing in and out of the dark and getting tired of dancing, to the musicians packing up their instruments across the dance hall and into the dark, going home, and not noticing the fact that we were left alone there, very deep in the darkness now, no longer in the misty shadows as Cuba Venegas sings but in the deep darkness now, in darkness fifty, a hundred, a hundred and fifty fathoms under the edge of light swimming in darkness, in the lower depths, wet kissing, wet all over, wet in the dark and wet, forgotten, kissing and kissing and kissing all night long, oblivious to ourselves, bodiless except for mouths and tongues and teeth reflected in a wet mirror, two mouths and two tongues and four rows of teeth and gums occasionally, lost in saliva of kisses, silent now, keeping silent silently kissing, moist all over, dribbling, smelling of saliva, not noticing, tongues skin-diving in mouths, our lips swollen, kissing humidly each other, kissing, kissing before countdown and after blastoff, in orbit, man, out of this world, lost. Suddenly we were leaving the cabaret. It was then that I saw her for the first time.

She was an enormous mulatto, fat-fat, with arms like thighs, with thighs like tree trunks propping up the water tank that was her body. I told Irenita, I asked Irenita, I said, who's the fat one? because the fat woman seemed to dominate the *chowcito*—and fuck! now I must explain what the *chowcito* is. (The *chowcito* was the group of people who got together to get lost in the bar and hang around the jukebox after the last show was out to do their own *descarga,* this Afro-Cuban jam session which they so completely and utterly lost themselves in that once they went down they simply never knew it was daylight somewhere up there and that the rest of the world's already working or going to work right now, all the world except this world of people who plunged into the night and swam into any rock pool large enough to sustain night life, no matter if it's artificial, in this underwater of the frogmen of the night.) So there she was in the center of the *chowcito,* this enormous fat woman dressed in a very cheap dress made of caramel-colored cotton, dirty caramel confused fused with the fudge judged with her chocolate skin wearing an old pair of even cheaper sandals, holding a glass in her hand, keeping time to the music, moving her fat hips, moving all her fat body in a monstrously beautiful way, not obscene but sexual and lovely as she swayed to the rhythm, crooning beautifully, scat-singing the song between her plump purple lips, wiggling to the rhythm, shaking her glass in rhythm, rhythmically, beautifully, artistically now and the total effect was of a beauty so different, so horrible, so new, so unique and terrifying that I bitterly regretted I didn't have my camera along to catch alive this elephant who danced ballet, that hippopotamus toe-dancing, a building moved by music, and I said to Irenita, before asking what her name was, as I was on the point of asking what her name was, interrupting myself as I was asking what her name was, to say, She's the savage beauty of life, without Irenita hearing me, naturally, not that she would have understood if she had heard me, I said, I asked her, I said to her, to Irenita, Tell me, *tú,* who is it? And she said to me in a very nasty tone of voice, she said, She's the singing galapagos, the only turtle who sings boleros, and she laughed and Vítor slipped up beside me from the side of darkness just then to whisper in my ear, Careful, that's Moby Dick's kid sister, the Black Whale, and as I was getting high on being high I was able to grab Vítor by his sharkskin sleeve and tell him, You're a faggot, you're full of shit, you're a shitlicking bigot, you're a snot Gallego, a racist cunt and asshole: that's what you are, you hear me? *un culo,* and he said to me, calmly, I'll let it pass because you're my guest and you're drunk, that's all he said and then he plunged, like someone slipping behind curtains, into darkness. And I drew up closer and asked her who she was and she said to me, La Estrella, and I thought she meant the star so I said, No, no, I want to know your name, and she said, La Estrella, I am *La* Estrella, sonny boy, and she let go a deep baritone laugh or whatever you call the woman voice that corresponds to basso but sounds like baritone—cuntralto or something like that—and she smiled and said, My name is Estrella, Estrella Rodríguez if you want to know, Estrella Rodríguez Martínez

Vidal y Ruiz, *para servirle,* your humble servant, she said and I said to myself, She's black, black, black utterly and finally eternally black and we began talking and I thought what a boring country this would be if Friar Bartolomé de las Casas had never lived and I said to him wherever he is, I bless you, padre, for having brought nigrahs from Africa as slaves to ease the slavery of the Injuns, who were dying off anyhow what with the mass suicides and the massacres, and I said to him, I repeated, I said, Bless you, padre, for having founded this country, and after making the sign of the cross with my right hand I grabbed La Estrella with my left hand and I said to her, I love you. La Estrella, I love *you!* and she laughed bucketloads and said to me, You're plastered, *por mi madre,* you're completely plastered! and I protested, saying to her, I said, No I'm not, I'm ferpectly so ber, and she interrupted me to say, You're drunk like an old cunt, she said and I said to her, But you're a lady and ladies don't say cunt, and she said to me, I'm not a lady, I'm an *artista* and youse drunk *coño* and I said to her, I said, You are La Estrella, and she said, And youse drunk, and I said to her, All right, drunk as a bottle, I said to her, I said, I'm full of quote methylated spirits unquote but I'm not drunk, and I asked her, Are bottles drunk? and she said, *No, qué va!* and she laughed and I said, So please consider me a bottle, and she laughed again. But above everything, I said to her, consider me in love with you, La Estrella, I'm bottle-full of love for you. I like the Estrella better than I love the estrus, also called heat or rut, and she laughed again in bucketloads, lurching back and forward with laughter and finally slapping one of her infinite thighs with one of her never-ending hands so hard and loud the slap bounced back off the wall as if outside the cabaret and across the bay and in La Cabaña Fortress they had just fired the nine-o'clock-sharp salvo like they do every evening at five past nine, and when the report or its echo ceased fire she asked me, she said to me, she said, You love me? and I said, Uh-huh but she went on, Kinkily? and I said, Kinkily, passionately, maddeningly, meaninglessly, foreverly but she cut me short, No, no, I meant, you love me with my kink, kinky hair and all, and she lifted a hand to her head meaning, grabbing more than meaning her fuzzy hair with her full-fat fingers, and I said to her, *Every* bit and piece of you—and suddenly she looked like the happiest whale in the whole world. It was then that I made my great, one and only, impossible proposition. I came closer to her to whisper in her ear and I said to her, I said, La Estrella, I want to make you a dishonorable proposal, that's what I said, La Estrella, let's do it, let's have a drink together, and she said to me, De-light-ed! she said, gulping down the one she had in her hand and already chachachaing to the counter and saying to the bartender, Hey, Beefpie, make it mind, and I asked her, What's mind and she answered, Not mind, baby, mind you I said mine, m-i-n-e, make it mine and mine is La Estrella's drink: no one can have what she has, not open to the public, see what I mean. Make it mine then, and she started laughing again in bucketfuls so that her enormous breasts began shaking like the fenders of a Mack truck when the engine revs up.

At that moment I felt my arm gripped by a little hand and there was Irenita. You gonna stay all night with La Gorda here? she asked, and as I didn't answer she asked me again, You gonna stay with Fatso, and I told her, *Sí,* nothing else, all I said was yes, and she didn't say anything but dug her nails into my hand and then Estrella started laughing in bucketloads, and putting on a very superior air, she was so sure of herself, and she took hold of my hand and said, Leave her alone, this little hot pussy can do better on a zinc roof, and to Irenita she said, Sit on your own stool, little girl, and stay where you belong if you don't mind, and everybody started laughing, including Irenita, who laughed because she couldn't do anything else, and showing the two gaps in her molars just behind her eyeteeth when she laughed, she exited into daylight.

The *chowcito* always put on a show after the other show had finished and now there was a rumba dancer dancing to the jukebox and as a waiter was passing she stopped and said, Poppy, turn up the lights and let's rock, and the waiter went off and pulled out the plug and had to pull it out again and then a third time, but as the music stopped every time he switched off the jukebox, the dancer remained in the air and made a couple of long delicate steps, her whole body trembling, and she stretched out a leg sepia one moment, then earth-brown, then chocolate, tobacco, sugar-colored, black, cinnamon now, now coffee, now white coffee, now honey, glittering with sweat, slick and taut through dancing, now in that moment letting her skirt ride up over her round polished sepia cinnamon tobacco coffee and honey-colored knee, over her long, broad, full, elastic, perfect thighs, and she tossed her head backward, forward, to one side, to the other, left and right, back again, always back, back till it struck her nape, her low-cut, gleaming Havana-colored shoulders, back and forward again, moving her hands, her arms, her shoulders, the skin on them incredibly erotic, incredibly sensual: always incredible, moving them around over her bosom, leaning forward, over her full hard breasts, obviously unstrapped and obviously erect, the nipples, obviously nutritious, her tits: the rumba dancer with absolutely nothing on underneath, Olivia, she was called, still is called in Brazil, unrivaled, with no strings attached, loose, free now, with the face of a terribly perverted little girl, yet innocent, inventing for the first time movement, the dance, the rumba at that moment in front of my eyes: all of my eyes and here I am without my fucking camera, and La Estrella behind me watching everything and saying, You dig it, you dig it, and she got up off her seat as though it was a throne and went toward the jukebox while the girl was still dancing, and went to the switch, saying, Enough's enough, and turned it off, almost tearing it out in a rage, and her mouth looked like it was frothing with obscenities, and she said, That's all, folks! Dancin's over. Now we'll have *real* music! And without any music, I mean without orchestra or accompaniment from radio, record or tape, she started singing a new, unknown song, that welled up from her breast, from her two enormous udders, from her barrel of a belly: from that monstrous body of hers, and I hardly thought at all of the story of the whale that sang in the opera, because what she was putting into the song was something other than false, saccharine, sentimental or feigned emotion and there was nothing syrupy or corny, no fake *feeling* or commercial sentimentality about it, it was genuine soul and her voice welled up, sweet, mellow, liquid, with a touch of oil now, a colloidal voice that flowed the whole length of her body like the plasma of her voice and all at once I was overwhelmed by it. It was a long time since anything had so moved me and I began laughing at the top of my voice, because I had just recognized the song, laughing at myself, till my sides ached with belly laughs because it was "Noche de Ronda" and I thought talking to Agustín Lara, Agustín, Agustín, you've never invented a thing, you've not ever invented a thing, you've never composed anything, for now this woman is inventing your song: when morning comes you can pick it up and copy it and put your name and copyright on it again: "Noche de Ronda" is being born tonight. *Esta noche redonda!*

La Estrella went on singing. She seemed inexhaustible. Once they asked her to sing "La Pachanga" and she stood there with one foot in front of the other, the successive rollers of her arms crossed over the tidal wave of her hips, beating time with her sandal on the floor, a sandal that was like a motorboat going under the ocean of rollers that were her leagues of legs, beating time, making the speedboat resound repeatedly against the ground, pushing her sweaty face forward, a face like the muzzle of a wild hog, a hairless boar, her mustaches dripping with sweat, pushing forward all the brute ugliness of her face, her eyes smaller now, more malignant, more mysterious under her eyebrows that didn't exist except as a couple of folds of fat like a visor on which were sketched in an even darker chocolate the lines of her eye makeup, the whole of her face pushed forward ahead of her infinite body, and she answered, La Estrella only sings boleros, she said, and she added, Sweet songs, with real feeling, from my heart to my mouth and from my lips to your ear, baby, just so you don't get me wrong, and she began singing "Nosotros," composing the untimely dead Pedrito Junco's melody all over again, turning his sniveling little *canción* into something real, into a pulsating song, full of genuine nostalgia. La Estrella went on singing, she sang till eight in the morning, without having any notion that it was eight until the waiters started to clear everything away and one of them, the cashier, said, Excuse me, family, and he really meant it, family, he didn't say the word for the sake of saying it, saying family and really meaning something quite different from family, but family was what he meant, really, and he said: *Familia,* we have to close. But a little earlier, just before this happened, a guitarist, a good guitarist, a skinny emaciated fellow, a simple and dignified mulatto, who never had any work because he was very modest and natural and good-hearted, but a great guitarist, who knew how to draw strange melodies out of any fashionable song no matter how cheap and commercial it was, who knew how to fish real emotion out of the bottom of his guitar, who could draw the guts out of any song, any melody, any rhythm between the strings, a fellow who had a wooden leg and wore a gardenia in his buttonhole, whom we always called affectionately, jokingly, Niño Nené after all the Niños who sang flamencos, Niño Sabicas or Niño de Utrera or Niño de Parma, so this one we called Niño Nené, which is like saying Baby Papoose, and he said, he asked, Let me accompany you in a bolero, Estrella, and La Estrella answered him getting on her high horse, lifting her hand to her breasts and giving her enormous boobs two or three blows, No, Niñito, no, she said, La Estrella always sings alone: she has more than enough music herself. It was then that she sang "Mala Noche," making her parody of Cuba Venegas which has since become famous, and we all died laughing and then she sang "Noche y Día" and it was after that that the cashier asked us *familia* to leave. And as the night had already come to an end, the *noche* already *día,* we did so.

La Estrella asked me to take her home. She told me to wait a minute while she went to look for something and what she did was to pick up a package and when we went outside to get into my car, which is one of those tiny English sports cars, she was hardly able to get herself in comfortably, putting all her three hundred pounds weight in a seat which was hardly able to take more than one of her thighs, and then she told me, leaving the package in between us, It's a pair of shoes they gave me, and I gave her a sharp look and saw that she was as poor as hell, and so we drove off. She lived with some married actors, or rather with an actor called Alex Bayer. Alex Bayer isn't his real name, but Alberto Pérez or Juan García or Something Similar, but he took the name of Alex Bayer, because Alex is a name that these people always use and the Bayer he took from the drug company who make painkillers, and the thing is they don't call him that, Bayer I mean, these people, the people who hang out in the dive at the Radiocentro, for example, his friends don't call him Alex Bayer the way he pronounced it A-leks Báy-er when he was finishing a program, signing it off with the cast calling themselves out, but they called him as they still do call him, they called him Alex Aspirin, Alex Bufferin, Alex Anacin and any other painkiller that happens to be fashionable, and as everybody knew he was a faggot, very often they called him Alex Evanol. Not that he hides it, being queer, just the opposite, for he lived quite openly with a doctor, in his house as though they'd been officially married and they went everywhere together, to every little place together, and it was in his house that La Estrella lived, she was his cook and sleep-in maid, and she cooked their little meals and made their little bed and got their little baths ready, little etceteras. Pathetic. So if she sang it was because she liked it, she sang for the pleasure of it, because she loved doing it, in Las Vegas and in the Bar Celeste or in the Café Nico or any of the other bars or clubs around La Rampa. And so it was that I was driving her in my car, feeling very much the show-off for the same reasons but the reverse that other people would have been embarrassed or awkward or simply uncomfortable to have that enormous Negress sitting beside them in the car, showing her off, showing myself off in the morning with everybody crowding around, people going to work, working, looking for work, walking, catching the bus, filling the roads, flooding the whole district: avenues, streets, back streets, alleyways, a constant buzzing of people between the buildings like hungry hummingbirds. I drove her right up to their house, where she worked, she La Estrella, who lived there as cook, as maid, as servant to this very special marriage. We arrived.

It was a quiet little street in El Vedado, where the rich people were still asleep, still dreaming and snoring, and I was taking my foot off the clutch, putting the car into neutral, watching the nervous needles as they returned to the point of dead rest, seeing the weary reflection of my face in the glass of the dials as if the morning had made it old, beaten by the night, when I felt her hand on my thigh: she put her 5 *chorizos* 5, five sausages, on my thigh, almost like five salamis garnishing a ham on my thigh, she put her hand on my thigh and I was amused that it covered the whole of my thigh and I thought, Beauty and the Beast, and thinking of beauty and the beast I smiled and it was then that she said to me, Come on up, I'm on my own, she said, Alex and his bedside doctor, she said to me and laughed that laugh of hers that seemed capable of raising the whole neighborhood from sleep or nightmares or from death itself, They aren't here, she said: They went away to the beach for the weekend, Let's go on up so we can be alone, she said to me. I saw nothing in this, no allusion to anything, nothing to nothing, but all the same I said to her, No, I've got to go, I said. I have to work, I've got to sleep, and she said nothing, all she said was, *Adiós,* and she got out of the car, or rather she began the operation of getting herself out of the car and half an hour later, as I was dozing off from a quick nap, I heard her say, from the sidewalk now, putting her other foot on the sidewalk (as she bent threateningly over the little car to pick up her package of shoes, one of the shoes fell out and they weren't woman's shoes, but an old pair of boy's shoes, and she picked them up again), she said to me, You see, I've got a son, not as an excuse, nor as an explanation, but simply as information, she said to me, He's *retardado,* you know, but I love him all the more, she said and then she left.

TRANSLATED BY DONALD GARDNER AND SUZANNE JILL LEVINE
WITH THE AUTHOR

NANCY MOREJÓN

Love, Attributed City

FOR THE READER, COMPAÑERO

here I say again: the heart of the city has not yet died
for us need never die
oh dream, the summer screens return
and the carpenters' hair blowing in the morning
merging now with all I leave in the wake of my steps

my heart is lodged in the city and its adventure

freely with all I leave in my wake poetry comes:
flower or demon
poetry comes freely like a bird
(I offer it a red tree)
and it alights fiercely on my head and eats
what is sclerotic in me;
but now it's not just the dawn, not just the
singing of birds
not just the city

here I'll tell of coastal waves and the Revolution
here poetry comes with a beautiful sword to make my
breast bleed

who am I

who hears the dream of my cursed youth
for whom do I speak, what ear will say yes to my words
the mouth of the poet fills with ants each time it yawns

who am I

the guerrilla, the roving madwoman, the Medusa, a
Chinese flute,
a warm chair, seaweed, the coast guard's cannon, anguish,
the blood of the martyrs, the ovum of *Ochún* on this earth

who am I

that I go again through the streets, among *orichas,*
through the dark and corpulent heat,
among schoolchildren reciting Martí,
among the cars, the hidden niches of the streets,
the summer screens, into the Plaza of the people
among the blacks, the *guardacantones,*
through the parks, the old city, the old, old neighborhood
of Cerro,
and my cathedral and my port

here I say again: love, attributed city

TRANSLATED BY KATHLEEN WEAVER

Note: In the Yoruba religion in Cuba, the gods are called *orichas,* and the goddess of fertility is *Ochún. Guardacantones* were ornate stone guards, mounted on the corners of buildings as protection from carriage wheels.

CALVERT CASEY

The Walk

"Come the first of the month," Ciro's mother said, "we will go to Anastasio's and you will try on a pair of long trousers." She remained silent for a few seconds, fumbling nervously for the big soup ladle which lay conspicuously within her reach, on the tablecloth. Having found it, she dipped it into the fuming *potaje,* bringing up the boiled slices of green banana and yucca, and then dipping them again, deliberately and to no visible purpose.

As on previous occasions when the visit to Anastasio had been mentioned, Ciro grew restless and mumbled impatiently:

"Yes, yes, Mother, you've said it before."

She gave a sharp short laugh and added: "You are growing up—you are not a boy any longer. Now, it's decided—come the first of the month, we'll go to Anastasio, and he'll fix a nice pair of blue trousers for you to wear."

Thus released, she ladled out the first course of the family meal, a copious affair which not even the sultry Cuban summer could discourage.

After this latest announcement, Ciro tried as hard as he could not to look at Zenón, his bachelor uncle who was sitting in his place at the opposite corner of the table, since every time mention was made of the long trousers Zenón would cast little confidential glances in his direction. The boy finally gave up, however, and met the other's winking eye. Ciro's uncle hooked his napkin into his collar and started to eat very slowly, gazing down at his plate in a contented trance, only looking up to wink at Ciro from time to time.

Ciro's maiden aunts, two stout pleasant women, were smiling. "He will look very handsome in his new trousers, no doubt," said Felipa, the younger one. She giggled, looking at Ciro with a roguish expression, opened her eyes very wide, and burst at last into open laughter.

"Felipa, Felipa, calm down," entreated her sister, herself giggling. Ciro's young sister was watching them, deep in the semistupor of her second teething.

It all worked up slowly but surely, through all those weeks, seemingly endless for Ciro, like a huge balloon inflated with a slow-motion pump. As he went about his daily errands, or left for school in the early morning, or walked into the house after a day out in Altagracia, the playing grounds near his home, Ciro became aware that the center of interest had been shifted from his eldest cousin's latest pregnancy and was now focussed sharply on him. The sudden unmentioned concern had left him in a spotlight, at whose center he stood, assailed by his aunts' giggles and his mother's sudden tenderness. There was an air of placid conspiracy in the family, a tacit understanding, a fat contentment, an ineffable mirth universally shared. It transgressed the limits of the household, trickled down the inner court to the neighbors, flowed past the iron grates of the balconies overlooking the street and poured finally into the entire neighborhood.

As the end of the month approached and the day of the visit to Anastasio grew nearer, a complacent smile had turned up on the faces of all of Ciro's uncles, and even on the faces of their wives and in-laws. He sensed his cousins eyeing him now in admiration.

Too, Ciro suddenly perceived that his Uncle Zenón's stature in the family had grown out of proportion. From a half-accepted and colorless bachelor in a large family of solemn patriarchs, he had become overnight an important figure considered with intimate affection by everyone. His sisters-in-law had suddenly taken to Zenón, with the very unanimity which had formerly marked their tolerance of his manner when they had first been admitted into the clan. On Sunday evenings now, as they mounted the stairs into the stifling front parlor, they greeted him amidst much fanning, wiping the cold sweat that trickled down between their breasts: "It's really Zenón! And how nice of him to spend the evening at home. The wise man of the family—wouldn't give up celibacy for anything." He was offered cigars by his brothers, who no longer found grounds for picking on him, and Felipa often looked his way intently, scowling with an affection never witnessed previously.

On a Saturday afternoon, as Ciro and his mother, back from Anastasio's, turned the familiar corner into the street where they lived and began mounting the slope to the house, he saw his two aunts leaning against the rail of the mezzanine balcony, their elbows propped on two pink brocade cushions. His mother looked up smiling.

"What happened?" the younger aunt asked.

"Everything is in order," Ciro's mother said, standing under the balcony, "Anastasio himself will deliver the trousers tomorrow morning."

"What color?" the other asked again.

"Blue, dark blue," Ciro's mother replied.

An expression of uncontrollable curiosity appeared on the face of Mrs. Figueras, their neighbor. She and Mr. Figueras were standing on their balcony, across the street, and evidently had been unable to grasp what had been said.

"Dark blue," Ciro's aunt hastened to brief them, "Anastasio himself will deliver the trousers in the morning."

"Is that so?" Mrs. Figueras offered, undoubtedly pleased at Anastasio's diligence.

Nothing else was said about the subject and the evening meal was eaten without any allusion to Ciro's attire, a deep unhurried satisfaction having settled over the family. Only once Ciro caught his mother looking at him, gazing down and then suddenly up at him again.

On Sunday afternoon—Anastasio having lived up to his word and repute—Ciro stepped briskly into his brand-new pants, which covered his ankles, deserting forever the loose-fitting trousers which his mother used to tie just below the knee. He washed his hands, combed his hair, and went out onto the spacious roof, where he was to meet his uncle after siesta.

The air was dry; the square red tiles embedded on the roof-floor calcinated slowly under the sun. A maze of flat roofs, occasionally broken by a lonely wash line waving in the distance, and separated by low thick walls, spread out of sight. Ciro sat on a low stool under the thin shade of a wooden trelliswork, waiting for Zenón. He appeared at five, wearing his Sunday finery: white and black shoes, striped shirt and tie, white linen suit stiffly starched, and white stiff hat. A blue sapphire was shining on the small finger of his right hand.

"Ready?" he asked, touching Ciro on the arm. Ciro smiled faintly, caught in the waves of cologne coming from under his uncle's hat and spreading in the hot afternoon.

"Don't be late for supper," Ciro's mother said without looking up at them for her corner of the main balcony.

"We won't, Mother," Ciro answered. His legs were a little shaky as they went down the stairs and into the street. He rubbed his hands against his thighs trying to dry the sweat off the palms, and felt his uncle's hand resting on his shoulder almost tenderly.

The afternoon breeze began to come in soft waves as they walked down the half-deserted streets lined by whitewashed walls, and hushed in the Sunday air. Anonymous women emerged here and there from their doors on a mid-afternoon reconnaissance, staring fixedly at them until Ciro felt uncomfortable. They crossed a big dusty square where a few trees stood dejectedly, walked along a narrow promenade, and slowly entered the old section of town. The sidewalk was very narrow here and they took to the road.

Ciro was seeing the *quartier* for the first time. The streets were no longer asleep in Sunday slumber. People walked, talked, and laughed aloud. On certain corners, large groups of young boys in shirtsleeves congregated and talked. They called each other by their first names, often making obscene gestures as they chattered. Groups of young girls strolled along, arms around one another's waists, deliberately ignoring the loud exchanges. The small coffee shops were full of men and women seated around tiny marble tables drinking coffee with milk and eating buttered bread. White electric bulbs glared furiously from the ceilings. Some of the customers had taken their chairs out to the sidewalks, from where they shouted their orders to the waiters inside.

Everyone seemed to know Ciro's uncle, and Ciro could hardly recognize him now. A mysterious change had overtaken him when they crossed the promenade. This was a new Zenón, and Ciro tried to think of the restrained man who sat daily at the family table abiding in silence the inane little jokes everybody made at his expense. He had expanded; he stopped here and there, shook hands with many people, laughed boisterously.

They stepped into one of the coffee shops and joined several people at a table. These were older people, well-fed and pleasantly garrulous, and Ciro was surprised at the ease with which his uncle fitted instantly into the mellow comradeship that linked them together. The uncle gave a short account of his health, and then almost immediately Ciro became, to his embarrassment, the subject of conversation. They patted him on the shoulder, took delight in his physique, felt his biceps and praised his good looks. His masculinity was the subject of firm, slowly delivered statements. The people sitting at the next table looked at Ciro appreciatively, and with some vague affection.

"Is he really your nephew?" one of the women at the table asked.

"Oh yes," Ciro's uncle protested, "but I can assure you: he is almost like a son to me."

"The boy looks exactly like you," the woman insisted. "What are you trying to tell us?"

"We know you, Zenón." An old man sitting next to Ciro was talking now. "You are too modest. Look at the boy's face. The very face of Zenón when I first met him." The woman had left her chair as the old man spoke, and taking Ciro by the chin she proclaimed the resemblance again, this time in an energetic voice.

"I bet he won't be as wicked as his father," she added. Everybody laughed at this. Ciro looked at his uncle, who seemed delighted.

"You are wrong," another woman in the group said. This one was fat and dark. "With his looks, the little one will very soon be well ahead of Zenón." The laughter was general now and attention was centered on their table.

"Don't be sad, Zenón," the woman went on, raising her voice. "Such is life. I bet he'll live up to your name, though." She winked one eye as she turned around to watch the effect of these words upon her audience. There was a roar of agreement. Zenón was clearly delighted. Smiling, he rose and shook hands with everyone. Then, amid shouts of good wishes, he and Ciro left.

They walked for a few minutes along the noisy thoroughfare, and then turned into a quiet little street lined with small one-storey houses. The iron grates had apparently been removed from the windows of these flats, but the tall shutter doors and built-in blinds had been kept, obviously to keep the places cool and guard them to some extent against intruders. A great deal of activity seemed to take place behind each pair of blinds.

They stopped before one of the houses, decorated with a rim of blue tiles; Ciro's uncle rapped on the blind and they were let in.

It was cool and dark inside. After a while, Ciro could make out a large room, poorly furnished, with a few heavy rocking chairs placed around a table. A gramophone was playing in one corner of the room. Two round vases of painted earthenware, filled with dusty wax flowers, stood on the table. A large framed lithograph of the Sacred Heart hung from the wall, and a leaf of holy palm had been nailed to the wooden frame.

Ciro saw three girls in the room. Two stood behind the slatted doors, peering through the blinds, and the other, a blond thin girl, was doing her hair with the help of a Negro boy who sat on the arm of her chair. The girls wore slacks, with small linen or cotton blouses covering their chests.

There was a huge ice-box in a small alcove next to the room, and a little old woman busied herself arranging bottles of beer in its compartments. The visitors were greeted warmly by the Negro boy and the young girls, who nevertheless remained seated and went calmly about their own business.

Ciro's uncle walked over to the old woman by the ice-box.

"Is she in?" he asked.

"She's in her room, I think; I'll call her. Shall I pour beer for you?"

She poured from a bottle and then looked at Ciro, without a word.

"No, thanks," he said, but at a gesture from Zenón she poured some in another glass and handed it to him.

A tall pretty woman arrived presently, having entered the room from a small court lined with painted buckets and pails seemingly intended for growing plants. She was big-boned, and walked with a pitching movement on a pair of tiny slippers, waving her arms to help herself forward. She had beautiful black hair, which she tied at the back of her head in a very tight *chignon,* and she was wearing a dressing gown. The black mass of hair pulling from her eyelids seemed on the point of snapping from her forehead.

"It is you, Zenón," she said smiling, "Ah, the son of a devil. He has forgotten us!"

"How could you say such a thing?" protested Zenón. They embraced affectionately, patting each other's back with noisy slaps.

"Have you had a drink?" she asked, and then turning to the old woman, "*Vieja,* are you keeping Zenón cool?"

"Do not worry, we are fine," Zenón assured her.

"Did you see my new acquisition? It wasn't here when you last came around," pointing to the big ice-box, its nickel moldings shining in the half-light of the room.

The gramophone was blaring very loud now. "Dago," the woman shouted to the Negro boy, "shut that thing. It's driving me mad."

The boy got up from the arm of the chair and walked to the machine. He was muscular and big and there was something comical in the way he wiggled his hips and in the thin stream of voice coming from the huge dark frame. He had been looking at Ciro all the time, grinning occasionally.

"And who is the young fellow?" the tall woman asked now, noticing Ciro for the first time.

"My nephew," Ciro's uncle announced.

"The one you used to tell me about? But he's big, a real big man now. He favors you, Zenón. *Vieja,*" she addressed the old woman again, "pour some more for this one here." She moved and spoke calmly, peering deliberately into Ciro's face with all-surveying eyes which often gave off a faint scintillation of amusement. She carried a handbag under one arm, which gave the impression, puzzling enough when it came to the rest of her attire, that she was about to leave. She shifted the bag and took a lit cigarette the old woman handed her.

"It's been a hellish day," she said.

"Yes, it's been warm and oppressive all day long," confirmed Zenón.

"On such a day one should remain under cold water."

"You are right," Zenón agreed, "one should."

She pondered awhile and then walked to the gramophone and played the same record again, very loud. The heat seemed unbearable in the room now. Ciro sat on one of the chairs, near the rustic bar built by the ice-box. The blond thin girl whom he had seen doing her hair when they arrived walked over to him after a while.

"Let's dance," she said. Ciro got up, took her by the waist, and started to dance with short clumsy steps. Nobody paid any attention to them and that made Ciro happier than he had been for quite some time.

"Your hands are damp," she said.

"Yes, they are," Ciro agreed.

They walked to the machine when the music stopped, and from the corner of his eye Ciro saw the other boy starting after them.

"Let me do it," the boy said, kneeling in front of the gramophone and fumbling with the tiny disks.

"Lay off, Dago!" the tall woman shouted from her place, turning her head, "lay off!" The boy left them, giggling, though visibly annoyed. He lifted his arms above his head as he walked away and broke unexpectedly into loud laughter.

"Dago is a little crazy," the girl explained as they danced again. Ciro said nothing. They danced for a while and then stopped to drink the beer the old woman poured. Ciro could hear his uncle and the tall woman chatting in a low voice.

She turned to consider them now from her chair. "Show him the place," she called to the girl, without addressing her by any name. "Take him around the house."

The girl grabbed Ciro's hand. "Let's go out back," she said. They left the room and crossed the tiny court with the painted buckets. Four small rooms overlooked the yard. There was a charcoal stove built into the rear wall, and protected with a zinc cover. Dago and one of the girls whom Ciro had seen standing behind the blinds were talking, sitting on the steps to one of the rooms.

They walked to the end of the little yard. "This is my room," the girl said. "It's cooler inside than out here." They went in and she closed the door behind her. A low wooden partition separated her room from the others, and they could hear Dago and the girl chat on the other side. "Sit down," the girl said.

Ciro looked around. There was a single chair with a porcelain basin and a jar sitting on it. Two or three slices of soap were on the floor around the chair. There was also a large iron bed with long posts rising almost to the ceiling; these were connected by rods, and a mosquito-net was strung across the top of the square frame. A crucifix hung from the wall over an unpainted night-table, and two small religious lithographs had been pasted to the wall on both sides of the crucifix. A small bouquet of red and yellow roses stood in a glass filled with water. A few dresses hung from a string nailed to the wall, opposite the bed.

Ciro sat down on the edge of the bed. The girl started to rearrange the flowers, emptied the glass in the basin and refilled it from the jar.

"I must keep them contented," she said, carefully placing the glass on the table again. "My saints, I mean. They are very good to me."

"Yes," Ciro agreed.

"Are you religious?" She took his hand now. "You must be." Ciro smiled again and said nothing.

"Your hands are still cold," she said.

"It's warm here, though," Ciro said.

"Yes, but it will be cooler in a few minutes. It's getting dark now."

"Yes, it's getting dark," Ciro agreed again.

She took a little handkerchief from one of the pockets in her slacks and began wiping the small crucifix and the lithographs on the wall.

"I was very sick last year, in this very room. And I prayed for a long time that they would save my life, and they did. I keep fresh flowers here, ever since. Do you go to mass?"

Ciro looked at her and gave no reply.

"Do you?" she insisted.

"On Sundays," he said.

"You do better than I. I rarely go, but I pray here."

Dago and the other girl were having a violent argument now, on the other side of the partition. Ciro could hear the torrent of words, uttered in the boy's high-pitched voice. "Dago is jealous," the girl said. She was sitting on the bed now. "He acts like that whenever he gets jealous."

"Like my new dress?" She pointed to a hook on the wall. Ciro looked up, lifting his eyes for the first time since they had started to talk.

"This one," she said, rising from the bed and taking down a green frock which looked too small for her. She was thin and fairly well built, except for an ugly brown burn on her left arm, which she didn't try to conceal.

"Like it? I love a new dress. Here, smell the material. Doesn't it smell good and clean? It makes you feel good."

"Yes, it is true," Ciro said, "it makes you feel good."

"I used to have an evening dress. That was some time ago, though. I had a picture taken. Here."

She opened the night-table drawer and took out a leather wallet from a batch of odd papers, curling tongs, and worn out puffs. She looked through the wallet and finally took out a small photograph. She was wearing a long gown in the picture and looked prettier and much younger. The ugly burn was showing on her arm. Ciro looked at her again, realizing that she was not very young any longer.

"It was taken at a big party, in Traganza."

"I know the place," Ciro said.

"There is a small pond and a stand where people dance, and they sell drinks near the stand."

"I know," Ciro was delighted at the girl's description of the familiar places he had inspected with morbid curiosity from the road.

"How come? I bet your mother doesn't know that." She was laughing now.

"I've seen it from the road, when we go diving to Dueñas."

"It's nice in Traganza."

"Yes," Ciro said, "but it is cooler in Dueñas."

"Oh no, it couldn't be nicer than it is in Traganza."

"No," Ciro insisted again, "it is much nicer in Dueñas. You may rest assured."

"You win." She was amused.

"That day in Traganza," she went on, "a friend of mine announced that I could sing, and they made me climb up on the stand."

Ciro had a sensation of extreme well-being now. The beer had delivered him into a soft mellowness, from which he had no desire to emerge. Dago had quieted down, though Ciro could still hear him walking past the door, presumably on little errands from the zinc cover to the room in front. A rooster crowed now and then in a nearby yard. Through an opening at the top of the door Ciro could see a piece of sky.

The girl was lying near him, on her back. Propped on one elbow Ciro watched her.

"Sing," Ciro said.

She began to sing in a low voice, looking up at the wood-panelled ceiling. Her hands crossed behind her head, she sang absently, or rather hummed to herself. Ciro wondered once whether she was aware of his presence at all. She went on singing for a long while, and then stopped. She untied her hair slowly and wove it back into a single loose braid on her shoulder.

It was getting dark in the room. Ciro thought of his uncle, but didn't make any movement. Finally the girl rose to her feet. "It's late now," she said. "Your uncle must be getting impatient out there."

"Yes, I must go," he said.

She got up, took a hairpin from the night-table drawer, pried it open with the aid of her front teeth and plunged it into her braid. The hair was smooth and very blond on the nape of her neck. She walked unhurriedly to the door and opened it. They went out into the little yard again, and retraced their steps back to the room in front. The doors to the other rooms were now shut. She put her arm around Ciro's waist and they walked very slowly as they came through the narrow hallway.

There was only one girl in the front room; she was peering into the street. The old woman stood by her ice-box. Zenón and the tall pretty woman were still chatting in a subdued voice, but they got up from their chairs when they saw Ciro.

"We must get ready to go now," Zenón said, "it's late." He walked to the old woman and handed her a few coins. She tipped her head to one side and then to the other, as though a little abashed. "Buy yourself cigarettes," he said, "and take good care of your ice-box. It's a very good ice-box, so spacious and shiny." He nodded to the tall woman. "Very fine," he added, "it is really very fine, you may have my assurance." She gave a pleased smile and proceeded to show her visitors to the door.

"You come more often to see us, Zenón," she said as they stepped out into the street; and then looking at Ciro: "You take care of this one too."

Ciro and his uncle walked back again through the old section of town and turned into the street leading to their house. It was really dark now, but from a distance Ciro could make out his aunts leaning against the balcony rail, their arms resting on the brocade cushions. A few minutes more and they were home. They went up the stairs and were let in.

"You are late for supper, you two," Felipa said. Ciro sat at the table and helped himself to a piece of the Sunday roast.

The other members of the family took their places around the table and started to eat.

"It was rather pleasant out," Ciro's uncle said.

"Was the square very crowded?" Felipa wanted to know. "Being Sunday it must have been." Ciro was aware of a vague deference in her bearing.

"There was quite a crowd," Ciro replied; and then frowning, "the usual one, they are always the same."

When dinner was over, Ciro sat on his stool at the far end of the front balcony. The street was empty now, except for the breeze rustling gently about him. He looked up at the summer sky and then, for a long time, he looked down in wonder at the street, where no noise could be heard.

TRANSLATED BY JOHN H. R. POLT

CLAVE 3

JOSÉ LEZAMA LIMA

Chapter VIII

from PARADISO

The interior of the school opened onto two courtyards that were connected by a small door, not unlike the one leading to the refectory in seminaries. One courtyard was for the lower school, for children between the ages of nine and thirteen. The lavatories were parallel to the three classrooms. Lavatory recess occurred at a fixed time, but since it is difficult to dominate chronometrically the Malpighian corpuscles or the final contractions of digestion, one sometimes had to signal the teacher to receive permission to relieve oneself. Professorial sadism, with no appeal in that situation, would show itself on occasion with Ottoman cruelty. There was the case, mentioned in whispers, of a student who asked to discharge his ammonium carbamate and ethereal sulfates, and having been denied permission, went into contortions that were discovered to be peritonitis—after the student's death. Now, whenever a student asked permission to "go out," he subtly tried to coerce the teacher, creating for himself the possibility of being an adolescent murdered by the gods and, for the teacher, that of being thought of as a demented satrap.

An older student monitored the courtyard: Farraluque, then in his last year of lower school, the product of a semititanic Basque and a languid Havana woman. He was a small-bodied adolescent with a sad, baggy-eyed face, but he could count among his few attributes an enormous member. He was in charge of overseeing the parade of younger students to the toilet, at which time a priapic demon took furious possession of him; as long as the procession went on, he danced, raised his arms as if clicking aerial castanets, all the while leaving his member outside his fly. He wrapped it in his fingers, cradled it on his forearm, pretended to strike it, scolded it or soothed it as if it were a suckling child. This improvised phallic display or ceremony was observed through the blinds on the upper floor by an idling domestic, who, half prudish and half vindictive, brought the inordinate imbalance of that priapic piece of gossip to the climacteric ears of the wife of the son of that Cuevarolliot who had fought so often with Alberto Olaya. Farraluque was dismissed from his post as monitor of lavatory recess and made to spend several Sundays in a row in the study hall; during the week, he pretended seriousness as he faced his fellow students, but even his face had been converted into an object of hilarity. The cynicism of his sexuality caused him to don a ceremonious mask, inclining his head or shaking hands with the circumspection of an academic farewell.

After Farraluque was temporarily exiled from his burlesque throne, José Cemí had an opportunity to witness another phallic ritual. Farraluque's sexual organ was a miniature reproduction of his visage. Even his glans resembled his face. The extension of the frenum looked like his nose, the massive prolongation of the membranous cupola like his bulging forehead. But, among upperclassmen, the phallic power of the rustic Leregas reigned like Aaron's staff. His gladiator's arena was the geography class. He would hide to the left of the teacher on some yellowing benches that held about twelve students. While the class dozed off, listening to an explanation of the Gulf Stream, Leregas would bring out his member—with the same majestic indifference as the key is presented on a cushion in the Velázquez painting—short as a thimble at first, but then, as if driven by a titanic wind, it would grow to the length of the forearm of a manual laborer. Unlike Farraluque's, Leregas's sexual organ did not reproduce his face, but his whole body. In his sexual adventures his phallus did not seem to penetrate but to embrace the other body. Eroticism by compression, like a bear cub squeezing a chestnut, that was how his first moans began.

The teacher was monotonously reciting the text, and most of his pupils, fifty or sixty in all, were seated facing him, but on the left, to take advantage of a niche-like space, there were two benches lined up at right angles to the rest of the class. Leregas was sitting at the end of the first bench. Since the teacher's platform was about a foot high, only the face of this phallic colossus was visible to him. With calm indifference, Leregas would bring out his penis and testicles, and like a wind eddy that turns into a sand column, at touch it became a challenge of exceptional size. His row and the rest of the students peered past the teacher's desk to view that tenacious candle, ready to burst out of its highly polished, blood-filled helmet. The class did not blink and its silence deepened, making the lecturer think that the pupils were morosely following the thread of his discursive expression, a spiritless exercise during which the whole class was attracted by the dry phallic splendor of the bumpkin bear cub. When Leregas's member began to deflate, the coughs began, the nervous laughter, the touching of elbows to free themselves from the stupefaction they had experienced. "If you don't keep still, I'm going to send some students out of the room," the little teacher said, vexed at the sudden change from rapt attention to a progressive swirling uproar.

An adolescent with such a thunderous generative attribute was bound to suffer a frightful fate according to the dictates of the Pythian. The spectators in the classroom noted that in referring to the Gulf's currents the teacher would extend his arm in a curve to caress the algaed coasts, the corals and anemones of the Caribbean. That morning, Leregas's phallic dolmen had gathered those motionless pilgrims around the god Terminus as it revealed its priapic extremes, but there was no mockery or rotting smirk. To enhance his sexual tension, he put two octavo books on his member, and they moved like tortoises shot up by the expansive force of a fumarole. It was the reproduction of a Hindu myth about the origin of the world. The turtle-like books became vertical and one could see the two roes enmeshed in a toucan nest. The roll of dice thrown by the gods out of boredom that morning was to be completely adverse for the vital arrogance of the powerful rustic. The last of the teacher's explanatory syllables resounded like funereal rattles in a ceremony on the island of Cyprus. Leaving at the end of class, the students had the look of people waiting to be disciplined, waiting for the Druid priest to perform the sacrifice. Leregas, foolish-looking, went out with his head tilted to one side. The teacher was somber, like a person petting the dog of a relative who has just died. When they passed, a sudden charge of adrenalin rushed into the teacher's arms; his right hand shot out like a falcon and resounded on Leregas's right cheek, and immediately afterwards his left hand crossed over and found the cocky vitalist's left cheek. Feeling his face transformed into the object of two succulent slaps, Leregas was unabashed; he leaped like a clown, a cynical dancer, a heavy river bird making a triple somersault. The same absorption that had held the class during the lighting of the country boy's Alexandrian Pharos followed the sudden slaps. The teacher, with serene dignity, trudged off to the office with his complaints; as he passed, the students were imagining the lecturer's embarrassment in explaining the strange event. Leregas plodded on, not looking around, and got to the study hall with his tongue hanging out. His tongue was a lively poodle pink. Now it was possible to compare the tegument of his glans with that of his oral cavity. Both were a violet pink, but the color of the glans was dry, polished, ready to resist the porous dilation of the moment of erection, while that of the mouth was brighter in tone, shining with the light saliva, as the ebbing tide penetrates a snail on the shore. He used his clownishness to defend himself from the finale of the priapic ceremony somewhat coyly, with some indifference and indolence, as if he had been rewarded for the exceptional importance of his act. He had not meant it to be a challenge, he simply had not made the slightest effort to avoid it. The class, in the second quarter of the morning, was passing through a period conducive to the thickening of galloping adolescent blood, assembled before the essential nothingness of nodding didacticism. Leregas's mouth was receptive, purely passive, and there saliva took the place of maternal water. The mouth and the glans seemed to be at opposite poles, and Leregas's clownish indifference allied him with the hidden femininity of his mouth's liquid pink. His arched eros collapsed completely under the pedagogical slaps. He remembered that the phalli of Egyptian colossi or the giant children spawned by the sons of heaven and the daughters of man did not correspond to their large size, but instead, as in Michelangelo's painted sex in the Creation, the hidden glans hinted at its diminutive dome. Almost all the spectators remembered the arching temerity of that summer morning, but Cemí remembered better the wild provincial's mouth, inside which a small octopus seemed to be stretching, disappearing into the cheeks like smoke, sliding down the channel of the tongue, falling to pieces on the ground like an ice flower with streaks of blood.

Leregas was expelled from school, but Farraluque, who had been condemned to forfeit three Sunday passes, provoked a prolonged sexual chain that touched on the prodigious. The first Sunday of his confinement he wandered through the silent playgrounds and the completely empty study hall. The passage of time became arduous and slow. Time had become a succession of too moist grains of sand inside an hourglass. Creamy, dripping, interminable whipped cream. He tried to abolish time with sleep, but time and sleep retreated until at last they touched backs as during the first moments of a duel, then pacing off the number of steps agreed upon, but no shots rang out. And the prolonged smell of

Sunday silence, the silent gun cotton that formed quick clouds, phantasmal chariots with a decapitated driver bearing a letter, all fell apart like smoke with each blow of his whip against the fog.

In his boredom Farraluque crossed the courtyard again, just as the headmaster's maidservant, who had an extremely agreeable face, was coming down the stairs. She apparently wanted to contrive an encounter with the chastened scholar. It was she who had observed him from behind the blinds, carrying the droll bit of gossip to the headmaster's wife.

When she passed by him, she said: "How is it that you're the only one who hasn't gone to visit his family this Sunday?"

"I'm being punished," Farraluque answered dryly. "And the worst part is that I don't know why."

"The headmaster and his wife have gone out," the maid replied. "We're painting the house. If you help us, we'll try to pay you for it."

Without waiting for a reply, she took Farraluque by the hand, walking by his side as they went up the stairs. When they got to the headmaster's apartment he saw that practically everything was covered with paper; the smell of lime, varnish, and turpentine sharpened the evaporations of all those substances, suddenly scandalizing his senses.

In the living room, she let go of Farraluque's hand and with feigned indifference climbed up on a stepladder and began to slide the brush dripping with whitewash along the walls. Farraluque looked around, and on the bed in the first bedroom he could make out the headmaster's cook, a mammee-colored mulatto girl of nineteen puffed years, submerged in an apparently restless serenity of sleep. He pushed on the half-open door. The neat outline of her back stretched down to the opening of her solid buttocks like a deep, dark river between two hills of caressing vegetation. The rhythm of her breathing was dryly anxious; the sweat of summer, deposited in each small opening of her body, gave a bluish gloss to certain areas of her back. The salt glistened in each of those depressions in her body. The reflections of temptation were awakened by the challenging nearness of her body and her own distance in sleep.

Farraluque undressed swiftly and leaped onto the patchwork of delights. Just then the sleeping woman, without stretching, gave a complete turn, offering the normality of her body to the newly arrived male. The unstartled continuity of the mulatto's breathing eliminated the suspicion of pretense. As the large barb of the small-bodied boy penetrated her, it seemed as if she was going to roll over again, but his oscillations did not break the circle of her sleep. Farraluque was at that point in adolescence when, even after copulation, the erection remains beyond its own ends, at times inviting a frenetic masturbation. The immobility of the sleeping woman now began to unnerve him, but then, peeping through the door of the next room, he saw the little Spanish girl who had led him by the hand, also fast asleep. Her body did not have the distension of the mulatto's, in which the melody seemed to be invading muscular memory. Her breasts were hard, like primal clay, her torso was tense as a pine tree, her carnal flower was a fat spider, nourished on the resin of those same pines, tightly wrapped like a sausage. The carnal cylinder of a strong adolescent boy was needed to split the arachnid down the middle. Farraluque had acquired some tricks and soon began to exercise them. The secret touches of the Spanish girl were more obscure and difficult to decipher. Her sex seemed corseted, like a midget bear in a carnival. A bronze gate, Nubian cavalrymen guarded her virginity. Lips for wind instruments, as hard as swords.

When Farraluque jumped onto the feathery spread in the second room, the rotation of the Spanish girl was the opposite of the mulatto's. She offered the plain of her back and her Bay of Naples. With ease, her copper circle surrendered to the rotund attacks of the glans and the full accumulation of its blooded helmet. This was evidence that the Spanish girl took theological care of her virginity, but that she had little concern for the maidenhood of the remaining parts of her body. The easy flow of blood during adolescence made possible a prodigy which, once normal conjugation was over, enabled him to begin another, *per angustam viam.* This new amorous encounter recalled the incorporation of a dead serpent by its hissing female conqueror. Coil after coil, the momentarily flaccid member was penetrating the body of the conquering serpent, like a monstrous organism of Cenozoic times, in which digestion and reproduction formed a single function. How frequently the marine serpent had come to the grotto of the Spanish girl was apparent from the relaxation of the tunnel, and Farraluque's phallic configuration was extremely propitious for that retrospective penetration, for his barb had an exaggerated length beyond the bearded root. With an astuteness worthy of a Pyrenean ferret, the Spanish girl divided its length into three segments, motivating, more than pauses in her sleep, the true hard breathing of proud victory. The first segment comprised the hardened helmet of the glans and a tense, wrinkled part that extended from the rim of the glans like a string waiting to be plucked. The second segment brought up the strut or, speaking more properly, the stem, the part most involved, for it would give the signal for continuing or abandoning the incorporation. But the Spanish girl, with the tenacity of a classical potter opening the broad mouth of an amphora with only two fingers, managed to unite the two small fibers of the opposing parts and reconcile them in that darkness. She turned her face and told the boy something that at first he did not understand but later on made him smile with pride. The vital luxury of Spanish women often leads them to use a number of Cuban expressions outside of their ordinary meaning, and the attacker on two established fronts heard her exhale pleadingly out of the vehemence of her ecstasy the phrase "permanent wave." This had nothing to do with barbershop dialectics. In asking, she meant for the conductor of energy to beat with the flat of his hand on the foundation of the injected phallus. With each of those blows her ecstasy was transformed into corporeal waves. A tingle in her bones was enlivened by the blow, with the fluency of muscles impregnated by a stellar Eros. The phrase had come to the Spanish girl as something obscure, but her senses had given her an explanation and application as clear as light through a windowpane. Farraluque withdrew his barb, which had worked hard on that day of glory, but the waves continued in the Hispanic squire until her body was slowly carried off in sleep.

The drawn-out vibration of the bell called people to the dining hall, but he was the only one sitting in the large chamber that had been prepared for four hundred students who were absent on the Lord's day. The marble table, the white china, the venerable dough of the bread, the whitewashed fly-speckled walls with their Zurbarán motifs, supplied the harmonizing counterweight for that orgiastic Sunday.

Monday night, the headmaster's cook was with the servant girl across the street. She was the only servant of a couple approaching the age that brings the attrition of reproduction. Day and night she watched over the immense tedium of her employers. Boredom was now the only magnet holding together weary people. When they copulated in disjunct time, the clock of their encounter squeaked from the rust of everyday displeasure, well-sharpened bad humor. The forty-year-old wife's frustration was poured out in endless droll conversations with the maid, while her feet itched in their struggle against a minuet. The maid repeated to her mistress the whole tale that she had received from the cook, complete with the memory of the feverish ecstasy of taking in such a large barb. The lady asked for repetitions in the tale, details concerning the dimensions, minute proofs of the progression of laments and hosannas in the pleasant encounter. She made her stop, go back over a fragment of the event, expand on an instant in which feigned sleep was on the point of changing into a war whoop or the murmur of a flute. But the lady demanded so much from the story, such detailed descriptions of lance and socket, that the maid told her with extreme humility: "Ma'am, a person can only tell about that when she has it right in front of her, but believe me, then you forget it all and later on you can't describe any of the details."

When ten o'clock arrived on that warm night, the maid began to shut the living-room windows, lowering the dusty blinds; then she poured a carafe of water for the lady's night table. She turned down the covers and fluffed up the pillows on the bed, which showed an unfurrowed voluptuousness. Half an hour later the lady was falling into a sleep cut off by anxious sighs. What strange butterflies were coming to alight on the very edge of her nocturnal rest?

The second Sunday for the castigated fellow passed with a cheer that rose and fell in the depths of bottled-water tedium. At sundown, a light breeze began to creep in cautiously. A monkey-like little boy, the brother of the aforementioned mammee cook, came into the school courtyard looking for Farraluque. He said that the lady in the house across the way wanted him to help her paint too. The priapic one was proud that his name was spreading from the small glory of the schoolyard to a broader fame in the neighborhood. When he entered the house, he saw a stairway and beside it two buckets of whitewash and farther on a brush, the bristles shining and paintless, keeping intact its pleasant aspect of a prop chosen for a still life by a painter of the school of Courbet. As in a stage setting, once more there was a half-open door. The mature madonna was artlessly feigning a sleep of sensual drowsiness. Farraluque felt obliged to show he didn't believe the cataleptic state would last, so, before he undressed, he let the whole scandal of the elastic progression of his rosy worm show through his hands. Without abandoning her pretended drowsiness, the woman raised her arms, crossing them rapidly, and then she joined the index and middle fingers of her hands in a square that broke apart as it faced the proximity of the phallic Nike. When Farraluque leaped into the square that was frothy with an excess of pillows, the woman bent to get closer and converse with the penetrating instrument. Her lips, dry at first, lightly moistened and began to slip along the filigree of the porous weave of the glans. Many years later he would remember the beginning of that adventure, associating it with a history lesson, where it was said that a Chinese emperor, while his troops paraded interminably behind hornpipes and war drums, caressed a piece of jade, polished with an almost insane craftsmanship. The wanton woman's vital intuition led her to show him an impressionable specialty in the first two of the eight different stages of the *Auparishtaka* or oral union according to the sacred texts of India. With the tips of two fingers she pressed the phallus down at the same time as she ran her lips and teeth around the edges of the casque. Farraluque felt like a dazzled horse being bitten at the root by a newborn tiger. His two previous sexual encounters had been primitive; now he was entering the realm of subtlety and diabolic specialization. The second requirement of the sacred Hindu text, in which she showed special proficiency, was in whirling the carpet of the tongue around the cupola of the casque, and then with rhythmic nodding movements coursing up and down the length of the organ. But with each movement of the carpeting, the woman was cautiously stretching it toward the copper circle, exaggerating her ecstasy, as if carried away by the bacchanal from *Tannhäuser* and directing the frenzy imperiously toward the sinister grotto. When she thought the combined nibbling and polishing were about to reach an ejaculative finale, she started to pull it toward the deep shell, but at that instant Farraluque, with a speed that comes only out of ecstasy, raised his right hand to the madonna's hair, pulled upward with fury and exposed the excited gorgon, dripping with the sweat extracted from the depths of her action.

This time he left the bed and with cat eyes looked into the next bedroom. The encounter had had a touch of a bite on the tail about it. Its completion only increased his desire for a new beginning; the strangeness of that unexpected situation and the extreme vigilance exercised over Circe, hard at work in the serpent's grotto, had curbed the normal affluence of his energy. A leftover tickling tugged at the back of his neck like an inexorable cork on a floating line.

With a haughty nakedness, he now knew what was waiting for him and he went into the next room. There he found the monkey-boy, the headmaster's cook's brother. Lying on his back, his legs merrily open, he displayed the same mammee color as his sister, offering an external ease, one full of ingenuous, almost indecipherable complications. He too pretended to be asleep, but with visible cunning and one uncorked and mischievous eye looked over Farraluque's body, pausing then on the culminating tip of the lance.

His mixed ancestry was revealed not by his asymmetrical face but in his small nose, his lips barely visible in a purplish line, and the green eyes of a domestic cat. His hair was an expanse of exaggerated uniformity, and it was impossible to isolate one thread from the whole thickness, like a night when rain is expected. His oval face closed with softness, attractive because of the smiling smallness of the features it sheltered. The tiny teeth were creamy white. He showed an incisor cut in the shape of a triangle, which, when he smiled, showed the mobility of the tip of his tongue, as if it were half of a serpent's bifid tongue. The mobility of his lips was sketched along his teeth, tinting them with a marine reflection. He wore three necklaces that hung down to the middle of his chest. The first two shared the whiteness of coconut meat, the third mingled wood-colored beads with five red ones. The sienna of his body deepened all those colors, giving them the depth of a brick wall in a golden noontime. The monkey-boy's astute position persuaded Farraluque to accept the challenge of the new bed, where the sheets had been waved by the rotations of the body displayed there like a distant sacred joke. Before Farraluque moved into the pleasant picture, he observed that when Adolfito (it is time for us to give him a name) rolled over, he kept his phallus hidden between his legs, leaving a hairy concavity tense from the pressure exerted by the phallus in its hiding place. When the encounter began, Adolfito rotated with incredible sagacity; when Farraluque tried to take aim, he avoided the fruit of the serpent; when, with his barb, he became determined to draw the monkey-boy's out of its hiding place, the boy would roll over again, promising him a calmer bay for his prow. But pleasure for the monkey-boy seemed to consist in hiding, in making an invincible difficulty for the sexual aggressor. He could not even succeed in what the contemporaries of Petronius had made fashionable, copulation *inter femora,* an encounter in which the two thighs provoke the spray. The search for a harbor maddened Farraluque, and finally the liquor, in a parabola of maleness, leaped onto the chest of the delightful monkey-boy, who spun over like a prodigious ballet dancer, showing at the end of the struggle his back and his legs, diabolically spread, while he rolled over once again and on the sheets rubbed his chest smeared with a sap that had no final use.

The third Sunday of his punishment, events began to spin and tangle from the morning on. Adolfito took advantage of his sister's being with the headmaster's cook to slip into the courtyard and talk to Farraluque. He had already persuaded the headmaster's two maids to let Farraluque leave the school when the sun went down. He told him that *someone,* enticed by his art of whitewashing, wanted to meet him. He gave him the key to the place where they were to meet, and leaving him, as if to reassure him, he told Farraluque that if he had time he would come and keep him company. Since by now what was meant by whitewashing was abundantly clear, he limited himself to inquiring about the *someone* he was supposed to visit. But the monkey-boy told him that he would find out soon enough, and clicked his tongue against the hollow of his triangular incisor.

The people of Havana, between five and six on a Sunday afternoon, smell the tedium shared by whole families, parents and children, who abandon the movies and retreat homeward. It is the moment, invariably painful, when the exception to the tedium makes way for the everyday habit of a man who ponders his destiny, not what directs and consumes him. Farraluque left the empty school courtyard and its weekend pause for the greater challenge of a state of boredom, the nervous system of a city. In the first corner café he watched a father rubbing the greasy residue of some ice cream off a little girl's blouse. Across the way, a nursemaid, all in white, was trying to pull a little girl away from the lamppost that had caught her red balloon with its black Islamic marks. Near the drain a boy spun a top, moving it over to the palm of his hand. Scratching his hand, he sat on the curb, and then he looked very slowly from one end of the street to the other.

Farraluque found the right number on Concordia Street. He inserted the small key, turned it softly, and took a step, almost stumbling into a forest of fog. Into what depths had he fallen? After his eyes adjusted, he could see that the place was a charcoal warehouse. The bins around the whole square area were filled with charcoal, divided up so that customers could carry it off in bags. Higher up, there were sacks from La Ciénaga, big as mountain crags, broad as filaments of cold light. And last, cakes of peat were mixed in with the charcoal to help spread the initial flame, which as it rose drew so many curses from the cooks of the last century, for one had to be adept to initiate the dialogue at the right moment between the most combustible wood fragment and the pinching, irritating flame.

He moved on and saw a tiny room lit by a small bull's-eye. A man was inside, about fifty years old, naked, his shoes and socks on, and a mask that made his face completely unrecognizable. Spotting the person he had been waiting for, he almost leaped into the other room, where the mist from the charcoal painted things. Like the priest of a springtime hierophancy, he began to undress the priapic one as if turning him on a lathe, caressing and greeting with a reverential sense all the erogenous zones, principally those that flashed their length. He was plump, white, with small waves of fat around the stomach. Farraluque observed that his double chin was about the size of his scrotal sack. The serpent was incorporated in a total, masterful way, and taking in the penetrating body, he turned red, as if, instead of receiving, he was about to give birth to some monstrous animal.

The apoplectic tone of this all-powerful incorporator of the outside world crescendoed in genuine oracular roars. His hands held high, he gripped the ropes fastening the charcoal sacks until his fingers began to bleed. He envisioned those prints where Baphomet, the androgynous devil, appears, possessed by a toothless pig, his waist encircled by a serpent that crosses over the site of his sex, inexorably empty, while the serpent shows its flaccid head in oscillating suspension. His phallus had not followed that biological law of evolution, namely, the greater the function, the larger the organ. This caused Farraluque to laugh, for what was to him a proud jewel, something to be displayed to three hundred students in the courtyard of the lower school, in his receptive companion was something to be concealed, its flaccidity disdained by the roots of life. At a certain moment, his phallus, accustomed to ejaculate without the heat of carnal envelopment, became agitated, for the interior of the charcoal repository was as hot as a boiler room on a navy ship. Their bodies were perspiring as if they had been in the most recondite tunnels of a coal mine. He inserted the vacillating tool in a crack in the charcoal, and his exasperated movements in the final moments of passion sent the coal dust scattering. He pulled on the ropes, he pounded the hollows of the sacks with his fists, he kicked at the charcoal that had been parceled out to sell to indigent customers. His frenzied tumescence brought on the final hecatomb in the charcoal repository. Coal dust flowed with the silence of a river at dawn, bringing behind it chunks of coal of imposing natural size, those that had not been broken down with shovels rolling as in a Polyphemic cave. Farraluque and the gentleman in the mask took refuge in the small room nearby. The noise of the peat cakes and the rough black chunks became more explosive and frequent. In the small warehouse, all kinds of charcoal began to bounce around and deposit irregular black stripes on the bodies of the two ridiculous gladiators joined by the softened iron of their now alienated sexes.

The pieces of charcoal hitting the floor made sounds that had no relation to their size; they broke apart with a crackling noise similar to a Great Dane chewing on a white rat. All the sacks had lost their balancing support, they had all been hit by the cursed retrospective furor of the gentleman in the mask. Farraluque and his companion would not be able to withstand the sinking mine in the small room. They covered themselves only with the articles of clothing essential for modesty. The masked gentleman left first, his wrinkled face still ruddy from the truncated adventure. At the corner, out of the corner of his eye, he made out the red balloon with black Islamic markings, still beating against the cynical, smiling lamppost.

Farraluque barely had time to put on his shoes, pants, and the jacket with a black spiral that ran down his back. He fastened the lapels to cover the hair on his chest. In the middle of the block, sitting whispering happily, he saw the boy with the top, and Adolfito. To recover from his scare, Farraluque sat down with the two urchins. Intending to penetrate his joy, the monkey-boy smiled complicitly, alluding to his sexual festivities; he was at that age in which copulation was always pleasurable for him, whether with an albino woman with an enormous protruding fibroma, or with the trunk of a palm tree. He did not associate sexual pleasure with an aesthetic meaning, not even with the fascination of a touch of friendship. In the same way, his active or passive presence in copulation depended on what the other person wanted. If he had been slippery with Farraluque, it was not out of moral prejudice, but to prepare for future adventures. In him, astuteness was a stronger instinct than maleness, which for him was indifferent and even unknown.

"Now do you know who the *someone* waiting for you was?" Adolfito asked him as he went off, pulling on the cords of the top of the boy he was talking to.

Farraluque shrugged, and only said, "I didn't feel like taking off his mask."

"Well, behind the mask you would have found the husband of the lady across from the school. The one you had to pull by the hair . . ." Adolfito finished with a smile.

The last day of classes before Christmas vacation arrived. José Cemí, after saying goodbye to his few school friends, went to sit on the bench across from his house for a while, watching the skaters pass on their way toward the Malecón. Around five he went inside, and at the ironwork gate between the main door and the one leading to the dining room, he came across his Aunt Leticia and Doña Augusta discussing the coming trip to Santa Clara.

"I'm not well," Leticia was saying, "and you have to come with me, because if you don't, you won't be a good mother." The conversation would calm down whenever Leticia persuaded herself that her mother would accompany her on the trip; at other times it became restless, and their voices rose and crossed; that was when Doña Augusta alleged that her home could not be abandoned, that her other children needed her, that she was tired of visiting the provinces when she had a house on the Prado. When her companionship became doubtful, Leticia's habitual hysteria would rise up, she would grit her teeth and sob, call for her salts, lie down on the sofa as if she were irresistibly dizzy. "All right," Doña Augusta said, condescending to pack her bags, "I'll go back with you again, everything I have will be abandoned. Rialta will be alone again with the children and sink deeper and deeper into her memories of José Eugenio. Your selfishness, Leticia, is the only illness you have, and a mother always ends up giving in to the selfishness of her children. When you drag me off, Leticia, my household is left abandoned, and that's the way we'll end up, scattered and in chaos."

Seeing Joseíto, as Leticia called José Cemí, come in, she turned to Rialta, saying: "If you want, I'll take Joseíto to spend a couple of weeks with me, he hasn't been in the country, he could visit some plantations and farms. He could ride horseback in the morning and it would do his asthma a lot of good. I think he's very introverted for his age. He has to go out more, meet more people, have friends. I don't think he likes anything better than to hear you people talking about Christmas in Jacksonville, about the death of his grandparents, and most of all about his father's death. You're making him timid that way. I've already noticed that when someone drops by for a visit he runs and hides." Actually, Leticia was not saying any of those things to persuade Rialta to give him permission to go with her on the trip to Santa Clara, but to have another family member in Doña Augusta's entourage, thinking that would strengthen her cause.

Cemí listened to the scene with indifference, for in family differences he preferred to have his mother decide. "I think it would do him good," Rialta answered, even though she did not really like to be separated from her children. "The country air might be good for his asthma, even though it's such a perverse illness that all those plants and flowers will probably make it worse. But he can only stay there a short time, because that's how it has to be," she said, changing her tone, "and if he spends more time I'll come to get him myself."

"Let's not get tragic," Leticia answered, hiding with a smile the disagreeable effect of Rialta's words. "He'll be back with you again in two weeks," Leticia said, "with less asthma and quite happy, all ready to take another trip."

Rialta agreed to make Doña Augusta's first days at Santa Clara more agreeable; if she was accompanied by one of her grandchildren, the separation from the rest of the family would not be so brusque. She knew that Leticia had an abusive temperament and was given to taking satisfaction for her smallest domestic whims. The resentment that had risen up in her from marrying an older man with whom she had never been in love, combined with the years she had had to spend in the provinces, an Olaya like her, a member of an aristocratic family with its own house on the Prado, had made her very stubborn, and she would aggrandize the details of her daily life, attempting to convert them into a cavalcade converging in her desires. At least now José Cemí and Doña Augusta would be forming part of her entourage at the leave-taking, that is, at the moment she returned to the provinces.

The first signal for the train to start sounded. Augusta, Rialta with her three children, Leticia and her husband with their two children, and Demetrio, always happy to see Leticia's husband, who reminded him of the pleasant days on the Isle of Pines. The horizontal line broke up, and the members of the family who were leaving on their trip into the interior got into the coaches. Ever since his father's death, Cemí associated separation with the idea of dying. As the years passed, paradoxically, the feeling of death, which was interwoven with his moments of inertia, the beginning of drowsiness, or resisting an unconquerable boredom, made him conscious of those periods of asthenia; and life became a plain on which a buzzing cloud was forming, with no beginning and no end, an expression of those states of mind that over the years he had reduced to the simple statement that life was a bundle tightly bound that became untied only when it fell into eternity.

The train was already moving off and the growing distance made him look at his mother's face as perhaps he had never done before. He observed the noble serenity of her face, revealed in her eyes and the pallor of her skin. Distance seemed to give her eyes their full meaning, the respect for her children and her deep family feelings. With the passage of time, her serenity, her patience, her lack of ignoble or self-serving haste to develop her children's virtues, she would become the sacred center of a family dynasty. Settling into his seat beside his grandmother, Cemí was able to observe the difference between the two faces. They had a similar basis, and on top of it subtle distinctions began to come out. Doña Augusta was still majestic and strong enough to dominate the whole family assembly. But the death that was already at work in her was even more majestic than her innate majesty. In her waiting, one could already see the face of her death, also waiting. The circles under her eyes and the folds on her face were growing heavy, hinting at the enmity between the Malpighian corpuscle and the four houses of the heart. Her dwindling fortune, Alberto's insolent foolishness before his death, the death of the Colonel, the irregular doses of Leticia's hysteria had upset her so that now her illness was winning out against her indifference to having it treated by doctors; she prepared for her somber farewell. Distance made his mother's face visible to him, rising to the fullness of her family destiny. The train's movement, in the speed of the images he saw, turned Doña Augusta's face into a myriad of little dots that dissolved an oscillating figure into a nothingness as concrete as a mask.

Cemí took a certain pleasure in his berth, unlike his aunt, who feigned nausea and petty annoyance with everything she saw and touched, reducing everything to its domestic use, the bed, the servants. What most attracted his attention all through the night, which he spent awake as he usually did when away from home, was the subsistence achieved by time, becoming visible, transmuted into an incessant gray line that went off into the distance. He closed his eyes and the gray line pursued him like a seagull that had been changed into the horizon line, rousing him with its cries in its midnight travels. Then the line, as it oscillated and reappeared, seemed to be shrieking.

Aunt Leticia had invited Ricardo Fronesis, the son of a very lordly lawyer, to visit; the father had a jovial Cuban manner, noble in its conscientiousness and faithful care for his clients' fate; he treated the gold-plated landowners the same as humble workers who came to go over their retirement papers. This lawyer was the kind of educated man who accepted or rejected cases in accordance with an upright and unsophisticated interpretation of the law. His provincial life consisted of the hours he spent in his library. The exercise of his profession was a long and meandering stroll in the morning outside his library, seeing some friends, a classic way of shoring up his idle hours. His father had been a native of Havana, very fond of travel, but when he died, his son realized that his career could be used to help his mother, so he decided to go to the provinces after his matrimonial adventure in Europe, because there the money he needed could be obtained with less painful competition. He was a friend of Leticia's doctor husband, though their friendship was not dictated by liking but by the unavoidable dealings which in the provinces are the unbreakable requisite of tedium and habit.

At seven o'clock in the morning Ricardo Fronesis was already knocking at Aunt Leticia's door. Somewhat surprised at his punctuality, the house stirred itself to receive the visitor. When José Cemí had to sleep in a relative's house, his eyelids were inured to wakefulness; thus it was he who went at once to greet Ricardo Fronesis, thereby avoiding the humbug of provincial introductions, including the enumeration of merits and horoscopes of illustrious family members, past, present, and absent. He quickly perceived that Fronesis was quite different from the boys he had dealt with hitherto at school and in his neighborhood. "My father always likes me to appear at the exact hour of the appointment, but like all the virtues we inherit, we're unfamiliar with the risks of fulfilling them. I arrive on time," he added with youthful grace, "and the whole house is asleep. But you can see now how those family virtues save us, you seem to have been awake all night and that makes me more than a visitor, the first person to break your insomnia and tell you that a new morning has begun."

Cemí admired the way the provincial adolescent bypassed introductions, putting the two of them on a friendly footing at the outset. He had spoken without hesitation, with the lordly assurance of a bourgeois who has been given a noble apprenticeship in the most exquisite courtesy. In no way had his courtliness reduced the virile lines of his body or the beauty of his face.

The rest of the outing to the Tres Suertes Plantation was all appearances, shunting conversation into the category of backdrop. The plastic element overcame the verbal. Aunt Leticia covered her face with a thick net, so absurd in a country outing that the birds, fearful of being caught in that web, seemed to flee before the car's advance along the road to the plantation. The triumphal morning, one of a dominant cleanliness, refused to justify the appearance of Leticia's husband in a duster that he wore gracelessly, with the kind of broad orange belt that was made fashionable in the days of Ralph de Palma, when metaphysical tables were consulted to ascertain whether the Moloch of speed would demand blood.

Tres Suertes was a farm that had been started around the middle of the nineteenth century and was raised to plantation status at the beginning of the Republic; but it was a far cry from the vast plantations whose rich sugar harvests were made to fill assigned quotas. Its owner was Colonel-of-Independence Castillo Dimás, who spent three months on the plantation during the harvesting and grinding season, three months on some keys he owned near Cabañas, a completely Eden-like locale, where he slept like a gull, ate like a shark, and bored himself like a marmot in the Para-Nirvana. He also spent three months in Havana with his mistress, an unctuous octoroon who had been elevated to a painted blonde and was endowed with a scandalous, shouting prolixity in conjugal pleasures. The colonel kept the best of himself for himself, as he was wont to say; three months for the garrets of Paris, where, like an Ophite, he rendered homage to the serpent of evil. When he discovered that visitors were coming to Tres Suertes, he would run to his house and come out all dressed up in his *guayabera* with ruffled front and his Murillo-blue pants, exchanging the crusty handkerchief in his right rear pocket for a white cloud with large initials and little angels in the corners.

In the midst of all that machinery there was a large vat with a mouth a yard and a half wide, and out of a spout the thick molasses slid, dense as the wounding heat. Around the spout, with the rapt attention of watching for fish in the liquid, the group of visitors was arranged in a circle according to Aunt Leticia's terrestrial hierarchy.

"There comes Godofredo the Devil," Fronesis said to break the monotony, though he tried to have only Cemí hear him. Walking in front of the group at the vat was an adolescent of extreme beauty, with reddish hair, like a sulphur flame. His face was very white, and the reflections of his hair's flame dimmed in a pink spiral that sank blushing into a chiaroscuro neck. He came over, or rather he stopped to look at the group at the vat, certain that his indifference was visible. His shirt was unbuttoned, his sleeves short, his pants rolled up, he wore no socks, and Cemí was able to see how the spiral that began with pink tones became sharper, until it reached a fruity red over all of his body, exposing the fortunate energy of the drive and the demons of that energy who were so dear to Blake. When Cemí heard Godofredo the Devil it seemed to him that he was hearing those names, Tiriel, Ijim, and Hela, that he had underlined in his first readings of Blake.

All the beauty of Godofredo the Devil was topped by a fury like that of the Tibetan bear, also called the Chinese demon, who spins round incessantly in circles as if to bite himself. One of his eyes was missing, and the Polyphemic eye that was left peered at everyone with a malign challenge, as if everywhere he went they knew his shame. The foggy eye was the right one, the one theologians call the canon eye, for a person who lacks it cannot read the sacred book during the elevation, and thus could never be a priest. It was as if Godofredo unconsciously knew the intrinsic value that the canons gave to that eye of his, for he was content to be Godofredo the Devil. Beyond the mist over his right eye, his hair was of a noble substance like that of the fiercest animals, like the bowstrings of archers in the entourage of the breaker of horses. His restless beauty gave him the look of a Greek warrior who, having been wounded in one eye, might have gone over to the Sarmatians in their cruel upheavals.

Handsome adolescent Polyphemus, when he saw that everyone was looking at his one raised eye, cursed from every pore of his unreconciled beauty.

Leticia's husband was lost in rambling statistics, talking to Colonel Castillo Dimás about the current crop, the trade agreements, the comparative percentage of molasses in this and previous years. That ridiculous topic of sugar, as men of that generation said, made sugar experts more important than the country itself as it disappeared under a landscape green with cane. Fronesis knew how to hide his boredom and all his expressionless looks contained a cultivated smile, a pleasant inheritance from his mother; whereas Leticia's oldest child did not know how to hide his boredom, and with a frequency that increased with the pace of the enveloping statistics, he yielded crocodile yawns.

The call of nature brought Leticia to a pretended romanticism. She ordered the driver to stop; whenever she organized one of these excursions into the country, she burst into longings for solitude and urges to embrace the bougainvillaea. No one else got out of the car, as though they shared the secret of her belated romanticism. When she came back, the dusk was growing, and where she had stood to clasp the bougainvillaea, a circle was seen to make the grass glow, and a small, exhausted cricket was unable to flow along the improvised current.

When Dr. Santurce's family said goodbye to Ricardo Fronesis, they expressed insistent but false desires to have him stay for dinner. Fronesis begged off, pleading a morning exam, but just as he was leaving, he turned to Cemí and, in a prelude to an enjoyable friendship, said that tomorrow after five he would call to take him to a provincial café where they might talk.

The next day Fronesis did not come by for him, but at a quarter to five he rang up to say that he was waiting at the Café Semiramis, next to the hotel with the colonial façade, of which it was a pompous prolongation.

For the first time Cemí, in his adolescence, realized that he had been summoned and led over to a corner to talk. He felt the word "friendship" taking on flesh. He felt the birth of friendship. That meeting was the fullness of his adolescence. He felt sought after by someone outside his own family. And Fronesis always showed, along with the good cheer that burst forth from his spiritual health, a stoical dignity, which seemed to withdraw from things, paradoxically, in order to achieve his ineffable charm.

Fronesis told Cemí at the beginning of their conversation that he had preferred ringing him up to stopping by for him, because he would have had to play the role of visitor, repeating with slight variations the visit to Tres Suertes. He also preferred talking to him alone; since they were both in their last year of preparatory school, there was a lot of magic thread to be cut. Fronesis rescued the dry cliché by inserting the word "magic," transforming a commonplace into a fey night in Baghdad.

Fronesis told Cemí that he spent every weekend in Cárdenas sculling. Cemí noticed the sharp angularity under his sleeves; the cloth hid a musculature exercised in swimming and competent in boating. These well-spaced exercises did not bring his muscles together in shameful clusters; instead, they sent blind energy pouring through his distributive channels.

The manly green of Fronesis's eyes became fixed on a point in the distance, and suddenly he exclaimed: "Here comes Godofredo the Devil again." Cemí glanced around and saw the redheaded, one-eyed man approaching. He was whistling a tune that scattered like the fragments of a gilded serpent.

"Godofredo the Devil," Fronesis began, "takes a strange pleasure in passing in front of people he thinks know his story. He won't look them in the face, a sign of his indifferent hatred, which he can show only by turning his face. My father, being a provincial lawyer at the center of almost every bit of gossip that passes around town, knows his terrible story. As Godofredo knows he knows, he imagines my father must have told me too, and so he supposes that any moment now I'm going to start telling you the story that ends up with his blind eye. He can't hold himself back whenever he sees me, and he tries to come close, but he always keeps his head turned like that, afraid that if I stare at him, he might lose the eye he has left.

"When he was fifteen, Godofredo the Devil had hallucinations about Pablo's wife. Pablo was the head machinist at Tres Suertes and, at the age of thirty-four, was seventeen years older than his wife, and this, combined with his Saturday-night drinking bouts, lent a certain irregularity to the nighttime hours they had together. On some summer nights Fileba, which is what she was called, could not liquefy the density of Pablo's sleep, thickened as it was by the load of spirits and his hoarse, rummy breath. To get away from her flirting, Pablo would pull a pillow over his head, and this stopped the pounding of Fileba's little hands from waking him up. Finally, fatigued, she would drop off with an ill-humored stiffness, dreaming about monsters carrying her away naked to the hilltops. She would wake up and Pablo would still have the pillow over his head. It was raining and the dampness kept her sleeping until the first singing of dawn.

"One Saturday, Godofredo took Pablo home and helped put him to bed. Pablo was so drunk that he almost had to carry him on his back. He noticed Fileba's paleness more carefully, her eyes enlarged by the mortification of so many nights. And he began to hang around the house like a wolf cub who knows that the girl of the house has tied the dove to the kitchen table by its leg.

"Thinking himself master of a secret, Godofredo began to court her. She refused to have trysts or to play the game of the precocious evil one. Another Saturday when he again brought Pablo home on his back, Fileba left Pablo at the door as he was about to take a step into the house. Pablo stumbled, fell headfirst onto the floor of the living room, so she put down a mat for him and brought him the usual pillow. While she was preparing a strong brew, she went out to take a look at the Saturday drunkard and noticed Godofredo making his Luciferine rounds, and that time she closed the windows and called in some neighbors to keep her company.

"That was when Father Eufrasio arrived at Tres Suertes, taking a disoriented priest's vacation. Too much study of concupiscence in St. Paul and copulation without pleasure had sucked the marrow out of him, putting his reason out of kilter. How to keep the other body at a distance in an amorous encounter and still attain the leap of supreme energy in the moan of pain was plaguing him like a turnstile spinning in a space ringed by great vultures. He went on vacation under the pretext of visiting a younger brother, the one in charge of the cane-cutting gangs, for a few days. The disorientation he was experiencing was not known to the denizens of Tres Suertes, so that his prolonged, immutable looks and his glassy silences were indecipherable to everybody around him, out there where the lowing of cows drives away all theological subtleties about the reproductive sensorium.

"With the priest's arrival, to pretend that at Tres Suertes they followed the same customs as townspeople, some girls began to call on him. Naturally they knew nothing about his derangement, or about his strange problem of concupiscence. Fileba's gentleness brought her along and Father Eufrasio was getting to hear all about the midnight pillows of Pablo the machinist. Whispered confidences demonstrated that she was supplicating carnal closeness, while Pablo was trying to put off the terrible attacks of her flesh, which he had to alienate to keep his vital reserves untouched. At the approach of the concupiscent act, he deflated at his virile tip, languishing hopelessly.

"Thus the nights that Pablo dedicated to the sabbat came to be used by Eufrasio and Fileba, and when Pablo the machinist got home, he could fall asleep without having to cover his head with a pillow like a shield. Meanwhile, Godofredo the Devil discovered that the couple disappeared every Saturday into a little nest owned by the priest's younger brother, who was unaware of the priest's novel methods for curing his concupiscent complexes.

"One day Godofredo went to get Pablo in the village bar before he downed his fourth glass. On the way back to Tres Suertes he was playing out the long thread of Fileba's betrayal. He told Pablo that if he had doubts, he might lurk nearby and actually watch the couple go into the house of sin. Pablo hid behind a mulberry tree, and Godofredo along the wall near the door, to prove, in the dim light, that the couple decidedly did enter the house of sin. Around ten o'clock, in the exaggerated smile of the crescent moon, not from the tamped-down path to the door of the house but from a shortcut, the couple appeared, lightened by the lunar whiteness, which gave them the pallor of sin.

"When Pablo the machinist, behind the mulberry tree, had proof of the truth, which sucked at him like an octopus, he went back to the bar, totaled up a staggering number of fourth glasses of straight cognac, and started shouting so loud that some country police arrived. Seeing it was Pablo, they covered him with their capes to keep the heavy dew off and took care of him till they were certain that the key that had been describing grand circles in the air finally came to rest in the keyhole. With a scintilla of clarity he fell on the living-room sofa where he and Fileba had posed for their newlywed pictures, a piece of furniture which had been bought secondhand for their wedding but which held firm on the tragic occasion of Pablo the machinist's collapse as he placed his demon in the service of his fate."

At that point in the tale, Cemí realized that Fronesis was making an effort to go on, but certain hesitations showed that he was entering the real whirlwind a little fearfully.

"Meanwhile, Godofredo the Devil felt around the walls and windows with his nails for a peephole to be able to watch the couple. At last he stationed himself at the window and peered through the lower corner. Like a marine apparition contemplated through the tube of a telescope, a strange combination of figures rose to view. Fileba, naked, lay on the bed weeping, showing the fullness of her body. But it was hardly suffused with pleasure; rather, she seemed indifferent, frigid. Eufrasio, his pants off, was still wearing his shirt and undershirt. A string was tied to one end of the bed and stretched to wrap around his testicles, purple from the gradual strangulation, as Eufrasio drew back with an almost liturgical slowness. His phallus, in the culmination of its erection, looked like a great votive candle that had been lit for a very sinful soul. His scorched, rigid cheeks were receiving infernal slaps. When the seminal reason of Augustine finally came out, the testicular strangulation was as much as the string could stand, and a sweaty moan struggling for silence trembled through the disoriented man's body. Fileba was crying, covering her mouth to keep from making noise, but her eyes shot out cold flashes, the congealed rays of a copper mine on an endless Siberian steppe, a glance like a halcyon's, dead in the stormy coldness, drifting into eternity wide-eyed. Thus she watched Eufrasio dress and leave the room without glancing at her. The distance of his body and the painful orgasm, which the deranged priest considered the fulfillment of unbreakable Pauline laws, had been attained to perfection.

"She ran home as fast as she could, shaking. Pablo was lying down with the light out and the pillow over his face. She tried to sleep, for endless hours pretended to sleep, but then she noticed that Pablo's hands weren't crossed over the pillow shield on his face, as usual in his Saturday-night exhaustion. She nervously presumed an unexpected ending; then she saw the flaccid hands of the one who accompanied her on a last night. She turned on the light. She saw in a shock that the pillow was soaked with blood, his shirt still wet. The machete on the floor near the slit throat had begun to oxidize with the coagulation of the blood. Pablo, before lying down to recuperate, had washed his face with the cool water of night. Fileba tugged at the pillow on the floor, but like a gorgon soaked in somber purple, it began to cast off threads and pools of blood. She quickly turned on all the lights and opened up the living-room window. Her shouts are still remembered by some of the people at Tres Suertes who were awakened at midnight.

"Around dawn, Godofredo the Devil slipped past Pablo's house. The whole neighborhood had crowded into the street, still alarmed by Fileba's shouts. He overheard the gossip and perplexities that were being woven about the machinist's suicide. He hastened off along the main road, and as he got farther from the plantation, he was being wrapped in an implacable army of vines. The trees and bushes cut off his path. Around his waist he wore a machete for his work as a cane cutter. He shouted and kicked at the trees, and flung himself on the vines, and they drew back from his slashes, coiling like rearing serpents. The vines around his waist, as he beat them, whistled like a hurricane wind. One among all those vines took its vengeance on him, and drawing back, it drove forward and engraved a cross on his right eye, the canon eye.

"That was how Godofredo the Devil lost his right eye and also lost his reason. His walks describe immense, implacable circles, with the radii zigzagging like bolts of lightning. When the rains of April come, he throws himself into ditches, his body stops trembling, and the humus puts his fever to sleep. The incessant rain also softens the flames of the red hair of Godofredo the Devil, the malignant flower of the crossroads."

TRANSLATED BY GREGORY RABASSA

HEBERTO PADILLA

Self-portrait of the other

Is it anxiety, nausea,
raptures?
Or is it just wanting
sometimes to shout out?
I don't know. I come back onstage.
I walk toward the footlights
as if toward yesterday,
        swifter than a squirrel,
with my child's drool
and a tricolor flag on my breast,
        agitator, irascible,
                among the students.

The truth is that they finally
                managed to lock me up
in that baroque garden I hated so much
and this opal gleam
                in my eyes
makes me unrecognizable.
The little gladiator (bronze)
which I have put on the table
—a scowling hero, master
of his short white blade—
and his snarling bitch

are now my only buddies.
But when my troupe of jugglers
appears
we will file through the bars
and I will break out.
Doors are things there are too many of!

Under the plastic moon
have I become a parrot
or a nylon clown
that bumbles and loses the password?
Or is it not true?
Is it a nightmare
that I myself could destroy,
opening my eyes
suddenly
and rolling through the dream in a barrel,
and the world mixed now with these seethings?
Or is it just wanting
sometimes to shout out?

The Right praises me
(in no time they will defame me)
The Left has given me a name
(have they not begun to have doubts?)
But at any rate
I warn you I'm alive in the streets.
I don't wear dark glasses.
And I don't carry time bombs in my pockets
or a hairy ear—a bear's.
Give me room, now.
Don't greet me, I beg you.

Don't even speak to me.
If you see me, keep to one side.

TRANSLATED BY ALASTAIR REID AND ANDREW HURLEY

A prayer for the end of the century

We who have always looked with tolerant irony
on the mottled objects of the end of the century:
the vast structures
and men stiff in dark clothes
We for whom the end of the century was at most
an engraving and a prayer in French
We who thought that after a hundred years there would be only
a black bird lifting a grandmother's bonnet
We who have seen the collapse of
parliaments
and the patched backside of liberalism
We who learned to distrust illustrious myths
and who see as totally impossible
(uninhabitable)
halls with candelabra
tapestries
and Louis XV chairs
We children and grandchildren of melancholy terrorists
and superstitious scientists
We who know that the error exists today
that someone will have to condemn tomorrow

We who are living the last years of this century
wander about unable to improvise
movements
not already planned in advance
we gesture in a space more straitening
than the lines of an etching;
we put on formal clothes again,
as though we were attending another parliament,
while the candelabra sputter at the cornice
and the black birds
tear at the bonnet of that hoarse-voiced girl.

TRANSLATED BY ALASTAIR REID AND ANDREW HURLEY

ES CASAL

The Founders: Alfonso

Wei wu wei
Do without doing

GREAT-GRANDDAUGHTER 1

My grandmother used to tell me that when her father was seventy years old and blind—this was fifty years after his arrival in Cuba—he would fly into a seething rage if he found so much as one piece of furniture out of place. He would roam the house like some infallible guardian of order in the world, setting chairs straight and checking that tables were in their proper position. Very erect, with his grey moustache cascading down over his hairless chin, he used his gnarled hands to see the world and to reconstruct it. Wearing his inevitable blue espadrilles, he walked with confident step, his impeccably ironed guayabera loose over his white drill trousers.

Five decades on from the hellish journey and, at last, the dream of respectability, somewhat modified, it's true, but made real, no doubt, in the geometric precision of the formal living room: the mahogany and wickerwork furniture, the piano, the six-foot-tall mirror, the vast tapestries and the chandelier filtering its unnecessary light through the hundreds—thousands?—of pieces of carved crystal.

Three excited taps of his walking stick would presage the coming storm—a chair left at a careless angle or, worse, an unfamiliar object blocking a path previously left open—followed by fulminations against the murderous intentions of the other inhabitants of the house.

Once order was restored, Alfonso López would flop into the armchair in the dining room.

ALFONSO I

You would flop into the armchair and when you felt the familiar pressure of the wickerwork on your bony spine, you knew that everything was in its place. Then, you would close your eyes (or leave them open, it made no difference) and look back, which is all you can do with your eyes closed and/or when you're blind and with seventy years behind you. You didn't smoke—ten years tending the leaves in the fields made you lose your taste for tobacco early on—although you had always lived off those who did smoke and it seemed to you that all the memories you had of your life came to you wreathed in smoke. As if every memorable event in your life had taken place in some small, smoke-filled room.

HISTORY I

The importation of coolies to Cuba began in July 1847 (Zulueta & Co. of London, a Spanish ship, the *Oquendo,* 206 Chinese) and progressed slowly at first, then with great vigor from 1853 onwards, continuing busily and, of course, profitably—there is no need to say for whom—until 1874, the year of the visit to Havana of the imperial envoy, the Mandarin Chin-Lan-Pin, investigator-into-the-fate-of-the-sons-of-the-great-empire-contracted-to-work-in-the-empire-of-New-Spain. Alerted by Eça de Queiroz, he decided to leave the deceptive capital and travel into the hinterland. As a result of his report, the trade contract was terminated.

The contract: four dollars a month for eight years. In southern China, during the death agony of the Manchu dynasty, that seemed like a fabulous sum. Besides, Manila wasn't so very far away and Tai-Lay-Sun was, of course, Manila. When the journey went on longer than expected—the voyage to Cuba took one hundred and fifty days—the dreams grew bitter. How many committed suicide? Others resorted to rebellion, only to die having gained control of ships they had no idea how to sail. There are legends, tales, about ghost ships, phantasmal clippers, spotted adrift on the high seas and boarded sometimes by sailors who were met by horrific scenes, the spectral spectacle of between three and five hundred corpses. Freedom and its price.

ALFONSO 2

Your father—Wu Liau—had been a follower of Hung Hsiu-chuan. You had heard him talk about the Kingdom of the Great Peace and about the Way and about Christ and the Revolution, probably in as confused a fashion as you remember it now. When your father was captured along with other rebels, a mandarin from Fukien sold him to Tanco, the Colombian who traded in coolies. Your father committed suicide, hanging himself the night before they were due to set sail. You vaguely remember the hard times that followed. Having six children and being the widow of a rebel was not much help in a country where poverty required so little encouragement, in an empire that was clearly in an advanced state of decomposition. So a few years later, you decided to take the place on the ship rejected by your father. Perhaps Taiping, the

Kingdom of the Great Peace, could flower across the seas, in the lands of New Spain. Perhaps you could return one day and be a man and not the plaything of mandarins and other petty tyrants.

Even forty years later, the Spanish expression "They made a Chinese fool out of you" still rankled. You heard your son Alejandro use it once quite innocently. You were already almost completely blind, but you still had the use of your hands and you clouted him so hard that he fell backwards into one of the flowerbeds in the courtyard. Manila, the Manila that became Havana without you realizing it: months and months of blueness—the Pacific is an inhuman, transhuman ocean—days and evenings and nights of sun and cold and salt seeping into your very bones; days and nights and evenings of pressing your face into the wooden deck to try and escape the stench of five hundred piled-up, half-naked bodies, and always that blueness and then land—which was not, however, *the* land—and the journey by train and then another ship and more blueness and, at last, New Spain.

How many people did you see die by your side? Some were carried off by strange fevers, others by terrible diarrhea, others simply, silently, slipped overboard. The dream of the Great Peace and the dream of death.

Now, however, that you could flop into the armchair and feel the wickerwork against your bony spine, now that you could prescribe exactly where the table with the vase on it should go, now that your dog came and lay across your blue espadrilles as soon as you sat down, now you finally felt at peace. And if this peace—the peace of espadrilles and of the formal living room, of the courtyard with the flower border and the begonias and the creeper and the penetrating smell of ylang-ylang on light summer nights—if this peace was not the Great Peace, it was at least yours . . . and it was enough.

Guilt? You have earned that peace, now that it makes no difference whether you have your eyes open or closed, for you have seen far too much in your time—too many wars and deaths in the years when your eyes still had light.

Wu Liau—you remember how they brought him and deposited him like a bruised bundle in the middle of the room before your own horrified eyes and your mother's screams. Thus ends the revolution—with a rope around your neck, a filthy shirt and two imperial guards dumping you unceremoniously on the ground without a word, with a hysterical widow and six orphans and you—the eldest son—crazy enough, one day, eight years later, commending yourself neither to God, the Devil nor to your ancestors, to go off in search of Tanco when you heard that he was back in Canton looking for workers.

You arrived in Cuba only to find yourself in the middle of another war. Your owner—sorry, your contractor—could not send you to the canefields (the fields in Oriente had been burned) and so he set you to work with tobacco in Alquizar, near Havana, where it was almost as if there was no war. Now you bore your owner's surname, López; they gave you the same Christian name too, Alfonso. A brand-new name, new and Spanish, for New Spain.

Later, they told you that according to Máximo Gómez: "There's no such thing as a Chinese deserter or a Chinese traitor." But then you had only just disembarked and you were terrified by all the sounds and stories of war, and the Kingdom of the Great Peace seemed farther off than ever. Rumors about what was going on in the countryside reached even your field—it wasn't your field, of course, but López's, but let's not quibble over details—even relatively peaceful Havana. Many, many Chinese men fought in Las Guásimas (you didn't know it then, of course, but they began fighting the very day you disembarked, 15 March 1874). Pablo Chang used to tell you that—he was the one who wanted to rebel and take you with him. There are even Chinese commanders,

Chang would say seductively, and suddenly you could imagine yourself as a mandarin, riding across the fields of Cuba at the head of hundreds and hundreds of horsemen, you in your embroidered clothes and wearing a cap adorned with glass buttons and a peacock feather. The bruised bundle of Wu Liau weighed too heavily in your memory, though, and by the time you had reached a decision, the war had ended. Later, you learned that Commander Sian used to travel barefoot and was the only one among his troops to own a poncho, threadbare and faded from countless washings. When he died, there was no one to place a coin in his mouth, nor even a coin to place there. And now, no one remembers them . . . People do not even know that any Chinese fought in the war.

So, after a small war and another big war and after mini-wars and after lean years and fat years . . . you have learned a lot. The husband of one of your daughters reached the rank of colonel in the 1895 war and what did he get for it? They shot that handsome Negro, Colonel Isidro, in the back . . . No, it certainly would not have been worth your while becoming a commander.

The Chinese men who threw themselves into the revolution obviously still had that Taiping madness going round and round in their heads . . .

HISTORY 2

The Empire was "shaken to its foundations" by the Taiping rebellion (1850–64) or, rather, the Taipings emerged out of the rotten foundations of the Empire. Hung Hsiu-chuan: visionary, prophet, military leader. An obscure peasants' revolt became a real revolution. No to the imperial aristocracy, no to Confucian ethics, no to ancestor worship, no to the Manchu dynasty, no to private property. Yes to agrarian reform, to equality for women and language reform. No to landowners and Mandarins. Yes to a revolutionary millenarianism tinged with a rather odd form of Christianity. The Taipings believed that their mission was to create heaven on earth—the Kingdom of the Great Peace that they solemnly proclaimed in Nanking when they took it in 1853.

The corrupting effects of power diluted the utopian puritanism of those early, difficult years, however; but what finally finished off the Taiping rebellion was the profits from the opium trade, which placed France and England firmly on the side of the Manchu dynasty, the Ever Victorious Army (made up of mercenaries led by an Englishman who called himself Charles George Gordon), and the landowners of Hunan who equipped the army of Tseng Kuo-fan, plus, perhaps, the fact that the rebellion was eighty years before its time. When Tseng Kuo-fan retook Nanking for the Empire, in 1864, it was clear that the extermination of the Taipings was only a matter of time.

ALFONSO 3

Stripping the leaves was women's work. That was what Amalia did. Amalia was certainly different; she was a mulatta, none too bright, it's true, but fierce as they come, the daughter of a black female slave freed by her white master-father. Amalia, a worker in what was then Cuba's biggest factory (a corner shop by today's standards) in Güira de Melena, spelled it out to you when you tried to lure her up into the hills: "Bit of paper, then talk," she said, mocking you, imitating your pidgin Spanish. And she explained to you how her mother had taught her that you have to be firm with men, which was why she wasn't going to open her legs just yet. "Not until we're married." You turned on your heel and marched off without saying a word. Who did that little mulatta think she was! You had two daughters already and no one had ever made you sign a bit of paper before. You thought: "She can have her treasure; however tightly shut she keeps her legs, it'll just be food for the worms one day anyway," and you spat through the gap where your left eyetooth used to be. You kicked the lemon tree so hard it nearly toppled over. Who the hell did that mulatta think she was! But you couldn't stop thinking about those prominent eyes, that small mouth and the jet-black hair caught up and held in place by a comb, and that mocking laugh and those hands and that intense cinnamon-colored skin that burned your eyes and even now burned inside your pants. You gave the lemon tree another kick. You turned around. You threw a stone up at her window. She looked out. "All right, we'll get married." She smiled at you. "When?" she asked. "Whenever you want," you said, smiling back.

"Any chance of an advance?" you asked, half-joking, half-serious. The window had already closed again when you heard her laughter. You shouted: "See you tomorrow," and leaped on your horse. That night you rode back and forth four times between her house and yours, unable to stop, your cock irremissibly erect, fighting to get out of your trousers. And you rode and rode; you felt as if you were drunk—and doubtless you were—drunk on Amalia and on the wind and on the doves and you rode until your exhausted horse's legs buckled under him, outside the door to the dairy—the dairy belonged to López, just as you once had—and you got off your horse and lay down on the ground next to him, and the following morning, they found the two of you still lying there, wet with dew, mouths open.

HISTORY 3

Between 1847 and 1874, some one hundred and twenty-five thousand "Asians" arrived in Cuba. It is estimated that about ten thousand managed to return to China. In 1899, when the American administrators completed the census and stopped immigration, there were some fourteen thousand Chinese, most of them "Californians"—that is, not coolies but Chinese immigrants who had arrived via the United States. In 1862, of the 346 suicides that took place in Cuba, exactly half—173 of them—were Asians. So, over a period of about fifty years there were one hundred thousand deaths (due to suicides, beatings, wars, fevers and, of course, old age, but how do you catalogue the deaths from sadness?).

Esteban Montejo mentions the Chinese: "A lot of us were slaves. Blacks, Chinese, Indians and various mixtures. The Chinese were always looking and thinking. The blacks were always moving around, doing something. If the Chinese ever had a moment to sit, they would sit down and think . . . on Sundays or feast days, we would dance and the Chinese would sit and watch us, as if they were trying to work something out in their heads . . ."

ALFONSO 4

They said in the village that the rebels meant business. At their head was Colonel Isidro, a huge Negro, who could strangle a horse with his bare hands, the scourge of both Spaniards and Creoles. All his men were black, they said, and when they struck at night, they would attack stark naked and machete in hand, in order to blend in with the darkness of the forest. By then, the war had reached Occidente. You remembered the Taipings and gave them tobacco and, sometimes, pigs, but you also remembered Wu Liau's corpse and decided to stay with your family. Amalia had given you a daughter, Carmen—your first child in wedlock—as well as the longed-for son, Sebastián you called him (the name you would have liked, but which they did not give you). Your eldest daughter, Eugenia, had come to live with you too (her mother died in a smallpox epidemic). So you had your family to look after—the peace, the Great Peace begins at home. You had had quite enough problems with your second daughter—Leonor—the one you had with that woman from the Canary Islands who lived in Colón. Leonor turned out to be a rebellious tomboy, very much like Wu Liau and a little bit like you. She disappeared one night on horseback and nearly rode the poor animal into the ground trying to reach Oriente. She didn't make it; instead she joined up with Pancho Pérez's troops near Esperanza, and you had heard nothing since. One extremely uppity daughter and Carmen, who, by some miracle, survived smallpox and now this Colonel Isidro striding about the countryside naked . . . The Great Peace remained as far off as ever, despite the new house which your neighbors helped you build in the twinkling of an eye, despite the small farm—by then yours—where you planted vegetables and fruit trees and raised pigs and experimented with growing rice as they used to in Fukien, despite your cigarette stall which was flourishing, what with the village and the war, which, it seems, encouraged people to smoke more not less.

And now it was the rainy season and, one day, you got home late and found Amalia sitting on the doorstep with Sebastián in her arms, waiting for you, and when you saw her anxious, frowning face, you knew at once that something was wrong. "That daughter of yours"—she weighed each word, emphasizing the "yours"—"you've got to talk to her." You sat down in silence and waited for her to speak. You took off your hat and hung it on one of the posts on the veranda. "That daughter of yours takes no notice of anyone and she's as crazy as Leonor." You shuddered. Leonor was a name that always made you feel as if you had been punched in the stomach and left gasping for air. Things must be really bad for Amalia to mention Leonor. You took off your left boot. "That daughter of yours, Alfonso, she's only a kid of eighteen and she's already mixed up with men." You took off your right boot, smiled and said gently: "Amalia, you were only sixteen when we got married." Amalia brought her hand down hard on the sill, making the doorframe shudder and shaking the stool you were sitting on. "Your daughter Eugenia is having an affair with Colonel Isidro." "Eugenia!" you thundered. She came to the door. She was wearing a red flower in her hair, a marpacífico. Years later you would often remember this scene and that flower was always the first thing to come to mind. "Sit down!" She pulled over another stool and set it down opposite yours. She looked you straight in the eye and you saw yourself reflected in eyes identical to yours. "What exactly is going on?" She held your gaze, as proud as yours. "I'm engaged, Papa. My fiancé wanted to come and talk to you and I told Amalia so that she could ask your permission, but she just flew into a rage." You were drumming your bare feet on the floor that your boots had left covered in mud. "Is it Colonel Isidro?" you asked and Eugenia nodded. You took off your belt and dropped it on the floor, machete and all. "I don't want you to be a widow before you're even married." You had rolled your sodden shirt up into a ball and were gripping it in your left hand and punching it with your right. "No one's going to kill Isidro. The man hasn't been born who could do that. We'll get married when the war is over, and that will be any day now. I just wanted you to know and to give us your blessing. No one else outside this house must know anything about it."

You tipped the stool back so that it was leaning against the wall. The front legs were in the air and your bare, muddy feet rested on the front bar. Your daughter was still holding your gaze. "You're a fool, Eugenia." She said nothing, but kept her eyes fixed on yours. You jumped to your feet and stood a few inches away from her. She looked up, still with her eyes trained on yours. Amalia thought you were going to hit her. Eugenia said later that she knew you wouldn't. You took her face in your wet hands and kissed her on the mouth. "Tell him to come and see me as soon as he can." Then you picked up your straw hat and strode into the house.

HISTORY 4

The end of the war did, in fact, come swiftly—the end came with the arrival of the Americans. And vice versa. That signalled another beginning too. Many of the remaining Chinese had settled in Havana, in what later became Chinatown. It began in 1858 when Chang Ling settled in Calle de Zanja and opened a cheap restaurant there and Laig Sui-Yi opened a fruit stall.

The "Californians" had started arriving in 1860 and they came with a few savings. They were the Chinese entrepreneurs, not just small businessmen but also illegal bookies and racketeers. By 1873 there was already a five-star restaurant on Dragones and a Chinese theater. In 1878 the first newspaper was started.

Chinatown became fully established in 1913 when the doors for immigration, closed by the administrators, were reopened. Between 1913 and 1929, thirty thousand Chinese arrived, this time as ordinary immigrants. The dream of New Spain and of a new Cuba was clearly a powerful one.

ALFONSO 5

It was Carmen's wedding day, the only time in your life when you got drunk. "You really pushed the boat out," the neighbors said. She was your last daughter to get married and you felt proud of a job well done. Five children (three daughters) and all of them decent folk. Not like your old friend, Salvador Monleón, the most respected patriarch in all Alquízar, who had so many children he didn't even know their names. He was a good stud was Salvador. He stayed on in the village when you all moved to Havana. No one knows exactly how many children he had, but on his birthday, you counted forty-five at the party, of all colors and sizes, some younger than his own grandchildren. It was Salvador who helped you when your contract had just expired and you almost had to sign on again because no one would employ you. He said: "I need an honest man who's not afraid of hard work," and he smiled as if to say that he knew you fulfilled both conditions. That was the day you began to be free. One of Salvador's daughters, Bértila, taught you to read and write Spanish, and it was in Salvador's house that you met Amalia, your wife, his wife's half-sister.

And on Carmen's wedding day when you saw him crouch down to come in through the door—he was a very big man—and saw him surrounded by the mist that was by then your constant companion, you knew with painful certainty that very soon you would never see him again and so you decided to get drunk with him on pure rum, in the name of all the good times you had had and of those that would never come again.

Since they had never seen you drunk, your children made a huge fuss. Carmen laughed hysterically and had such a terrible fit of hiccups she nearly had to cancel her honeymoon. Eugenia was angry and jealous that you should get drunk at Carmen's wedding, whereas at hers you had never touched a drop. Leonor sat down in an armchair beside you and matched you drink for drink—a whole bottle of cheap rum. At that point, Colonel Isidro arrived and said to her: "You certainly live up to your rank as general" (that's how they always addressed Leonor after the war, although, in fact, she only ever made lieutenant). He joined you and Leonor and you each took a swig of brandy, straight from the bottle. And when Leonor said: "I could drink you both under the table," you and Isidro accepted the challenge and bet a whole roast suckling pig for the whole family, to be paid for by the first to pass out, and two gallons of rum, to be paid for by the second. When the hour of reckoning came, you and Isidro were both sprawled on the floor and Leonor said: "You see, you don't need balls to drink," but when she went to get up, she keeled right over and they left the three of you out in the courtyard because you all stank to high heaven of brandy.

GREAT-GRANDDAUGHTER 2

Alfonso refused to live in Chinatown when he moved to Havana. He rented a house nearby, though, and sometimes he would go in search of smoked pork and sweet bread and sugar candy and glazed fruits.

ALFONSO 6

And now you can flop into the armchair and feel the wickerwork against your bony spine and you can look back and see, through the smoke, that you lived through a lot of bad times, but a lot of good times too. You know that it is 1924 and you never expected to get this far. You stroke the handle of your walking stick and take a deep breath; you can fall asleep without fear now. After all, you have had the rare privilege of surviving and being able to die sitting in your armchair, surrounded by five children, five grandchildren, two dogs and a turtle.

GREAT-GRANDDAUGHTER 3

Ah, the great bearded dragon with eyes of fire and gaping mouth! Let's dance the dragon through the streets hung with little colored lights and paper flags. Let's dance the dragon through the fireworks and the rockets. And let's wait for them to award the prize and the greenbacks and, finally, there'll be the party with rice wine to drink. But the dragon, after the parade, after the dreams, the dragon, deflated now, the dragon . . . always ends up biting his own tail.

TRANSLATED BY MARGARET JULL COSTA

LINO NOVÁS CALVO

As I Am . . . As I Was

As I recall, it all began at the end of September. My birthday was about to arrive, and my mother was making me a new shirt. As she sat working on it, her face turned pale and she began to cough. Her eyes grew wide and she stood up, clutching her bosom. Then she walked into the other room.

The doctor was not called. When she seemed worse and her temperature was fluctuating wildly, my Aunt Sol came to see us, bearing news of some kind. She stood in the doorway, an expression of secrecy on her face, and looked into the room where my mother lay in bed. When my mother saw her, she became radiant. Then she began to weep silently.

Aunt Sol left immediately. When she was gone, my mother got up and put on her best dress. She arranged her hair and applied makeup. But at dusk Aunt Sol came back, and the animation in my mother's face suddenly disappeared. They spoke in low voices for a moment. Aunt Sol was exhausted; her eyelids closed as she said: Maybe they're mistaken about the date. He could be coming on another ship.

She went slowly toward the door. My mother stood in the middle of the room, her hands across her chest. Thanks, anyway, Sol, she said weakly.

That was the beginning. For a period of several months I was obliged to watch these changes. And I understood nothing. Or perhaps I should say that I understood them without explaining them to myself. I knew that each month *someone* was supposed to be arriving on a ship, but this someone did not come. Meanwhile my mother would fall ill and then suddenly recover, or at least it seemed that she did. Another arrival date would be approaching, bringing with it a fresh hope. Then Aunt Sol would appear, looking disappointed, and my mother would go back to being ill once again.

But she did not complain of feeling sick, merely sometimes of being tired. She never stopped sewing. One day after Sol had left she said: It was all the work of the Devil. There's no help for it!

I can see her now, pale and thin, taller than the little door at the end of the room. I imagine her going out with her head bent over and then coming into the other room through the little doorway, as if she were emerging from a crypt. At that time the two of us lived alone at El Cerro. She had told me: I'm going to take in a lodger. She'll live in the sitting room. She's a seamstress too. We've got plenty of space, and I can do my work in our room.

This room faced the little garden, where I played with the other children of the neighborhood. The seamstress who came to live in the sitting room was a solid woman with shiny black skin. My mother shut the door between the two rooms, and we went in and out through the garden to the street behind.

We don't need the sitting room, she would say. And that street in front of the house is full of holes and there are puddles when it rains. In the back you can see the country. You can watch the sun go down.

I did not feel that she was talking to me. She had brought the sewing machine in and installed it in our room, and the stacks of unfinished work were in the bathroom. The women who ran the shops no longer came to the house. Sometimes she went out early to deliver finished things and pick up new work. There was not much of that. She worked slowly now. Sometimes I would look in through the window from the garden and see her from behind. She would stop the sewing machine and sit there stiffly, merely looking at the wall. When she began to pedal again she would keep her bust erect, as a person does when he has been seized by a paralyzing pain.

One day she told me: I'm going to send you to your Aunt Sol's house for a few weeks. Or maybe to your Uncle Martín's. I've got to go away to the country and do some work there. It may take me several weeks.

I had never gone to the country. I had not mentioned it to her except once in a while back in Spain, and again coming over on the ship, and finally here in El Cerro, in that lean-to. I said: And my other uncles?

They're all right. They're somewhere around. The trouble is that they think I'm bad. It was the Devil that did it!

Martín came that evening. He had visited us before, passing through. He was a languid man with a dark, sad, pockmarked face, and he did not like to talk. I always saw him wearing a wide belt that held files, pliers and hammers. As he was leaving he said to my mother: You think about it. Send me the boy if you want.

She added quickly for my benefit, but speaking to her brother: I'm coming right back, you know. It's just some work I've got to do there in Artemisa. But it might be better for him with his Aunt Sol. It's country there, and there are flowers.

Martín squinted at us both. Then he looked around the room as if in wonder. As you like, he said. But anyway, you know.

He went out slowly, a bit hunched over, through the little garden. She turned out the light, set me on the edge of the bed, and let herself fall into the rocking chair.

Your uncles are good men, she told me. Maybe I was the bad one. But I didn't want them doing favors for me; neither they nor anybody else. I brought you here so you wouldn't have to grow up with Adán. He's the one who's bad. God forgive him! God forgive us all! It was the work of the Devil!

I did not understand what she was saying. I had heard her speak of Adán before, and although I had never seen him, I knew he was my father. She went on.

He's your father, but if ever you see him, just remember one thing. He never recognized you. Besides, you don't look like him. You're a Román.

She was silent, and I felt that she was weeping somewhere inside. Then, raising her voice, she exclaimed irritably: Go to bed! I don't know why I'm telling you all this.

The following day she was herself once again, dignified, reserved and haughty. When I think of it now, it seems strange that a personality such as hers should have belonged to a village woman. But nothing about her made one think of the country. Furthermore, she lived in such a state of tension that one did not think of what she was, but only of what she felt. She astonished those around her. One day she said to the black woman: You're surprised that I know how to speak and dress properly. According to you I ought to be working as a maid!

The woman opened her eyes very wide, shrugged her shoulders, and began to mutter. My mother turned to a client who was there and whispered: I realize that sometimes I lose my temper. I was very young when I went through all that. There was nobody to help me. All my brothers were in Cuba.

She would get up and dress before dawn, looking ghostlike but beautiful in her light-colored, flowing dress, with those unmoving green eyes and her black hair all around her head like a halo. To me she seemed very tall—taller than Martín and taller than the black woman—perhaps because she was being whetted for death.

A serving maid! She reiterated on another occasion. No one in my family has ever been a servant. God forbid!

Uncle Martín returned the following night. My mother seemed to be full of life. That morning Sol had sent a neighbor, Romalia, with a message. Once again a ship was about to arrive.

I've put off the trip to Artemisa, she told my uncle. Today's Saturday, I'd like to spend Sunday here, and I may stay on for another week. But the boy's going to Sol's. She has more room where she lives. I don't want to go off and leave him shut into your little cubicle. It's like a grave in there.

They were both silent. Martín shut his eyes briefly and went out, his head bent forward in front of him. He looked back sadly at me, but he did not look at her. And he never again saw her alive!

In the morning Sabina the black woman called timidly at the door in the partition. Teresa! Teresa! Are you all right?

That night I had slept like a drugged person. Perhaps that actually was the case. As I was going to bed my mother had given me a herbal brew she had made. At times in my sleep it seemed that I heard her coughing, but I was not certain. My sleep was leaden. Sometimes I had dreams in which I thought I heard moans, but there was no way of knowing whether they were real or imaginary. In the morning my mother was up, her hair all arranged, wearing a clean starched houserobe with flower designs on it. She partially opened the little door and with great aplomb looked at the black woman.

Yes, thank you, Sabina. I'm all right. I had a nightmare, that's all. And she repeated: Thank you, Sabina!

Never yet had I heard her say she was ill. Nor had the doctor come to the house. Sometimes she would be away all one morning or afternoon. Finally she explained to me that now she was sewing at other people's houses as well as at home.

I've put off the trip to the country until next week. I have some clothes here I've got to finish first. She spoke without looking at me, and she moved carefully, as if she suspected that something inside her were about to break. Sitting down at the sewing machine, she began to hem a piece of cloth. Now and then she stopped and stared fixedly out through the doorway, across the countryside. Once she caught me staring at her, and said severely: Come on, drink your milk and go and play. Pretty soon you've got to go for your lesson.

I did not go to school. It was a long way from our house, whereas the woman who taught me lived across the street. She gave me classes after breakfast and again after lunch.

Be careful! my mother went on. We don't want them throwing stones at you again.

I went outside, but not to play. I threw myself onto the grass and began to sniff, the way a dog does. I had an exceptionally acute sense of smell, and certain of the neighbors, aware of this, had remarked upon it. Once I had claimed that a room smelled of a dead body, and three days later the old woman who lived in it had died. My mother knew about this.

When I returned at noon, Sabina was with her. They were sorting the sewing. Romalia was there as well. She was a sad, bony, toothless woman, with a little round belly that stuck out in front.

My mother handed her a package, saying: Take this to my sister Sol. Tell her to come by here tomorrow.

She turned to explain to Sabina: My half-sister. I have only one brother, Antón, and he works for her in the garden. My half-brothers are all over the place. Martín, in the sack factory down there. Javier, riding around in his mule cart. And Sol, my half-sister, in Jesús del Monte. Románes everywhere!

She tried to smile, but by now her smile had become a mere grimace. She was horribly pale, and the makeup she had put on only augmented her pallor. But she forced herself to stand erect, as a healthy person does. Seeing me in the doorway, she said: And this one. This one too is named Román. He has no other family name. And he doesn't need any other!

And she added to herself in a deep, angry voice: A spineless jellyfish!

The others, Sabina and Romalia, listened to her quietly, saying nothing, pretending to be unconcerned. But their eyes went from her to me.

My mother repeated: A jellyfish! I can't see how . . . But God forgive me!

She looked downward, crossing her hands on her breast.

And God forgive him, too!

Slowly her voice had grown softer; her body hunched over slightly. Then she became aware of this, straightened herself, and said in a strained, almost imperious voice: Go along, Romalia. Take the bundle with you. Tell Sol to come tomorrow. Perhaps one of these days I'll be going along to the country.

Romalia backed up little by little, staring at us. She went out through Sabina's room. Sabina remained seated on the stool near the sewing machine, leaning first one way and then the other in order to see us better. Then my mother said to me: I've been thinking, I may stay quite awhile in Artemisa. I've been offered better work there. In the meantime, where would you like to stay? With your Aunt Sol or your Uncle Martín? Sol has country; there are flowers.

It was getting dark. She went to the door and looked out at the countryside for a long time, without speaking. When she turned back, it seemed to me that her eyes were moist, but she would not let me see them. She walked to the end of the room and began to ladle out the food that had been bought at a stall in the street. And she began to hum.

The next morning Aunt Sol arrived. She was nothing like my mother: older, somewhat blond, and with the wide body and the gross voice of a country woman. She looked at my mother with the same expression of surprise and compassion that I had seen in the neighbors' faces.

I'll wait another week, said my mother. Today's the twentieth. On the twenty-seventh the *Alfonso XII* is docking, isn't it?

She saw me and changed the subject. If I stay there, she told them, send him to school. He'll have to study. He's never going to take to farm work.

Then, in a burst of confidence, she said: Today I feel well. Really, I do feel much better. Do you think the *Alfonso* . . .

For the first time I was aware, if only vaguely so, of the reason for her alternating depressions and exaltations. Another ship was on the way.

Sol said: Don't you worry about the boy. We'll take care of him.

And perhaps you won't have to, my mother said, her face flushing, forgetting that I was there. These last days I've been praying all the time.

Then an idea occurred to her, and her face clouded over. It's true that maybe I don't deserve it. They say I'm bad.

She regained control of herself and stood up with a grimace. Each day she changed her dress, and that day she was wearing the prettiest one. But she was busy making another, and she had bought a bottle of perfume. This scent made me more aware of another odor, still extremely faint, but unmistakable, that was beginning to be noticeable in the house. Then I realized that she was getting worse; for months she had been failing. At the moment she was lively, she looked younger, but she was like a light that flickered on and off. She had no muscles left—only skin, bones and tendons.

When Sol said good-by she seemed to be leaving against her will. Tell me the truth. How do you feel? You still don't want me to take him?

My mother seemed to be slightly delirious as she spoke. She was not looking at the others, and from time to time she seemed to be addressing someone who was not present.

I was saying to Sabina, there are terrible people in the world. They trample you underfoot, then tease you and humiliate you. And nobody calls them to account for it. There's no justice.

She shook her head, clutched her bosom, and cried in a low voice: God forgive me!

After a silence she said: No. Don't take him yet. We'll wait another week. Will you do me this favor once more? Go to the dock. . . .

Sol went away shaking her small head. I saw her clench her fists, and I heard her murmur to herself: Poor sister! It's not right that she should have all this trouble!

My mother did not follow her out. When the door was shut she stood against it, facing the little doorway opposite. On the other side of the partition Sabina's sewing machine no longer hummed. Without looking at me, my mother said: That package on the chair there. It's the dress for the lady at number eleven. You take it over to her.

I went out, but I stood on the other side of the door, listening. I heard Sabina go in.

You look much better today, said the black woman. But if I were you I wouldn't put off going to the hospital any longer. You'll be better taken care of there.

There was a silence, and my mother said: I want to stretch the time as far as I can. I want to be with the boy. But I don't want him to see me haggard and ugly. I want him to remember me as I am . . . as I was. When I come back I'll look younger again. I'll be like a young girl. She paused. But it's still not certain that I'll go. Something may still happen, you know.

When I got back to the house I found her leaning over, clutching the edge of the table. Then she went behind the curtain, and for a long time I heard her heavy breathing. But the following day she got up looking rested, and put on the new dress she had finished making. Aunt Sol came in early, very lively. They talked together in low voices. Soon Sol hurried out, and my mother seemed to be waiting for her to return. The fire had come back to her eyes, and she moved with a lightness she had not shown for many months. She showered, put her new dress back on, and made up her face. Then she sat down again at the sewing machine and began to sing under her breath. All afternoon she gave no sign of having noticed my return to the room. Sabina opened the door a crack and looked in at her with concern.

Come in, Sabina, come in. You know, I feel fine. And I think we're going to have a visitor.

She did not make any explanation. I went out and in, and for several hours she did not seem to be aware of my presence.

You know, Sabina, no one can judge anyone. Each one of us has his own soul, and sometimes it's not what others think it is. If we have a visitor, we'll invite you to the party. Because we're going to have a little party. You're a good friend, Sabina.

Then I saw that she was weeping, and that it was because she was happy. The black woman moved her eyes from one side to the other as if she expected to see a ghost.

I tell you my sister Sol heard that a certain personage was coming on the *Alfonso XII.* And if it's true . . .

Then she looked in the direction of the door, remained poised, immovable for an instant, and in a lower tone of voice added doubtfully: I don't mean to be presumptuous. I'm like the Chinese. Let us wait and hope. Do you know this child's name? Román is his second name, my father's name. But he must have another. Everybody has two family names. Why did he have to be something less than other people? His other name is Pérez. My sister says a certain important person is arriving on the *Alfonso.* And if he's coming, I know why. You'll see, Sabina! You'll see yet how everything will all be settled!

I was stretched out on the floor behind the curtain, sniffing. She did not seem to realize this.

You'll see, Sabina, you'll see, said my mother.

Slowly the black woman shut the door behind her, as one does with sick people. But she was frightened. I ran around the outside of the house and went in through the street entrance to stand in front of Sabina's open door. She was piling up pieces of clothing and saying to herself: an important person, a certain important personage . . . The poor thing's out of her mind!

She saw me and stopped talking. I ran out. Something was bothering me. Perhaps it was the new smell. When I got back to the room my mother had turned on all the lights. She sent me to take a shower, and dressed me in my best suit.

Put this on, just for today, she told me. It's Sunday. And you're growing. What's the use of saving your clothes? Besides, we may have a visitor. You'll see! You'll see!

She was exhilarated. She had been working up to this little by little. Soon she was quite beside herself with excitement. Then, suddenly, she was still. Nothing happened. No one came. It was so quiet I could hear a fly go past me in the air. But some message had reached her innermost being, and when, hours later, Aunt Sol came back with the news (or rather the lack of news), it was as if she had already prepared herself to hear it.

My aunt said: It's no good, Teresa. Things are the way they are. What's the use of pretending? There must have been a mistake. He's not coming here. He's gone to Buenos Aires!

My mother stood looking at her. She had no expression. In the past few hours her face had gone dead, like a fire that has burned itself out. It was only a ghost of itself, no longer a face, but a mask. Yet her voice was still firm when she said: It's all right. You can take the boy with you. I think I'll go where I have to go.

At the time (and for long afterward) it was this memory of my mother that stayed in my mind. But then, slowly, it began to dissolve, and in its place I was left with the other picture, the one she had meant to leave with me the day when she had said: I don't want him to remember me haggard and ugly. I want him to remember me as I am . . . as I was.

TRANSLATED BY PAUL BOWLES

NICOLÁS GUILLÉN

Josephine Baker in Cuba

Smoothly rubbing his hands together in a polished display of attentiveness, the employee confessed his impotence with a hypocritical, almost sad smile: "You must understand how embarrassed we feel. You have no idea how sorry we are. However, there isn't a single room available. . . ."

And then he added mysteriously: "Imagine! At the height of the tourist season!"

An embarrassing silence followed. A silence soft and thick as a heavy rug. The presumed guest stood there for a few moments, unsure, drumming his fingers on the thick glass of the countertop. By his side, a slim black woman, still young, her small head topped by a gray beret, questioned him in French. She was none other than Josephine Baker—"the world-famous *vedette*" according to the boisterous announcements promoting her performance in Havana. The man was her husband, Jo Bouillon, white, an orchestra conductor. Nearby, several Cuban friends who had met them at the airport understood the situation all too well but were helpless in their indignation.

What had happened? Nothing but a now familiar occurrence in the sociology of Americans of pure European blood. The splendid Hotel Nacional was refusing lodging to the great artist because of the color of her skin. Of course they had rooms available. But what excuse could the management have offered the blonde North Americans—who cannot stand to be close to "colored people" in their own land—when they found themselves obliged to eat in the same hall as that filthy creature here in Havana? Of course, the teeming tribe of Smiths that overruns this exclusive mansion now and then produces a sudden gentleman, an improvised lord who blows his nose in a napkin or who sticks a fork piled high with rice into his mouth like a domestic fakir. But the whiteness of his skin is beyond all doubt: a slightly pinkish white resembling that of certain tumors just before they are sliced open by a surgeon; their eyes swim in a bluish water; their hair, plastered against their skulls, runs the full gamut of yellows, from ripe wheat to dysentery.

So Mrs. Baker and her husband left the hotel and went to take a room in another, more modest, hotel where the Cuban Constitution offered them greater guarantees. What more could you ask for? As occurs with the fiction of international law by which embassies are extensions of the country to which they belong, so are there many places here where our laws are not worth the paper they're written on. The Hotel Nacional, for example, is Yankee territory. In Havana it stands for a piece of Virginia or Georgia, places where to be black is barely a humanized form of being a dog. Having said that, let us be fair: it must be noted that at no time did Mrs. Baker run the risk of being lynched as she would have in Richmond or Atlanta. Is this not a clear sign of progress, for which we Cubans should pride ourselves?

The next day, the star of the Folies-Bergères, Parisian to the bone although she was born in the United States, speaking English with a slight inflection from the Boulevard Saint-Michel and placing the stress—in the French manner—on the last syllable of her surname, made her debut in the América Theater before a packed and convulsed hall. The audience received her with a truly torrential standing ovation. Despite her years—now numbering fifty-four—Josephine Baker is still Josephine Baker. Lithe, lively, fiery, and bursting with spirit. Only now, she dances fully clothed.

"Where are the bananas?" a spectator shouted from the balcony.

"I ate them all during the war!" Josephine responded.

And she continued dancing, her marvelous body wrapped tightly in a practically polar, almost Antarctic white suit, a suit like snow slashed by the sun and filled with shining stones. Diamonds? Apparently so. . . . Flowing from her shoulders was a black and white cape that the *vedette* moved like the wings of an enormous butterfly. The ensemble—she herself said so—cost thirty thousand dollars. No wonder, for her complete wardrobe is worth eighteen million francs.

Thus every appearance Josephine makes is like the rising of the sun. No sooner does she emerge than a murmur of amazement rises from the audience like a cloud of words. Hundreds of eyes ambitiously examine her body from head to toe. Immediately, she fills the set with her sensual presence, her broad smile, her mischievous eyes overflowing with fresh, crowd-pleasing charm, her warm, mellow voice like a hand knowingly caressing the most sensitive regions of the skin. Then the murmur turns to a charged, phosphoric anguish that finally explodes in a tempest of thunder and lightning. This takes place every single afternoon, the theater packed to the rafters, the box office sold out by an endless line of men and women, and Josephine, in the admiring embrace of all Havana, squeezed to the point of suffocation.

It goes without saying that the presence of Josephine Baker among us has already enriched our repertoire of popular anecdotes. They say that on the day of her first performance, people were waiting for her for more than thirty minutes in the Radiocentro building where she was to rehearse. Her eminence notwithstanding—and perhaps because of it, for this happens at times—someone there was one not to mince his words and reprimanded her as was her due for being late. Immediately, Josephine—buoyant, smiling, sophisticated—apologized in Spanish with such grace, such elegance, that the tension dissolved right away. The artists from this radio station immediately surrounded her in an atmosphere of warm sympathy. Present as well was the producer of a certain sponsored program for which the *vedette* had been hired: Señor José Antonio Alonso.

"Señora Baker," he said. "We thought you might sing three numbers for us. Is that all right with you?"

"Just two, Señor Alonso," responded the artist.

"However," the producer insisted, "in these types of performances it is customary to do three numbers."

"I'm sure it is," Josephine responded, "but two, that's it."

Señor Alonso agreed—what could he do!—and then they went on to settle certain technical details of the transmission.

"You will sing the first number, Señora Baker, then there will be a commercial message and afterward, you—"

The producer, distressed, could not finish his sentence. With a firm smile, Josephine had interrupted him.

"No, Señor Alonso. Only two numbers, one right after the other. Between my first and my second number not a word shall be spoken. . . ."

And so it was.

The very modern América Theater has the most luxurious dressing rooms in Havana. When the great black *vedette* was shown to hers, she protested: "Oh no! I can't go in there. I need mirrors on all the walls, a rug on the floor—but a big rug, one that covers the entire floor—and flowers, lots of flowers. I can't live without flowers."

Only a few minutes later, she was satisfied.

Josephine Baker was great friends with Eliseo Grenet, the acclaimed composer of popular music who had died a month earlier. "He wouldn't wait for me," she said with moist eyes while still in the airport. The next day she visited the cemetery to place a bouquet of roses on the grave of the author of "Mamá Inés." She has said that she will bring the "sucu-sucu" with her to Paris and debut it there, "as he would have wanted, as he would have done."

"Do you like Havana?" a reporter asked her the other day. One of those reporters present in every aerodrome and seaport throughout the world whose function it is to ask equivalent stupidities of illustrious travelers.

"Quite," Mrs. Baker answered courteously. "I have always been obsessed with this country, so warm, so full of fire, with such a dazzling sun. Only . . ."

"Only what?"

"Only . . . it's so cold!"

So it was. The thermometer had been registering—already in November—fifty-seven degrees . . .

TRANSLATED BY MARK SCHAFER

CLAVE 4

VIRGILIO PIÑERA

The Face

One morning I got a phone call. The person on the other end said he was in grave danger. To my obvious question: "With whom do I have the pleasure of speaking?" he replied that we had never seen each other and never would. What does one do in a situation like this? Tell the caller he's dialed the wrong number, of course, then hang up. That's what I did, but a few seconds later, the phone rang again. I told the persistent caller to please dial the number he wanted carefully and even added that I hoped not to be bothered again, since it was too early to start joking around.

Then he told me in a voice full of anguish not to hang up, that this wasn't any kind of joke, that he hadn't dialed the wrong number, that it was true we didn't know each other, for he had picked my name at random from the phone book. And, as if to anticipate any further objection, he told me that all of this was happening because of his face; that his face had a power of seduction so strong that people would shun him—disturbed, as if fearing irreparable harm. I confess that this business interested me; at the same time, I told him not to lose heart, for everything in this world has a cure. . . .

"No," he told me. "It's an incurable affliction, an aberration without remedy. Mankind has shunned me; even my own parents abandoned me some time ago. I only deal with the lowest of the human species, that is, with servants. . . . I'm reduced to the solitude of my house. I hardly ever go out any more. The telephone is my only consolation, but people have so little imagination. . . .

Without exception, everyone takes me for a lunatic. There are those who hang up, uttering unpleasant phrases; others let me speak and my reward is an outburst of laughter; there are even those who call people over to the phone so they, too, can enjoy the poor lunatic. And so, one by one, I lose them all forever."

I was moved, but I was also thinking that I was talking to a lunatic. Nevertheless, his voice had such a tone of sincerity, sounded so pained, that I refrained from bursting out laughing, from shouting and hanging up without further explanation. A new doubt struck me. Could he be a prankster? Or could it be a joke by one of my friends trying to spark my imagination? (I'm a novelist.) Since I'm an outspoken person, I let it all out.

"Well," he said philosophically, "I can't get that idea out of your head. It's reasonable for you to be suspicious, but if you have confidence in me, if pity moves you to stick this out, you'll soon be convinced of the sad truth I have just confided to you." And without giving me time to object again, he added: "Now I await the sentence. You have the final word. What's it going to be?" he whispered in terror. "A burst of laughter, shouting?"

"No," I hastened to say. "I won't forsake you. You've gotten me interested. However," I added, "you can call me. I'll only speak with you twice a week. I have thousands of things to do. Unfortunately, my face is one that everyone—or almost everyone—wants to see. I'm a writer, and you know what that entails."

"Praise the Lord!" he replied. "You stopped me at the edge of the abyss."

"But," I interrupted, "I'm worried that our conversations will have to be suspended for lack of anything to talk about. Since we don't have anything in common, neither friends nor common circumstances; since furthermore, you aren't a woman (you know how women like to be courted over the phone), I think we'll be yawning out of boredom within five minutes."

"I've thought of that," he replied. "It's the risk people take who can't see each other face to face. . . . Well," he sighed, "there's no harm in trying."

"But," I objected, "if we fail, you're going to feel bad. Don't you see that the cure could be worse than the disease?"

I couldn't dissuade him from his strange idea. Then an even more peculiar idea occurred to him: he suggested that we attend various shows in order to exchange impressions. This proposition, which at first rather annoyed me, ended up sounding interesting. For example, he told me he'd be attending the opening of a certain movie at a certain hour. . . . I didn't fail to attend. I hoped to make out that face, seductive and dreadful, among the hundreds of people filling the movie theater. At times, my curiosity was so intense that I imagined the police blocking the exits, determining if there was a person with a seductive and dreadful face in the theater. But would this be an infallible method for the police? Both the enchanting youth and the fiendish assassin can have a seductive and dreadful face. With these reflections I calmed down, and when we returned to our telephone meetings and I told him of these rebellions, he begged me in a sobbing voice never to dare to see his face, not even in jest; that I could be sure that as soon as I saw his "astonishing" face once, I would refuse to see him again. That he knew I would go on about my business, but that I should think of all he would lose. That if I cared at all about him as a defenseless human being, I would not try to see his face. And at that point, he became nervous and asked that in the future we not attend the same shows.

"Fine," I told him. "Granted. If you prefer it that way, we'll no longer be 'together' anywhere. But under one condition. . . ."

"One condition . . . ," he repeated feebly. "You're placing conditions and requirements on me. I can imagine what the request is going to cost me."

"The only thing that you wouldn't accept is for us to see each other face to face. . . . And no, I would never insist on that. You interest me enough that I would never box you in."

"Well, what condition is it then? Whatever situation you might imagine will be foolhardy. Think about it," he begged me. "Think about it before you make matters worse. Anyway," he added, "we're so safe on the telephone."

"The hell with your telephone!" I nearly shouted. "I absolutely have to see you. No, please!" I apologized, for I sensed that he'd nearly fainted. "No, I don't mean to say that I have to see your face! I would never dare to look at it; I know that you need me, and even when I'm literally dying to contemplate your face, I'll sacrifice that desire for your safety. Rest assured. No—what I mean to say is that I'm also suffering. You aren't the only one your face plays tricks on—it plays tricks on me, too. . . . You want to make me see it; you want me to leave you, too."

"I hadn't expected that," he replied in a voice as thin as a thread. "Damned face, playing tricks on me even when it's hidden! How could I imagine you'd be desperate to see it?"

There was a long pause; we were too moved to speak. Finally, he broke the silence: "What are you going to do now?"

"Resist as long as I can, as long as is humanly possible . . . as long. . . ."

"Yes, until your curiosity can't bear it any longer," he interrupted with pronounced irony. "It can bear more than your mercy can."

"Neither one nor the other," I nearly shouted at him. "Neither one nor the other is true! . . . I haven't been moved 'exclusively' by pity for you. There has also been a lot of sympathy on my part," I added bitterly. "And as you see, now I feel as wretched as you do."

Then he thought it a good idea to break the tension with a joke of sorts, but its effect was to depress me. He told me that since his face had the power to make me "lose control," he considered our conversations over, and that in the future he would look for a person who didn't have that unhealthy curiosity to see his face. "Never!" I implored him. "If you did do such a thing, I would die. Let's continue as we have up until now. Only," I added, "make me forget my desire to see your face."

"I can't do anything about it," he replied. "If I fail with you, it will be the end."

"But at least let me be near you," I begged. "For example, I suggest you come to my house. . . ."

"Now you've got to be joking. Now it's your turn to be the joker. Because that's a joke. Right?"

"What I'm proposing to you," I explained, "is that you come to my house, or I go to yours, so we might speak face to face in the darkness."

"I won't do it for anything in the world!" he said to me. "If you're already going crazy on the telephone, how will it be when we're within inches of each other?"

But I convinced him. He couldn't refuse me anything, nor could I refuse him anything. The "encounter" took place at his house. He wanted to be sure that I wouldn't play any tricks on him. A servant who came to meet me in the hall searched me carefully.

"By order of the master of the house," he informed me.

No, I wasn't carrying a flashlight or matches: I never would have resorted to such desperate measures, but he was so afraid of losing me that he couldn't gauge how ridiculous and offensive his precautions were. Once the servant was sure that I wasn't carrying any kind of light, he led me by the hand and at last seated me in an armchair. The darkness was so complete that I couldn't see my hand in front of my face. I felt a little immaterial, but was nevertheless doing fine in the dark. In any case, I was finally going to hear his voice without having to use the phone, and—even more moving—he would be within inches of me at last, seated in another armchair, invisible but not disembodied. I was burning with the desire to "see" him. Could it be that he was already seated in his armchair or would he be long before making his entrance? Had he changed his mind, and would the servant be returning now to tell me this? I began to get anxious. Finally, I said:

"Are you there?"

"Long before you came," his voice replied, which I sensed was a short distance from my armchair. "I've been 'watching' you for a while."

"I've also been 'watching' you. Who would dare offend heaven by asking for any greater happiness than this?"

"Thank you," he replied in a trembling voice. "Now I know you understand me. There's no longer room in my heart for suspicion. You'll never try to break through this darkness."

"That's right," I said. "I prefer this darkness to the darkness of your face. And as for your face, I think the time has come for you to explain a little about it."

"Why, of course!" and he shifted in his seat. "The story of my face has two periods. When I was its ally, and when I became its mortal enemy. During the first period, together we committed more horrible deeds than an entire army. Because of my face, knives have been buried in hearts and poison sunk in guts. Some have gone to remote countries just to be killed in unequal combat; others have lain in their beds until death carried them off. I must stress the following peculiarity: all those wretches expired blessing my face. How is it possible that a face that everyone runs from in horror might at the same time be an object of final blessings?"

He was silent for a good while, like someone trying in vain to find an answer. At last, he continued with his story:

"This bloody sport" (in the beginning, passionate) "was little by little becoming a terrible torture to my very soul. Suddenly, I knew I was isolating myself. I knew that my face was my atonement. The ice of my soul had been melted; I wanted to redeem myself, but my face, on the other hand, tightened even more, its ice grew thicker. While I aspired with all my soul to possess human tenderness, my face was proliferating its crimes with redoubled passion until I was reduced to the state in which you find me now."

He got up and began to walk around, I had to tell him to calm down, for in this darkness he would soon be flat on the floor. He explained to me that he knew the room by heart, and as proof of this, he would perform the "tour de force" of inviting me to have coffee in the dark. I heard him moving cups around. A weak glow told me he was just putting a pot of water on an electric burner. I looked at that luminous point. I did it as a simple reflex; furthermore, he was so well positioned that such a weak glow couldn't reveal his silhouette. I joked that I had the eyes of a cat, and he replied that when a cat doesn't want to see a dog, its eyes are like those of a mole. . . . Receiving a human being in his house and offering him the sacred civilities of hospitality, in spite of his face, made him so happy that he expressed his pleasure with a joke: he said that since the coffee would take a little while, I could amuse myself "by reading one of the magazines sitting within reach on the red table with black legs. . . ."

Days later, reviewing the visit in my mind, I realized that it was characterized by a great emptiness. But I didn't want to see things too darkly, and I imagined it was just because I was unaccustomed to the situation. In fact, I told myself, everything is happening as if that ultimate prohibition on seeing each other's face didn't exist. What importance is there, after all, in a mere physical abnormality? On the other hand, if I did see his face, I would probably lose my sanity and lose him in the process. But as far as that's concerned, if his soul isn't in conflict with his face at the moment, I don't see what power his face could have over anyone else's face. Let's suppose that I finally see his face, that his face tries to demolish mine. It wouldn't succeed, for isn't his soul there, ready to stop his face's assault? Isn't it there, ready to defend me, and—what is more important—to hold on to me?

At our next meeting, I presented this whole line of reasoning to him—reasoning which seemed to me so convincing that I didn't doubt for a moment that he would get up to flood his dark room with light. But instead, I was surprised to hear him say:

"You've thought of all the possibilities, but have forgotten the only one that couldn't be rejected. . . ."

"What?" I yelled. "Is there still one more possibility?"

"Of course. I'm not sure that my soul would defend you against the attacks of my face."

I felt like a ship that has almost been grazed by another ship. I sank into the armchair; farther than the armchair, I sank into the thick mud of that horrible possibility. I said to him:

"Then your soul isn't pure?"

"It is. I have no doubt. But if my face reveals itself? Now then, if my face should show itself, I don't know whether my soul would come out for or against it."

"Do you mean to say," I yelled, "that your soul is dependent on your face?"

"If that weren't the case," he replied, sobbing, "we wouldn't be sitting here in the dark. We'd be looking at each other's faces under a dazzling sun."

I didn't reply. It seemed useless to add another word. On the other hand, in my mind, I accepted the challenge of that seductive face. I now knew how to defeat it. It would neither lead me to suicide nor to leaving him. On my next visit, I would remain permanently at his side; at his side, without the darkness, his room full of light, the two of us facing one another.

There is little more for me to add. A while later, I returned to his house. As soon as I was seated in my armchair, I told him I had poked my eyes out so his face wouldn't separate our souls, and added that since the darkness was now superfluous, the lights could very well be turned on.

TRANSLATED BY MARK SCHAFER

REVISED BY THOMAS CHRISTENSEN

GUSTAVO PÉREZ-FIRMAT

Six Mambos

from LIFE ON THE HYPHEN:
THE CUBAN-AMERICAN WAY

MAMBO NO. 1
Lost in Translation

*Take the phrase literally. Turn the commonplace into a place. Try to imagine where one ends up if one gets lost in translation. When I try to visualize such a place, I see myself, on a given Saturday afternoon, in the summer, somewhere in Miami. Since I'm thirsty, I go into a store called Love Juices, which specializes in nothing more salacious or salubrious than milk shakes made from papayas and other tropical fruits. Having quenched my thirst, I head for a boutique called Mr. Trapus, whose name—*trapo*—is actually the Spanish word for an old rag. Undaunted by the consumerist frenzy that has possessed me, I enter another store called Cachi Bachi—a name that, in spite of its chichi sound, is a slang word for a piece of junk,* cachivache. *And then for dinner I go to the Versailles of Eighth Street, a restaurant where I feast on something called Tropical Soup, the American name for the traditional Cuban stew,* ajiaco. *My dessert is* *also tropical, Tropical Snow, which is Miamian for* arroz con leche; *and to finish off the meal, of course, I sip some Cuban-American espresso (don't go home without it). In this way I spend my entire afternoon lost in translation—and loving every minute. Translation takes you to a place where cultures divide to conga. My effort in this book is to show you the way to such a place. Step lightly, and enter at your own risk. Who knows, you might just end up becoming the missing link in the Desi Chain.*

MAMBO NO. 2
Spic'n Spanish

Miami Spanish includes a term that, so far as I know, is unique to the city of sun and solecisms: nilingüe. *Just as a* bilingüe *is someone who speaks two languages (say, Spanish and English), a* nilingüe *is someone who doesn't speak either: "ni español, ni inglés." Such a person is a no-lingual, a nulli-glot. My example of nilingualism is Ricky Ricardo. Ricky's occasional Spanish utterances are shot through with anglicisms:* falta *for* culpa, introducir *for* presentar, parientes *for* padres, *and so on. Sometimes the anglicisms seem deliberate (so that the monolingual viewers understand what he is saying), but at other times they're plain mistakes.*

A curious thing: as Ricky got older, his English didn't get any better, but his Spanish kept getting worse. Equally curious: the same thing happened to Desi Arnaz. In 1983 Arnaz was picked "king" of the Cuban carnival in Miami, Open House Eight. By then, his Spanish was as frail as his health. He now had an accent in two *languages.*

In Spanish to know a language well is to "dominate" it. But my mother tongue has it backward: people don't dominate languages, languages dominate people. By reversing the power relation, English comes closer to the truth. When someone speaks English better than Spanish, we say that he or she is "English-dominant," an expression in which the language, and not the speaker, has the upper hand. But in Ricky no language achieved dominance; English and Spanish battled each other to a tie (a tongue-tie). A nilingüe *treats his mother tongue like a foreign language and treats the foreign language like his other tongue. T. W. Adorno once said: "Only he who is not truly at home inside a language can use it as an instrument." Ricky Ricardo is a multi-instrumentalist. He is homeless in two languages.*

MAMBO NO. 3

Desi Does It

Going through her father's house after his death, Lucie Arnaz found a box of papers and memorabilia that she donated to the Love Library at San Diego State University, where Desi had lectured several times. The Desi Arnaz Collection contains a few home movies, an old film short entitled Jitter-humba, *several drafts of* A Book, *and assorted notes that Arnaz took when he was working on his autobiography. Originally intending to write either a sequel to* A Book *(to be called* Another Book*) or a novel (probably to be called* A Novel*), Arnaz marked some of these jottings "Other Book" or "Novel." The notes contain not only many self-revealing moments and juicy gossip (like a list of Lucille Ball's alleged lovers), but also some of Desi's best quips.*

Seeing Gary Morton, Lucy's second husband, on a TV talk show, he writes: "About Gary on TV with Lucy: Seems to be suffering from a massive inferiority complex to which he is fully entitled." To his children, Lucie and Desi, Jr., he once remarked: "The only reason you are here is because I woke up one night and couldn't think of anything else to do." About his famous quarrels with Lucy, he says: "Lucy and I had some great battles but at times when someone asked me why we fought, I had to answer, 'I don't know. She wouldn't tell me.'" Most pertinent, perhaps, are his thoughts on being a writer: "Writing a book is, I discovered, not an easy

ʻhing to do. It also proves that the brain is a wonderful thing. It starts up when you are born and stops when you sit down at the typewriter."

But my favorite is the simple aphorism "History is made at night." It seems appropriate that the box ended up at a place called the Love Library.

MAMBO NO. 4
The Barber of Little Havana

When I first became interested in the mambo some years ago, I was puzzled to find that a well-respected British reference work, The Faber Companion to 20th-Century Popular Music, *gave Pérez Prado's first name as Pantaleón rather than Dámaso. More puzzling still, after describing Pérez Prado's career in accurate detail, the entry concluded, "His elder brother Damos* [sic] *was also a bandleader and composer who specialized in the mambo." Later I discovered that Pérez Prado actually had a brother named Pantaleón, who was also a musician. Still later, while going through some music magazines from the 1950s, I found that Pantaleón had actually toured Europe claiming to be* the *Mambo King, an imposture that ended only when Dámaso threatened to take legal, rather than musical, steps.*

For many years there has been a barbershop on Eighth Street in Miami called Barbería Pérez

Prado. Its elderly owner bears a striking resemblance to Dámaso; some say he is Pérez Prado's brother, Pantaleón. But when questioned by visitors, the barber of Little Havana disclaims any connection. Will the real mambo king please stand up and grunt?

MAMBO NO. 5
Mirror, Mirror

One of the landmarks of Cuban Miami is a restaurant called Versailles, which has been located on Eighth Street and Thirty-fifth Avenue for many years. About the only thing this Versailles shares with its French namesake is that it has lots of mirrors on its walls. One goes to the Versailles not only to be seen, but to be multiplied. This quaint, kitschy, noisy restaurant that serves basic Cuban food is a paradise for the self-absorbed: the Nirvana of Little Havana. Because of the bright lights, even the windows reflect. The Versailles is a Cuban panopticon: you can lunch, but you can't hide. Who goes there wants to be the stuff of visions. Who goes there wants to make a spectacle of himself (or herself). All the ajiaco *you can eat and all the jewelry you can wear multiplied by the number of reflecting planes—and to top it off, a waitress who calls you* mi vida.

Across the street at La Carreta, another popu-

lar restaurant, the food is the same (both establishments are owned by the same man) but the feel is different. Instead of mirrors La Carreta has booths. There you can ensconce yourself in a booth and not be faced with multiple images of yourself. But at the Versailles there is no choice but to bask in self-reflective glory.

For years I have harbored the fantasy that those mirrors retain the blurred image of everyone who has paraded before them. I think the mirrors have a memory, as when one turns off the TV and the shadowy figures remain on the screen. Every Cuban who has lived or set foot in Miami over the last three decades has, at one time or another, seen himself or herself reflected on those shiny surfaces. It's no coincidence that the Versailles sits only two blocks away from the Woodlawn Cemetery, which contains the remains of many Cuban notables, including Desi Arnaz's father, whose remains occupy a niche right above Gerardo Machado's. Has anybody ever counted the number of Cubans who have died *in Miami? Miami is a Cuban city not only because of the number of Cubans who live there but also because of the number who have died there.*

The Versailles is a glistening mausoleum. The history of Little Havana—tragic, comic, tragicomic—is written on those spectacular specular walls. This may have been why, when the mirrors came down in 1991, there was such an uproar that some of them had to be put back. The hall of mirrors is also a house of spirits. When the time comes for me to pay for my last ajiaco, *I intend to disappear into one of the mirrors (I would prefer the one on the right, just above the espresso machine). My idea of immortality is to become a mirror image at the Versailles.*

MAMBO NO. 6

English Is Broken Here

Some years ago a Cuban radio station in Miami aired an advertisement promoting an airline's reduced fares: "Piedmont Airlines quiere limpiar el aire sobre sus bajas tarifas." "Limpiar el aire?" "Clean the air?" This phrase is ungrammatical in two languages. First mistake: perhaps influenced by the Spanish poner en limpio *(to clean up), the author of the ad must have thought that the English idiom was "clean the air" rather than "clear the air." Second mistake: he then decided that "clean the air" could be translated word for word into Spanish. Third mistake: he rendered "about" as "sobre," which in context sounds too much like "over" or "above." Hence: "Piedmont Airlines wants to clean the air above its low fares." But this sentence does have a certain flighty logic, especially considering that it went out over the airwaves. Piedmont's clean-air act is an interlingual utterance that remains up in the air, that cannot make up its mind whether to land in the domain of Spanish or English.*

Another comedy of grammatical errors will bring

us back to earth: there is a Cuban-owned pizza chain in Miami called Casino's Pizza. When Casino's was launched (or lunched) a few years ago, its publicity campaign included a bilingual brochure. I quote the first sentence of the Spanish text: "Su primera mirada, su primer olor, su primer gusto le dirá que usted descubrió La Pizza Ultima." Since "La Pizza Ultima" (the last pizza) doesn't make much sense in Spanish (it should have been "la última pizza" anyway), upon first reading this anglicized sentence, I had the impression that the final phrase was an incompletely digested translation of "the ultimate pizza." In order to check out my hunch, I went to the English text: "Your first sight, your first smell, your first taste will tell you that you've discovered La Pizza Ultima."

So what happened to my hypothetical Ultimate Pizza? It seems to have been eaten in translation. The same phrase that sounds like an anglicism in Spanish is offered as a hispanicism in English! Food for thought: the English phrase presupposes a Spanish phrase that presupposes an English phrase that doesn't exist. This is paradox-lover's pizza, one that consumes itself in the cracks between languages. Like the Piedmont ad, "La Pizza Ultima" refuses to be English but cannot be Spanish. If Beny Moré is the "bárbaro del ritmo," the authors of these ads must be bárbaros *of barbarism. Sometimes the American dream is written in Spanglish.*

SEVERO SARDUY

from FROM CUBA WITH A SONG

DOLORES RONDÓN

Since it's such a hot day, it won't do us any harm to take a walk in the cemetery: marble is cooling, almost like lemonade. There are no café tables or one-armed bandits in this garden of stone, but we'll come to that. In this part of Camagüey, in the center of Cuba, there's no end of oil portraits, of dead black men looking rosier and healthier than they ever did alive, or of two-story chapels, or reading material. Here at this crossroads, for example, you can read Dolores Rondón's poem:

Dolores Rondón did here
reach the end of her career,
come mortal, and ponder
on where lies true grandeur.
Pride and arrogance,
power and prominence,
all is bound to perish.
And you only immortalize
the evil you economize
and the good you may cherish.

A Hard Profession, Dolores's. Courtesan and poet. Courtesan all her life. Poet for a day. But time dissolves it all, like the sea into the sea. Of the courtesan, and her ups and downs, which were those of the senator Mortal Pérez, nothing remains. But the poet views us, from death.

Under the poem two angels face down hold up a lighted lamp.

A lighted lamp over a ribbon inscribed in Latin.

A ribbon inscribed in Latin tied around a bunch of flowers.

And all in marble!

But let's give our two narrators the floor. Let them present the life of Dolores Rondón. They won't do it in chronological order, but in that of the poem, which, after all, is the true one.

DOLORES RONDÓN DID HERE

In the provinces, the recent republican era

NARRATOR ONE *(chorus leader with a squeaky, biting voice):* Ah yes, going back to writing again, what an emetic! As if all this had some purpose, as if all this would penetrate some thick skull, occupy some driveling reader curled up in his armchair before the soporific stew of everyday living!

NARRATOR TWO *(high-sounding, solemn chorus leader, with a deep-chested voice):* That's it, decipher it or bust: all has a purpose, all is final, all returns to all, that is, to nothing, nothing is all *(his throat rasps)* . . . with this play on words I mean that your emetic is very useful, useful because emetic, in short, with words you modify things, behaviors, the behavior of the *(he stops short, stamps his cothurnus on the floor).*

NARRATOR ONE *(very high pitched):* Behavior, future, modify: lame words. Please, it only hurts when I laugh. You have a mangy dog, I say mangy for example, well then, you take the dog, which is the word, and throw a pail of boiling water on him, which is the exact sense of the word. What does the dog do?

What does the word do? And so we have dog-word, water-sense: These are the four parts. Take them! Who pins the tail on the donkey? Here is the summary of my metaphor: lame words for lame realities that follow a lame plan drawn up by a lame monkey.

NARRATOR TWO: I'm slow I admit, but I don't get who the monkey is.

NARRATOR ONE *(in coloratura soprano):* My son, please, when will you learn! *(He looks for an easy comparison.)* Now then: words are like flies, toads, as you know, eat flies, snakes eat toads, bulls eat snakes and men eat bulls, that is to say . . .

NARRATOR TWO: Men eat flies!

NARRATOR ONE: It's not that easy, but enough, we didn't meet here today for that, but to discuss, under the denomination of the Patron Saint of Small Animals, to discuss I say, the case of the mulatto Dolores Rondón.

NARRATOR TWO *(answering a riddle):* The one who reached the end of her career?

NARRATOR ONE: They're one and the same. Let's talk about her.

CLEMENCY *(redheaded and waxen youth with a high and hysterical voice):* With chapter and verse!

HELP *(redheaded and waxen youth with a high and hysterical voice):* With toad tack!

MERCY *(redheaded and waxen youth with a high and hysterical voice):* With monkey fine stone and cats fly cabala!

NARRATOR ONE *(protesting):* Oh no, out of the question! I will not stand for those three queens, horrible creatures.

NARRATOR TWO: Come on, for God's sake (a figure of speech), more simplicity, more modesty. Throw your spangles into the well and listen quietly. These are Dolores's witnesses, her attendants. Let them express themselves.

HELP *(leading a protest by the trio, real leader of the masses style, very confident):* We strive to come out!

MERCY *(sprecht-gesang):* Like the tortoise from his shell,
like the chicken from his egg,
like the corpse from his hole, yes!

NARRATOR ONE *(frightened before the apparition of the three acolytes):* Please!

DOLORES *(Wifredo Lam, mulatto woman, voice between a guitar and an obatala drum):* You've got to get out. *(Without any graduation: a street near the station. Run-down hotels. A smell of tobacco and mangos. In the lemon-colored air the red cap of the porters, the clicking of spurs. Street cries. Jewelry vendors. Perhaps the horn of an old Ford.)* Get out of the hole. If you don't change, you get stuck. You've got to keep moving. No, it's not the mud that bothers me, nor the heavy rains, nor the puddles, nor the oxcarts, nor the electoral campaigns; it's the other people buying and selling, buying machetes, soap, knockers, scissors, earrings, rags, old cots and bottles; the others eating and sleeping.

(The street disappears just as it had appeared.)

NARRATOR ONE: Now do you see? She despises the essential, the place of her birth.

NARRATOR TWO: Shut up, stupid. The essential is somewhere between the *guanábana* and the *mango.*

DOLORES *(conscious of the narrators' interruption):* I'm getting out of here and I've come to sell all I've got: a wristwatch and a fine Grade A rooster. I can make it to Camagüey easy on what I get. This is it. I'm doing like Christopher Columbus, who burnt his ships behind him. I'm a high-class dancer, let the others have the box step rumba. Learned, I am, well-read, no. My saints I know by heart, and I play the right numbers. Show and place.

HELP *(quickly):* Hey, what's all this about "play"?

MERCY *(erudite):* Each animal is a number of the lottery, one is the horse, nine the snake.

CLEMENCY *(in false falsetto):* Which eats toads, which eats bulls.

DOLORES: I am the legimitate daughter of Ochún, queen of the river and the sky. You got to move fast. You got to keep moving ahead, like a train. You got to get out of here.

NARRATOR ONE: That's what she thinks, that she's going, but she's staying here, here's where her career ends.

NARRATOR TWO *(grandiloquent):* She's going, she's going so that the poem may come true, so that, as I was saying, fate may exist, and the emetic be useful.

DOLORES *(who has overheard the conversation):* What? What are those two old goats over there saying? That I'm staying? That here's where my career ends? We'll see about that. Hey there, Spaniard baby! Yeah you, with the beret.

MORTAL *(blondie, piñata eyes, the man from Castille, with his pure Castillian diction):* Are you calling me?

HELP *(recitative, the voice of a hoarse soprano, glad to see the poem is following its course):* Opposites attract!

MERCY *(and he powders his nose):* Their vertices touch!

CLEMENCY *(crowned with marble garlands):* Like the snake its tail!

HELP, MERCY, CLEMENCY *(dissonant requiem):* Like the beginning its end! *(The three in* guanábana *hats, holding baskets of sugar cones, jumping over the tracks, the train is coming!)*

REACH THE END OF HER CAREER

In the provinces, after the fall of Mortal

NARRATOR TWO: Now look where we are! What did I tell you? Her attendants abandoned her, leaving her to her executioner just as they left her to her lovers before, always to the best bidder.

NARRATOR ONE: It's not their fault, they didn't mean to. They revealed the place where Dolores meets her lovers and that's all. For a few coins, for a few cartons of Chesterfields and an Elizabeth Arden lotion they've sold her, the frivolous lads. They didn't know what they were risking, they didn't know that death was watching at every step. But let's not name Lady Bones, the Lonely Ánima, let us not anticipate her arrival. Trusting, they were, are, victims of the mustached fury. They should be warned: Oyá is dread and comes by every day with her cart, mistress of the ways of the wind, of the keys to the cemetery. Dolores is going to die, perhaps is already dying so that the poem may come true. In the heat, in a bug-ridden bed she is dying, without the air conditioning she lived her better days in, always on Very Cold, without her Simmons mattresses, the best in comfort, without the rosewater that once perfumed her. Lady Bones, make her . . .

HELP *(realizing the evil he has done):* All must perish!

MERCY *(and he sprays himself from head to toe with an atomizer):* We are nothing!

CLEMENCY *(and he combs his hair):* From dust to dust!

DOLORES *(With this monologue Dolores receives death. She no longer fears the grandiloquent tone, ridiculous images, folklore, verbosity itself. Dolores enters death in a major key, as she once entered life. She draws out certain words, the names of saints, in this "lyrical declamation." Tearful comicality. Here the rhetoric, and on the patios in the background, the cha-cha-chá):* The river returns to the source, the light to dawn, the wounded beast to the forest. Each one in his water. Each bird in his air. I return to the bottom of the sea, in the god Obatalá's white dressing gown, in the night, flag of the dead. I am a tree, I threw a shadow. Darkness frightens the birds, but day is coming, roosters' watch. Valley of shadow, come to me! The son of Eleguá lacks neither bread, nor pasture, nor the chosen water of repose, nor her husband the fragrant fruit. Guitars, I was wood; let my death warm ye. Maracas, break, untuned goddesses. The saints had said it with their daily signals: the broken glass of water, the frisky horses, the black in the mirrors. I didn't hear. I didn't believe. I didn't open the door. Ye were calling. Let the king of the heavens open to me now with the same smile with which I now open, not to every day's lover, but to the murderer. The gods provide for the Damp House the same as they do for the earth. There will be heat, there will be wine and coffee in death. Neither bread, nor pineapple, nor open mamey, nor beheaded roosters will be wanting in my tomb. Nor the oration of the nine days, nor mourning, nor the abundant banquet with guayaba and cheese. Let there be rum at my wake. Rum and rumination. No weeping, no teeth gnashing, no torn clothing. King, receive me; I go without fear. Wind swallow me. Scatter me in the rain . . . And yet, dark servants, beasts who have betrayed me, may war decimate ye, lightning blind ye, leprosy corrode ye. Ye have promised without keeping your word, gods of whites. Dagger, be brief. Do not repeat my blood.

(The cha-cha-chá goes off.)

HELP: A ridiculous farewell monologue. Lacking in Camagüeyan spontaneity.

MERCY: Let the dead have fame, but the living love!

CLEMENCY: What I wouldn't do for a nice cold beer!

NARRATOR TWO: Dumb Fates. Owl faces.

NARRATOR ONE: It's late. Let's go. There's a Caridad del Cobre fair and tonight everybody's drunk.

(Dolores screams. The cha-cha-chá begins again.)

(In the brothel next door, Help, Mercy, and Clemency dance it and wave their tresses—slow whirls of flame—patting their lips, biting their fingers, pulling off their cartilage bone necklaces, breaking off their eyebrows, their faces now quartered, pale masks.)

COME, MORTAL, AND PONDER

In the provinces, before the election

NARRATOR ONE *(ironical):* Remember the dog?

NARRATOR TWO *(as lost as a nun in a garage):* What dog? The one in the manger?

NARRATOR ONE: No, the other more mongrel one, that came shooting out in the first line when they threw a bucket of boiling water on him.

NARRATOR TWO: Good Heavens! Of course I remember. What's become of him?

NARRATOR ONE: You'll know soon enough. Wait. Look: they're already there, they're already arriving.

NARRATOR TWO: Who are those people?

NARRATOR ONE: The nomination people, Mortal's people.

NARRATOR TWO: The watch of the living and the dead! *(Multitudes in the square. Cheers, applause. Pennants. Arches of triumph pop up all over the place.)*

MORTAL *(aspiring candidate to the municipal council. The voice of the first line has become authoritarian):* I . . . (*but there are defects in the microphone, in the radio. First like "static," to such a point that you can hear only one syllable, then the dial goes through all the stations. Sharp whistle.)*

(Singing commercial) Candado Soap leaves your clothes *(spoken, a feeble voice)* or in the Gentleman of the R *(intellectual's voice)* Wallraf-Richartz-Museum *(spoken)* and in a situation that is internal ext *(sung, Ella Fitzgerald)* in the moon.

MORTAL *(continuing the speech):* I, suh *(but the "static" returns).*

NARRATOR TWO *(afraid):* Looks like the gods are against him. He can't even begin his message.

NARRATOR ONE *(a quick giggle):* Message? For there to be a message *(repeating something he doesn't understand, and that he's just read somewhere)* there must be: number one, intentionality; two, a consciousness of the transmitter; three, a code; four.

MORTAL *(continuing his speech):* I, son of this Province, on this day have received the nomination as candidate to the municipal council of Camagüey, the loveliest land that human eyes have ever seen, to occupy a position in the government of the Republic *(applause).* Others will say that . . .

NARRATOR ONE *(erudite):* The parts of a speech are known: introduction, thesis, antithesis, refutation, and summary.

MORTAL: It's easy to promise prosperity before you're in power; for us power will not be a triumph but a sacrifice, just as the Nation is an altar, not a pedestal. We will confront those who waste and stake the national treasury in risky pacts or disturbing and reckless exchanges with planned finance and welfare programs for our peasants which includes the building of cheap housing, roads, schools, and medical aid, not to forget school breakfast *(applause),* the creation of dance centers, circuses, cockfights, fairs *(applause)* as you have all requested with unanimous enthusiasm.

NARRATOR ONE *(laughing at* MORTAL *for using the word enthusiasm without knowing its root):* Listen to that!

MORTAL *(after listening to him):* Yes, with unanimous enthusiasm, all you illustrious citizens of this glorious and twice heroic town. The voice of rebellion *(in that moment a dog crosses the square where the meeting's taking place, howling like a condemned soul out of Dante's Hell, among applause and cheers, while* HELP, MERCY, *and* CLEMENCY *scream and lose their feathers.)*

HELP, MERCY, CLEMENCY: Watch out! He has rabies!

NARRATOR ONE *(priestly):* Canis hydrophobus, Dominus Tecum!

HELP, MERCY, CLEMENCY: Amen!

NARRATOR TWO: Aha, those vipers again, those venomous poisons, fresh, newly bathed, bleached salmon and wearing zebra-skin boots, I knew I smelled Camels and Shoulton Old Spice. There they are, after perpetrating the most bloodcurdling crime in Camagüeyan history, the most ignoble betrayal, a fratricide that's so . . . I cannot find the adjective.

HELP, MERCY, CLEMENCY *(witches' cackles before a concoction of vinegar and salty toads).*

HELP: Poor devil, he doesn't understand a thing. He has no discrimination whatsoever. Look, it's enough to enumerate in one stroke all your errors: they are colossal, dropsical, whale-sized. Look, it's enough to point out four *(sure of himself, an academic reading his paper):* error number one, concerning the material being:

MERCY: We are neither fresh nor newly bathed, since there's not a drop of water in the whole town and we merely wiped ourselves with a rag dipped in alcohol. On the other hand, our dazzling wigs, which all are admiring as they ought, are not salmon colored as in the naïve appraisal you have uttered, but rather grated carrot color, which is not the same.

HELP: Error number two, concerning the material peripheral being:

CLEMENCY: It is neither Camels, a cigarette we loathe for its verbal allusion known to us all and which reminds us of the nickname of our childhood, nor is it Shoulton Old Spice, but rather Fleur de Racaille de Caron: *en perfumes on sait très bien à quel saint se vouer.*

HELP: Error number three, concerning the phrasing of the insult and propriety in the use of words, since each one, as we know, has its own meaning—which is what excludes all synonymy—and this can neither be changed nor transferred.

MERCY: In fact, it has nothing to do with a fraticide, since no kindred ties us to the one you believed torn to pieces; we have not perpetrated it, we shall simply be the "intellectual authors," and, on the other hand, the adjectives bloodcurdling, ignoble, belong to a past aesthetic . . . but let's not enter into details.

HELP *(radio announcer, angel of the apocalypse with a tenor sax, entangled in bunches of ribbons, haloed, barefoot on a sword):* And lastly, the fourth error, the least forgivable, concerning the spiral quality of the time of the being:

CLEMENCY: The famous crime, the fratricide of which you speak, in spite of having been the theme of line number two, we now being on three, has not yet taken place. It would be inane to think that the numerical order corresponds to the time sequence; that is, we have not yet revealed anything, the senator to whom Dolores's destiny will be bound has not yet appeared, since in this meeting he announces his aspiration to be a councilman. Lastly, even if this had taken place after Dolores's death, we would not have celebrated by coming to a meeting, but instead would have remained close to her body.

NARRATOR TWO: Well then, what the hell are you doing here?

HELP, MERCY, CLEMENCY: The same as always—that is—taking care of Dolores—faithful and eternal as we are—moral support—lads-in-waiting—etc., etc.

NARRATOR TWO: Ah, then Dolores is coming to the meeting?

HELP: She's coming, but not exactly to complain, like us, about the lack of water, indeed not to make any complaint at all; she's coming simply because the Spaniard promised (in line one, since that one does take place before this moment, and just before)

NARRATOR TWO: And the spiral?

HELP *(without answering him, looks out of the corner of his eye, which is elongated by a golden line):* if he wins the election for councilman which of course will happen, in order for the poem to come true step by step *(which is already beginning to bore us),* and without obstacles *(for which I beseech you end this line right now)*

NARRATOR ONE: It shall be done in a few lines.

HELP: to take her to Camagüey, and what's more, if we understand correctly (since, in parenthesis, that damn peninsular accent is a pain in the neck), he promised that once there, he was going to ask for her hand, since he can't mean cut off her hand as far as we know since it has nothing to do with the cutting off of hands as with delinquent slaves, which she isn't. So that. But let's finish.

NARRATOR TWO: Dolores, there she is!

DOLORES *(puffing, from all that running):* What a trip, holy cow! Bouncing like the dancing turkey in the circus on an electric iron! I've been bounced around in a tobacco cart drawn by two oxen over hill and dale, night and day, but I've finally arrived. And it's worth it. I'm the first, the founder of Mortal's Fan Club. I'll have six hundred pictures of him in my room, a lock of his blond hair in a locket. *(And changing her tone.)* Boy, am I hungry. Anybody have a sandwich for me?

NARRATOR ONE: Nobody, Nobody. No cheese for Jerry. Not even a scrap of ham for Tom. Tens of thousands like you have come. From the most out-of-the-way places. Haitians and Jamaicans in railway caravans. Singing and leaping from car to car, on sacks of white sugar. The trains like wakes of fire in the night, whistling, repeating Mor-tal-Pé-rez!

MORTAL *(in complete possession of the microphones and the public, under a rain of purple lampoons):* There'll be more than you've seen since the Deluge!

(Last applause and cheers. Help, Mercy, and Clemency demand improvements, pinch each other, take off their eyebrows, and prick each other. The dog passes by again.)

HELP, MERCY, CLEMENCY: Water! Water! Water! *(And they squirm and do somersaults in the sand, they swallow red stones and slobber, the thirsty things—they think they see turrets, an oasis.)*

ON WHERE LIES TRUE GRANDEUR

At Dolores's house

NARRATOR ONE *(shaking a maraca):* He won! He won!

NARRATOR TWO *(does a somersault, falls off the hammock):* What's up?

NARRATOR ONE: Oh, I woke you up. It's just that I'm a little ahead of time. We have to shout in a few lines, at a party.

NARRATOR TWO: Are we going to a party? What about destiny? And Dolores?

NARRATOR ONE: Precisely, we've occupied all the previous lines pushing them aside with our empty talk, but since they are the essential theme of the poem we must make ourselves scarce.

NARRATOR TWO *(a bit scared):* What do you mean, make ourselves scarce? Not appear anymore?

NARRATOR ONE *(clarifying):* We will appear, yes, but as anonymous servants: hairdressers, dress designers, people who don't add up to being. As for the three Etruscan conductors of souls, who were yesterday a marvel . . . *(Without any transition: creole country dance. Guitars. The party people, the Matamoros Trio arrive; rum with lemon. The sallow girls break their hips.)* . . . are today Dolores's dressmaker, pastry cook, and antique dealer: scissor, poison, and termite. *(The din approaches.)* Let's go! Now's when you have to shout! With feeling! Allegro vivace!

NARRATOR ONE and TWO *(allegro vivace):* He won! Mortal Pérez won!

DOLORES *(very lyrical):* Open doors and windows! The first to go are these shoes which were so tight on me, this shoulder bag, these pans. And now: bring in the water!

HELP: But honey, you know there's not a single drop in this damn town!

DOLORES: That's not the water I mean. Peroxide water: we're gonna be blonds!

MERCY: We're gonna be white!

HELP: We're gonna be pale!

CLEMENCY: Blond like corn, like light beer!

DOLORES: We got to pack. Yes, we're moving to a better house. In a fancy neighborhood. We're going to Camagüey, to Havana. In a sleeping-car suite. Call the dressmaker, say it's Dolores Rondón calling . . . Dolores Rondón . . . what a name for a councilman's wife . . . Dolores de Pérez . . . Lola Pérez Rondón . . . There's nothing you can do about it. We are the name we're born with. *(In the party, someone steps on a dog; it howls.)*

MERCY: Here's the dressmaker!

DRESSMAKER *(who is Help in disguise. In her new metamorphosis, the Fate comes with enormous scissors, her head shaved, like a mannequin, wearing a headband—a measuring tape. Lines of black stitches run across her chest.):* Light and Progress!

DOLORES: Oh, it seems to me I know you. Where have we met before? Now I know: at the wake of . . .

DRESSMAKER *(takes a step back, to get her off the track):* Me at a wake? Never. Chrysanthemums nauseate me, candles make me choke, coffee attacks my liver, sleepless nights make me sallow, etcetera.

DOLORES: I must be wrong then. But let's talk about the important things, about what they're wearing in Havana: we want bottle green silk, the kind of fur that makes you cough, necklaces, gloves, hats with flowers, and little birds and those sunglasses you can see through without being seen.

DRESSMAKER: Like old crossbones!

DOLORES: What?

DRESSMAKER: Like the cross-eyed, who cover their eyes, but they see, they keep seeing, they see too much.

DOLORES: Oh, right. *(shouting)* Hey what's happening, isn't there anything to drink in this house? A daiquiri for the dressmaker!

(Cheers to victory, to MORTAL.*)*

PRIDE AND ARROGANCE

In the capital of the province

HAIRDRESSER: There must be method to your madness. There must be method. Change lovers, Dolores. Hair color. Houses. But not gods. Your speaking high-class and not mumbling like a councilman's wife should, putting in two gold teeth for pure show and without ever having had the slightest toothache, drinking scotch on the rocks and Tom Collinses, pretending to be blind so as not to recognize your friends, going to bed with your blond servants, abandoning the poor Spaniard to the dizzying heights of the mayor's office, where, as everybody knows, he follows your advice and recruits an army of mambo dancers in your image and likeness from the farthest corners of the province . . . all this is permitted. All of it. But there must be method. You must keep up the appearance of method. There must be method within the lack of method. I'm tripping on my words. I mean that you mustn't forget the glass of water, the sunflowers, the roosters. I mean you mustn't forget the offerings to the gods.

DOLORES *(with her head in a plastic dryer. Operatic. With pride and arrogance.):* What's with the servants? First that old bag the antique dealer snickering at me, all because I asked for twisted chairs and a Simmons mattress. Then toad eyes, the housekeeper, who didn't recognize me in a two-piece suit. Then the pastry cook with her rice pudding *(and on a long high note);* I want a Banana Split! And now you, the Attila of hairdressing, after mangling my tresses, my beautiful straight hair, my skull, my whole head; after applying stinking pomades to straighten it, electric dryers to curl it, massages to straighten it again, curling irons; after leaving me scabby, scalped, bald as an egg . . . now it's method. Now it's saints. Now that they're preparing another banquet, another candidacy, another partyswitching, another caucus *(she's complaining, the poor thing)* . . . How much further, Catalina, will you carry the abuse of our forbearance? Madness, Method. Loaded words. Which of the two has the bigger mouth? Which swallows the other? Does madness swallow, digest, expel method? Does method gag on madness? Do both devour, fear, flee each other? I don't know. I only know that the kitchen pots are under the bed and the chamber pots on the stove. That's the method. I only know that you've left me bald.

THE HAIRDRESSER *(almost crying):* No, Dolores. You've had too much to drink. Bloody Marys unhinge you. It's not true about your hair. We straightened it, we made it blond and purple like a piece of cloud, then we turned it into flames. You weren't satisfied. You wanted concentric ringlets, upside-down towers, ship prows. You wanted a Flavian hairstyle. You said: "I am Titi." Hence the aluminum dryers, the high voltage, the muriatic acids, the curling iron, the stench. That's the way of method. You wanted to be a bird, a gazelle, you loathed your slanty eyes. Hence the spinach mascara, the baby pineapple cream, the simultaneous massages, and the Helena Rubinstein beauty sunfluid. We did what we could. That's the way of method. The well-rounded, clean, classified, filed, alphabetically ordered way, in the belly of method. That's how it is.

DOLORES *(Valkyric):* No! You won't stop me, you won't tie me down like a goat. If you don't change, you get stuck. I'll keep moving ahead, always ahead, like a train. This very day I'll pack my bags. I'm going. From here to Havana. This dusty city without ships, I without Chinese restaurants, I can't stand it any longer. I want chop suey, fried rice, chicken with almonds, glazed pork. I'll go wherever the wind takes me. To Peking, to Hong Kong. Bald as you've left me. Cross-eyed, lame: no matter what, I'll reach my destiny on time, like an American train.

Life is a soap dish; if you don't fall, you slip. I'm going. We'll win the municipal, provincial, senatorial, national elections. I'll be the wife of a senator. I'll have more and more admirers: That's Hip Power for you!

And to you, servants who refuse to follow me, who despise victory, who want to stay buried here like the snake in its cave, to you I leave these blond pieces of straw, my last hairs, those wires you've twisted over my head; you who despise the capital, the swell life,

POWER AND PROMINENCE

you who in the eleventh hour abandon me, in the hour of the great election, the soya beans, and the egg roll, I free you of job and wages. Faithful, the only among a whole staff of boisterous, demanding, angry, irritated, and mad servants, my three advisors follow me: the dressmaker, pastry cook, and antique dealer. The elegance, and sweetness, of past and present. Three sacrificing souls. At least there'll be pastries, frozen meringues, and Mandarin oranges. I'm going to the ships. Bald, lame, but to Havana.

(The drumming of typewriters. Traffic lights. Ships. Sirens fading in and out.)

NARRATOR ONE: Do you hear it? Havana. She wanted it, she herself hastens her own destiny, jumps toward it like a fish toward the shore. She wants Havana, she wants the swell life, she wants, as she says, to imitate our illustrious Cuban classic, the adventurous Countess of Merlín. Well here is the beginning of the end: here's Havana!

DOLORES *(with the emphasis of all political apotheosis):* Faithful servants, dear shadows of myself. Let's begin the senatorial stage with a bang. I knew I'd be a senator's wife. There are the votes, there is Mortal acclaimed by the caucuses, the parties, the people themselves! The days of the province, the dust, the rooster, are way behind us. The bathtub. I want a bath. A bathtub full of rum. And then they can fan me with giant leaves. This is the life the four of us deserve. Today we'll throw gold coins to the little black boys! Bring the wig, the tightest corset, the spangle, the orchid that arrived this morning from Miami. I'm going to the Presidential Palace! *(The telephone rings.)*

THE DRESSMAKER *(answering the phone):* She's not in, Mrs. Senator is not in! *(She snickers, hangs up with a bang.)*

NARRATOR TWO *(remorseful):* You got to admit it. Dolores has reached her baroque period. She's outdoing herself, beating her own record. This is all going to end like a Chinaman's spree. Her reading has done her a lot of damage. It's driven her insane. It's okay for her to learn English, which, in parenthesis, she speaks like a Haitian; it's okay for her to order perfumes and frozen flowers from Miami, but the Cuban classics have been the strongest of all. What digestion. There she is, having herself fanned by two fat Negresses after a rum bath. Just like the "Countess of Berlín," she says. Good God!

TRANSLATED BY SUZANNE JILL LEVINE

REINALDO ARENAS

from BEFORE NIGHT FALLS

THE FLIGHT

There was no bathroom in the cell—it was outside—and the detainees were constantly asking for permission to go. The police officer stood by the cell door, padlock in hand, to watch the others. On one of those occasions, while the officer was waiting by the cell door, another officer arrived and announced that he had brought hot espresso, a privilege in Cuba, where coffee is rationed at three ounces a month per person. The announcement started a great commotion at the station; all the police officers rushed to the coveted Thermos bottle. The officer guarding the gate also went, leaving the open padlock on the gate. I quickly unbolted the lock and, crouching, escaped from prison.

I ran out through the back door, which led to the shore, freed myself of my clothes, and jumped into the water. I was a good swimmer then. I swam away from shore and to Patricio Lumumba Beach, near my aunt's house. Once there, I saw a friend with whom I had had a few erotic adventures. I told him what had happened, and he managed to get me a pair of shorts from one of the lifeguards. Dressed that way, I immediately showed up at my aunt's house. She was absolutely flabbergasted to see me there; it was only a short time since I had been arrested and taken away in a patrol car. I told her it had all been a mistake that was cleared up right away and I only needed to pay a fine; I had come home to get the money. But my money was no longer there; my aunt had taken it. I demanded, somewhat violently, that she return it. A little intimidated, she gave me back only half of it.

I ran toward the beach to meet my black friend, but it was swarming with policemen. They were evidently searching for me. Luckily, it did not occur to them at first to look for me at home, which enabled me to pick up the money and destroy everything there that might compromise me. The friend who had gotten me the shorts hid me in one of the booths at the beach, then checked my house and confirmed that it was surrounded by policemen with guard dogs. He told me to jump into the water and hide behind a buoy, where the dogs would not be able to find me. I stayed there all day, and in the evening my friend signaled me to come out of the water. He bought me a pizza with his own money; mine was completely soaked. He then hid me in the lifeguard's booth. The following day the beach was crawling with policemen looking for me; I could not come out of my hiding place. My friend provided me with an inner tube, a can of beans, and a bottle of rum. In the evening we walked through the pines to la Concha Beach. He had also gotten me a pair of swim fins, and the only solution seemed to be that I leave the country on an inner tube. Before jumping in, I hid my money under some rocks near the shore. My friend and I said good-bye. "Good luck, my brother," he said. He was crying.

I tied the tube to my neck with a piece of rope. He had fitted the tube with a gunnysack in such a way that I could sit on it. A small jute bag held the bottle of rum and the can of black beans. I stowed the bag securely, and got into the water. I had to make my escape from the very beach where I had spent the most beautiful years of my youth.

As I was swimming out, the ocean was turning increasingly rougher: it was the choppy November surf, announcing the arrival of winter. All night I swam out, but at the mercy of the waves my progress was slow. When I was about three or four miles away from shore, I realized it would be difficult to get anywhere. On the high seas I had no way of opening the bottle, and my legs and joints were almost frozen.

Suddenly a boat appeared in the darkness, heading straight at me. I jumped off and submerged so I could hide under the tube. The boat stopped about twenty yards from me and extended a huge claw—it looked like a giant crab—which plunged into the water. Apparently it was a sand hauler trying to dig up sand. I heard voices and laughter, but they did not see me.

Clearly there was no point in going on. Farther out I saw a line of lights: the coast guard, fishermen, or more sand haulers. They formed a sort of wall on the horizon. The waves were getting rougher and rougher. I had to try to get back.

I remember seeing something shiny in the deep and was afraid a shark might take a bite out of my legs, which, of course, I tried to keep out of the water. A few hours before dawn I realized that the whole thing was absurd, that even the tube was a hindrance; that I could almost get to the United States faster by swimming freely than by riding on that tube, without oars or direction. I got off the tube, and swam for more than three hours toward shore, the bag containing the bottle and can of beans tied to my waist. I was almost paralyzed and my greatest fear now was to get cramps and drown.

I reached the coast at Jaimanitas Beach and noticed some empty buildings. I hid in one of them; never had I felt such intense cold or such deep loneliness. I had failed and would be arrested any minute now. There was only one way for me to escape: suicide. I smashed the bottle of rum and with the pieces of broken glass slashed my wrists. I thought it was the end, of course, and lay down in a corner of the empty house, slowly losing consciousness. I felt that this was death.

Around ten o'clock the following day I woke up thinking I was in another world. But I was in the same place where I had attempted, unsuccessfully, to end my life. Though I had bled profusely, at some point the bleeding had stopped. With the shards of the broken bottle I opened the can of beans; they restored my strength somewhat. Then I washed my cuts in the sea. The inner tube had also washed ashore, not too far away.

I started walking along the beach, without any clear sense of direction, and suddenly came upon a group of men, close-shorn, lying on the sand. They looked at me a little surprised but did not say a word. I realized they were forced laborers, prisoners at a farm in the Flores section. I had walked by them barefoot and with cuts on my arms; they could not have thought I was a mere bather. Finally I arrived at La Concha, and recovered the hidden money.

On my way to the place where I had hidden the money, I heard someone calling me: it was my black friend, who was signaling me to come. I quickly told him what had happened, and he said we could still go at once to Guantánamo; it was his hometown and he knew the area well. Lying under the pines, he traced a map of Caimanera in the sand and told me how I could reach the U.S. naval base.

It was imperative now to get clothes to wear. I saw one of my cousins at the beach, and told him I needed some. He warned me that the police were looking all over for me. The stupidity of the police was incredible; they were searching in vain for me in the very same area where I was. My cousin said he would try to get me something. He left the girl he was with and soon came back with a complete outfit. It was a voluntary, unexpected gesture of kindness I found quite surprising.

I dressed quickly and went with my black friend to his home in Santos Suárez. It was a huge house, full of glass cabinets. He cut my hair very short, almost to the skull; I looked like a different person. When I saw myself in the mirror, I was shocked. Instead of my long hair I now had short hair parted in the middle. He also exchanged the shirt that my cousin had given me for a rougher-looking one. According to him, this was the only way I could avoid being arrested before reaching Guantánamo.

With the money I had, and a little more that his grandmother gave him, we went to the train station. It was not easy to buy tickets for Santiago de Cuba or Guantánamo; you always had to reserve way ahead. But he managed to get them by talking to an employee and slipping him a few pesos.

Again I was in one of those slow, steamy trains to Santiago de Cuba. The black guy immediately made friends with everyone who shared our seat; he had bought a bottle of rum and started drinking. At some point he told me it was a good idea to socialize with everyone around to escape notice.

He spent the whole trip, which lasted three days, drinking and sharing with the others, laughing and telling jokes. He quickly made friends with other black men, some of whom were in fact very beautiful. I would have liked to get off the train and make love with him in any hotel, the way we used to at Monte Barreto; in moments of danger I have always felt the need to have someone close to me. He said it would be difficult to get a hotel room in Santiago, but that we could perhaps find accommodations in Guantánamo.

At Santiago we took a bus for Guantánamo, but first we ate some of those croquettes sold at cafeterias in Cuba and jokingly called "palatial" croquettes because they had a tendency to stick to your palate in such a way that it was almost impossible to dislodge them.

We arrived at Guantánamo, a town that seemed horrendous to me, flatter and more provincial even than Holguín. The black man took me to a tenement, which looked like a den of criminals. He told me to take off all my clothes because he had acquired another set even more rustic than mine. He also asked me to give him all my money; it made no sense for me to take that Cuban money with me if I was going to enter United States territory. I did not like the idea, but I had no choice. He took me to the terminal from which I could take the bus to Caimanera, and refused to accompany me on this trip. He had given me all the necessary instructions: to get off at the checkpoint, turn right toward the river, walk along the riverbank and when the lights of the airport became visible, hide in the bushes till nightfall, swim across the river and proceed on the other side until reaching the ocean; then stay hidden around there all day, and the following night, jump in and swim to the naval base.

It was not hard to remain unnoticed inside the bus; the black man had been right in disguising me the way he did. After I got off, to avoid being seen I walked almost on all fours for many hours. Around midnight, while I was crawling through those wild bushes, startled quail and other birds would fly off. I crawled on. Suddenly I heard a thunderous noise; it was the river. It was a great joy to look at the water. My black friend had not deceived me; the river was there. I continued walking along the riverbank; it was very swampy. I still had in my hand a piece of bread the black man had told me not to eat until I was ready to jump in. At dawn I finally saw the lights of the airport; they seemed like party lights to me. They would go on and off, as if they were beckoning me. It was time to get into the water.

While walking next to the river I kept hearing crackling sounds. I do not know why, but it seemed to me that the Moon was telling me not to go into those waters. I continued walking until I got to a place where I did not hear those crackling sounds anymore, and looked for a good spot to enter the river. Suddenly, strange green lights began appearing in the bushes. They looked like lightning, except they did not come down from the sky but sprang out of the ground, next to the tree trunks. I kept on walking and seeing green lights. A few seconds later I heard machine-gun fire; the bullets seemed to be grazing me. I later found out that those green lights were signals; they were infrared lights. The guards had discovered that someone was trying to cross the border; they were trying to locate and, of course, to exterminate the intruder. I ran to a tree with a dense canopy and climbed as high as I could, hugging the trunk. Cars came, full of soldiers with dogs, looking for me. All night they searched, at times rather close to my hiding place. At last, they left.

I spent the whole day and the following night up in the tree. It was hard to get down without being seen, especially since the area was already on alert. At dusk I finally climbed down. Tired, I had to gather all my strength to get back to Guantánamo, and from there plan a different, perhaps less hazardous, escape route that would get me to the naval base. I dragged myself through the mud and, once close to the highway, fell asleep in the shrubbery. Early the next day I washed my face and cleaned my clothes as best I could, returned to the number 1 checkpoint, and took the bus back to Guantánamo. I arrived in town with no idea where to look for my black friend, and wandered aimlessly through the streets, a dangerous proposition in my case. I had no money. At the Guantánamo train terminal I came across the black guy. He looked scared; evidently he thought I was either dead or at the naval base. He told me that it would be impossible to make another try, that the place he had directed me to was really the best one, and that every place was being watched much more closely now, according to his friends. He told me I had been very lucky after all, because some boxes that I mentioned having seen were mines, and if I had stepped on one, it would have blown me to bits. But I refused to give up; a return meant accepting failure. I decided to try again. The area was under closer surveillance, but I had nothing to lose. It had been absurd to listen to the Moon. This time I entered the water and by the light of the Moon I was able to see where the crackling sounds had come from: the river was infested with alligators. I have never seen so many sinister-looking animals in such a small expanse of water. They were just waiting there for me to get in so they could devour me. It was impossible to cross that river. Again I returned to Guantánamo covered with mud. No doubt the bus driver thought I was a coast-guardman working for State Security who had been newly transferred to that region.

For three days I walked around Guantánamo, without any food. I didn't have a penny, and continued to sleep at the train terminal. I never saw the black man again. I met some young men at the terminal who were planning to go by train to Havana as stowaways. They told me all one had to do was to hide in the men's room when the conductor came by. I had no other choice, so I decided to make the trip that way.

We boarded the train and the three of us hid in the men's room when the conductor came. It was not long before they became sexually aroused, so I was able to enjoy those excited guys while the train moved slowly through the hills of Oriente. The train would stop at every town and I would get off. Then the train continued, and whenever the conductor passed by, about every four hours, we would hide in the men's room, they would get excited, and those beautiful legs would get entangled with mine. I told them I was a draft evader trying to return home to Havana. They were real draft evaders who wanted to go to Havana because they thought it would be easier to escape notice there than in Guantánamo, their hometown. At one of the stops where we got off, Adrián, one of the young men, gave me an ID. He told me he had another one, and that it might come in handy. The ID had his picture on it, but those photos are so unclear and impersonal that they could look like anyone. From then on I was Adrián Faustino Sotolongo. At Cacocún I left the train and started walking toward Holguín. It was a long stretch. I finally hitched a ride on a truck full of laborers who did not ask any questions. I arrived home at daybreak.

I was returning home alone, persecuted, defeated. My mother opened the door; she screamed at the sight of me, but I asked her to keep quiet. She began to cry silently, and my grandmother fell to her knees and started praying, asking God to please save me. My other aunts said that I should hide under the bed. My mother brought me a piece of chicken and said it pained her greatly to see me like this, under the bed like a dog, hiding to eat. All this distressed me so much I could not have a bite, even though for several days I had had no food at all.

My grandmother was still on her knees, asking God to help me. I had never felt so close to her; she knew that only a miracle could save me. At some point there was an opportunity for me to talk with her, but I did not know what to say. I had not seen her since my grandfather died; she had loved him very much even though he beat her quite often. When she came into the room for a moment, I crawled out from under the bed and hugged her. She told me she could not live without my grandfather Antonio, who had been such a good man. I cried with her; he had beaten her almost every week, but they had lived together for fifty years. Evidently, there had been a great love between them. My grandmother had suddenly aged.

The following day my mother and I left for Havana. Vidal, one of my uncles by marriage, walked us to the train station and lent us some money. I had hoped that perhaps Olga, to whom I had given the address of the Abreu brothers, had been able to make some contacts abroad on my behalf. I had already sent her the Mayday telegram we had agreed upon: "Send me the flower book." She knew that meant I was asking them to get me out by any means.

I was able to sleep on the train. I had never taken a train trip with my mother, and never traveled in a sleeper. She said, "How sad to take such a beautiful trip under these circumstances." My mother was always complaining about everything, but this time she was right. I thought about how beautiful it would have been to enjoy the scenery without the feeling of being persecuted. How pleasant it would have been to travel at my mother's side if I had not been in such a predicament. The simplest things now acquired extraordinary value for me. During the entire trip my mother tried to persuade me to give myself up; she said it would be best for me. She was telling me that one of her neighbors who had been sentenced to thirty years had been released after only ten, and now was free and walked by her house every day, singing. I could not see myself singing in front of my mother's house after ten years in jail; this was not a really promising future. I wanted to get out of that hellhole in any way possible.

When we arrived at the Havana train terminal I was arrested by two undercover cops. My mother was terrified. Her skinny body was shaking. I took her thin hands in mine and told her to wait for me, that everything would be all right. The policemen took me to a small room and asked a few questions. I told them that I had come from Oriente and that my name was Adrián Faustino Sotolongo, and showed them my train ticket and ID. They told me I resembled someone they were looking for who had escaped from a police station in Havana. I answered that it would not be logical for me to be the suspect because I had just arrived in Havana, and the person they were looking for would obviously try to get out of Havana, not come to the city. My reply made sense and I had produced proof of a different identity, so they let me go, after having taken God knows what measurements of my neck. My mother was out there trembling, looking more pathetic by the minute. I told her that we had to separate, that she should stay with my aunt Mercedita, who lived in East Havana. I would call and let the phone ring once. If she received that signal, it meant that she should return to the terminal, where we could meet to work out some plan.

I would try to hide in the home of a friend. I had hopes that if somebody talked with the French ambassador, perhaps he could arrange for me to be granted political asylum at the French embassy; perhaps the ambassador could hide me in his home and obtain an exit permit for me. After all, all my books had been published in France. I was hoping that my mother would go to the home of a French citizen who had been one of my professors, and with whom we had established a certain friendship; it would be easy for him to speak with the ambassador. We had left Holguín with a letter addressed to the ambassador; it was a crazy idea, but perhaps it might work.

I called on Ismael Lorenzo, who lived with his wife. He was very generous and told me I could stay with them. He and I had planned our escape many times, thinking of the Guantánamo naval base. He said it was a miracle that I did not get caught, because when the infrared rays send their signal, the army men do not stop until they have captured their man. He explained to me the real advantage of those infrared rays, that the signal is triggered by heat and the heat source can be any living creature near the detectors. The search team probably thought it had been an animal and therefore had given up.

Lorenzo's home was under surveillance because he had submitted an application for a permit to leave the country, and the Committee for the Defense of the Revolution paid him frequent "friendly" visits. I did not want to endanger his position. After spending a night there, I went to see Reinaldo Gómez Ramos. He looked at me, terrified. He knew of my escape, of course, and told me it would be absolutely impossible for him to take me in, that I had to leave immediately.

I returned to the terminal and called my mother. We agreed to meet at a nearby park. My uncle Carlos had arrived from Oriente; he was aware of my situation. Carlos was a member of the Communist Party, but for him the family came first and he was good to me. He offered to go with my mother to see the French professor and show him my letter.

They returned a few hours later. They had seen the professor, who was very responsive and within a couple of hours had taken my mother and Carlos to the ambassador. But the ambassador's reply was absolutely negative; he said he could do nothing for me, though he kept my letter. That was the news they brought me.

I gave my mother and Carlos the address of the Abreu brothers. It was absurd for me to remain at the bus station; that was the center of police activity, where they asked for everyone's ID. At night, when I saw the patrol cars, I had the feeling that they were all looking for me. I decided to hide in Lenin Park; it was a park used for many official events and perhaps the last place where the police would look for a political fugitive. I wrote a short message to Juan Abreu. I gave him a date and time when we could meet on the left side of the amphitheater in the park. The amphitheater was surrounded by bushes where I could hide safely.

I did not have to explain much to Juan about my plans to escape with Olga's help. I told him that perhaps she would send someone over from France to get me out of the country. Abreu looked at me and replied, "That person is already here; he arrived three days ago. We were all desperately looking for you. I stopped by your aunt's and she almost had me put in jail." He added that he would see the person the following day; that he seemed to be a very intelligent Frenchman who spoke perfect Spanish.

The Abreu home was being watched closely; everybody knew they were among my best friends. The Frenchman had shown up there with a bottle of perfume, and said that he had a message from Olga about the "flower book." He had managed to give the hotel police the slip and, without knowing Havana, after taking three or four different buses to confuse the police, had reached the home of the Abreus. Juan Abreu told him the truth, that I was a fugitive and my whereabouts were unknown. The Frenchman's entry permit allowed him to stay a few more days. I had reappeared at just the right time.

My friends in Paris, Jorge and Margarita, informed by Olga of my situation, had decided that it was necessary to immediately find someone unknown to the Castro regime who could go to Cuba and try to get me out. They had contacted Joris Lagarde, the young son of friends of theirs, who was an adventurer and spoke perfect Spanish. He had traveled all over South and Central America hunting for treasure supposedly buried by Spanish conquistadors or lying at the bottom of the sea. He theorized that certain galleons had gone down off the coast of Maracaibo and that there was plenty of gold and sunken treasure just waiting for an expert diver. He was an excellent swimmer and also knew a lot about sailing. Lagarde was the right person to come to my rescue. Jorge and Margarita had purchased a sailboat and a compass, and Olga added some hallucinogenic drugs to keep me high. They bought Lagarde tickets to Mexico, as a cover-up, with a stopover in Cuba. He was to explain to the authorities that he was going to take part in sailing races in Mexico, and that he would like to train along the Cuban shoreline. That plan would justify the boat. He had arrived in Havana at the same time I was attempting to escape through the Guantánamo naval base.

Around midnight Lagarde and Juan arrived at Lenin Park. He was really a fearless young man and did all he could to get the sailboat into Cuba, but the airport authorities told him that although he was allowed to visit Cuba, the sailboat had to remain in custody until the time of his departure for Mexico. A boat was, of course, a forbidden mode of transport in Cuba. Only high officials were allowed to use boats, and some of them had left in those boats for the United States.

Again my hopes to leave Cuba were dashed. Joris Lagarde gave me his own lighter and all the foreign cigarettes he had, as well as the compass and the boat's sail. He promised he would go to

France and come back for me somehow. We talked all night. He felt bad about leaving me stranded and told me we would meet again in four days, before his departure.

The next day Juan brought me a razor, a small mirror, Homer's *Iliad,* and a small notebook so that I could write. I immediately wrote a communiqué that began: "Havana, Lenin Park, November 15, 1974." It was a desperate appeal, addressed to the International Red Cross, the UN, UNESCO, and the countries still privileged to hear the truth. I wanted to report all the persecution I was being subjected to, and began as follows: "For a long time I have been the victim of a sinister persecution by the Cuban regime." I went on to list the censorship and harsh treatment that we Cuban writers had suffered, and to name all the writers who had been executed; the case of Nelson Rodríguez, the imprisonment of René Ariza, the fact that the poet Manuel Ballagas was held incommunicado. In one paragraph I explained the desperate situation I was in and how, as persecution was escalating, I was writing those lines in hiding, while waiting for the most sinister and criminal state apparatus to put an end to my existence. And I stated: *I want now to affirm that what I am saying here is the truth, even though under torture I might later be forced to say the opposite.*

Lagarde arrived at the appointed day and hour to see me, and I gave him the communiqué with instructions to have it printed in every publication possible. I also gave him a letter to Margarita and Jorge, asking them to publish all the manuscripts I had sent them in which I openly denounced the Cuban regime. The Abreu brothers also took advantage of Lagarde's visit to get as much of their work as possible out of the country. We agreed that I would stay in hiding as long as feasible, until Lagarde could return and rescue me somehow.

He returned to France with the news of my situation, and all my friends mounted a campaign on my behalf. The document was published in Paris in *Le Figaro,* and also in Mexico City. I had conceived the idea that Margarita and Olga send telegrams with my signature to various government officials in Cuba, telling them that I had arrived safely. Thus, while I slept in the culverts at Lenin Park, Nicolás Guillén received a telegram reading: "Arrived OK. Thanks for your help. Reinaldo." The telegram was sent from Vienna.

All this confused them for a week, but then they realized that I had not escaped, and they tightened their surveillance of my friends. The Abreus' home was surrounded and the terror led them to unearth the manuscripts of all my novels and burn them, together with all the unpublished work they had written—approximately twelve books. Nicolás and José felt they were being so closely watched that they did not dare come to see me in the park.

Several of my friends who were now informers (Hiram Prado was one) had called on Nicolás Abreu where he worked as a movie projectionist, to inquire about me. The police not only were watching José; they threatened to put him in jail if he did not disclose my whereabouts. The person directing the group in charge of capturing me was a lieutenant by the name of Víctor.

Once an undercover cop sat next to José Abreu on the bus. The cop started to praise the United States and then added that Reinaldo Arenas was his favorite author. José just changed seats, without saying a word. When the surveillance intensified, Juan would go to the place where we had agreed to meet and instead of waiting for me, he would just leave me something to eat.

I started writing my memoirs in the notebooks that Juan had brought me. Under the title "Before Night Falls" I would write all day until dark, waiting for the other darkness that would come when the police eventually found me. I had to hurry to get my writing done before my world finally darkened, before I was thrown in jail. That manuscript, of course, was lost, as was almost everything I had written in Cuba that I had not been able to smuggle out, but at the time, writing it all down was a consolation; it was a way of being with my friends when I was no longer among them.

I knew what a prison was like. René Ariza had gone insane in one; Nelson Rodríguez had to confess everything he was ordered to and then he was executed; Jesús Castro was held in a sinister cell in La Cabaña; I knew that once there, I could write no more. I still had the compass Lagarde had given me and didn't want to part with it, although I realized the danger it posed; to me it was a kind of magic charm. The compass, always pointing north, was like a symbol: it was in that direction that I had to go, north; no matter how far away it might take me from the Island, I would always be fleeing to the north.

I also had some hallucinogenic drugs that Olga had sent me. They were wonderful; however depressed I was, if I took one of them, I would feel an intense urge to dance and sing. Sometimes at night, under the influence of those pills, I would run around among the trees, dance, sing, and climb the trees.

One night, as a result of the euphoria that those pills gave me, I dared to go as far as the park amphitheater, where none other than Alicia Alonso was dancing. I tied several branches to my body and saw Alonso dance the famous second act of *Giselle.* Afterward, as I reached the road, a car stopped all of a sudden in front of me and I realized that I had been discovered. I crossed near the improvised stage platform, which was on the water, dove in and came out on the other side of the park. A man with a gun was following me. I ran and climbed a tree, where I stayed for several days not daring to come down.

I remember that while all the cops and their dogs were searching for me in vain, one mutt stood under my tree, looking at me happily without barking, as if it did not want to let them know where I was. Three days later I came down from the tree. I was ravenously hungry; but it would have been difficult to contact

Juan. Strangely enough, on the very tree in which I had been hiding there was a poster with my name, information about me, my picture, and in large letters the heading: WANTED. From the information supplied by the police, I learned that I had a birthmark under my left ear.

After those three days of hiding, I saw Juan walking among the trees. He had dared to come to the park. He told me my situation was desperate, that in order to mislead the police he had spent the day switching buses to get to the park, and that there appeared to be no way out. Moreover, he had not heard from anyone in France, and the international scandal caused by my escape was amazing; State Security had sounded the alarm. Fidel Castro had given the order to find me immediately; in a country with such a perfect surveillance system, it was inconceivable that I had escaped from the police two months before and was still on the loose, writing documents and sending them abroad.

In water up to my shoulders, I would fish with a hook and line that Juan had brought me. I would make a little fire to cook the fish near the dam, and try to stay in the water as much as possible. It was much harder to find me that way. And even in that situation of imminent danger I had my erotic adventures with young fishermen, those always ready to have a good time with anybody who cast a promising glance at their fly. One of them insisted on taking me home—he lived nearby—so that I could meet his parents. I first thought it was because of the wristwatch I had, another present from Lagarde, but I was wrong; he simply wanted to introduce me to his family. We had dinner, had a good time, and later returned to the park.

The hardest part was the nights. It was a cold December, and I had to sleep out in the open; occasionally I would wake up soaking wet. I never slept twice in the same place. I hid in ditches full of crickets, cockroaches, and mice. Juan and I had several meeting places because a single spot would have been too dangerous.

Sometimes at night I would continue reading the *Iliad* with the help of my lighter.

In December the water behind the dam dried up completely and I sought protection against its great walls. I kept a sort of mobile library there; Juan had brought me a few more books: *From the Orinoco to the Amazon River, The Magic Mountain,* and *The Castle.* I dug a hole at the end of the dam and buried them there; I took care of those books as if they were a great treasure. I buried them in polyethylene bags, which could be found all over the country; I think they were the only item the system had produced in abundance.

While hiding in the park I got together now and then with the young fisherman I had met there; he was alarmed by the excessive surveillance of the place. He told me that, according to the police, a search was in progress for a CIA agent hiding there. He also told me that other fishermen and State Security were spreading various stories to alarm the people of the area so they would inform State Security if they saw any suspicious-looking character. They were saying that the person they were looking for had murdered an old lady, raped a little girl; in short, he was supposed to have committed such heinous crimes that anyone would inform on him. It was unbelievable that he had not been captured yet.

THE CAPTURE

Since I scarcely had eaten in the last ten days, I ventured down a path leading to a little store in the town of Calabazar with the *Iliad* under my arm. I think at that moment I felt suicidal. That, in any case, is what a friend whom I had met in the park had already told me. His name was Justo Luís, and he was a painter. He lived nearby and was aware of everything that was happening to me; the night I saw him he brought me something to eat, cigarettes, and some money, and said: "Here you are giving yourself away; you have to go somewhere else."

In Calabazar I bought ice cream and quickly returned to the park. I was finishing the *Iliad.* I was at the point when Achilles, deeply moved, finally delivers Hector's body to Priam, a unique moment in literature. I was so swept away by my reading that I did not notice that a man had approached me and was now holding a gun to my head: "What is your name?" he asked. I replied that my name was Adrián Faustino Sotolongo, and gave him my ID. "Don't try to fool me, you are Reinaldo Arenas, and we have been looking for you in this park for some time. Don't move, or I'll put a bullet in your head," he exclaimed, and started to jump for joy. "I'm going to be promoted, I'm going to be promoted, I've captured you," he was saying, and I almost wanted to share in the joy of that poor soldier. He immediately signaled other soldiers nearby and they surrounded me, grabbed me by the arms, and thus, running and jumping through the underbrush, I was led to the Calabazar police station.

The soldier who had captured me was so grateful that he selected a comfortable cell for me. Although my mind told me I was a prisoner, my body refused to believe it and wanted to continue to run and jump across the countryside.

There I was in a cell, the compass still in my pocket. The police had taken the *Iliad* and my autobiography.* Within a few hours the whole town was gathered in front of the police station. The word had spread that the CIA agent, the rapist, the murderer of the old lady, had been captured by the Revolutionary police. The people were demanding that I be taken to the execution wall, as they had so loudly shouted for so many others at the beginning of the Revolution.

Those people actually wanted to storm the police station, and

*It seems that R. A. was able to recover the *Iliad* later.

some of them climbed on the roof. The women were especially incensed, perhaps because of the rumored rape of the old lady; they threw rocks at me, and anything else they could find. The cop who arrested me yelled that Revolutionary justice would take care of me and succeeded in calming them down a little, although they still remained outside in the street. At that point it was dangerous to take me out of there, but the police finally managed to do so with a heavy escort of high-ranking officers. I then met Víctor, who had been interrogating all of my friends.

Víctor had received orders from the high command to transfer me immediately to the prison at Morro Castle. As we drove through the streets of Havana, I saw people walking normally, free to have an ice cream or go to the movies to watch a Russian film, and I felt deeply envious of them. I was the fugitive now captive, the prisoner on his way to serve his time.

TRANSLATED BY DOLORES M. KOCH

ZOÉ VALDÉS

The Ivory Trader and the Red Melons

". . . like an angel created by man, leaping forth upon the joyous and meandering sands then disappearing into the torrid royal blue seas. . . ."

—CINTIO VITIER

She wasn't over-ample, nor especially wide-hipped, not even exotically brunette. Her eyes were not exactly Egyptian and her breasts wouldn't squeeze into her neckline. She was eighteen years old and—as her closest confidante the Pole would tell her—merely the soft-touch lover of a fifty-nine-year-old bureaucrat. The "tit fetishist" (in Cuba, an ageing chaser of young girls) rented her a room containing a Russian-manufactured color television; promised her a video on his return from the next foreign trip; and went to collect her in his Lada from school, until she decided to abandon her studies. She decided to abandon them in order to come closer to the legendary BB. BB always acted contrariwise, when everyone was marrying, she was divorcing, and now that everyone was divorcing, she wanted matrimony to set the seal on her serious relationship. She'd read as much in the latest *Paris-Match* the Pole had lent her.

She spent her days and nights alone. Her mother had given up on her ever since she found out that her youngest daughter was sleeping with her boss, with whom (in parentheses) she herself had outrageously flirted, strictly in the interests of providing her offspring with a better life. The old man took it upon himself to convince her that her mother's spite was quite logical given her double humiliation, as both mother and lover. Some future day she'd get over it, as time would tell, as it did so much. So she just kept reading and reading the books lent by the Pole. On his constant trips to Eastern Europe her Old Man only brought her cotton frocks, the cheapest makeup and unfashionable shoes. The Pole made fun of her, wondering where on earth she'd dredged up her fancy man.* The lack of a father might afford some explanation. The Pole never understood why she always acted so contrary, since amorous relations (in inverted commas) with bureaucrats had gone out of fashion; they didn't deliver and delivered less than ever now that there were cars but no petrol. And from one day to the next, they'd put their hands in the till, they'd get their marching orders, until bye-bye trips, and keep your pyjamas buttoned.

Her one and only friend was the Pole, her confessor and confidante. Now their game was called "taking in laundry" and it meant finding a foreigner to marry. For the Pole this was easy, she'd studied and was a writer (although no one had ever seen a book by her), and she spoke English, Japanese, French, German, Italian, Hungarian, Russian and Esperanto, because you have to be ready for anything. One whiff of an Italian and the Pole was there. The French are very romantic, that's true, but they deliver up their Paloma Picasso, their two meals with oysters, then a look to leave with. The Spaniards sugar the pill with chorizos from the dollar shop. The Germans consider that the best form of payment is to perfect your accent. The Japanese massage your neck and press a photo album on you as they leave—the most generous adding, by way of ineradicable souvenirs, some of the most technologically advanced equipment on offer and some ear acupuncture to soothe anxiety. The English are all married and broke, and forever riddled with guilt. The Canadians go for the beach. Those from the

*There's a Cuban saying, supposedly addressed to young girls, which onomatopoeically runs, "Busca un temba que te mantenga" (Get yourself a forty-plus old lag to support you).

former socialist camp were still unexplored territory, still no good at playing games. The Italians constituted a case apart. Yes, they married without preliminaries, a direct approach and without false promises of a Venetian palace. The Pole spoke from experience of numerous close friends who, after taking in laundry, had scaled great heights with the authentic heirs of Dante.

She was called Beatriz. She didn't want to stir, didn't want to do anything. She loved the Old Man, although she occasionally wished he were dead. She still didn't know what she did want. She slept a lot. It's true she was charmed by the taste of the chocolates the Pole introduced her to, the Baci, meaning in English "kisses," each one wrapped in a verse from a different poet. Within a month she learned that the verses were repeated, but she also discovered many poets she'd never previously read, like Rimbaud for example. And she read and read, without preconception or pretension, which is the best way to read.

They were making a film about slavery in the Cathedral Square. The blacks, the heavyweights for over a quarter of a century, were endowing too great an authority on their role of slaves. Meanwhile, the fair moustachios, while intent on graduating in the Engineering Faculty, sabotaged the delicate minuets of their creole performance with rock and roll and coffee-stained pages of arithmetical calculations.

The blacks had no more notion of being slaves than the whites of playing masters. On top of everything, they'd gathered to learn how to move to a different rhythm. The Producer puffed herself up, twitching with nerves—the one thing no producer should ever be allowed to suffer from—dressed in period in order not to jar with the rest, frustrated over and over again with the repeated clambering up and down into the carriage, hand extended, very much the grande dame, striving to explain to the extras, the blackest in the city, how a nineteenth-century Andalusian lord would behave when confronted by the refined young lady who was preparing to descend, smothered in mother-of-pearl appliqué.

From there the rest absconded to an assembly of lunatics where they devoured frozen black beans. Others fled, ostensibly to a fictitious guard duty, in truth to a session of rum and dominoes.

It was now midday and the Director desired that at all costs the noontime tropical heat be converted into deepest night. To achieve this, she penned the actors up in a chapel and wafted sandalwood smoke around the place. The Assistant Director suffered a detached retina, and the place moved into a Leningrad June night, scented with antibiotics and decomposing cane liquor—emerald in its vase blown of Venetian glass.

Meanwhile Beatriz got dressed any-old-how. She pulled on a pair of boring Swedish clogs, gathered up thirty musty twenty-centavo coins, bunged the litre-size cut-glass perfume bottle into a Bally's shoe shop plastic carrier, and set off in search of yoghurt. And that was how she made her entrance, dressed in cotton stays and a skirt some five inches above the knee, her toenails painted a pearly white (one of the tit fetishist's requirements), her feet incarcerated in their northern wood, a strip of office cloth tying back her scraggy ponytail, bearing an old carrier bag, relic of a remote and expensive European furrier (the Pole always presented her with the wrappings to the presents she received); inside the carrier bag, having bribed the dairy assistant and jumped a queue that went the length of the block—the litre of curdled milk was in the process of reheating. Thus in the most fin-de-siècle style she could muster, Beatriz entered the slavery stage set without even noticing; and of course, being there, fucked it up.

"A present-day—blonde—Chinese . . . ?!" screeched the Director, panicking wildly.

At this point another sandalwood cloud erased Beatriz from the naturalistic scenery required by the actors' state of trance. The Producer rapidly crowned her with a shiny, frizzy black wig, coated her in brown stain, flung a white smock over her and even shoved a cigar in her mulatta's refined mouth. The bottle of yoghurt went from hand to hand and ended up hidden behind a bunch of green bananas, supposedly attached to the estate in that other period where mildew and machete strokes had implacably withered them.

Which was when, further on and seated at an ivory table resting on its bronze base, furiously meditating on her cup of lemon tea, Beatriz encountered the scruffy image of a fellow contemporary, chin cupped in the palm of a semi-open hand and elbow pressed into the eternity of a page. Beatriz registered that they resembled siblings or, more likely, those lovers who, with all that loving come to resemble one another, thus ending up loving themselves most of all, and eliminating the need for mirrors. Such a situation could never happen to the Old Man. No way.

First Beatriz lightly lifted her right foot from the verge of nothingness, then took a leap into durable reality. She fled beneath the waterspout of the fountain, casting off the trappings of the mestiza outfit. Nobody observed her departure, or maybe they thought it was merely an exquisite exit premeditated by the eye of the genius behind the camera lens.

Beatriz focused on the Contemporary, but realized that the most important matter in hand was to collect the yoghurt. She opened up her shawl and crawled on all fours towards the greengrocer's, where, taking advantage of the general uninterest, she seized her flask and once again slunk catlike back to her epoch.

The Contemporary rested his eyes on the young woman dressed in filthy rags, now creeping towards his table with a Bally shoe-bag in her hand. It occurred to him to rhapsodize, "What natural pearl is this in the sand!" and to note it down on the paper napkin stained with the tea sweating at the base of his cup. And he experienced a compelling desire to be invited down to the beach.

The young woman scrambled to her feet and spat out a small stone. She decided that the most sensible thing would be to put the litre of yoghurt on the table, sit down beside whoever was going to be her new friend and invite him to have a drink of it. Beatriz surprised herself at the rapid realization of her plan. The Contemporary refused her invitation with disdain. He made a suitably sweeping gesture, as if to say that neither tea nor yoghurt were the kind of fluids he enjoyed. Again, no way. Beatriz studied the pronounced "r" of the Contemporary and it occurred to her that she'd struggled with that rolled consonant ever since childhood: "R as inciga*r,* R as in ba*rr*el; the ca*rr*iages *r*un *r*apidly on the *r*ailway t*r*acks." Her aunt had obliged her to recite the refrain through a mouthful of stones because she believed that vicars' r's could be cured just like stammering. The upshot was that Beatriz was left with the sensation that she was infinitely striving to spit out a wayward pebble which was preventing her from saying what she wanted.

She began to wax lyrical. Through reading she discovered the visionary trails laid open by words. She caught at images, romantically assuming that they could have been written for her. She had intermittently been bitten by the writing bug, but here again the Pole was way ahead of her, and so she pretended to forget about it, confusing even herself. She could never have been someone in another century who confused the state of being with the role of being. Being, against all odds, seduced her at least as much as surrendering to the possible in that unwonted terrain, egotistical and profound, of love and art. But she was definitively not an artist and had never fallen in love to the point of slicing her jugular. She loved the Old Man like she loved her mother, because he had been put there, there in her life. Putting herself in the precise position of a clairvoyant, she got it right the second time around and proposed a trip to the seaside to her Contemporary.

They walked smartly over the cobbled surfaces of old-fashioned streets, seeking out the taxi avenue. They still hadn't figured out how to cope with walking side by side, still less when combining it with strenuously attempting to recount something sufficiently fascinating to rush them headlong into a profound mutual understanding.

He impertinently paraded his gift of being a foreigner, brandishing his jetlag in her face, rubbing in the ease with which he crisscrossed frontiers. He reported on the tragedy of a pistol duel with his best friend in one of Europe's most beautiful squares. That was what Beatriz wanted, a best friend. To play once more in a patio scented with the fragrance of scorched jasmine. He replied without a yes or a no. The Contemporary was hell-bent on marinating his lungs in the sea air, bronzing himself "in lost climates . . . swimming, walking barefoot on grass . . ." He was quoting himself. Without exactly meaning to, he spoke as though about to fall in love. Nor, for her part, did Beatriz pursue him with this in mind. But a certain curiosity as to who knew if . . .

"Are you married?" she asked calculatingly.

"I can't remember . . . What has that got to do with us?"

"I've got an old man. When I'm old, then I'll have a young one . . ."

"That's hardly original. You'll just be one more . . ."

"I know I'll always just be one more."

"At last I've discovered someone I can exchange idiocies with."

A chasm of interruptions swallowed up the magic of their conversation. People were turning to look admiringly at this new couple, even asking the time in order to fathom whether they were tourists or not, checking out their accents. After this once-over, they followed on another twenty meters behind, demanding peppermint chewing gum to freshen their breath. Beatriz sealed their ears with a strategically soft whistle, as though from a strangulated porcelain doll. The frequent absence of intelligent conversation was rendering her stupidly childish, artificially ingenuous. She had furthermore observed how deliberately coming out with stupidities could be an intelligent game. They were aware of the aroma of tilapia fish giving rise to a distinct moistening of their lips. Between that smell lodged in their clothes and the open rundown tenements, the dusty street came to an end and they emerged on to asphalt and a fresh dimension, sparkling with beer bottletops encrusted there over the decades. The Contemporary attempted to hail passing taxis.

"Those are the 'specials,' they won't stop. Hold out a twenty-dollar note—we call them draculas—and 'specials' will appear out of the blue, ready to take you to the ends of the earth. Or so says my friend the Pole."

"I don't have 'draculas.' Mine seem to be all 'frankensteins.' "

"Ah, so you have the hang of our slang. Brilliant," Beatriz said coldly. "Get out your twenty dollars and you'll see."

A minute later they were on their way to the eastern beaches, their complex currency stowed in the pocket of his linen trousers and the yoghurt fermenting in its plastic bag. The taxi driver agreed to take them on the clear understanding that he never got mixed up in business with whores. After a while he asked the Contemporary if he were a troglodyte. Beatriz, all too familiar with that kind of mistake, agreed that yes, her friend was a polyglot.

"In any case, it's all the same . . . you get my drift . . . you're in the business . . ." and humming "La vie en rose," he left them to discuss the weather and the remotest possibility of violent rains.

The taxi coasted the beach at full speed, running on adulterated bitumen. They felt the silent incandescence in their bones and the day slipping away without a move made. Beatriz listened quietly and the Contemporary moved only his lips, imperceptibly. Sweat flowed between breasts and groins. The taxi driver folded his hanky in four and, with one hand liberated from the steering wheel, he tied it around his neck, Mao-style. Supermacho, boldly daring, he at least was making moves, his shirt unbuttoned to the navel, displaying his hairy chest, thrusting it out to impress. Sweat had sapped the starch from his uniform, which (as he told them) his wife ironed and ironed like a workhorse for him. He felt sticky and spat out the brownish spittle of his last gulp of coffee.

Beatriz took another look at the Contemporary, but he was studying the countryside, grimacing as if refusing to acknowledge so much beauty all at once. They selected the beach furthest from the city and squealed to a halt there with a screech of rubber. The taxi driver apologized for exceeding the speed limit, reminding them that he could not go hungry all day long, without so much as warming his guts. There he dumped and overcharged them, and with one slam of the door sprung the intimation that on an island adventure is godlike.

Beatriz wanted to know more, but it troubled her to keep asking. She wanted to get on and get to bed, since in bed you can discover so much. They walked beneath the palms, collecting seaweed streamers and snail shells. Eventually they sat down on the seashore and she stripped off, exploiting their juvenile crisis. She was bent on converting this interlude in their lives into a black-and-white film, scripted by Cocteau.

"I'm not undressing to be provocative, it's so you'll notice how my real beauty lies within . . . so that we may talk and wrestle with our thoughts, not with our bodies . . ." (She also delighted saying the opposite of what she was thinking.)

"That's sheer provocation, then," he said, without appearing in the least nervous.

The Contemporary was either the desired presence or else a glass image, particularly constructed to reveal her secret, the reason she felt herself to be an historical attribute. And he was moving closer to her, without once registering the existence of her splendidly ambiguous body.

"Do you enjoy making love with an old man?"

She nodded hesitantly. "I know you only get *half* the pleasure.

Not during penetration, only when your clitoris is sucked. I know that you're still unaware of your body and of your desires."

"When will I know them? What do you see in my body? You don't frighten me staring at my private parts like that."

To him it wasn't private and he recounted in dissolute tones how he had burned out his emotions early on, with the single intention of avoiding compromising responses. He also told her how he had written the material essential to forging his soul in the most ardent proof of solitude, deciding not to single out any one object for his verses, burying them in their own rhythms. He decided to sell a role to himself: that of being someone else inside himself, in order to escape into his inner self, travelling with the reflexes of a champion who experiences the intimate pleasure of the boxer who ejaculates after knocking out his opponent. And Beatriz actually believed for a moment that she had captured an angel, only then the image of the Pole came into her head. Today she would try to be like her.

"Talking of ejaculation, I'm an expert in procuring them—with my mouth."

He wasn't into that, to waste his seed fronting the sea and discovering a sucker, albeit one of fragile nakedness. He was voyaging to shake out the last ray of sunlight and to enter that fateful and blessed slumber of destiny there on the beach. Beatriz had confused making a friend with the perfect shaft of conquest. For her, perfection was a matter of first fucking and then moving. Without mercy. That much she'd learned from her Old Man.

"I'm thirsty," he announced, looking for a café in the distance.

"D'you think I should study? I left school . . ."

"You study a lot, you spend your whole time reading. That's obvious from the wrinkles in your fingertips. Those who are self-taught clench their fists and sleep in a fetal position with their hand in their crotch and . . . surround themselves with older companions . . . the reason is the lack of teachers. You don't belong to the classroom but to the world . . . You see? I find it intriguing to play the imbecile . . . I'm thirsty!"

The yoghurt in its plastic carrier had been forgotten in the car and there were no signs of tourist oases in their surroundings. The world seemed a worse place for those obliged to be irredeemably traversing it, and the Contemporary remembered his time as a bum when he ate leftovers from the rubbish bins of the rich, inhaled damaging substances and slept under Parisian bridges in a state of bestial inebriation. The girl was sucking her middle finger, causing saliva to wet his lips. But not even this technique, apparently intelligently undertaken, managed to move the Contemporary in an erotic direction, given his further consideration that a kiss delayed the pleasures of caresses and that gentle friction was the prelude to an imminent erection.

"You're one of those women without a man, because you behave like a man, and that scares men away."

"Are you homosexual?"

"You see? Ardor and impulse will forever complicate your chances of communicating with others. We're too boring a planet for that kind of question."

"I think I'm bisexual but I've never done it with a woman . . . the very thought makes me all jittery! The Old Man suggested it once, but . . ."

"Please. There are things one doesn't discuss."

"I haven't any friends, that's why I'm telling you all this. I spend days on end without speaking to anyone. In peace, solitude and dumbness."

Beatriz began to whimper quietly, taking up fistfuls of sand and throwing them angrily away from her. The Old Man had forbidden her to go out with her lifelong friends, arguing that they were too effeminate and that he didn't want to see them there in that room he paid for out of his own pocket. As for fag hags, you should know them for what they are, cruising, upfront dykes, and it didn't suit him to be associated with such a trendy group, he was too old for all of that.

Anyway, one noon—the Old Man made love at noon because he was on a diet and never swallowed a mouthful during the morning—one noon, in the midst of a hysterically sadomasochistic destruction of Beatriz's fresh young body with pinches, bites, scratches, slaps and blows (his revenge on old age), the Old Man whispered a request so disconcerting about inserting her finger and calling him a whore that she could only uncomprehendingly reply with, "Pardon?"

"Stick in your finger and call me a whore . . ."

Beatriz flung him off her, both feet together kicking him in the belly and in the direction of the mirrored wardrobe.

"So that's how you inform against my friends, you bribe them into becoming informers, driving them away from me, and now you're asking me to fuck your arse and call you a whore! Yes, that's it, you're no better than a whore, an old whore, how d'you like that?"

Beatriz was still more surprised when he didn't react; on the contrary, he kept his face pressed up against the mirror, as though wasted by the pleasures of urinating, he sighed and his cock sputtered a feeble dribble. She cried and cried. He went over to her, embracing and kissing her gently on the forehead.

"Thank you. You've achieved what no one else has managed in a long while, made me come like that on my own, just with insults . . . I'd like it if you hit me from time to time . . ."

Beatriz cried harder. No comfort was at hand since, worse still, the Old Man closed the conversation with the following words in a menacing tone, "And let there be no mistake, I'm a real man, a proper macho."

Beatriz cried and cried, for she realized the extent that most important people's brains are full of shit. And instinctively the one thing she did not want was to have her brains full of shit.

She stopped silently crying when she saw a figure pushing a cart off in the distance. Beatriz made frantic signals and the Salesman approached hastily towards his one aspiration: a sale.

"Red watermelons!" the Contemporary called out euphorically.

To which the Salesman added, almost mechanically, "And tamales too, underneath the melons," he explained, looking around conspiratorially. "If you buy the tamales, please eat them discreetly, you know how things are, the whole hassle about the maize and where I get it, then the hassle about the pork and where I get *that* . . ."

The Salesman had the eyes of a cat and a skin like you see only in the photos in Italian fashion magazines. He was a classic macho beauty. No mystery, only beauty.

Contrary to the Contemporary's reaction, when the Salesman caught sight of Beatriz's nakedness, only semicovered with sand, his candor was aroused and the smoothness of his looks dissolved in an excess of prophetic grimaces that went from the swelling of the veins in his neck to *that age-old skyward throbbing of the traitor below.* The Contemporary let out the most horrible guffaw and the crest dived for the floor. Not that amid all this the Salesman would admit defeat, but stood as ecstatic as a Greek bronze. It was then that Beatriz knew she could use him to catch her friend. But jealous intrigues didn't work with the Contemporary, who with all his worldly experience, already fully recovered from his fright, sat himself indolently down on her shirt and began devouring melons.

"Does nobody want a tamal? Give me one of your cigarettes, French, they'll have to be French if you are . . ." The newfound presence was asking, shamelessly.

Chewing on the black melon seeds, the Contemporary poked around in his pockets and retrieved three proud filtered Gauloises. It was the first time she had smoked and she couldn't deny the intensity of the sensation.

"You, what's your line of work?" the Salesman asked Beatriz's friend.

"I'm not sure what you'd call work . . . I'm an ivory dealer."

The other man's face lit up like the expression of a cat before a mirror; he kept exhaling mouthfuls of smoke and turned unpleasantly to Beatriz ominously, as if to inflict punishment, an air of warning that intimated, "You're fucked, I'm going to devote my afternoon to this, I've spoilt your romp." Then he continued, overbearingly interrogating the other. The other had entered a state of ecstasy, sucking noisily on the skins of the luscious fruit. The Contemporary answered him with actions and, feeling overladen with liquid, he lifted up his cock and pissed at the luminous heavens.

"So far and so high, with the pardon and absolution of the heliotropes . . ." he finally pronounced, sighing deeply.

The Salesman couldn't concur in someone else peeing higher than himself, so he strained and failed, then hid his face against the burning sands and put the valor of his reputation as the conqueror of forbidden and frigid maidens into mourning.

Beatriz observed the sea with funereal laments, crushing the voluptuous temptation to coil herself around the waves. The sea appeared as an error, meaning death. She began to imagine she was an actress in the process of designing a new reality beholden to this existence. She stood and watched the sea and then, with renewed reluctance, those two midday bodies: one of which rejected her without knowing why and the other dying for the chance to touch her. She left them resigned to the sea air. Walking towards the water, she defended her premonitions.

This was what would be truly new for her, happening for the first time, even though it was sure to be repeated one day. Submerged to the top of her crown, she breathed alternately through her nose and her mouth, until instinct propelled her to the surface once more, coughing phlegm from between bruised lips. Nobody noticed her poor acting, or perhaps to put it more simply that she was such a weakling. Suicide is not accomplished with such deliberation, still less before two spectators of like calibre. Once recovered from reacting against the reflection of what she herself called her mediocrity, she swam underwater. She liked to think while she swam. Why was she still panting after love with the Contemporary? Why kill herself so theatrically? She swam until she hit a pair of knees blocking her passage. Brought up sharp against them, she emerged clutching that pubis, the chest, and the face of the Contemporary. His eyes were closed and he was laughing ironically.

"Bathe me, arouse me . . . I'm so weary of big cities, of stigma . . . *merde!* Even the breeze causes me anguish, and still I live on inert, feeling more than ever the lack of a heart, as though it were a leg that they'd amputated . . . Valor is a bourgeois ruse, you put on a brave front and you're ready to kill. Give me a postmodern world to contradict them with . . . I'm weary, I want to write, sell red watermelons, to love . . . The fact is that I'm happy with weariness, that way I feel perfect, unique, envied and powerful. It's a lie: I loathe power, I loathe all of it! And a fist in the face by broad daylight is what they deserve. That's what I'd like to give them right now. I'm preoccupied with hating too much to feel love. I don't need to go gently, curses on all politicians and I'll never, never be happy . . . Melancholia is my protest . . . Bathe me, arouse me!"

Beatriz was scared by all this sounding suspiciously like anarchism, like nonconformity with the system, like voluntarism, but a few seconds later she reflected that perhaps it was his way to win over a woman. Beatriz stepped back just far enough to land him an indecisive punch.

"So why are you stripping off then?" the Salesman whispered to Beatriz, having silently swum up and caught her unexpectedly from behind. The Contemporary embraced them, sobbing theatrically, but suddenly his crying dried up in unleashed guffaws.

This rapture so infected the others they threw him broadside into the waves, then pursued him, racing against each other, into the sparkling indigo sea.

Once detained, the Contemporary embraced them both again, first kissing Beatriz on the lips. Meanwhile, the Salesman licked his chops like the cat that got the cream. Then the Contemporary stared fixedly into the feline eyes of the Salesman and kissed him fiercely on his clenched, resistant lips. When he was himself once more, his opponent squared up to him and flung him a punch straight in the face. The Contemporary's nose streamed blood, darkening a rough, complaining sea. The Salesman grabbed the girl with one hand, pulled her away and issued a direct warning: "Watch out, you'd better not trust this one. In your place, I'd call the police!"

Yet another one out to deceive her. Why not take it all transcendentally?

"Whoever told you that if one man kisses another it's necessary to inform the police? And don't the Russians kiss each other on the mouth? I've seen Gorbachev on television . . ."

"Ah, no, no! I never had too much time for our Soviet comrades, and now they're down, don't even mention either them or Gorbachev! My thing is the melons and tamales; he's your problem, and as for me, I'm off!"

The Salesman swam like lightning, then disappeared with his little handcart through the curtain of trembling palm fronds.

The pallid arm covered in light freckles stretched out and drew back a veil of sudden clouds. A storm of sewing needles impudently stitched a double horizon.

They waited, cut off on the shore, fearful of attracting the electricity of a lightning bolt through the contact of their feet with the shells. The cloud's silhouette was that of a cannonball and sped energetically along. The sky, and of course the sun's viscosity reappeared. The waters washed the wound. The sea green diluted over the Contemporary's face, accentuating his vanity. The girl invited him to return, tugging his hair, and he replied with a wave, although mentally paralyzed.

"Let yourself be loved," pleaded Beatriz.

For him to let himself be loved implied allowing himself to be dominated, and his aim was to profile the souls of others with an authoritatively bloody finger. The girl squeezed out her hair and knotted it at the base of her neck. She shrugged her shoulders and left him standing. She too then set off in the direction of the Victor.

Vertigo was suffocating the Contemporary. He celebrated his solitude in the middle of the sea, beating very gradual breast-strokes in Beatriz's wake. When he reached her, he found her dressed and saltily sticky.

"I appreciate your homage to Kabuki. I too enjoy living theatrically. It's the best way to assume a double morality. For example, I always indulge in a game whereby when someone says something to me, I switch it around so that I can more or less get the gist of what they really believe."

"Do you need the truth?"

"Yes, it's a defect of mine."

"I don't belong to this era and I urgently need to return to my own," he muttered, gasping in the brine, his hair slipping over the blisters on his shoulders.

"Don't worry about it, and if one day they get around to interrogating me, I'll tell them it was all a dream."

"And if it all was?"

"Then I'd be free of the interrogation. Who's interested in dreams?"

They walked towards the bus stop.

"Beatriz, it was a pleasure to accompany you to the beach and to get to know you."

"You don't know me. For me too it was a pleasure. It's the first time I've seen a poet's face. They hardly ever—almost never—appear on television."

Once it arrived, the crowd swept them hungrily down the bus, fighting for space inside. The human tide found in their favor and they clambered horizontally on board through the window. In the blink of an eye they were squashed in like sardines in a tin, crushed beneath sandy armpits and greasy jaws. The doors concertinaed around the last passenger's back, who, although he wasn't deaf, found it necessary to blow his mind with a transistor on at full volume pressed to his ear.

"Tell me if you found in my past . . ."

The Contemporary attempted to explain: "Poets are afflicted with an endemic disease. When invited to appear on television, they become invisible before the cameras, just like vampires before mirrors, no one can bear confronting the invisible. It'll be the cause of the next war. I arrived courtesy of the dreams of the film director . . . I'm a tourist of chance, of the imagination."

"A reason for forgetting or for loving me . . ."

The sound of the undulating sweet sugarcane field released scented memories of crinkled baobabs. Beatriz didn't hear the Contemporary's voice, bellowing in her ear, "I don't belong to any particular space . . . I dare to set about revolutionizing the world too precociously . . . revolutionizing the world through the verses of an inspired adolescent. Who would have thought it!"

Astounded by the indifferent response he'd precipitated in intellectual circles, he then retired to Africa to trade in ivory. Beatriz longed to boast: "These things happen. Look at Rimbaud."

"That's me. The other. That was when time exploded in my brain."

Beny Moré,* the one and only, sang on soothingly, beguilingly, insinuatingly.

*An enormously popular romantic balladeer and dance singer of the 1940s and 1950s.

"You ask forgiveness . . ."

In the future someone would dream of transporting him with a load of slaves to the set of a film being made on a deluded island. The Cinema Director's dream had been so authentic that the punishment dictated by rheumatic visions was to fail in its consecration, fragmenting its impact by scattering the characters across different centuries. Why did he always have to be defending himself?

"That's why I transgressed another dreamlike desire: yours."

"The Cinema Director maybe, but me, what have I in common with you if all you tell me is true?"

"Curiosity. Knowledge."

"If it suits you . . ."

Compelled by impulse. Cursed be he who puts a brake on an angel's dreams. Beatriz knew that she had something in common with him in at least one respect: the two of them were ambitious and poorly regarded among others who are neither clearheaded nor overconcerned as to where their ambitions are heading. Overly metaphysical. Beatriz felt she was going for the dealer like the last hair on a bald man's head, a point of no return. The Contemporary was so flesh and blood, he strode across the paving stones with such energy, that he cut the breeze, and it occurred to her that perhaps the Cinema Director and she only existed in his dreams. Tourists from the past passing through the mind drugged by the desire to peer into the far beyond.

On the other hand, the dead had never appeared to her as they had to the Pole, who frequently told her of it. But in the here and now she trembled with a fierce aversion to squandering the opportunity to catch hold of an affair, because whichever way, one of them must be the other's dream. And what was it she wanted? Love or adventure? Naturally there's no difference, this much she knew thanks to the encounter. But never with him. Nor with the Old Man. Lately things had been happening to her, that from there on in, she thereafter couldn't share with anyone. Life was becoming a big secret. She was going to be alone after all.

And why do we rush around here and there, forever looking for love? Never again, that was what she wanted to think: never to be thought of again. Only two things were clear to her: did she understand love, did she understand death? Was it necessary to understand or was it simply something that occurred sometime after an immediate and terrible now? And why was she worrying over understanding, she who had never attempted to understand anything? If the Old Man had found out about this, he'd have flayed her alive, not for having gone off to the beach with someone else, but because that someone else was a foreigner, and above all because he couldn't stand women who thought for themselves.

"Don't call what you have a heart . . ."

They got out of the bus and retraced their steps to the film set. The guy with the radio followed closely behind them.

"Does it also bother you they dragged it out of you that you've virtually no past, that you can only express yourself when life's daily violences force you to?"

"Beatriz, people are entirely composed of their pasts."

"In which case, what the hell is the future?"

"A fabrication to distract us."

"You depress me."

They had arrived. The Cinema Director opened her notebook and wrote the most exquisite last page.

"You ask me about my past, what it was like . . ."

The Contemporary also jotted his final sentence down in his notebook. Then he shut it forever, not one line too many between its covers.

"Before loving you have to have faith . . ."

The same present-day characters masked with the past welcomed them in a sandalwood haze. Serene and ambiguous slaves let their masters' arms slip around their hips. Laced in their stays, aristocratic ladies indulged beneath the crushing bondage of their corsets. Under duress.

"Surrendering life for love . . ."

The Contemporary handed his notebook to Beatriz. She read its title with surprise: *Mauvais Sang.* And the dedication: *For Beatriz, who is me, solitary and future.* And his enigmatic signature. And a date from the past.

"It's for your eyes only. Just like with television, anyone else who looks at its pages will find them blank."

And he smiled. The Cinema Director gave the order to get on set and everyone scurried to their posts. The Producer swelled up, fearing a lack of respect from outside the epoch. The Assistant, suddenly aroused by a mouthful of salad dressing, grunted loudly on finding that someone had cut down on the mayonnaise in his tea-time sandwich. And life ground into gear, without dreams, without . . .

"Without dying, that's caring, that's something you don't possess . . ."

Beatriz gave her friend a shove in the back, a gilded postmodern foot assailing a vertical reality.

"To love I don't need a reason . . ."

Beatriz by now no longer wished to let herself be loved.

"Another contemporary. Cut!" shouted the Director, her feet on the ground.

As reality advanced, more members were lost in the admiration of angels. And he took the lad by the hand, extricating him from his slave makeup. Seated together at the marble table with its bronze base, he there erased it with a drop of tea, as easily as unpinning the wings of an angel.

"I'm overwhelmed, so overwhelmed, my heart."

The Contemporary stood petrified within the Fantin-Latour portrait, utterly hysterical, uncomprehending, repenting of his return. Only Beatriz could see him.

Beatriz witnessed a fabulous ambition. She extended her arm

and pulled the cloud aside. She readied herself to approve the obligatory subject. Double Standards. She'd never been a good student. It all left her pretty cold. But at heart, at heart she knew it was important to derive the maximum possible from it.

She flipped back her seat and made out she'd only just noticed that she'd escaped to the cinema with the money intended to buy yoghurt. That was why she loathed money, it always rendered her guilty. She pretended to leave the cinema humming a tune that had nothing to do with the film. Or maybe it did.

She began to feel or to make believe she felt a need for something trifling and bought herself an ice cream. She was alone, sweaty and blameworthy, and the seaside didn't suit her. She convinced herself that she was seeking a thousand pretexts for going into a bookshop, or for listening to the entire classical repertoire of the planet, to go and see someone, to dance, or even return to the cinema.

She kept chewing it over. Love. Love. Forgetting that love couldn't exist because nobody had a quiet spot to look themselves in the eye any longer. Lost because of a dream, because of a film, because of reality. Because of herself. She made as if she repeated this last phrase to herself because it was healthier to develop awareness and a spirit of self-criticism.

She chucked aside her ice-cream cone. Plenty of people were watching her despite the fact that she had cast it aside calmly, thoughtfully, in slow motion. Beatrice pretended to be looking for a way out. Out of herself or out of where? She affected to be looking for the answer in herself.

In any case, loneliness was the Old Man making love with a pornographic magazine between them, the constant and impatient anxiety. Loneliness was avarice, not ambition. Even a foreign fan was loneliness.

She went into a café, bought cigarettes, smoked in order to be even more bored with herself, to feign the passing of time, as though she were watching its flight. She couldn't even let the Pole in on what had happened. She'd only make fun of her: a fuck for a book of poetry, hilarious! The Old Man would have to be informed that his lover had been in contact with a bisexual Frenchman, and a writer at that! They would oblige her to answer for herself. To flee. She wouldn't respond. And she wouldn't flee. Now she would learn the full extent of her strength. Putting it into operation wasn't a game. It could break her. No.

TRANSLATED BY AMANDA HOPKINSON

CLAVE 5

Salsa

ERNESTO MESTRE

The Bakery Administrator's Daughter

from THE LAZARUS RUMBA

Once, in Guantánamo, there had been fifteen Studebakers like the powder-blue Studebaker that had belonged to the murdered police captain. Once, before the triumph of la Revolución, before el Rubio had sprouted filaments of old gold under his armpits and on his chin and around his navel, before he had worked for the yanquis inside the naval base, before Colonel MacDougal had expelled him under suspicion of spying for the Batista government, before he had ventured to the Sierra, hungry and barefoot, his services at first rejected by a guerrilla comandante because he did not own a gun, before el Rubio had ever dreamed of owning a car, any car, much less a yanqui car, much less a Studebaker, there had been fifteen of them in the small provinciality of Guantánamo. *Imagínense, quince Studebakers en este pueblecito de guajiros.* Actually over half of the Studebakers belonged to soldiers in the yanqui naval base, but in those days passage to and from the paradise of tin roofs was common—many Cubans, like el Rubio, worked inside the base and many soldiers visited the town when on leave—there was no Cerca Peerless, no mines, no river infested with crocodiles, no bay infested with sharks, no watchtowers.

The flaky upper-crust families, the type of families that put ads in the local newspapers looking for "white Spaniard maids," or those families less aristocratic, less bleached in their lineage, who had connections with the ruling regime, the type whose mothers and daughters, y hasta la anciana abuelita, dyed their hair the color of el Rubio's natural hue, resplendent and ochery as just-sifted riverbed gold, had made a ritual of leasing the fifteen Studebakers from their owners on the fifteenth anniversary of each daughter's birth, the day she was welcomed into womanhood. Fifteen couples would be invited to ride in the fifteen yanqui cars to the feast in the Centro Municipal near Parque Martí, where along with the father and her daughter they would dance to a mamboed version of a Strauss waltz.

After the triumph of la Revolución, some of the families that had not fled had tried to continue this ritual but were thwarted when they found that el Rubio would not lease his Studebaker (which had come into his possession when one of Batista's henchmen, a sergeant in the Rural Guard, had fled with his family on the eve of la Revolución, leaving behind any possessions that could not be stuffed into one of his fourteen suitcases, or hastily sewn into the lining of his evening jackets, worn dutifully as dresses by his four young daughters, or into the virgin crevices of his own body) for the purpose of this outdated bourgeois ritual. Thus the celebrations went on for a few years, marred, misnumbered, truncated, sometimes with seven Studebakers, sometimes with four and finally with as few as two, the fifteen couples crowded into the spacious cars like clowns in a circus. Finally, when el Rubio had amassed enough power and been appointed chief of the revolutionary police, he sabotaged the engines of the two remaining Studebakers and forbid, by decree, the celebration of *las fiestas de los quince.* Never having sired a child, never having known the luxurious joy of doting on a daughter, he had underestimated the will with which Cuban fathers want to please their daughters. The celebrations went on, more outrageous than before. The shells of the two remaining Studebakers were bought and fixed over twin mulecarts, and once more the fifteen privileged couples jammed in, their suits and dresses grown more and more shabby with the passing years, badly tailored, the lining of suits poking out of the hems like hounds' tongues, the seams of the dresses clustered and bulged like the flesh of creeping slugs; and too many of these dresses the señoritas proudly wore, their chins cocked, their faces painted, their hair stiffened like baked meringue, their gazes askant, as if they were attending a ball at Versailles, bore the vestigial traces, in their heaviness, their loud patterns, their patchwork, of drapes and furniture upholstery. It was murmured in the local CDR, after the minute book had been shut, that in less than five years of progress, la Revolución had left every window of Guantánamo naked and every chair or sofa bare as a skinned rabbit. Still, they celebrated. Against the decree, in badly tailored suits and hull-thick dresses they celebrated. Two lame mules hung with cowbells tugged the husks of two Studebakers, their rusty exteriors garlanded with hibiscus and branches of crape myrtle, their hollowed interiors jammed with fifteen couples armed with claves, castanets, and maracas, past the Department of State Security, past the office of the man who had decreed against them, and they aimed their great joyous noise at him, daring him to rejoice along for another *niña* had become *una mujer.*

Y las mujeres son la gran alegría de este mundo. La mujer was what the Creator created after He had created everything, after He had rested, and with this final masterpiece He topped even Himself, so went one of Father Gonzalo's sermons during one of the illegal celebrations. Yet illegal as they certainly were, el Rubio could not hector any of his men to take action against them. As soon as they heard the clickclack of the claves, the raptap of the castanets, the swishwhoosh of the maracas, they laid down their arms and grew deaf to any orders and threats that el Rubio barked at them. They too were fathers of Cuban daughters. Not even el Rubio's loafish bullmastiff Tomás de Aquino (no father himself, for his grotesque belly had made it impossible for him to mount any bitch) could be persuaded of the seriousness of the decree and at each pass of the mulecart Studebakers, he got off his monumental behind and followed the caravan, adding his baritone howl to the percussive harmony.

El Rubio was patient. He kept the decree on the books. But he stopped barking orders and threats to his men, he let them lay down their arms, let the two-cart Studebaker caravan pass, let Tomás de Aquino follow doltishly along. He listened with a tolerant ear to his bullmastiff's over-the-top, harsh-tuned, off-the-tracks, traitorous aria. He listened to the subtle threats in the suggestions of the ladies from the local CDR that the decree, if looked at in the wrong light by the wrong Party higher-up, could *itself* be deemed counterrevolutionary. All the while he said nothing and let the people, with the lashing of their tongues, set their own trap.

There was an administrator of a bakery who had a daughter just shy of fifteen. The administrator was rumored to be terminally ill. And it was said that as a farewell gift to his daughter, he was planning to throw the greatest *fiesta de quince* ever seen in Guantánamo, even more extravagant than those celebrated by the wicked aristocracy in the days before la Revolución. This was absurd of course, for the administrator, even though there were always long *colas* at the bakery and he was more accustomed to the orange fire within his brick ovens than to the yellow fire in the heavens, was paid a measly sum of pesos that was just enough for him and his family to get by. Still, on the evening before the appointed day, seven cases of Dom Pérignon were carried in by two mulatto men through the back door of his house on José Martí Street near the shores of the Bano River. A few minutes later a massive slaughtered pig was carried in on a pole, through the same back door, by the same two mulatto men. (Cashier clerks at the bakery, el Rubio recognized them.) And then a second pig almost as large, and then three bunches of unplucked white gallinas, tied together by their legs and hung upside down like dead flowers. A barrel was rolled in, possibly rum, and bags of fruits and vegetables and rice followed, then branches thick with flowers, deep red and pinkish white. More black-market goodies than el Rubio had ever seen amassed at one time. He watched from the driver's seat of his powder-blue Studebaker, hidden at the edge of a blooming guava grove near the river. Every time the mulatto men disappeared into the house, waved in by the bony liver-spotted hand of the old administrator, el Rubio put down his binoculars and wiped the lenses with his shirt. He saw more than he could believe, for after all the food was smuggled in, another truck pulled up, and the two mulatto men started unloading hunks of shiny red metal and polished chrome and black-leather bucket seats and whitewall tires whose bands were pearly and unspotted as a bride's new dress. And then another truck from which was unloaded three sets of conga drums and enough brass trumpets and trombones and fugelhorns to supply a small symphony orchestra.

"Qué cojones," el Rubio muttered. He tried to wake up Tomás de Aquino sprawled on the passenger's seat next to him, just to make sure he was not the only one who witnessed this abominable spectacle, but the bullmastiff flicked his ears and exposed his yellowed fangs. Had Tomás de Aquino known that there was so much comestible booty gathered together in one place, had he listened to his master and raised his large helmet of a skull, he might have charged the criminals with the proper courage of the police dog that he certainly was not; but Tomás de Aquino was wont not to pay any heed to his master, and he went on snoozing in the passenger seat, content, as most of the Islanders, on dreaming of riches that he knew would never be his.

El Rubio continued to watch till the day turned bright and the whiff in the morning breeze of sizzling pig hide awoke Tomás de Aquino, who struggled up and sat on his haunch and poked his cavernous wet nostrils into the air, mewing each open, as if the smell of the thing alone could ease his eternal hunger. Before

Tomás de Aquino broke into a hunger seizure, el Rubio rolled up both windows and mud-tailed out of the guava grove. He decided he would let them have their last supper. He asked one of the vigilantes of the local CDR to take note of everyone who attended the fiesta. She returned to him that night with a list of over a hundred citizens who had attended as guests, the twelve citizens who had served as musicians, and the five citizens who had been employed as servants. She was tipsy, un poquito jumada. She said she had gotten too close (vaya, she had needed to get close for champagne corks launched from the patio were whizzing into the street endangering any passerby) and the administrator's wife (*una mulata buen moza, with fleshy hips and sumptuous breasts, she won't be a widow long, eso es seguro*) had caught her peeking through a crack in the red-brick patio wall; but instead of reprimanding her, she had invited her in.

"Vamos, entra, rejoice and party like a true cubana. You comuñangas, all of you, have forgotten what fun it is to be Cuban! My husband has decided to remind you before he goes to his grave. Vamos, entra. Alleluia, my daughter is a woman today!"

El Rubio nodded, he said that perhaps she should consider adding her own name to the end of the list. The vigilante sobered up instantly, her eyes widened, she insisted she had done it out of duty, to get a closer look, a better count. Y vaya, once she was in she could not refuse their hospitalities, else they get suspicious. El Rubio said he would take her sense of duty into account, but added her name to the list anyway. The morning after, he went to the house on José Martí Street and arrested the bakery administrator.

At the trial, the names were made public. The administrator's name was Roque San Martín. His daughter's name was Benicia. She was legendary among the long-tongued neighbors, for since the day of her birth her father had not allowed scissors to touch her chocolate hair and it had grown to graze her ankles. He himself, it was said, combed the knots out of it every evening. Roque San Martín's coffee-colored, wondrously curved and much younger wife was called Yeyé. Each of the guests that attended the feast, beginning with the vigilante, was called by the revolutionary tribunal to testify against their generous host and his family. Only a handful ignored the summons. Only a handful listened to the urgings of Father Gonzalo (who it was revealed later had been briefly at the feast to bless the debutante). In a sermon on the Sunday after the arrest, he proclaimed, mirroring the twisted logic of el Rubio's charges, that there had been no feast on St. Anthony's Day, that he had not been there when he went there to bless the child-woman and that all those he saw there, at the greatest fiesta de quince he had ever attended, even during the era of the aristocrats, had certainly not been there either. This, he said, is the way el Rubio and the tribunal should be addressed. Any and all statements infected with nonsense. But only a handful listened to the urgings of Father Gonzalo. Of the 104 guests who had been at the feast, over ninety, including the vigilante, including the two mulattoes who worked for Roque San Martín and helped him purchase the black-market booty, gave concise, clear and descriptive statements of what had transpired on the evening of St. Anthony's Day.

Sure enough, from what the tribunal heard, from what it saw (for there had been three photographers hired for the occasion, two who dutifully turned in their negatives to the tribunal), Roque San Martín had made true on his herculean boast—not even in the wicked prerevolutionary days had Guantánamo seen anything like the fiesta for Benicia's fifteenth birthday. As the guests arrived they were handed a single camellia, some white, some red, some bicolored. The guests were then escorted by Yeyé into the main patio where the roasting pit was set in one far corner, and in another corner the two mulatto bakers were assembling an automobile, an Italian convertible. Rum was scooped from the very cask with a wooden ladle, set in the third corner, and distributed liberally, so that it wasn't long before things got rolling, before the guests got anxious for the debutante and her father to appear, for someone to pick up the trumpets and trombones and fugelhorns gently laid on the stools atop the band platform in the fourth corner, for someone to jump behind the drums and pound them, like a tumble-rough lover, like a giant-handed masseuse, to their better life.

"Sí, sí, ya viene la música. . . . But first, antes que nada," Yeyé announced, silencing the expectant guests. "The bath."

A shutter on the second-floor window of the house flew open and the sickly Roque San Martín stepped out into the small semicircular balcony. He was clearly on his last days, his face so deflated that it hung on his skull like a hood, his chest sunken and his spine bent inward like the opening of a final question, the last three wisps of hair on his pate like weedgrass that had endured a long drought. Still, he had found the strength to don his most elegant linen guayabera and now that he was outside he found it proper to put on his most stylish Panama and was liberally sucking on a dark long Hoya, which his wife wouldn't let him smoke inside the house. He found the strength to lean forward on the wrought-iron railing and smile, a frightening gummy smile, and he signaled to the guests gathered on the patio below, with the back of his free hand, as if he were a nonagenarian pontiff on the balcony at St. Peter's Square. The guests cheered his presence like wearied pilgrims and they raised their rum-filled glasses to him. They shouted that with God's help he would overcome his illness and see his grandchildren, that God owed it to them, for He had not worked a miracle in Guantánamo in a long, long time.

Roque San Martín grew serious at hearing this. He sucked on his Hoya and spoke with the abandon of the faithless. "Ay no me jodan señores y señoras. Cancer is a most terrible fate. My innards are a nest of scorpions . . . besides I am atheist!—and the only time I believe in God is when I look into Benicia's brown eyes, when I bury my nose in the fragrance of her hair. Her beauty has been all ours, her mother's and mine, for fifteen years, and under our stern aegis it has blossomed, ya verán, ya verán . . . for the time has come, the shield must be removed, from here on her beauty is the world's and her admirers will be as countless as the stalks in a cane field." But, as if unable to imagine his daughter wooed and pursued by so many, Roque San Martín fell into a fit of hacking and coughing, his frail frame doubling in on itself like a spent world, his lit Hoya slipping out of his fingers, bouncing off the wrought iron railing and spiraling down to the patio like a misguided missile. Yeyé moved towards the spot underneath him, as if to catch him in case he too came tumbling down. Roque San Martín pounded his chest and gargled in a gulp of air and waved her off. "No es nada," he wheezed.

"Do you need help with the tub?" Yeyé called.

"No coño, I said, no es nada. I am fine. Dying, but fine."

There was cautious laughter below. "Así estamos todos en esta maldita Isla."

"Bueno, basta, the time has come." Roque San Martín summoned all his powers and disappeared into the penumbral room behind him, from whence in a few moments emerged, as if moving of its own will, the great white bow of the magnificent bathtub in which the girl-woman Benicia lay, the back of her head resting on the edge, her long, long never-scissored hair falling over the front, her face hidden from the guests below, her nervous giggles audible. Feeble, dying, Roque San Martín pushed the monumental bathtub out onto the balcony till its stern touched the iron railing and his daughter's brown and thick and knotless locks fell halfway down the balcony, unswayable by the gentle spirits of the early summer breeze, smooth as a cataract of caramel.

"Aquí va, aquí va," Roque San Martín called from the shadows, popping open bottles of champagne with the vigor of a young barman, the corks shooting over the red brick wall into the street, and emptying them into the tub. "Aquí va, coño, put your masks on and witness the first bath of the woman, my daughter the woman! Put your masks on, carajo, respect her dignity."

Benicia's giggles erupted into outright shrieks as the chilled foamy baptismal French bathwater rose on her virgin body, till it lapped up against her bare nipples like a prophecy of the many eager suitors to come. And before the guests knew it, the band had snuck onto the platform on the fourth corner and began to play a mambo, and their attention shifted from the balcony, so that only a few recalled seeing (their carnival masks in place so that eyes that saw would not be seen seeing) Roque San Martín lift his shrieking shivering daughter from the bathtub (naked and newly a woman as she was, her melonous buttocks goose-pimply) and straddle her in his fleshless arms and carry her into the darkness of the room, and, again, before anyone knew it, they were down on the dance floor, she in a flowing white linen dress, her hair doubled and tripled into a bun, carrying her father through the dance as if he were a lifeless strawman.

From there the feast went on, there were photographs of Benicia in the driver's seat of the motorless Italian convertible, photographs of a rainstorm of camellias that flooded the bucket seats and frame by frame buried the driver up to her neck, photographs of balloon-cheeked trumpet players, à la Louis Armstrong, whose joyous notes seemed to tear through the black and white flatness, photographs of the guests possessed by the spirits of the drums, their eyes white, their mouths agape, their knees bent and their arms akimbo, a fuzzy photograph of the two-faced parish monsignor as he touched the forehead of the debutante with moistened fingers, and finally, photographs (these that irked the tribunal most) of the two monumental plump-haunched pigs hung over the roasting pit, their hide charred, their flesh visibly tasteable.

Certainly, the tribunal concluded in a caustic note after reviewing all the evidence, the bakery administrator could go to the grave pleased that he was a fouler aristocrat than all the foul aristocrats who had ever tarnished the history of the Island. ¡Pura degeneración! And before it passed its harsh sentence—fifteen years imprisonment for the administrator (one year for each of the eight counts of embezzling from the bakery, one year for each of the four counts of illegal sales and purchases, one and a half years for his irreverent tirade on the witness stand in which he hurled insults at el Rubio, among the kindest being that the poor police captain did not want girls to become available women because he wanted all the young hombrecitos for himself, and one and a half years for the incestuous overtones of the champagne bath—the tribunal expressed its fondest wishes that the convicted, terminally ill as he was rumored, would live to serve every minute of his sentence), three years imprisonment for his wife (for shamefully letting her daughter be used as a pawn in her husband's sick, immoral and rebellious masque), and complete loss of custody of the child Benicia whose virgin hair was shorn, military-style above her ears, and whose upbringing would be resumed by the Communist Youth League of the province of Oriente (it was not, the tribunal expressed its fondest hope, too late to make her a loyal compañera)—it set in stone el Rubio's decree against quince celebrations; from here on, celebration of the feast was strictly prohibited, its venomous bourgeois roots unearthed by this incident, and anyone caught in any semblance of a celebration of a girl's fifteenth birthday would be prosecuted to the fullest extent of the revolutionary code.

Y a propósito, the tribunal's judgment went on, *to rid us of the temptation, perhaps it would be wise to abolish the fifteenth year of a young woman's life altogether, so that legally (if not chronologically), she leapfrogs from fourteen to sixteen, thus erasing any vestiges of this sham ceremony from the annals of our history. A cubana is a woman, una mujer propia y derecha, when she devotes her moral nature to the principles of la Revolución, not, magically, when she turns fifteen, and her father sees fit to pawn her off to other men. La Revolución has always sought to vanish the horrid discrepancies between the sexes inwrought in our culture. The way a girl becomes a woman should he no different from the way a boy becomes a man, through her deeds in service of her society. All this, of course, deserves further consideration and it is beyond the scope of our power to implement, though we will send a letter to the Central Committee and to the Minister of Culture in the capital with our recommendations.*

Young women, of course, still turned fifteen after fourteen. The Central Committee and the Minister of Culture in the capital never answered the tribunal's letter. How could they, with a sober face? Young women, still, when the time came, turned fifteen. No committee or minister on heaven and earth could change that. ¿Quién se atreve a usurpar la naturaleza?—¡ni el Señor mismo! But now there were no fiestas, no father with the rebellious heart of Roque San Martín, no daughter like Benicia who would ever feel the tickle-joy—under the armpit, in the shallow pit of the navel, on the rosy hills (esas colinas inexploradas, jamás pisadas) of her woman parts—of a million frisky bubbles of Dom Pérignon.

So on what man would fall the burden of commemoration? To what sad soul would the banished angels of womanhood reveal themselves, when girls after fourteen (and musn't they?) naturally turned into women of fifteen?

On no man, no man . . . for what man had the cojones with which to lavish a daughter with feastly love after the heavy sentence that fell on Roque San Martín, what bull had not withered into an ox? So on no man, no man at all . . . but on a short-haired gorbellied loose-sphinctered flat-muzzled misery of a beast. Angels, especially banished angels, have the strangest preferences for who should serve as their messengers in this world. And so they appeared, one afternoon not long after Roque San Martín's trial, to the bullmastiff Tomás de Aquino. He, no visionary, was lounging on the sun-warmed bricks of his master's inner courtyard, thoughtless almost (as was his wont) except for the close attention he was paying to the expanding bubble of fetid gas that was vacillating in his belly, unsure of whether to escape out the back door or the front. And would not his namesake, the angelic doctor, have lectured el Rubio's bullmastiff that it is exactly when we are paying the most dire attention to the basest matter that heavenly creatures see it best fit to visit us, that it is only in those moments of desperate scrutiny to our impure flesh, esta carne como ropa vieja, that we are vulnerable at all to God's better beauty, to the grace of the immaculate? It was so for the soot-footed Virgencita in her dusty dwelling, it was so for the old gray-haired Elizabeth in her long and barren marriage, and it is so for all beings. The wind, any guajiro knows, howls fiercest past shuttered windows.

But in our story, another wind, a reeking wind lengthened in swirls—like the vaporous tail of a plummeting fiend—in Tomás de Aquino's midsection so that he had to shift the heft of his thick torso over to his left and cast his prodigious haunch heavenwards to facilitate release; all this, forcing his huge head askance, setting his jaundiced eyes directly into the sunlight that torrented through the iron-grill roof of his master's inner courtyard; and there from the pure nimbusy yellow of afternoon light to the sick yellow of excess bile passed the banished angels of womanhood and possessed this most brutish seed of a vile murderous race (for no man, no man at all, found them worthy for their avenging task).

On that afternoon, less than a week since the sentencing of Roque San Martín and his family, less than two weeks since the last quinceañera feast on St. Anthony's Day, so suddenly and heavenly struck, Tomás de Aquino let out a monstrous tympanic fart and he rolled back his leathery lips and exposed his vulpine fangs and assumed the mantle of his mission.

He sang.

No, no, no, chico, not sang. That is too casual and watery a word. Tomás de Aquino did not sing, not if a song is melody and harmony and rhythm, not if a song is the metered whispers and thunders of a river, not if a song is a deep-tissue massage to the noise-sore soul. No, this was no song, no cantata, no madrigal, no aria, no hymn. Perhaps a fugue, yes a fugue maybe. Qué va, no, not even that. This was discord, jagged vengeance of the sort unmatched by all furies of pandemonium, unimagined by even the most modern composers; so Tomás de Aquino most certainly did not sing. Later, they were to name the sky-piercing wail that first burst from his lungs that afternoon like the cry of a thousand tortured demons *el llanto de los quince* (the wail of the fifteens), as if all women that had not become, or *would* not become, women, by decree, had lent their caged voices, their ululant tongues, all the anger of their thwarted womanhood, to this basest of beasts named after the most celestial of saints. Later, mothers and grandmothers, sisters and aunts, cousins and neighbors (indeed all women who had properly become women when it had been legal to do so) were to join Tomás de Aquino in el llanto de los quince, so that the unsevered silence that was once common during the height of the siesta, at the low night hours when roosters slumber and diarists scribble, in the brief moments just after prayer, all were swallowed by the thousand-voiced harsh protest against el Rubio's inhuman decree. Yet on that first afternoon, it was Tomás de Aquino alone, no man, no man at all, and no woman either, but he, humble flatulent he, whom the banished angels of womanhood visited.

And many years after Tomás de Aquino had drowned in a pool of his own vomit, his death synchronized to the second with that of his master who never had the luxury of knowing that his last anguished opium-laced breath would be his last, many years after the feasts of quinceañera had become common again, the decree against them still on the books but degenerated into the sort of law that it is wiser not to enforce, better left, like old parchment, unperused, it was Benicia San Martín, her hair grown past her shoulders again, her old beauty somewhat rough-hewn by her boxed blooming years spent sleeping in bunkers, wearing olive fatigues, and marching in combat boots, who architected the great feasts of quinceañeras, who, after graduating from the Communist Youth League, had been wise enough to set up her own business, a business that had nothing to do with her training as an electronics technician, a business that was, without mincing words, the family business, a business that fed and clothed her and her reunited family, her delirious mother Yeyé—the stunning mulata of the once-sensuous lips droopy now and slippery with dribble, of the irresistible curves forever shrouded now by the stale urine-stained sheets of the bed she would not abandon—and her decrepit father, who had been released from a Santiago jail and given back his house and welcomed back by his family, who against his better judgment obeyed the wishes of the tribunal to endure till he had served every minute of his sentence, though he had only served half of it, because at some point he had seen the light and signed a document that detailed his conversion to the creeds of la Revolución, that with its marvelous drugs and brilliant surgeons had excised all traces of cancer from his polluted body, and now, sound as a dollar but hollow as a peso, wandered the hallways of his house like a phantom, in a ripped soiled undershirt and low-hung underpants, raising chickens in the drape-drawn living room, condemning his daughter's *illegal affairs* and boldly proclaiming that he was only waiting, waiting till his daughter's hair again touched her ankles so that he may step in peace into his grave, *y maldito sea el día that she had ever become a woman y se me metió en el coco a mi celebrarlo, y maldito sea San Antonio and all his days,* a business with no government license, legitimized instead, yanqui-style, with a business card, a whorish red allegro script on a white background, which she handed surreptitiously to any inquirer, palm to palm, folded in two, as careful as if it were three crisp yanqui hundred dollar notes, which is what it was worth, sí, como no, as much as nine thousand pesos on a monthly basis, for so large was the urge to celebrate a new womanhood after the murder of el Rubio and the silencing suicide of Tomás de Aquino.

The banished angels of womanhood, suddenly unbanished, shifted their allegiance to Benicia, La Reina de los Quince, the fairy godmother of present and future quinceañera celebrations, who would do her all to make sure that a young woman would remember this day for the rest of her life, especially for the older ones, the ones in their late teens and twenties who had missed out on their celebrations during the ban period and now came to her with their own bundle of pesos or wrinkled black-market dollars, to reclaim their right. The business was run from the palace of la Reina, the same house where Roque San Martín had staged his infamous St. Anthony's Day feast and now raised chickens and tormented the clientele with his derelict appearance, with his gargly taunts that nothing his daughter would do could match what he had done, that the champagne bath at eight hundred pesos was a sham, soda water tinted with a little bit of coffee and sweetened with a few drops of cane juice, that the linen dress the quinceañera could rent, at 150 pesos, had been altered and re-altered so many times that it had more stitches than a baseball and more stains than the shroud of Turin and stunk worse than a whore's bedsheet, that the makeup the new women would wear for the photo session, personally applied by Benicia, for a mere thirty pesos, had been concocted from the waste and blood of his chickens, that the hibiscus and rose bushes and potted palms set up in the patio for these same photo sessions, at five hundred pesos (even though his daughter was no photographer by trade—*a television repairwoman, carajo, that's what they made her!*), were fakes, as plastic and devoid of fragrance as a capitalist's soul, that the waltzes she played for her measly parties were from records so scratched and from phonographs so antique that the marvelous Strauss "Tales from the Vienna Woods" sounded more like "Wails from the Corner Brothel."

And what could Benicia San Martín, as the quinceañera's mother placed her hand on her daughter's chin and turned her daughter's eyes away from the mad old man, say to the father who had brought her so much joy on that St. Anthony's Day so long ago? What but a most mild retort?

"Cállese, papacito. Cállese, por favor. This woman just wants to make her daughter happy, like you once made me happy." And at this, Roque San Martín would hunch his bony shoulders and snivel like a boy and wipe his hands, stained with the blood of slaughtered chickens, on the seat of his underpants, and shuffle back into the living room, and mutter to his daughter that her hair was far too short for anyone to believe that she was a fairy godmother of any kind.

Y quién sabe, perhaps Roque San Martín was right, for the more Benicia let her hair grow, down past her wing-bones stretching towards the foothills of her buttocks, not as dark now, not as thick, streaked with long strands of yellowy gray, like threadings of gold in a countess's gown, the more her business thrived, till she was able to afford real camellia and gardenia bushes and a faux-brick well, which she set up in the center of her patio for the quinceañeras to lean against during the photo sessions, and new Irish linen dresses in six different sizes and styles and boxes of makeup, which she purchased from the local theater company, and even, near the collapse of her business, a Rolleiflex camera, which was said to once have belonged to the town's most famous and notorious photographer, Armando Quiñón (somehow having been pilfered from the bonfire that destroyed all his things on the day of his suicide), that made it almost impossible to take a bad picture, and she even, once or twice, found enough real champagne on the black market for the quinceañera to take a puddle-bath and was able to hire a quartet from the town's symphony to play live waltzes at the fiestas.

So it was wallowing in so much relative success, to the surprise of her father, who now made it a point not to show his face when prospective clients came over, to even tidy up the living-room coop and box all the gallinas in the kitchen, her hair now past the lift in her buttocks, that Benicia San Martín headed to the house on the corner of Maceo and Narciso López Streets. Her client, a boyish girl, named Teresa Cruz, had failed to show up for her preliminary makeup and photo session. Perhaps, Benicia thought, her mad abuelita, the once respected and respectable doña Adela, widow of the libertine Teodoro, mother of the most famous dissident on the Island (though Benicia thought her father better deserved that honor), had not finished the dress, for she had insisted on not renting one of Benicia's newly purchased dresses for her granddaughter.

"I will make her my own from the moth-eaten shreds of her mother's wedding dress," she had said on her visit to Benicia's patio. "That at least I can do for the poor girl. It is said that madwomen make the finest dressmakers!" And she smiled wickedly and pressed a bundle of pesos, mingled with dollars (to give it heft), into Benicia's palm and shuffled off on her two canes.

Roque San Martín, who had been peeping through a lifted drape in the living room, prophesied to his daughter that soon, much too soon, the Island would be full of people like him and the mad old Adela, too weak to walk but too proud to die. This, he shouted to his daughter, was the glory and future of la Revolución, a nation of immortal invalids.

"Por favor, papacito," Benicia said, not looking at him, separating the dollars from the pesos, "if the vigilantes hear you saying such things they'll throw you right back in jail."

"No, no, mijita, we are the tamed, the cured, the undead. We are no good to them in their jails, better to have us raising gallinas and knitting shut holes in moth-eaten dresses. Let them cast their sad nets elsewhere. Hacia usted, mijita . . . hacia usted, and all your illegal affairs."

"¡Sshhh, sumuso, papacito, por favor! Los vigilantes have ears cupped to every wall!"

And such she feared was the reason the girl Teresita Cruz had not shown up for her appointment. Someone had found something out and whispered it to someone who whispered it to someone else who whispered it in a wrong ear. Such were the perils of running a private business not sanctioned by the government, and Benicia had coursed through them many times before (greasing the greasable palm, tickling the ticklish hand—a full quarter of her profits she reserved in her coffers for bribes), but she had never been challenged by the return of the piteous wail known as el llanto de los quince. She, like the many, had thought it had died forever with the death of el Rubio and his grotesque bullmastiff. But on the porch steps of señora Adela's house, as she arrived to investigate why the girl Teresa had not shown up for her preliminary makeup and photo session, she heard it again. And she asked herself if hounds too have more than one life. And even as she pleaded with the angels of womanhood not to abandon her side, she resisted the temptation to cup her ears, for she knew others heard it too, and she knew that the girl inside that house would never turn fifteen, her life never rightfully and ceremonially steered into womanhood, and that this, this again would be the fate of all the not-yet-women of Guantánamo, for they too heard it, even the unborn, all infected by this song that was not quite a song, not quite anything but the high-pitched noise of mourning, like the squeals of a violin tuned to the echoes of Inferno's steepest canyons, they too heard it and mimicked it, and so Benicia knew, right then and there, on the front porch steps of the house at the corner of Maceo and Narciso López Streets that she was ruined, ruined till the day they would bring home the lamenting mother (to whom the banished angels of womanhood had now turned), in a pine box, on the six o'clock from Santiago, for not till then would any girl in Guantánamo become a woman again.

So resigned, Benicia San Martín made some quick calculations in her head. She figured that for her ever-blooming camellia and gardenia bushes, for her faux-brick well, for her fifteen finely tailored Irish linen dresses, for her Rolleiflex, for her battered tocadiscos and collection of Strauss waltzes, through la bolsa, she could procure enough yanqui dollars to sustain her ailing family for about a year. "After that, papacito's gallinas better start laying golden eggs!"

To make sure Roque San Martín would see that day, she went home, and with a kitchen knife, butchered off her gray-threaded brown locks. When he saw her, Roque San Martín shook his head and said only that it was very unfit for a young woman to live so long with the incontinent ghosts of her parents. Then, just as matter-of-factly, with a most dignified patience, he set out to teach his gallinas how to cackle *el llanto de los quince.*

"Who knows, it may one day serve as our national anthem," he said to them, "for what right-minded girl would want to reach the age when she would need to bear children on this god-forgotten futureless Island!"

MARÍA ELENA CRUZ VARELA

Love Song for Difficult Times

Antonio
how much it hurts being a man.
—ALBIS TORREZ

So hard to say I love you madly.
Until I reach my marrow. What would happen to my body
if I lose your hands? What would happen to my hands
if your hair is lost? So hard. Very hard
a love poem on these days.
It happens that you exist. Ferocious in your evidence.
It happens that I exist. Counterfeited. Insisting.
And it happens that we exist. The law of gravity doesn't forgive
us.
So hard to say I love you these days.
I love you with urgency. I want to make a statement.
Without doubts. And without traps.
To say I love you. Like that. Plainly.
And that our love shall save me from the nocturnal howl
when, like a maddened she-wolf, the fever will grab me.
I don't want to be hurt by the absence of tenderness.
But love. So hard to write that I love you.
Like this. *"Between so much gray, so many hunchbacks together."*
How can I aspire to transparency.
To retake this worn-out voice.
This ancient custom of saying I love you.

Like this. Plainly. Anciently. I say.
If everything is so hard. If everything hurts so much.
If one man. And another man. And again another. And another.
Destroy the spaces where love is kept.
If it weren't hard. Hard and tremendous.
If it weren't impossible to forget this rage.
My clock. Its tick-tock. The route to the scaffold.
My ridiculous sentence with this false cord.
If it weren't hard. Hard and tremendous.
I would cast this verse with its cheap cadence.
If it were this simple to write that I love you.

TRANSLATED BY MAIRYM CRUZ-BERNAL WITH DEBORAH DIGGES

The Exterminating Angel

Here the terrible thing. The beauty that overwhelms.
The destructive thing. The angel that rubs me.
Enlightened ring. Pure white presence that the astonished archer
hurls at us between two lightning bolts. I am unhappy. Mortal.
I suspect the profound treason under the mask of my body.
I initiate myself into what is terrible. I shine.
The other women that I am do not determine me. Because
every angel announces extermination. I cling to the beams.
I let them lacerate my poor back. Feet of mine: crawl.
This is my Vía Crucis. Another step. A step to the vestibule of
hell.
How to let pass the tender pungent caresses of fire.

And how can I not adore the body for the body itself. The man
himself.
The vibrating bulrush. Variations of that act in which I am
elevated.
Acrobatic fatality. What is beautiful. What is terrible.
The unbearable eternity exhales its bubbles. For I am but a weak
breath of air.
So imploring. Going down in the body for the body.
Trying to escape. But there is no way out.
A glimpse of the remnants from the old splendors appear.
Perhaps there will be no more light. Maybe no more fire.
Perhaps I will return to the country of eternal snow.
To my orphaned costume of winter. An angel in the medley.
Careful accord from a poor blinded bard.
Ready to recite my filth.
To patent my acts. My unpublished terrors.
An angel is the forge. Have fear of beauty.
It is concentrated lightness and weight.
Here, the terrible thing. The beauty that destroys.
I barely know if I can endure it.

TRANSLATED BY MAIRYM CRUZ-BERNAL WITH DEBORAH DIGGES

JOSÉ MANUEL PRIETO

from NOCTURNAL BUTTERFLIES OF THE RUSSIAN EMPIRE

LIVADIA

I kept taking dream journeys, plowing through the sea, covering thousands of miles in trains so long that on curves you could look across at the engine at the front of the arc, pulling an endless line of coaches. Me riding in the ninth, having tea. For a few brief seconds, while the train went around the corner, I tilted my head, pressing my cheek to the windowpane and watching the engine throb laboriously. Afterward I had the feeling that my car was continuing on by itself, with the cries on the platform, the very look of the city I'd left, all carried along as if in a single block. Aboard I was like a time traveler in a capsule cutting through various ages like a stack of pancakes. Hours in the car, hours talking to my fellow travelers, shrank to nothing when I arrived at my destination, evaporating the moment I stepped onto the station platform. One trip from the Black Sea to the Baltic, three days of biting cold, disappeared as if by magic the moment I saw the first golden cupolas of St. Petersburg. The worst was waking up after a dream trip full of strange beauties—all swindlers trying to steal my bags—worn out from wrestling with them, a terrible anxiety pressing down on me. I opened my eyes not knowing where I was and lay staring around a room without a single painting or personal touch. In the corner I saw copper heating pipes: two tubes thick as a finger that fed the radiator in my room. Had those parallel lines provoked my prolonged glide along the rails in the dream? The little window I'd left open when I came to bed was rattling, the shadow of a beech tree fell across the glass, a woman in the garden was shouting in Tartar. I had finally reached the end of my journey: Livadia.

Without enough energy to rise, I looked out the window at a beach dotted with early-morning bathers, many with dogs. I was keenly aware of everything; I hadn't been here long enough to have registered the changes, this pension room, Livadia. It hurt to see those swimmers with their dogs, I confess. I didn't have a house, my books were gone, I didn't even have a dog. These strangers coming out of the woods bothered me, walking their dogs on the beach. I don't think anyone in the pension had one. All rovers, like me, without a dog.

Before moving to this pension I had checked out the Oreandra, a hotel in Yalta. I left in disgust: I would never stay in such a high-priced place, a hotel for foreigners (a *jungestill* built in 1905 where the rooms cost more than a hundred a night). I was not exactly a foreigner. I had lived in Russia too long. I knew, for example, that if you want a room, you have to look at the ads on lampposts, the concentric layers of signs tacked up there. I needed a pension that had rooms for single men (Russian, many specified, but that was a small snag, no problem). I pulled up layer after layer, as carefully as if they were the Dead Sea Scrolls. They worked loose easily, soft from the rain. I found a sign about a pension in Livadia—perfect—with the name and number repeated on a fringe at the bottom, so you could tear off a strip. Only one strip left, that wasn't so good: the room could be gone.

I went back to the Oreandra. From a phone booth in the lobby, I looked out the window and saw that the day was turning nice again: big beams of light shot out like fans from the bottom side of gray clouds, that sort of thing. If you had been looking out this same window an hour earlier, you would have seen a downpour splashing on the flagstones, but when I dialed the number and someone picked it up on the second ring, the sun burst out from behind a cloud, the rays so bright they hurt, and I had to half-shut my eyes. The booth had a list of prefixes—typewritten with penciled corrections—for the major Russian cities. I could say I was calling from Simferopol, I realized, for a better bargaining position, so I'd be under less pressure, the rain less of a threat.

"I'm calling about the ad." (Why else would I be calling? I ought to introduce myself first, but that meant a name. I could invent a name: say, Andrei Gavrilov. Maybe I should start with a greeting: "Good afternoon, but it's probably already evening . . ." No, straight to the point, no preliminaries.)

"Yes," she responded dryly. (Fifty or fifty-five years old, fleshy, full breasts, in a dark housedress and slippers at the moment. Flinty blue eyes. I could just picture her.)

"Can you tell me about it?"

"I don't give out information on the phone." (Seventy, no, more than seventy years of Soviet rule).

"But do you have any rooms?" (Several years in Russia myself. I can elbow my way on to a city bus, if need be, and haggle over a kilo of figs in the market, with the best of them.). "I have a letter of recommendation," I added. The lie occurred to me as I watched a multicolored helium balloon go up across the bay.

"Oh, good!" Meaning, that changes things, and in more than one sense: she knew it was false, totally false, but wasn't that a testimonial to my ingenuity? Anyway, they didn't use letters of recommendation in Russia anymore. Since 1917, maybe a little later. Only the state wrote letters for or against you, promoting you to a ministerial post or dumping you in a distant outpost, ruining your reputation and your career. She suspected I was a foreigner, which gave her a bit of confidence, enough to open the door a crack, so she could throw me out, face first onto her lawn, telling me:

"I don't think it will be possible. We don't have any vacancies. But you can come by anyway."

Before I left the phone booth, I ran my finger down the list for the Astrakhan prefix. A second balloon was now rising, rocking back and forth, as slowly as a coin falling to the bottom of a glass (not quickly, the way a bubble rises from the bottom of a glass—how odd!). The revolving door of the Oreandra pushed me toward the street with feigned friendliness, but instead of hurrying out before it slapped me on the back I continued the circle and returned to the lobby. I had decided to write myself a letter of recommendation on the spot, at one of the tiny marble tables in the lobby.

I used my best Russian penmanship, imitating the shaky handwriting of a seventy-five-year-old man, Vladimir Vladimirovich, a friend in St. Petersburg. A single paragraph was all I needed, and I turned it out in the stiff superficial style of official letters, applications for jobs (and dismissals from them). And addressed it to Maria Kuzmovna (just like that, Maria, Kuzma's daughter, with no last name), the name on the ad.

The coast road ran past blue mountains with pine trees growing up them (and the sea below). Sometimes there was a clearing and I would have a perfect view of the tourists' sailboats and a large-hulled ship coming into the harbor. The wind carrying the balloons across the bay hit me in the face, a few raindrops still floating in it, but warm again. The asphalt ribbon of the highway slipped off onto the shoulder without a curb, irregularly, like it was pinned down by pine needles. A good road. I was glad it was asphalt not concrete, very much alike, but the asphalt was softer, making my walk easier. The lady at the front desk in the Oreandra had told me that a trolleybus went to all the little towns and beaches on the coast, Livadia and beyond, as far as Alupka. A strange route for a trolley. I let her tell me where to catch it—go five blocks down, wait at the movie house—and decided to walk.

It would take a half hour, I figured, by the road through the pines. I walked against the traffic. That way I could see the cars coming toward me (as a safety precaution), and the shuddering of the cable long before the trolley appeared around a long curve, an ancient model, its wires held on by rope.

Following its line I couldn't get lost. I walked past several pensions, practically on the road. The trolley didn't make regular stops, just pulled over when the driver saw anyone who wanted to go into Yalta, or the other way, to the mineral baths in Alupka. I had been to Yalta before, but it didn't count. I had made a quick circuit of the peninsula, driving along the coast in a prewar convertible, hardly stopping at all. Without visiting Livadia, for instance. There is a Grand Palace in Livadia, built in 1911. Surrounding it is an English garden with the road down the middle. I stepped onto its grass and ran downhill, full tilt, so I wouldn't fall. I slowed down at a gravel path. "It's not far from the Palace, in fact, just 800 meters from the left wing." Nice location, near a palace. I went a little farther, down to the sea. And found the two-story house I wanted: "Livadia" (the pension's name, too).

The Black Sea was a good place to live, lots of family-style pensions, very cheap since the crisis. The only problem was that these pensions, these solid houses built on stone foundations, with ten to fifteen rooms plus a kitchen, were not really family-run. Not any more. Not since the turn of the century. Now they were administered by the state, with the rooms listed on the vacation plans of unions from all over. Schoolteachers and retirees could stay practically free, paying with vouchers for meals, plus every service from laundry to midnight snacks: a cold glass of milk and some cookies.

Vladimir Vladimirovich had spent a month there, I told Maria

Kuzmovna. She didn't remember him, naturally, but my dollars, which she could change into the new local money, widened the opening my fake reference had given me. I just let her know I didn't approve of the old voucher system. I would pay in cash and in advance for board and bedding.

She didn't have to read the letter twice, I noticed, not this Kuzmovna. Her fear was gone, most of it anyway. She was just cautious, probably had to be, without the false trust so many people invested in the newly opened market. The swarms of old soviet economic police were being replaced by fiscal inspectors, and I had seen many people slip up on deals that seemed safe. She gave me a sharp look. She was about fifty, with a broad chest like a landing strip for airplanes with soft tires, nearly flat. She yelled: "Mikhail Petrovich!"—another retiree in loose shirt and sandals—"Come here please." She wanted a witness to our deal. So at least she wasn't overcharging me. She wanted to know the purpose of my visit. No answer. She had to ask, she explained, since I was staying so long. I said, "I need a room with a view." It could mean anything: a poetic nature, an interest in astronomy, a respiratory disease. "I have a room facing the sea," she admitted at last. She folded the letter and put it away, slipping it into the pocket of her dress. Mikhail Petrovich, the retiree in the round glasses, couldn't be her lover: he was too old and feeble to move Kuzmovna's massive hips. I was in. A pair of unsuspecting vacationers showed up for the room, pockets full of vouchers, and she sent them packing: someone's always messing up, Moscow or somewhere, sending two guests for the same spot (lie!); try the big sanatoria, maybe, or the Palace.

I soon discovered that the boarders exchanged notes, which they attached to the doors of their rooms on little self-adhesive papers with a strip of glue that stayed sticky. I went sneaking from door to door, reading these little notes, forming impressions of the other guests. Kuzmovna's always had a peremptory tone: "Mikhail

Petrovich, don't ever leave the oven on again!" Kuzmovna was bright enough ordinarily, but could not seem to learn my name. I let on that it was Joska, which ended the stammers provoked by a strange name, and soon notes started to appear, topped by that simple name, and decked with three exclamation marks (indicating amazement, urgency, incredible importance): "Don't forget to empty the wastebasket!" or "How many times must I tell you, your breakfast gets cold by eight-thirty in the morning?"

LIVADIA

The woods led down to the beach. I was cold walking through them, among the pines. When I came out on the beach, I was shocked by the heat, unimaginable under the trees. Just the sort of contrast you would remember years later, and made a (mental) note: "This sure beats the tropics, those dry lonely beaches." At least I liked it better now, the nice combination of sunny beach and woods, the chance to withdraw to the shadows, light a fire in a clearing. The mere hint (mental) of the August sun made me queasy. By September, maybe before, the market would be full of fruits. That, too.

I had traveled too much the past two years, I thought, when I was back under the trees. I had hurried away from great cities, with their museums and galleries, without seeing them, in and out in three days, not a moment to spare. Always rushing to catch a plane, the ferry leaving at 18:37, the train at 13:45. Always in some cab, the backseat heaped with bags, flying toward the dock, the station, the airport. Or else, I had floated through too many cities: Helsinki, Prague, Vienna, Stockholm, Berlin, buying and selling, immersed in liquidation sales when the Wall gave way, chasing after cut-rate antiquities in Kraków, barely alighting in its cobbled streets, soaring to Vienna on sandals winged with 500 percent profits. My sole activity: crossing the membranes of states (borders), taking advantage of the different values between one cell (nation) and another. And after a few days' inactivity, taking off charged with oxygen, a terrific payoff with a minor toll on my nerves. I did not, for example, take the opium bars an Uzbeki tried to push on me in Samarkand. I had read how every hour in prison seems endless, and also, of course, about men in solitary confinement with nothing to do, a lifetime of letter-writing ahead.

The problem of borders fascinates me, the practical angle, of course. In one night hundreds of people, hundreds of smugglers, crossed the Estonian border. A dream. The newspapers didn't say a word about the incident or its political significance. Russia had set its colonies free, shrinking away from its customs posts, its barbed wire, its dogs. Crossing into Estonia or any of the other Baltic republics, you were suddenly in a foreign country. Across the border a dark mass of smugglers had gathered, suitcases stuffed with illegal merchandise, trucks with tarps covering their loads. Like the army of the night preparing an attack, with every precaution. In Ivangorod, the ancient fortress that now marked the end of Russian territory and the start of the Hanseatic League, you could walk down the main street in broad daylight and not see the preparations: the forces camped along the border, the jeeps with their lights out and their map boxes open, the index fingers tracing a sinuous route by which a few soldiers were taking out three helicopters with muffled blades. People had been filtering across this "transparent border" (as *Izvetia* called it) for a long time, gradually "draining the lifeblood from Mother Russia" (*sic*), but one moonless night the first divisions of smugglers began pouring out of the heart of Russia, overrunning the country like an an army of lemurs, and months later in Warsaw or Berlin, people were still talking about it. A single night. Some of them took more than one trip. A cargo of osmium oxide, for example, a rare earth, at seventy thousand dollars a kilogram, making a killing overnight. Estonia and the other Baltic republics took the weapon fate had given them and paid Russia back with smuggled goods. I traveled through Ivangorod when memories of that night were still fresh, inspiring long hours of stories in the train-station café. That day was over, but some people had seized it, as well as a fortune. I heard about it the afternoon I arrived, a few months too late, from a drunk selling fried meatballs, twirling his aluminum fork, and talking about crossing that border on foot, no problem. "A walk in the park!" (he winked), but with just two bottles of vodka in the pockets of the checked jacket he was wearing. By now, he told me, he could have been a millionaire in Tallin . . . "Kolya! My friend Kolya . . . We drank together here many times . . . Zubrovka . . . I visited him three days ago in his office in Narva, five minutes from here: two secretaries, *nogui, vo!* (legs up to here, this long), cellular phone. The transparent border!" he spit out furiously.

It was no less transparent now, but you needed quick wits to go through: you might have to toss the goods and run. Russia had brought in soldiers from all over, garrisons in the Urals or Bashkirya, raw recruits with no real sense of customs, ready to take your watchband to stop the looting of their country.

A curious incident, something that happened to me on one of my trips: a woman in Brussels tried to return some goods I supposedly sold her in Liège, some bad caviar. I had never gone to Liège, nor would I want to. Nor had I ever sold any caviar. Well, all right, one time someone gave me a bargain on a few tins of the finest caviar—beluga, anyone who eats caviar knows what that means. But this woman, on that trip to Brussels, saw me in the plaza by myself, cool and assured, singing the praises of my goods. (I'm embarrassed to admit, but at first, when I was starting out, I stood in plazas selling my merchandise, before I found clients who would buy whole shipments from me, items like Hasselblad cameras, two hundred dollars apiece. I should add that I'm interested in optics, that's why I went to Russia, to study optics, but I didn't graduate.) The lady could have been seeing double, suffering from some kind of optical aberration, maybe a temporary disphasia. Like déjà vu, the same physical principle. The theory is that one eye (we'll say the right, but it can be the left) sees the image first, a split second ahead—a young man in a khaki jacket, a black watchcap over his ears, excellent teeth flashing a disdainful smile, thinking he won't make very much here, he should go big time—and his image travels along the optic nerve to the brain, where it is received, processed, and stored; and then a bit later, the left optic nerve gets a second image (which looks the same, but is actually different, secretly altered—the young man thinking he ought to get better stuff, a bigger profit, at least a hundred grand a year), and that one reaches the brain, and hey! seen that one before!; and next thing you know the person, the fifty-year-old fury walking toward me, is sure she's met me, and what's worse, I'm the man from Liège, the one who sold her the lumpy caviar that tasted like asphalt.

It took me completely by surprise, like déjà vu, providing an aftertaste, a faint hint or a big hit, of nostalgia or euphoria. The woman didn't have the nerve to throw her caviar in my face—she had the cans in her bag, maybe planning to present them in the lower house of the Belgian parliament, material evidence in a complaint about smuggling, tainted goods coming into the country from the east, Russland. Seeing me there—and inexplicably taking me for whoever had sold her the caviar in Liège—she spoke to a pair of teenagers, explaining the dirty trick I'd played, shaking an angry finger as she came toward me (twisting the top of my thermos in irritation, gripping it with the fleshy fingertips protruding from my cut-off gloves), and spat out a big speech in Walloon, brandishing the cans I had never seen (much less sold). Then she switched to plain English: pay her back or she'd call the cops. I started to explain that I never sold caviar, it wasn't my line.

And showed them the sort of things I sold, handing infrared telescope sights to the boys, who might want to follow their debut as bodyguards with a little turn at surveillance. Since the stuff had sidestepped customs, the woman wanted to have it out with me—the accused swindler—herself. Let's just see, I thought, if she'll call the police. I gave her a cutting answer, in English (I must say, English has an edge, I like that, at least in the tough novels I've read, Mickey Spillane, plenty sharp): *"What's the problem? The money? You want your money back? Okay. Give me those damned cans and get your money back."* I knew I could unload them on some other Sunday stroller short the francs for caviar from Belgian shops. I'd never been to Liège, I hadn't sold her those cans, but the old lady tapped them with a crooked finger and pointed at my chest, establishing a mysterious link between me, the caviar, and an unknown city (Liège).

She took me for someone else, I figured. A month later, in Stockholm, a man came up to me, quite friendly, claiming we had met on the ferry, saying I had promised him some folk music tapes from southern Russia. He seemed to be suffering from some delusion, too, like the Chinese who can't tell Western faces apart, or maybe it was a blindspot, like the Westerners who can't tell Chinese faces apart—although I don't look Chinese; that's just an example.

Later it was my turn: I was sitting in the bay window in a Greek restaurant, right here in Livadia, and simultaneously seemed to be in some faraway place. Like when you're sitting in an armchair at home and suddenly feel like you're in a pasture in Inner Mongolia, all the same physical sensations, wind bending the tall grass, small ponies grazing. I would really like to find an explanation for this phenomenon.

TRANSLATED BY CAROL AND THOMAS CHRISTENSEN

ANA MENÉNDEZ

In Cuba I Was a German Shepherd

The park where the four men gathered was small. Before the city put it on its tourist maps, it was just a fenced rectangle of space that people missed on the way to their office jobs. The men came each morning to sit under the shifting shade of a banyan tree, and sometimes the way the wind moved through the leaves reminded them of home.

One man carried a box of plastic dominos. His name was Máximo, and because he was a small man his grandiose name had inspired much amusement all his life. He liked to say that over the years he'd learned a thing or two about the meaning of laughter and his friends took that to mean good humor could make a big man out of anyone. Now, Máximo waited for the others to sit before turning the dominos out on the table. Judging the men to be in good spirits, he cleared his throat and began to tell the joke he had prepared for the day.

"So Bill Clinton dies in office and they freeze his body."

Antonio leaned back in his chair and let out a sigh. "Here we go."

Máximo caught a roll of the eyes and almost grew annoyed. But he smiled. "It gets better."

He scraped the dominos in two wide circles across the table, then continued.

"Okay, so they freeze his body and when we get the technology to unfreeze him, he wakes up in the year 2105."

"Two thousand one hundred and five, eh?"

"Very good," Máximo said. "Anyway, he's curious about what's happened to the world all this time, so he goes up to a Jewish fellow and he says, 'So, how are things in the Middle East?' The guy replies, 'Oh wonderful, wonderful, everything is like heaven. Everybody gets along now.' This makes Clinton smile, right?"

The men stopped shuffling and dragged their pieces across the table and waited for Máximo to finish.

"Next he goes up to an Irishman and he says, 'So how are things over there in Northern Ireland now?' The guy says, 'Northern? It's one Ireland now and we all live in peace.' Clinton is extremely pleased at this point, right? So he does that biting thing with his lip."

Máximo stopped to demonstrate and Raúl and Carlos slapped their hands on the domino table and laughed. Máximo paused. Even Antonio had to smile. Máximo loved this moment when the men were warming to the joke and he still kept the punch line close to himself like a secret.

"So, okay," Máximo continued, "Clinton goes up to a Cuban fellow and says, 'Compadre, how are things in Cuba these days?' The guy looks at Clinton and he says to the president, 'Let me tell you, my friend, I can feel it in my bones. Any day now Castro's gonna fall.' "

Máximo tucked his head into his neck and smiled. Carlos slapped him on the back and laughed.

"That's a good one, sure is," he said. "I like that one."

"Funny," Antonio said, nodding as he set up his pieces.

"Yes, funny," Raúl said. After chuckling for another moment, he added, "But old."

"What do you mean old?" Antonio said, then he turned to Carlos. "What are you looking at?"

Carlos stopped laughing.

"It's not old," Máximo said. "I just made it up."

"I'm telling you, professor, it's an old one," Raúl said. "I heard it when Reagan was president."

Máximo looked at Raúl, but didn't say anything. He pulled the double nine from his row and laid it in the middle of the table, but the thud he intended was lost in the horns and curses of morning traffic on Eighth Street.

Raúl and Máximo had lived on the same El Vedado street in Havana for fifteen years before the revolution. Raúl had been a government accountant and Máximo a professor at the University, two blocks from his home on L Street. They weren't close friends, but friendly still in that way of people who come from the same place and think they already know the important things about one another.

Máximo was one of the first to leave L Street, boarding a plane for Miami on the eve of the first of January 1961, exactly two years after Batista had done the same. For reasons he told himself he could no longer remember, he said good-bye to no one. He was thirty-six years old then, already balding, with a wife and two young daughters whose names he tended to confuse. He left behind the row house of long shiny windows, the piano, the mahogany furniture, and the pension he thought he'd return to in two years' time. Three if things were as serious as they said.

In Miami, Máximo tried driving a taxi, but the streets were a web of foreign names and winding curves that could one day lead to glitter and another to the hollow end of a pistol. His Spanish and his University of Havana credentials meant nothing here. And he was too old to cut sugarcane with the younger men who began arriving in the spring of 1961. But the men gave Máximo an idea and after teary nights of promises, he convinced his wife—she of stately homes and multiple cooks—to make lunch to sell to those sugar men who waited, squatting on their heels in the dark, for the bus to Belle Glade every morning. They worked side by side, Máximo and Rosa. And at the end of every day, their hands stained orange from the lard and the cheap meat, their knuckles red and tender where the hot water and the knife blade had worked their business, Máximo and Rosa would sit down to whatever remained of the day's cooking and they would chew slowly, the day unraveling, their hunger ebbing away with the light.

They worked together for seven years like that, and when the Cubans began disappearing from the bus line, Máximo and Rosa moved their lunch packets indoors and opened their little restaurant right on Eighth Street. There, a generation of former professors served black beans and rice to the nostalgic. When Raúl showed up in Miami in the summer of 1971 looking for work, Máximo added one more waiter's spot for his old acquaintance from L Street. Each night, after the customers had gone, Máximo and Rosa and Raúl and Havana's old lawyers and bankers and dreamers would sit around the biggest table and eat and talk and sometimes, late in the night after several glasses of wine, someone would start the stories that began with "In Cuba I remember." They were stories of old lovers, beautiful and round-hipped. Of skies that stretched on clear and blue to the Cuban hills. Of green landscapes that clung to the red clay of Güines, roots dug in like fingernails in a good-bye. In Cuba, the stories always began, life was good and pure. But something always happened to them in the end, something withering, malignant. Máximo never understood it. The stories that opened in sun, always narrowed into a dark place. And after those nights, his head throbbing, Máximo would turn and turn in his sleep and awake unable to remember his dreams.

. . .

Even now, five years after selling the place, Máximo couldn't walk by it in the early morning when it was still clean and empty. He'd tried it once. He'd stood and stared into the restaurant and had become lost and dizzy in his own reflection in the glass, the neat row of chairs, the tombstone lunch board behind them.

"Okay. A bunch of rafters are on the beach getting ready to sail off to Miami."

"Where are they?"

"Who cares? Wherever. Cuba's got a thousand miles of coastline. Use your imagination."

"Let the professor tell his thing, for God's sake."

"Thank you." Máximo cleared his throat and shuffled the dominos. "So anyway, a bunch of rafters are gathered there on the sand. And they're all crying and hugging their wives and all the rafts are bobbing on the water and suddenly someone in the group yells, 'Hey! Look who goes there!' And it's Fidel in swimming trunks, carrying a raft on his back."

Carlos interrupted to let out a yelping laugh. "I like that, I like it, sure do."

"You like it, eh?" said Antonio. "Why don't you let the Cuban finish it."

Máximo slid the pieces to himself in twos and continued. "So one of the guys on the sand says to Fidel, 'Compatriota, what are you doing here? What's with the raft?' And Fidel sits on his raft and pushes off the shore and says, 'I'm sick of this place too. I'm going to Miami.' So the other guys look at each other and say, 'Coño, compadre, if you're leaving, then there's no reason for us to go. Here, take my raft too, and get the fuck out of here.'"

Raúl let a shaking laugh rise from his belly and saluted Máximo with a domino piece.

"A good one, my friend."

Carlos laughed long and loud. Antonio laughed too, but he was careful to not laugh too hard and he gave his friend a sharp look over the racket he was causing. He and Carlos were Dominican, not Cuban, and they ate their same foods and played their same games, but Antonio knew they still didn't understand all the layers of hurt in the Cubans' jokes.

It had been Raúl's idea to go down to Domino Park that first time. Máximo protested. He had seen the rows of tourists pressed up against the fence, gawking at the colorful old guys playing dominos.

"I'm not going to be the sad spectacle in someone's vacation slide show," he'd said.

But Raúl was already dressed up in a pale blue guayabera, saying how it was a beautiful day and smell the air.

"Let them take pictures," Raúl said. "What the hell. Make us immortal."

"Immortal," Máximo said like a sneer. And then to himself, The gods' punishment.

It was that year after Rosa died and Máximo didn't want to tell how he'd begun to see her at the kitchen table as she'd been at twenty-five. Watched one thick strand of her dark hair stuck to her morning face. He saw her at thirty, bending down to wipe the chocolate off the cheeks of their two small daughters. And his eyes moved from Rosa to his small daughters. He had something he needed to tell them. He saw them grown up, at the funeral, crying together. He watched Rosa rise and do the sign of the cross. He knew he was caught inside a nightmare, but he couldn't stop. He would emerge slowly, creaking out of the shower and there she'd be, Rosa, like before, her breasts round and pink from the hot water, calling back through the years. Some mornings he would awake and smell peanuts roasting and hear the faint call of the manicero pleading for someone to relieve his burden of white paper cones. Or it would be thundering, the long hard thunder of Miami that was so much like the thunder of home that each rumble shattered the morning of his other life. He would awake, caught fast in the damp sheets, and feel himself falling backwards.

He took the number eight bus to Eighth Street and 15th Avenue. At Domino Park, he sat with Raúl and they played alone that first day, Máximo noticing his own speckled hands, the spots of light through the banyan leaves, a round red beetle that crawled slowly across the table, then hopped the next breeze and floated away.

Antonio and Carlos were not Cuban, but they knew when to dump their heavy pieces and when to hold back the eights for the final shocking stroke. Waiting for a table, Raúl and Máximo would linger beside them and watch them lay their traps, a succession of threes that broke their opponents, an incredible run of fives. Even the unthinkable: passing when they had the piece to play.

Other twosomes began to refuse to play with the Dominicans, said that tipo Carlos gave them the creeps with his giggling and monosyllables. Besides, any team that won so often must be cheating, went the charge, especially a team one-half imbecile. But really it was that no one plays to lose. You begin to lose again and again and it reminds you of other things in your life, the despair of it all begins to bleed through and that is not what games are for. Who wants to live their whole life alongside the lucky? But Máximo and Raúl liked these blessed Dominicans, appreciated the well-oiled moves of two old pros. And if the two Dominicans, afraid to be alone again, let them win now and then, who would know, who could ever admit to such a thing?

For many months they didn't know much about each other, these four men. Even the smallest boy knew not to talk when the pieces were in play. But soon came Máximo's jokes during the shuffling, something new and bright coming into his eyes like daydreams as he spoke. Carlos's full loud laughter, like that of children. And the four men learned to linger long enough between sets to color an old memory while the white pieces scraped along the table.

One day as they sat at their table closest to the sidewalk, a pretty girl walked by. She swung her long brown hair around and looked in at the men with her green eyes.

"What the hell is she looking at," said Antonio, who always sat with his back to the wall, looking out at the street. But the others saw how he resumed the stare too.

Carlos let out a giggle and immediately put a hand to his mouth.

"In Santo Domingo, a man once looked at—" But Carlos didn't get to finish.

"Shut up, you old idiot," said Antonio, putting his hands on the table like he was about to get up and leave.

"Please," Máximo said.

The girl stared another moment, then turned and left. Raúl rose slowly, flattening down his oiled hair with his right hand.

"Ay, mi niña."

"Sit down, hombre," Antonio said. "You're an old fool, just like this one."

"You're the fool," Raúl called back. "A woman like that . . ." He watched the girl cross the street. When she was out of sight, he grabbed the back of the chair behind him and eased his body down, his eyes still on the street. The other three men looked at one another.

"I knew a woman like that once," Raúl said after a long moment.

"That's right, he did," Antonio said, "in his moist boy dreams—what was it? A century ago?"

"No me jodas," Raúl said. "You are a vulgar man. I had a life all three of you would have paid millions for. Women."

Máximo watched him, then lowered his face, shuffled the dominos.

"I had women," Raúl said.

"We all had women," Carlos said, and he looked like he was about to laugh again, but instead just sat there, smiling like he was remembering one of Máximo's jokes.

"There was one I remember. More beautiful than the rising moon," Raúl said.

"Oh Jesus," Antonio said. "You people."

Máximo looked up, watching Raúl.

"Ay, a woman like that," Raúl said and shook his head. "The women of Cuba were radiant, magnificent, wouldn't you say, professor?"

Máximo looked away.

"I don't know," Antonio said. "I think that Americana there looked better than anything you remember."

And that brought a long laugh from Carlos.

Máximo sat all night at the pine table in his new efficiency, thinking about the green-eyed girl and wondering why he was thinking about her. The table and a narrow bed had come with the apartment, which he'd moved into after selling their house in Shenandoah. The table had come with two chairs, sturdy and polished—not in the least institutional—but he had moved the other chair by the bed.

The landlady, a woman in her forties, had helped Máximo haul up three potted palms. Later, he bought a green pot of marigolds he saw in the supermarket and brought its butter leaves back to life under the window's eastern light. Máximo often sat at the table through the night, sometimes reading Martí, sometimes listening to the rain on the tin hull of the air conditioner.

When you are older, he'd read somewhere, you don't need as much sleep. And wasn't that funny because his days felt more like sleep than ever. Dinner kept him occupied for hours, remembering the story of each dish. Sometimes, at the table, he greeted old friends and awakened with a start when they reached out to touch him. When dawn rose and slunk into the room sideways through the blinds, Máximo walked as in a dream across the thin patterns of light on the terrazzo. The chair, why did he keep the other chair? Even the marigolds reminded him. An image returned again and again. Was it the green-eyed girl?

And then he remembered that Rosa wore carnations in her hair and hated her name. And that it saddened him because he liked to roll it off his tongue like a slow train to the country.

"Rosa," he said, taking her hand the night they met at La Concha while an old danzón played.

"Clavel," she said, tossing her head back in a crackling laugh. "Call me clavel."

She pulled her hand away and laughed again. "Don't you notice the flower in a girl's hair?"

He led her around the dance floor, lined with chaperones, and when they turned he whispered that he wanted to follow her laughter to the moon. She laughed again, the notes round and heavy as summer raindrops, and Máximo felt his fingers go cold where they touched hers. The danzón played and they turned and turned and the faces of the chaperones and the moist warm air—and Máximo with his cold fingers worried that she had laughed at him. He was twenty-four and could not imagine a more sorrowful thing in all the world.

Sometimes, years later, he would catch a premonition of Rosa in the face of his eldest daughter. She would turn toward a window or do something with her eyes. And then she would smile and tilt her head back and her laughter connected him again to that night, made him believe for a moment that life was a string you could gather up in your hands all at once.

He sat at the table and tried to remember the last time he saw Marisa. In California now. An important lawyer. A year? Two? Anabel, gone to New York? Two years? They called more often than most children, Máximo knew. They called often and he was lucky that way.

"Fidel decides he needs to get in touch with young people."

"Ay, ay, ay."

"So his handlers arrange for him to go to a school in Havana. He gets all dressed up in his olive uniform, you know, puts conditioner on his beard and brushes it one hundred times, all that."

Raúl breathed out, letting each breath come out like a puff of laughter. "Where do you get these things?"

"No interrupting the artist anymore, okay?" Máximo continued. "So after he's beautiful enough, he goes to the school. He sits in on a few classes, walks around the halls. Finally, it's time for Fidel to leave and he realizes he hasn't talked to anyone. He rushes over to the assembly that is seeing him off with shouts of 'Comandante!' and he pulls a little boy out of a row. 'Tell me,' Fidel says, 'what is your name?' 'Pepito,' the little boy answers. 'Pepito—what a nice name,' Fidel says. 'And tell me, Pepito, what do you think of the revolution?' 'Comandante,' Pepito says, 'the revolution is the reason we are all here.' 'Ah, very good, Pepito. And tell me, what is your favorite subject?' Pepito answers, 'Comandante, my favorite subject is mathematics.' Fidel pats the little boy on the head. 'And tell me, Pepito, what would you like to be when you grow up?' Pepito smiles and says, 'Comandante, I would like to be a tourist.' "

Máximo looked around the table, a shadow of a smile on his thin white lips as he waited for the laughter.

"Ay," Raúl said. "That is so funny it breaks my heart."

Máximo grew to like dominos, the way each piece became part of the next. After the last piece was laid down and they were tallying up the score, Máximo liked to look over the table as an artist might. He liked the way the row of black dots snaked around the table with such free-flowing abandon it was almost as if, thrilled to be let out of the box, the pieces choreographed a fresh dance of gratitude every night. He liked the straightforward contrast of black on white. The clean, fresh scrape of the pieces across the table before each new round. The audacity of the double nines. The plain smooth face of the blank, like a newborn unetched by the world to come.

"Professor," Raúl began. "Let's speed up the shuffling a bit, sí?"

"I was thinking," Máximo said.

"Well, that shouldn't take long," Antonio said.

"Who invented dominos, anyway?" Máximo said.

"I'd say it was probably the Chinese," Antonio said.

"No jodas," Raúl said. "Who else could have invented this game of skill and intelligence but a Cuban?"

"Coño," said Antonio without a smile. "Here we go again."

"Ah, bueno," Raúl said with a smile stuck between joking and condescending. "You don't have to believe it if it hurts."

Carlos let out a long laugh.

"You people are unbelievable," said Antonio. But there was something hard and tired behind the way he smiled.

It was the first day of December, but summer still hung about in the brightest patches of sunlight. The four men sat under the shade of the banyan tree. It wasn't cold, not even in the shade, but three of the men wore cardigans. If asked, they would say they were expecting a chilly north wind and doesn't anybody listen to the weather forecasts anymore. Only Antonio, his round body enough to keep him warm, clung to the short sleeves of summer.

Kids from the local Catholic high school had volunteered to decorate the park for Christmas and they dashed about with tinsel in their hair, bumping one another and laughing loudly. Lucinda, the woman who issued the dominos and kept back the gambling, asked them to quiet down, pointing at the men. A wind stirred the top branches of the banyan tree and moved on without touching the ground. One leaf fell to the table.

Antonio waited for Máximo to fetch Lucinda's box of plastic pieces. Antonio held his brown paper bag to his chest and looked at the Cubans, his customary sourness replaced for a moment by what in a man like him could pass for levity. Máximo sat down and began to dump the plastic pieces on the table as he always did. But this time, Antonio held out his hand.

"One moment," he said and shook his brown paper bag.

"Qué pasa, chico?" Máximo said.

Antonio reached into the paper bag as the men watched. He let the paper fall away. In his hand he held an oblong black leather box.

"Coñooo," Raúl said.

He set the box on the table, like a magician drawing out his trick. He looked around to the men and finally opened the box with a flourish to reveal a neat row of big heavy pieces, gone yellow and smooth like old teeth. They bent in closer to look. Antonio tilted the box gently and the pieces fell out in one long line, their black dots facing up now like tight dark pupils in the sunlight.

"Ivory," Antonio said. "And ebony. It's an antique. You're not allowed to make them anymore."

"Beautiful," Carlos said and clasped his hands.

"My daughter found them for me in New Orleans," Antonio continued, ignoring Carlos.

He looked around the table and lingered on Máximo, who had lowered the box of plastic dominos to the ground.

"She said she's been searching for them for two years. Couldn't wait two more weeks to give them to me," he said.

"Coñooo," Raúl said.

A moment passed.

"Well," Antonio said, "what do you think, Máximo?"

Máximo looked at him. Then he bent across the table to touch one of the pieces. He gave a jerk with his head and listened for the traffic. "Very nice," he said.

"Very nice?" Antonio said. "Very nice?" He laughed in his thin way. "My daughter walked all over New Orleans to find this and the Cuban thinks it's 'very nice?'" He paused, watching Máximo. "Did you know my daughter is coming to visit me for Christmas, Máximo? Maybe you can tell her that her gift was very nice, but not as nice as some you remember, eh?"

Máximo looked up, his eyes settling on Carlos, who looked at Antonio and then looked away.

"Calm down, hombre," Carlos said, opening his arms wide, a nervous giggle beginning in his throat. "What's gotten into you?"

Antonio waved his hand and sat down. A diesel truck rattled down Eighth Street, headed for downtown.

"My daughter is a district attorney in Los Angeles," Máximo said after the noise of the truck died. "December is one of the busiest months."

He felt a heat behind his eyes he had not felt in many years.

"Feel one in your hand," Antonio said. "Feel how heavy that is."

. . .

When the children were small, Máximo and Rosa used to spend Nochebuena with his cousins in Cárdenas. It was a five-hour drive from Havana in the cars of those days. They would rise early on the twenty-third and arrive by mid-afternoon so Máximo could help the men kill the pig for the feast the following night. Máximo and the other men held the squealing, squirming animal down, its wiry brown coat cutting into their gloveless hands. But God, they were intelligent creatures. No sooner did it spot the knife than the animal bolted out of their arms, screaming like Armageddon. It had become the subtext to the Nochebuena tradition, this chasing of the terrified pig through the yard, dodging orange trees and rotting fruit underneath. The children were never allowed to watch, Rosa made sure. They sat indoors with the women and stirred the black beans. With loud laughter, they shut out the shouts of the men and the hysterical pleadings of the animal as it was dragged back to its slaughter.

"Juanito the little dog gets off the boat from Cuba and decides to take a little stroll down Brickell Avenue."

"Let me make sure I understand the joke. Juanito is a dog. Bowwow."

"That's pretty good."

"Yes, Juanito is a dog, goddamn it."

Raúl looked up, startled.

Máximo shuffled the pieces hard and swallowed. He swung his arms across the table in wide, violent arcs. One of the pieces flew off the table.

"Hey, hey, watch it with that, what's wrong with you?"

Máximo stopped. He felt his heart beating. "I'm sorry," he said. He bent over the edge of the table to see where the piece had landed. "Wait a minute."

He held the table with one hand and tried to stretch to pick up the piece.

"What are you doing?"

"Just wait a minute." When he couldn't reach, he stood up, pulled the piece toward him with his foot, sat back down, and reached for it again, this time grasping it between his fingers and his palm. He put it facedown on the table with the others and shuffled, slowly, his mind barely registering the traffic.

"Where was I—Juanito the little dog, right, bowwow." Máximo took a deep breath. "He's just off the boat from Cuba and is strolling down Brickell Avenue. He's looking up at all the tall and shiny buildings. 'Coñoo,' he says, dazzled by all the mirrors. 'There's nothing like this in Cuba.' "

"Hey, hey, professor. We had tall buildings."

"Jesus Christ!" Máximo said. He pressed his thumb and forefinger into the corners of his eyes. "This is after Castro, then. Let me just get it out for Christ's sake."

He stopped shuffling. Raúl looked away.

"Ready now? Juanito the little dog is looking up at all the tall buildings and he's so happy to finally be in America because all his cousins have been telling him what a great country it is, right? You know, they were sending back photos of their new cars and girlfriends."

"A joke about dogs who drive cars—I've heard it all."

"Hey, they're Cuban superdogs."

"All right, they're sending back photos of their new owners or the biggest bones any dog has ever seen. Anything you like. Use your imaginations." Máximo stopped shuffling. "Where was I?"

"You were at the part where Juanito buys a Rolls-Royce."

The men laughed.

"Okay, Antonio, why don't you three fools continue the joke." Máximo got up from the table. "You've made me forget the rest of it."

"Aw, come on, chico, sit down, don't be so sensitive."

"Come on, professor, you were at the part where Juanito is so glad to be in America."

"Forget it. I can't remember the rest now."

Máximo rubbed his temple, grabbed the back of the chair, and sat down slowly, facing the street. "Just leave me alone, I can't remember it."

He pulled at the pieces two by two. "I'm sorry. Look, let's just play."

The men set up their double rows of dominos, like miniature barricades before them.

"These pieces are a work of art," Antonio said and laid down a double eight.

The banyan tree was strung with white lights that were lit all day. Colored lights twined around the metal poles of the fence, which was topped with a long loping piece of gold tinsel garland.

The Christmas tourists began arriving just before lunch as Máximo and Raúl stepped off the number eight. Carlos and Antonio were already at the table, watched by two groups of families. Mom and Dad with kids. They were big; even the kids were big and pink. The mother whispered to the kids and they smiled and waved. Raúl waved back at the mother.

"Nice legs, yes," he whispered to Máximo.

Before Máximo looked away, he saw the mother take out a little black pocket camera. He saw the flash out of the corner of his eye. He sat down and looked around the table; the other men stared at their pieces.

The game started badly. It happened sometimes—the distribution of the pieces went all wrong and out of desperation one of the men made mistakes and soon it was all they could do not to knock all the pieces over and start fresh. Raúl set down a double three and signaled to Máximo it was all he had. Carlos passed. Máximo surveyed his last five pieces. His thoughts scattered to the family outside. He looked to find the tallest boy with his face pressed between the iron slats, staring at him.

"You pass?" Antonio said.

Máximo looked at him, then at the table. He put down a three and a five. He looked again, the boy was gone. The family had moved on.

The tour groups arrived later that afternoon. First the white buses with the happy blue letters WELCOME TO LITTLE HAVANA. Next, the fat women in white shorts, their knees lost in an abstraction of flesh. Máximo tried to concentrate on the game. The worst part was how the other men acted out for them. Dominos are supposed to be a quiet game. And now there they were shouting at each other and gesturing. A few of the men had even brought cigars, and they dangled now, unlit, from their mouths.

"You see, Raúl," Máximo said. "You see how we're a spectacle?" He felt like an animal and wanted to growl and cast about behind the metal fence.

Raúl shrugged. "Doesn't bother me."

"A goddamn spectacle. A collection of old bones," Máximo said.

The other men looked up at Máximo.

"Hey, speak for yourself, cabrón," Antonio said.

Raúl shrugged again.

Máximo rubbed his knuckles and began to shuffle the pieces. It was hot, and the sun was setting in his eyes, backlighting the car exhaust like a veil before him. He rubbed his temple, feeling the skin move over the bone. He pressed the inside corners of his eyes, then drew his hand back over the pieces.

"Hey, you okay there?" Antonio said.

. . .

An open trolley pulled up and parked on the curb. A young man with blond hair, perhaps in his thirties, stood up in the front, holding a microphone. He wore a guayabera. Máximo looked away.

"This here is Domino Park," came the amplified voice in English, then Spanish. "No one under fifty-five allowed, folks. But we can sure watch them play."

Máximo heard shutters click, then convinced himself he couldn't have heard, not from where he was.

"Most of these men are Cuban and they're keeping alive the tradition of their homeland," the amplified voice continued, echoing against the back wall of the park. "You see, in Cuba, it was very common to retire to a game of dominos after a good meal. It was a way to bond and build community. Folks, you here are seeing a slice of the past. A simpler time of good friendships and unhurried days."

Maybe it was the sun. The men later noted that he seemed odd. The tics. Rubbing his bones.

First Máximo muttered to himself. He shuffled automatically. When the feedback on the microphone pierced through Domino Park, he could no longer sit where he was, accept things as they were. It was a moment that had long been missing from his life.

He stood and made a fist at the trolley.

"Mierda!" he shouted. "Mierda! That's the biggest bullshit I've ever heard."

He made a lunge at the fence. Carlos jumped up and restrained him. Raúl led him back to his seat.

The man of the amplified voice cleared his throat. The people on the trolley looked at him and back at Máximo; perhaps they thought this was part of the show.

"Well." The man chuckled. "There you have it, folks."

Lucinda ran over, but the other men waved her off. She began to protest about rules and propriety. The park had a reputation to uphold.

It was Antonio who spoke.

"Leave the man alone," he said.

Máximo looked at him. His head was pounding. Antonio met his gaze briefly, then looked to Lucinda.

"Some men don't like to be stared at is all," he said. "It won't happen again."

She shifted her weight, but remained where she was, watching.

"What are you waiting for?" Antonio said, turning now to Máximo, who had lowered his head into the white backs of the dominos. "Let's play."

That night Máximo was too tired to sit at the pine table. He didn't even prepare dinner. He slept and in his dreams he was a green and yellow fish swimming in warm waters, gliding through the coral, the only fish in the sea and he was happy. But the light changed and the sea darkened suddenly and he was rising through it, afraid of breaking the surface, afraid of the pinhole sun on the other side, afraid of drowning in the blue vault of sky.

"Let me finish the story of Juanito the little dog."

No one said anything.

"Is that okay? I'm okay I just remembered it. Can I finish it?"

The men nodded, but still did not speak.

"He is just off the boat from Cuba. He is walking down Brickell Avenue. And he is trying to steady himself, see, because he still has his sea legs and all the buildings are so tall they are making him dizzy. He doesn't know what to expect. He's maybe a little afraid. And he's thinking about a pretty little dog he knew once and he's wondering where she is now and he wishes he were back home."

He paused to take a breath. Raúl cleared his throat. The men looked at one another, then at Máximo. But his eyes were on the blur of dominos before him. He felt a stillness around him, a shadow move past the fence, but he didn't look up.

"He's not a depressive kind of dog, though. Don't get me wrong. He's very feisty. And when he sees an elegant white poodle striding toward him, he forgets all his worries and exclaims, 'O Madre de Dios, si cocinas como caminas . . .' "

The men let out a small laugh. Máximo continued.

" 'Si cocinas como caminas . . . ,' Juanito says, but the white poodle interrupts and says, 'I beg your pardon? This is America—kindly speak English.' So Juanito pauses for a moment to consider and says in his broken English, 'Mamita, you are one hot doggie, yes? I would like to take you to movies and fancy dinners.' "

"One hot doggie, yes?" Carlos repeated, then laughed. "You're killing me."

The other men smiled, warming to the story as before.

"So Juanito says, 'I would like to marry you, my love, and have gorgeous puppies with you and live in a castle.' Well, all this time the white poodle has her snout in the air. She looks at Juanito and says, 'Do you have any idea who you're talking to? I am a refined breed of considerable class and you are nothing but a short, insignificant mutt.' Juanito is stunned for a moment, but he rallies for the final shot. He's a proud dog, you see and he's afraid of his pain. 'Pardon me, your highness,' Juanito the mangy dog says. 'Here in America, I may be a short, insignificant mutt, but in Cuba I was a German shepherd.' "

Máximo turned so the men would not see his tears. The afternoon traffic crawled eastward. One horn blasted, then another. He remembered holding his daughters days after their birth, thinking how fragile and vulnerable lay his bond to the future. For weeks, he carried them on pillows, like jeweled china. Then, the blank spaces in his life lay before him. Now he stood with the gulf at his back, their ribbony youth aflutter in the past. And what had he salvaged from the years? Already, he was forgetting Rosa's face, the precise shade of her eyes.

Carlos cleared his throat and moved his hand as if to touch him, then held back. He cleared his throat again.

"He was a good dog," Carlos said and pressed his lips together.

Antonio began to laugh, then fell silent with the rest. Máximo started shuffling, then stopped. The shadow of the banyan tree worked a kaleidoscope over the dominos. When the wind eased, Máximo tilted his head to listen. He heard something stir behind him, someone leaning heavily on the fence. He could almost feel the breath. His heart quickened.

"Tell them to go away," Máximo said. "Tell them, no pictures."

RAFAEL CAMPO

What the Body Told

Not long ago, I studied medicine.
It was terrible, what the body told.
I'd look inside another person's mouth,
And see the desolation of the world.
I'd see his genitals and think of sin.

Because my body speaks the stranger's language,
I've never understood those nods and stares.
My parents held me in their arms, and still
I think I've disappointed them; they care
And stare, they nod, they make their pilgrimage

To somewhere distant in my heart, they cry.
I look inside their other-person's mouths
And see the sleek interior of souls.
It's warm and red in there—like love, with teeth.
I've studied medicine until I cried

All night. Through certain books, a truth unfolds.
Anatomy and physiology,
The tiny sensing organs of the tongue—
Each nameless cell contributing its needs.
It was fabulous, what the body told.

NOTES ABOUT THE AUTHORS

REINALDO ARENAS (1943–1990) was born to a poor rural family in Holguín, Cuba. His first novel, *Singing from the Well* (1967), marked the beginning of a five-novel sequence. Arenas was also the author of numerous other novels, novellas, short stories, essays, experimental theater, and poetry. Imprisoned and tortured after the Revolution, Arenas escaped Cuba in 1980. His memoir, *Before Night Falls* (1993), was published after his suicide.

MIGUEL BARNET (b. 1940) is a pioneer of Latin American "testimonial" literature. He is the author of *Biography of a Runaway Slave* (1966), a classic of its genre, which tells the story of a 103-year-old former slave in Cuba, and *Rachel's Song* (1969), among other works. Barnet is a prolific poet, novelist, and ethnologist as well as the founder and director of the Fundación Fernando Ortiz in Havana.

ANTONIO BENÍTEZ-ROJO (b. 1931) spent many years as a statistician before turning his attentions to journalism and literature in the mid-1960s. He was a significant critic and writer in Cuba until his defection in 1980. His book *El mar de las lentejas* (1979) was banned on the island after its publication. Benítez-Rojo has taught at numerous U.S. universities and is currently a professor at Amherst College. His critical study of Caribbean literature, *The Repeating Island: The Caribbean and the Postmodern Perspective,* was published in 1989.

LYDIA CABRERA (1900–1991) was an anthropologist and short-story writer who spent seventeen years in Paris, where her interest in the African culture of Cuba was sparked. Upon her return to Havana in 1939, Cabrera began an exploration of Afro-Cuban folklore and mythology which resulted in her first major work, *Cuentos negros de Cuba* (1940). Other works followed, most notably *El Monte: Notas sobre las religiones, las supersticiones y el folkore de los negros criollos y el pueblo de Cuba* (1954). After the Revolution, Cabrera settled in Miami.

GUILLERMO CABRERA INFANTE (b. 1929) was an early supporter of the Revolution and director of its first literary journal, *Lunes de Revolución,* and also worked as a film critic. Cabrera Infante was sent to Europe as a diplomat, defected in 1965, moved to London, and remains one of Fidel Castro's staunchest critics. He is well known for his novels, essays, and film criticism, particularly *Three Trapped Tigers* (1967), *Infante's Inferno* (1979), *Holy Smoke* (1988), and *Mea Cuba* (1992).

RAFAEL CAMPO (b. 1964) is the son of Cuban immigrants. He is a physician and a professor at Harvard Medical School as well as a poet, essayist, and memoirist. Campo is the author of four volumes of poems, including *What the Body Told* (1996) and *Landscape with Human Figure* (2002), as well as a collection of essays, *The Poetry of Healing: A Doctor's Education in Empathy, Identity, and Desire* (1997).

ALEJO CARPENTIER (1904–1980) was biculturally Cuban and French and is considered one of the leading literary voices of twentieth-century Cuba. He is most renowned for his novels, among them *The Kingdom of This World* (1949), *The Lost Steps* (1953), and *Explosion in the Cathedral* (1962), as well as for his work as a musicologist, avant-garde radio programmer, and cultural and political theorist. His seminal book, *Music in Cuba* (1946), was recently translated into English. He died in Paris.

LOURDES CASAL (1938–1981) was born in Cuba of mixed African, Spanish, and Chinese heritage and moved to the United States at a young age. She was a poet and fiction writer as well as a psychology professor in New Jersey. Casal founded the literary magazine *Areíto* and spearheaded the Antonio Maceo Brigade in the 1970s, which brought Cuban-Americans like herself, who were sympathetic to the Revolution, back to the island.

CALVERT CASEY (1924–1969) was born in the United States and raised in Cuba. His first stories were written in English, but he ultimately chose Spanish as his primary artistic language. His dark, exquisite stories have been compared to those of Kafka and Poe. Although Casey was part of the intelligentsia in the early days of the Revolution, he was later exiled and lived in Rome, where he committed suicide at the age of forty-five.

MARÍA ELENA CRUZ VARELA (b. 1953) grew up on a farm in Matanzas province. By the time she was forty, she had published four books of poems and had been awarded the National Award for Poetry. In 1991, Cruz Varela was expelled from the writers' union and attacked for her human rights activities. She was forced to leave Cuba in 1994 and currently lives in Spain. A bilingual collection of her poetry, *Ballad of the Blood,* was published in 1996.

NICOLÁS GUILLÉN (1902–1989) was primarily a poet who addressed race, folklorism, and social protest in works such as *El gran zoo* (1967). In 1936, he was jailed in Cuba for publishing "subversive materials" and moved to Spain, where he remained during the Civil War. After the Revolution, he became Cuba's ambassador-at-large as well as the president of its Writers' and Artists' Union.

JOSÉ LEZAMA LIMA (1912–1976) was a giant of contemporary Cuban letters. His poetry, essays, and fiction, particularly his novel *Paradiso* (1966), have been enormously influential among Latin American writers. Called a "Proust of the Caribbean," Lezama Lima was an early supporter of the Revolution. Although he later became a scapegoat of its intolerant cultural policies, he remained in Havana until his death.

DULCE MARÍA LOYNAZ (1902–1997) was born to privilege in Havana and began publishing poetry in 1920 in the newspaper *La Nación*, the same year she first visited the United States. Thereafter she traveled extensively through North America, Europe, the Middle East, and South America before settling in her family's Vedado mansion for good. Loynaz is the author of several volumes of poems, including *Juegos de agua* (1947) and *Poemas sin nombres* (1953), and a novel, *Jardín* (1951).

JOSÉ MARTÍ (1853–1895) was both a champion for Cuba's independence and the father of its contemporary literature. As a teenager he was imprisoned for his involvement in the independence movement and exiled to Spain. Later he became a newspaperman in New York and tirelessly worked in behalf of Cuba's freedom. His poetry, journalism, and essays fill more than two dozen volumes, but he is best known for his books of poems *Ismaelillo* (1882), *Versos sencillos* (1891), and his posthumously published *Versos libres* (1913). He died in battle.

ANA MENÉNDEZ (b. 1970) was born to Cuban exiles who settled in Los Angeles in the 1960s. Menéndez has worked as a journalist in Florida and California and also studied creative writing in New York. Her first collection of short stories, *In Cuba I Was a German Shepherd,* was published in 2001.

ERNESTO MESTRE (b. 1964) is the author of the novel *The Lazarus Rumba* (1999). He was born in Guantánamo, but his family emigrated to Spain and then to Miami when he was eight years old. Mestre teaches at Sarah Lawrence College and lives in New York City.

NANCY MOREJÓN (b. 1944) studied French literature at the University of Havana and has worked as a journalist, theater reviewer, and essayist. She has written extensively on issues of class and race, including a book on the nickel miners of Nicaro, Cuba. Many of her poems have been translated into English, most recently in the collection *Looking Within: Selected Poems, 1954–2000.* She lives in Havana.

LINO NOVÁS CALVO (1905–1983) was born in Spain but moved to Cuba as a child. For many years he worked as a journalist, translator, and teacher both in Cuba and in Spain. In 1960, he left Cuba for the United States, where he taught college and continued working on his short stories. Novás Calvo translated Faulkner's *Sanctuary* into Spanish, among other works.

FERNANDO ORTIZ (1881–1969) was one of Cuba's foremost intellectuals. A former member of the House of Representatives, he was forced to flee the island in 1930 due to his opposition to the Cuban dictator Gerardo Machado but later returned to Cuba. Ortiz published widely on a number of subjects—history, biography, musicology, archaeology, and most notably, Afro-Cuban culture. He is best known for his *Counterpoint: Tobacco and Sugar* (1940), which was translated into English in 1947.

HEBERTO PADILLA (1932–2000) worked as a foreign correspondent in London and Moscow during the early years of the Revolution and came to know many other writers while living abroad, including Sartre, Yevtushenko, and García Márquez. In 1971, he was imprisoned on charges of espionage and forced to publicly recant. After years of house arrest, Padilla left for the United States in 1980. He was the author of numerous volumes of poems, fiction, and an autobiography, *Self-Portrait of the Other* (1980).

GUSTAVO PÉREZ–FIRMAT (b. 1949) was born in Cuba and moved to the United States at the age of eleven. Pérez–Firmat is primarily a literary critic and scholar who has also written poetry, fiction, and a memoir, including *The Cuban Condition* (1989) and *Life on the Hyphen* (1994). He is currently a professor at Columbia University.

VIRGILIO PIÑERA (1912–1979) was never known to hold a job and survived largely on the kindness of friends and relatives. In 1950, he moved to Buenos Aires, where he began publishing his short stories and novels, among them *René's Flesh.* Piñera returned to Cuba in 1957 but was arrested in 1961 for "political and moral crimes." Although he was released, his work was silenced, and Piñera died impoverished and relatively unknown.

JOSÉ MANUEL PRIETO (b. 1962) was born in Havana and lived in Russia for twelve years. He has translated the works of Joseph Brodsky and Anna Akhmatova into Spanish and is a professor of Russian history in Mexico City. His novel, *Nocturnal Butterflies of the Russian Empire*, was published in 1999.

SEVERO SARDUY (1937–1993) was culturally Spanish, African, and Chinese, a fact that greatly influenced his poetry, fiction, criticism, and even his painting. Sarduy left Cuba in 1960 on a government scholarship and never returned, becoming a fixture of French intellectual circles. As an editor for a French book publisher, he brought Latin American literature to the attention of European readers. He is best known for his novels, *From Cuba with a Song* (1967) and *Cobra* (1972).

ZOÉ VALDÉS (b. 1959) was born in Havana and worked for many years at the Cuban Film Institute and as a member of the Cuban delegation for the United Nations Educational, Scientific, and Cultural Organization (UNESCO) in Paris, where she currently resides. She is a poet, novelist, and short-story writer. Among her works are *Yocandra in the Paradise of Nada* (1995) and *Dear First Love* (2002).

A PERSONAL DISCOGRAPHY

Jesús Alemañy, *Cubanísimo* (Rykodisc, England)
Cachao, *Master Sessions, Vols. 1 and 2* (Sony, US)
Félix Chappotín y Su Conjunto, *Sabor Tropical* (Big World, US)
Celia Cruz, *La Incomparable Celia* (Palladium, US)
Cuarteto Machín, *Échale Salsita* (Tumbao, US)
Machito and His Afro-Cuban Salseros, *Mucho Macho* (Pablo Records, US)
Beny Moré, *Colección de Oro* (Philips, Colombia)
Los Muñequitos de Matanzas, *Vacunao* (Qbadisc, US)
Orquesta Revé, *La Explosión del Momento* (Real World Records, US)
Isaac Oviedo, *Routes of Rhythm, Vol. 3* (Rounder, US)
Ignacio Piñeiro and His Septeto Nacional (Tumbao, US)
Pérez Prado, *Havana 3 A.M.* (BMG, US)
Ritmo y Candela, *African Crossroads* (Round World, US)
Paquito d'Rivera, *40 Years of Cuban Jam Session* (Messidor, Germany)
Arsenio Rodríguez, *Dundunbanza, 1946–1951* (Tumbao, US)
Sexteto Habanero, *Las Raíces del Son* (Tumbao, US)
Sierra Maestra, *Criolla Carabalí* (Sonido, France)
Los Van Van, *Lo Último en Vivo* (Qbadisc, US)

VARIOUS ARTISTS

¡Ahora Sí! Here Comes Changüí (Corason, US)
Antología de la Música Cubana (K-Cha Records, US)
Buena Vista Social Club (World Circuit, US)
Cuba, I Am Time (box set of four CDs) (Blue Jackal, US)

Cuban Counterpoint: History of the Son Montuno (Rounder, US)
Cuban Percussion Kings (Babalao Records, US)
Estrellas de Areito, Los Héroes (World Circuit, US)
Hot Music from Cuba, 1907–1936 (Harlequin, England)

Grateful acknowledgment is made for permission to reprint previously published material:

Reinaldo Arenas, excerpt from *Before Night Falls*, translated by Dolores M. Koch. Copyright © 1992 by the Estate of Reinaldo Arenas. Reprinted with the permission of Viking Penguin, a division of Penguin Putnam Inc.

Antonio Benítez-Rojo, "A View from the Mangrove," from *A View from the Mangrove,* translated by James Maraniss. Copyright © 1998 by the University of Massachusetts Press. Reprinted with the permission of the publishers.

Lydia Cabrera, "The Hill of Mambiala," from *Rhythm and Revolt: Tales of the Antilles,* edited by Marcela Breton, translated by Lisa Wyant. Copyright © 1995. Reprinted with the permission of Isabel Castellanos.

Guillermo Cabrera Infante, "Lorca the Rainmaker Visits Havana," from *Mea Cuba*, translated by Kenneth Hall with the author. Copyright © 1992 by Guillermo Cabrera Infante. English translation copyright © 1994 by Farrar, Straus & Giroux, Inc. Reprinted with the permission of Farrar, Straus & Giroux, LLC. Excerpt from *Three Trapped Tigers,* translated by Donald Gardner and Suzanne Jill Levine. Copyright © 1971 by Donald Gardner and Suzanne Jill Levine. Reprinted with the permission of Marlowe & Company.

Rafael Campo, "What the Body Told" from *What the Body Told.* Copyright © 1996 by Duke University Press. Reprinted with permission.

Alejo Carpentier, "Prologue" from *Review: Latin American Literature and Arts* 47 (Fall 1993). Copyright © 1993 by the Americas Society. Reprinted with the permission of *Review: Latin American Literature and Arts*. "Journey Back to the Source," from *The War of Time,* translated by Frances Partridge (New York: Alfred A. Knopf, 1970). Translation copyright © 1970 by Victor Gollancz, Ltd. Reprinted with permission.

Lourdes Casal, "The Founders: Alfonso," translated by Margaret Jull Costa, from *Voice of the Turtle: An Anthology of Cuban Stories,* edited by Peter Bush (New York: Grove Press, 1997). Copyright © 1973 by Lourdes Casal. Translation Copyright © 1996 by Margaret Jull Costa. Reprinted with the permission of the translator.

Calvert Casey, "The Walk" from *The Collected Stories,* translated by John H. R. Polt. Copyright © 1998 by Duke University Press. Reprinted with permission.

María Elena Cruz Varela, "Love Song for Difficult Times" and "The Exterminating Angel," from *Ballad of the Blood,* translated by Mairym Cruz-Bernal and Deborah Digges (New York: The Ecco Press, 1996). Translation copyright © 1996 by Mairym Cruz-Bernal and Deborah Digges. Reprinted with the permission of Deborah Digges.

Nicolás Guillén, "Josephine Baker in Cuba," translated by Mark Schafer, as found in *The Oxford Book of Latin American Essays,* edited by Ilan Stavans. Copyright © 1997 by Ilan Stavans. Reprinted with the permission of Oxford University Press, Inc.

José Lezama Lima, excerpt from *Paradiso,* translated by Gregory Rabassa, pp. 197–219. Copyright © 1968 by Ediciones Era, S. A. Translation copyright © 1974 by Farrar, Straus & Giroux, Inc. Revisions copyright © 2000 by Gregory Rabassa. Reprinted with the permission of Farrar, Straus & Giroux, LLC.

Dulce María Loynaz, "Eternity" and "Certainty," translated by David Frye. Copyright © 2002 by David Frye. Reprinted with the permission of the translator.

José Martí, "Love in the City" and excerpts from *War Diaries,* from *José Martí: Selected Writings,* edited and translated by Esther Allen. Copyright © 2002 by Esther Allen. Reprinted with the permission of Viking Penguin, a division of Penguin Putnam, Inc.

Ana Menéndez, "In Cuba I Was a German Shepherd," from *In Cuba I Was a German Shepherd.* Copyright © 2001 by Ana Menéndez. Reprinted with the permission of Grove/Atlantic, Inc.

Ernesto Mestre, "The Bakery Administrator's Daughter," from *The Lazarus Rumba.* Copyright © 1999. Reprinted with the permission of Picador.

Esteban Montejo, "Life in the Woods," from *The Autobiography of a Runaway Slave,* edited by Miguel Barnet, translated by Jocasta Innes. Translation copyright © 1968 by The Bodley Head, Ltd. Reprinted with the permission of Pantheon Books, a division of Random House, Inc.

Nancy Morejón, "Love, Attributed City," translated by Kathleen Weaver, from *Where the Island Sleeps Like a Wing* (Oakland: The Black Scholar, 1985). Copyright © 1985 by Kathleen Weaver. Reprinted with the permission of the translator.

Lino Novás Calvo, " 'As I Am . . . As I Was,' " translated by Paul Bowles from *Eye of the Heart: Stories from Latin America,* edited by Barbara Howe (New York: Avon Books, 1974). Reprinted with the permission of the translator.

Fernando Ortiz, excerpt from *Cuban Counterpoint: Tobacco and Sugar,* translated by Harriet de Onís. Copyright © 1947 by Alfred A. Knopf,

Inc. Reprinted with the permission of Alfred A. Knopf, a division of Random House, Inc.

Heberto Padilla, "Self-portrait of the other" and "A prayer for the end of the century," from *Legacies: Selected Poems,* translated by Alastair Reid and Andrew Hurley. Copyright © 1982 by Alastair Reid and Andrew Hurley. Reprinted with the permission of Farrar, Straus & Giroux, LLC.

Gustavo Pérez–Firmat, "Six Mambos," from *Life on the Hyphen: The Cuban-American Way*. Copyright © 1994. Reprinted with the permission of the University of Texas Press.

Virgilio Piñera, "The Face," from *Cold Tales,* translated by Mark Schafer. Copyright © 1987 by Estela Piñera. Reprinted with the permission of the translator and Marsilio Publishers.

José Manuel Prieto, excerpt from *Nocturnal Butterflies of the Russian Empire,* translated by Carol and Thomas Christiensen. Translation copyright © 1999 by Carol and Thomas Christiensen. Reprinted with the permission of Grove/Atlantic, Inc.

Severo Sarduy, excerpt from *From Cuba with a Song,* translated by Suzanne Jill Levine (Los Angeles, Calif.: Sun & Moon Press, 1994), pp. 56–77. Copyright © 1967 by Severo Sarduy. Translation copyright © 1994, 1972 by Suzanne Jill Levine. Reprinted with the permission of Sun & Moon Press, Los Angeles.

Zoé Valdés, "The Ivory Trader and the Red Melons," from *Voice of the Turtle: An Anthology of Cuban Stories,* edited by Peter Bush (New York: Grove Press, 1997). Translation copyright © 1996 by Amanda Hopkinson. Reprinted with the permission of the translator.